Advance Praise for *Sex Happens*

"This novel is new and edgy!" Allison Volk

"I loved it. It was intriguing, and I'm waiting for her next book." Sue Podany

"I stayed up all night reading it." Michele Viera

"I could relate!" Stacey Padres

"I couldn't put it down." Bo Urbansky

"You'll make time to read this!" Eileen Davidson

"This novel proves life doesn't end with divorce." Suzie Schudder, MD

"This novel is for women looking to discover themselves." Ann Bennett

Carol Soloway's first novel is like a comet entering the fiction scene! *Sex Happens* had me captivated from the first page as I entered her world of love, broken promises, sex, lies, deceit, divorce, heartbreak, friendship, and so much more. It is absorbing, insightful, thought-provoking, and a gratifying page-turner.

—Sandra Biskind, International #1 best-selling author of the
CODEBREAKER PLATINUM Series

Sex Happens is a page-turner that makes you feel every emotion of the heart-wrenching experience that is divorce. Many women who have had to heal their hearts from infidelity will feel the connection and learn lessons from the emotional roller coaster ride of the divorce process. It's life-transforming and real!

—Renée Piane, Author of *Get Real about Love*
—*The Secrets to Opening Your Heart & Finding True Love*

So you are happily married? Enjoy every moment of your bubble of safety and comfort—it can be destroyed in one conversation. You will be thrown into a whole new world that will challenge everything you've trusted to be real. Will you be able to cope? Dr. Carol Soloway's riveting novel will give you one woman's answer. You will not be able to stop reading this lusty, exciting, heart-stirring novel until you've read to the very last page.

—Tessa Kershnar, MFCC

I rarely read fiction, as I am a nonfiction type of gal. But I was surprised that when I started reading Carol Soloway's novel, *Sex Happens*, I couldn't put it down. I now understand what it means when someone says that a novel is a page-turner! What intrigued me most about Carol's book is how real and authentic it is. Surprises kept showing up throughout the book. It's a book that is relatable and written in an engaging manner that kept my interest all the way to the last page. Bravo for writing such an exceptional book, Dr. Carol!

—Ruth Klein, Featured in *O, The Oprah Magazine*. Author of 6 best-selling books. Woman of Achievement Award—National Association of Professional Women

I had the opportunity to read *Sex Happens* this weekend. Woke up at 7 a.m., made my coffee, and settled back with the first 100 pages. I'm so impressed with her writing style. She captured my attention and never let it go! Other than walking downstairs for more coffee, I never put it down. I'm a fan! If you like Danielle Steel, Harold Robbins, or Sidney Sheldon, you'll love Carol Soloway. Destined to be a best-seller!

—Diana Sabatino, Managing Director of eWomenNetwork, Orange County

Many novels tell us an interesting story. Others take us on a roller coaster ride with twists and turns. But some also make us look deep within ourselves and give us insight. *Sex Happens* does it all!

—Sandy Ponsot

Sex Happens is a must-read, a page-turner, an edge-of-the-seat gripper. I enjoyed everything, especially the "juicy" parts.

—Bonnie Graham, Read-My-Lips Blog Radio

Sex HAPPENS

CAROL SOLOWAY

Printed and bound in the United States of America

ISBN: 978-0-692-78540-9

Dedicated to Wayne, my husband, my rock, my everything.

CHAPTER 1

S*ex happens in hotel rooms,* Alexandra Rose thought as she slid her new lipstick-red negligee out of the Victoria's Secret bag and folded it into her suitcase. Stroking the silky nightgown made her long for those lost moments in her marriage that seemed to have slipped away. She craved their urgent taking of each other just as much as she hungered for their intimate explorations, when they'd touch each other with a familiarity that was like putting lotion on one's own body. Most of all, she missed their gentle sex in the middle of the night—his leg brushing against hers, she'd turn to him, and he'd caress her with a touch as gentle as a kiss.

Just as she closed her suitcase, Jon, her four-year-old son, ran into the room. "Mommy, don't leave me." He looked up at her with tears in his warm brown eyes.

Alex bent down and hugged her son, already missing him.

"Why do you have to go?" Jon threw his arms around her legs.

She tousled his curly brown hair. "You know your daddy's been at a medical conference all week, and I'm flying out to meet him so he doesn't have to drive home alone."

"Daddy's big, and he doesn't need you." Jon ran out of the bedroom.

Although she hated to leave the children, she was excited about joining her husband, Gabe, in Las Vegas and celebrating their twentieth anniversary. She opened the night table drawer, took out the Tiffany box, and slipped it into her purse, certain the sterling silver money clip was the perfect anniversary gift for him. It had been so long since they'd spent time together, just the two of them. The weekend would be wonderful, magical. It had to be.

Alex walked to the bureau and picked up her wedding picture. The way her husband looked at her with a love so real it was palpable made her chest tighten. She held the picture in her hand and traced his handsome face, longing for the return of that look, that warmth, that love.

Jon returned with his backpack. "I'm going with you."

She swooped him up in her arms and kissed him. Then she opened the top drawer of the bureau, the drawer where she kept the little gifts for the boys. Although she didn't believe in spoiling them, occasional rewards for being especially good or doing well in school were, in her opinion, well-placed bribes. The older boys were thrilled with gift cards, and Jon delighted in the little cars.

"Jon, close your eyes."

"Eyes closing." He shut his eyes so tightly his entire face scrunched up.

She placed a little red Hot Wheels car in his hands and told him he could open his eyes.

Looking down, he saw the little car and threw his arms around her. "Yippee! You're the best mom in the world, but I'm still going with you."

"Cookie Face, do you know how much I love you?" She cupped his face in her hands, lifted his chin, and kissed his nose. He and his two brothers were her world. Her life had been completed the moment her first son had been placed in her arms. And the birth of each son brought not only life but joy and love to the family. Yes, she could almost smell the freshly bathed newborn—the most delicious scent in the world.

Baseball cap on backwards, Daniel, her middle son, walked into the bedroom, holding a paper with an A+ at the top. "As I'd hoped," he said.

"What'd you write about?" she asked.

"Honey and how much the whole family loves her even though she's dead." He handed her the report.

As she started to read, her eyes teared. Honey was the family's beloved golden retriever, but she was Alex's solace, her warmth. Just thinking about Honey made her heart ache. The boys wanted another dog, but she wasn't ready. Honey wasn't replaceable. She was as dear to Alex as her boys. "Danny, you really were Honey's favorite. You were the one who always walked her and fed her."

"Mom, she loved you the most." Daniel smiled at her.

"Didn't she love me the bestest?" Jon asked and then looked to his brother. "Danny, we don't want our Mommy to leave us like our Honey. Right?"

Daniel patted his little brother's head. "Jon, you can sleep in our room, and we'll make a tent. We'll camp out."

Alex smiled at Daniel. He always tried to help his little brother. Daniel had Alex's sparkly brown eyes and brown hair. His was straight, while hers was curly. He was intrepid and drew people to him effortlessly, while she was just as warm but more cautious, reserved.

"No way," Eric, the oldest, called from in the hallway. "Jon is not sleeping in our room. And when am I getting my own room?"

"Eric, you'll have your own room soon. Your dad and I promised you."

11

"Mommy, what if you don't come back like our Honey?" Jon grabbed her legs. "Then I won't have a mommy."

"I'll always be your mommy," she promised.

Ever since Honey had run out in front of a car and been killed, Jon had become fearful whenever Alex left him with a babysitter. She knew how sad he and his brothers were about Honey, and she tried to help them cope with the loss by having each one write a farewell note to send to heaven.

Eric had protested. At thirteen, he was becoming defiant. But finally, he'd written, "Honey, I'll miss you."

Daniel, sensitive beyond his eleven years, had written, "I hope you're as happy in heaven as you were living with our family. I'll always love my sister, Honey."

Jon, who couldn't write, had refused to tell Alex what he wanted to say. He'd insisted Honey wasn't in heaven because she kept coming into his bedroom at night, and she'd even licked his face. Alex had told Jon he'd been having dreams about Honey. He'd shaken his head and covered his ears. She'd explained when you really want something so much that your heart hurts, then when you go to sleep, your mind sometimes gives it to you for a little while.

Eric put his hands on his hips. "Mom, you didn't wash my uniform. Again."

"Calm down," she said. "Your uniform and stuff are all laid out in the laundry room as usual."

Although she was dedicated to running her chiropractic practice and treating her patients, the boys came first. She'd managed to go to almost every game, attend every parent–teacher conference, and be there for them whenever they needed her. Of course, that meant more time away from her practice, but as hard as she tried, she knew she couldn't do everything.

As the doorbell rang, Eric looked at Alex. "And I don't want Mrs. Davis, that weirdo babysitter lady, coming to my game."

"I expect you to be polite to her," Alex said and rushed downstairs to open the door for Mrs. Davis.

After kissing the boys good-bye and promising she and their dad would be home early Sunday, Alex took a cab to the airport.

Excited about the weekend, she thought about how much she still adored Gabe. From the moment they'd met twenty-five years ago, she'd been in love with him. She recalled the night she met him. She was a freshmen in college, and her friend Jeremy's date had cancelled on him right before his fraternity dance. He'd begged Alex to go with him. She'd reluctantly agreed.

As Alex and Jeremy had approached the dance floor for their first dance, Jeremy had tripped and fallen, pulling her down with him. Her high heel had gotten caught on her dress. She fell onto the dance floor, cutting her shin and twisting her ankle. When she looked up, she saw Gabriel Rose kneeling down in front of her, one knee bent as though he were proposing.

"You'll be fine," Gabe had promised and patted her knee with his starched white handkerchief.

There was something about him, something intriguing, something that'd made her believe everything would be fine. Yes, it was his aquamarine eyes that had attracted her, his brilliance that had intrigued her, but it was his warmth that had made her fall in love. She'd become his wife, and the family they'd created would unite them forever—of that she'd been certain—until recently.

Lately, Gabe had been distracted, distant, almost annoyed every time she tried to talk to him or touch him. That was why they needed this weekend to return them to that couple in the wedding picture on their bureau.

13

CHAPTER 2

A fter the short flight, Alex eagerly proceeded to the line for a taxi. As the cabdriver weaved in and out of traffic on the crowded Las Vegas Strip towards the Bellagio Hotel, Alex delighted in the glitzy glamour: the neon silhouettes of the dancing girls and the promise of sensual delights flashing before her.

She walked through the Bellagio lobby with its incredible ceiling decorated with blown glass in yellow, blue, purple. When she went to the reception desk, the clerk requested her driver's license before giving her the key to Dr. Gabriel Rose's room.

As soon as she opened the door and saw their lush room with the king-size bed and sumptuous white comforter, she was certain they'd make love here tonight. She thought about how long it had been since they'd had sex. First, they'd been too busy with the children and work during the day, and they'd fall asleep the minute they got into bed. Weekends were filled with the boys' sporting events and their social obligations. Then, there was an awkwardness about initiating sex, and before they knew it, weeks had passed, then months.

She put her suitcase on the bed and saw the note on the bureau:

Reservations at 7:00 pm at Le Cirque.

It was just like Gabe to have arranged dinner at the finest restaurant in the Bellagio. He always took care of everything— meticulously. She appreciated his attention to details. It always made her feel cared for, loved.

She read the description of Le Cirque in the hotel brochure, promising, "an evening that would remain in your memory for years to come." Yes, she was living her dream, and tonight, she was going to make him fall in love with her all over again.

After a luxurious bath, she brushed her wavy brown hair back off of her shoulders. Then she stepped into her short black dress and zipped it up. She decided she needed to wear Spanx. While her legs were still shapely and her tummy flat, there were tiny bulges at her sides. Since her practice had gotten busier, she and her partner often worked through lunch. After work, she'd rush home to the boys, leaving no time for workouts or tennis.

Although Alex and Gabe were members of the tennis club, Gabe told her he'd lost interest in tennis; therefore, he stopped going to the club. Tennis was where she excelled. When she and Gabe would play together, they'd move in perfect harmony, her natural athleticism complimenting his years of lessons and practiced perfection. She decided she would try to convince him to return to the tennis club. They needed to spend more time together, play together again.

Distractedly, she opened the top drawer of the vanity. The familiar scent of Gabe's cologne surprised her. He never wore cologne when he went to work or business meetings, insisting it wasn't professional. He only used it when they went out and was careful to spray it ever so lightly. The cap was off. It just wasn't like him. He must have brought it for tonight, she decided.

She glanced at the clock. Late, she stepped into her stilettos, rushed out the door, and started toward the elevator. Then she ran back to the room to get her earrings. Gabe had given them to her for their tenth anniversary. She wondered what he'd bought her for this anniversary.

Heart pounding with excitement, she took the elevator to the restaurant. The dramatic décor mixing vibrant oranges with golds affirmed Gabe's taste for elegance and opulence, a trait she didn't share but appreciated.

As soon as she walked up to the reservation desk, she saw her husband, perfectly tailored in his blue Armani suit, Reagan-red tie, and pristine white shirt. Time had caressed his face with gentle lines, but Gabriel Rose, handsome as the day they'd met, still took her breath away.

Gabe stood up as she approached.

It was so right to have come, she thought.

He walked over and pulled her chair out for her.

She smiled. He was the consummate gentleman—always and forever—of that she was certain. She moved to kiss his lips.

He turned his head and kissed her cheek.

She thought maybe he was just being proper since they were in the restaurant and there might be other physicians nearby. No, she was his wife. There was no reason for him to have turned his head. Surprised, she didn't smell even a trace of his cologne. Then she caught herself. She wasn't going to spoil the weekend.

"How was your speech?" she asked, certain it was perfect.

"Went well."

"I'm sure you impressed them." She was so proud of him. She knew how dedicated he was to his patients and how hard he'd been working on his invention, which, he was convinced, would revolutionize cardiac care.

"I had to be very cautious ..."

"But you're patented," she said.

"I can't take a chance. Someone could steal it and make a small tweak."

"No one would do that," she said with her usual optimism.

He shook his head. "You really don't know what people are capable of when they want something."

She knew Gabe always got what he wanted. Whenever he set his mind to something, nothing ever stopped him. "Well, they loved it, right?"

"Um." He looked down at his menu. "How are my boys?" he asked.

No. Not now, she thought. She loved the boys more than life, and she loved being a mother and wife, but tonight she wanted to be his lover.

"I asked about the boys," he repeated.

"Wonderful, but they missed you this week."

"Alex, we did a good job with the boys."

Wondering why he was describing their parenting in the past tense—almost wistfully—she agreed. "And Eric brought up having his own room again."

"We'll see about that. Right now, I'm not changing anything in the house." He called the waiter over.

"Gabe, I love the house. It's perfect."

During dinner, they talked about how clever Gabe was for purchasing their wonderful house and how well behaved and adorable their boys were. But she wanted to talk about them— their marriage—their lost intimacy. She wanted to hear him tell her how much he missed her, longed for her, loved her. She decided that would happen. The weekend would unwind as it was supposed to.

After their chocolate mousse, she winked at him. "Want to go dancing or ...?"

"I'm going to gamble."

"But—"

"Alex, I haven't had a chance the whole week with all the seminar preparation."

She studied him, trying to figure out whether he was telling her the truth. For all she knew, he could have gambled every evening during the conference. He was always secretive about money, and he'd insisted on controlling the finances right from his very first paycheck. His parents had had a nasty divorce. His mother had hired a Park Avenue attorney who'd demanded all of his father's financial records. When his mother had learned his father had embezzled money from his partners, she'd decided to tell the partners, even though it'd meant she'd also lose everything. His father had had to pay off his partners or go to jail. Gabe had told Alex he'd seen the other side of marriage—the dark and ugly side—and he vowed he'd never allow anyone to do that to him.

She followed him to the casino.

After an hour, as Gabe sat at a blackjack table under a canopy of turquoise-and-burgundy silk, she leaned close and seductively invited him up to their room. His eyes fixed on his cards, he waved at her like one does an annoying fly. "Later," he promised.

She took the elevator to their room, undressed, and put on her new negligee. She waited for two hours. Finally realizing the futility of her expectation, she threw her negligee on the floor, put on one of Gabe's T-shirts, and sobbed.

CHAPTER 3

At three in the morning, Gabe finally returned to the room. He neatly folded his clothes over the chair, climbed into bed, and fell asleep.

Devastated, Alex couldn't sleep. Finally, she turned toward Gabe sleeping peacefully beside her, his tuxedo-black hair against the white pillow. Slipping her hand under the white comforter, she trailed her fingers down his body.

"Alex, I'm done with your romantic weekend." He turned his well-chiseled face away.

"Gabe, it's our anniversary."

"I'm sorry," he said softly, almost gently. "Alex, it's not you."

But she knew it was her. It had to be.

He got out of bed and walked to the bureau. As she watched him steal away the possibility of intimacy, she hugged the comforter to her. In despair, she stared down at the red negligee laying on the floor.

He picked up his cell phone, read a text, and turned to her. "We have to leave now."

"We're booked until tomorrow."

"Alex, there's a problem at the hospital. They need me." He turned away, went into the bathroom, and closed the door.

She got out of bed and grabbed his cell phone. There was a text from the hospital, instructing him that one of the interns had breached some protocol, and he had to return. Reassuring herself that he'd told her the truth, she put his cell phone on the bureau and crept back into bed.

From the bathroom, the usual sound of Gabe humming in the shower was unmelodic, almost angry. She knew he'd been anxious about both his invention and his impending partnership in the most successful cardiac practice in Orange County, California, but lately, she'd been apprehensive about how distant and secretive he'd become.

"Aren't you going to shower?" Gabe asked, returning from the bathroom, the towel slipping down from around his waist.

"I'll wait until we get home. It'll be nice to see the boys and ..."

"I miss Honey too," he said.

Their eyes met, and they shared a knowing sadness.

"The boys'll be fine," he said and tightened the towel around his waist. "Children are resilient."

She wanted to believe him, but she wasn't sure. The boys seemed to be coping with the loss of Honey, but there'd been an overwhelming sense of grief, a pervasive tension in the house for the past several months. There even seemed to be something more than the loss of Honey that was invading the serenity of their beautiful family.

Gabe took his clothes from the bureau and turned to go back to the bathroom.

Wondering why he'd chosen to dress in the bathroom, she got out of bed and reached for the white shirt, raspberry cashmere cardigan, and jeans she'd draped over the chair.

Showered and shaved, clad in sharply creased jeans and a Lacoste golf shirt, Gabe returned to the bedroom and stepped into his preppy loafers. He grabbed yesterday's clothes from the other chair, threw them into his suitcase, and closed it.

"You look nice," she said.

"Um." He picked up the remote. "I hate these automatic checkouts. We're going downstairs." He lifted his suitcase off the luggage stand and rolled it out of the room. Then he turned back and motioned to her. "Now."

Although she was used to his abrupt tone whenever there was a problem or emergency at the hospital, she almost started to cry. Disappointed the weekend had ended without the reconnection she'd hoped for and knew they needed, she rolled her suitcase to the elevator, and they rode down to the lobby in silence.

While Gabe waited in line at the registration desk, Alex gazed up at the kaleidoscope of colored glass shapes that covered the Bellagio's ceiling. This time, the balloons made her think of a circus. A circus. The bright shapes were everywhere, hundreds of them, swirling around her. Alex shuddered and tried to not to think about the time she'd been frightened by a fat lady in the circus, but the memory ghosts were always trying to wrap their tentacles around her and pull her back to horrific childhood memories.

"The valet's here with the car," Gabe said, jarring her back to the present.

After ten silent minutes in traffic, she glanced back at the glass towers of the Las Vegas strip, the twinkling miniatures a mockery of her grandiose plans for a magical weekend.

Gabe turned up the Neil Diamond CD. She reached for his hand and entwined her fingers through his. He moved his hand away and gripped the steering wheel.

She tensed.

He leaned across the burl-wood console and muted the CD. "I'm going to tell you the truth."

"The truth?" Alex repeated. Suddenly cold and clammy, she knew this moment would be tattooed onto her heart forever.

"I'm leaving you," he said.

Panic gripped her, and she felt as though she was going to faint. She thought he could just as easily have said, "I'm going to kill you," because that was how it felt. She thought about grabbing the steering wheel and sending them off the road at high speed. And if they both died, then "until death do us part" would come true. The story of Alexandra and Gabriel Rose would end as it was supposed to end—together.

She couldn't imagine waking up without Gabe every morning, going to sleep between cold sheets, or no longer cuddling next to him when he returned to their bed after an emergency at the hospital in the middle of the night.

Sure, she'd suspected something was wrong, but she'd never thought it would come to this. She'd thought maybe they'd gotten too busy, and he was preoccupied with his invention and impending partnership. There wasn't anything wrong. There couldn't be.

"I don't want this to end." Tears filled her eyes.

"It did," he whispered.

Heart pounding, tears streaming down her face, she thought this couldn't be real. This had to be a dream. Her life couldn't be ripped from her this easily. She pulled down the visor, slid the mirror open, and stared at her reflection. She ran her fingers through her hair and then froze. Pain and terror reflected back.

"I'm sorry." He handed her his handkerchief.

She took it. She knew exactly how he liked his handkerchiefs pressed. Although few men carried cloth handkerchiefs anymore, he'd insisted on a clean, perfectly ironed handkerchief every day. *Amazing how all the little details anchor us to a person,* she thought. Yes, she knew everything about him—or so she'd thought. She laughed.

"I'm glad you're taking it so well," he said.

"No, I'm vacillating between anger and terror. I hate you for doing this, and—"

"I told you I was sorry."

"Sorry isn't enough. Why don't you just take the cigarette lighter and burn my other wrist?"

Only Gabe—well, of course, her sister, too—knew about the scar on her right wrist. Now his words were more searing than any burn. She'd never felt such pain. Her head was throbbing, she was chilled, and her heart was beating so quickly she thought she'd faint.

He took her hand, and from the gentle sadness of his touch, she knew she'd lost him.

She pulled her hand away. "You'll never find anyone who'll love you as much as I do."

"I already did."

Shocked, she felt totally out of control. Without any warning, she was watching their marriage disappear like part of a magic act. There was a pressure on her chest, and she couldn't take a breath. No, it wasn't happening to her; it couldn't be. But it was; it really was.

"Who?" she asked.

"Linda," he whispered.

"Linda," she repeated. Visions of Linda, the hospital administrator, and Gabe flashed before her. She tried to recall the Christmas party. Gabe and Linda had been talking to each other for a long time, but Alex had just thought he was acquiring another ally for his impending partnership. That was all he seemed to be focused on—or was it? "Why?" she asked.

"Linda and I just happened to—"

"Sex doesn't just happen!" she yelled, frustrated and scared.

"You're certainly right on that one," he said, almost cruelly.

"Gabe, last night you were too busy gambling to even come to bed."

"And why'd you go out and buy that sexy red negligee for the weekend? Where was that all these years?"

She felt a sadness to the very depths of her heart and asked, "With the boys coming into the bedroom at night when they were sick or had bad dreams, how could I wear something like that? Wasn't our sex life good?"

"It became more like scratching an itch." He shrugged.

"That was cruel."

"Sometimes the truth is cruel."

She glanced out the window at the monotone tan desert. Had she been that to him—uninteresting? Boring? Why was he really leaving her? She couldn't watch their love turn, right before her eyes, from warm, soft colors to cold, endless nothing. From the moment they'd met, she'd felt safe, anchored to the world. Hoping he'd change his mind, come to his senses, she wondered aloud, "Is sex really that different with someone else?"

"Find out for yourself," he said, an edge to his voice, as though his decision required him to steel himself against her.

"I will," she said, but couldn't imagine sex with anyone else. Sex was the part of her only he knew. She looked at him, the only lover she'd ever known, and almost afraid to hear the answer, she asked, "How did it happen?"

"Linda and I were at a meeting, and we started talking. You know ..."

"No, I don't fucking know," she screamed. She was asking him what had happened to them, their marriage, their life, but he was explaining how he and Linda had fallen in love. She was no longer part of his story. And for her, there was no story without him.

Then, as though he didn't hear her, he continued with what appeared to be a speech he'd been rehearsing while she'd slept securely in their bed.

"Linda and I," he said with a familiarity that made it clear they'd been together for a long time.

"You and Linda," she repeated. Angry, confused, she wondered whether there'd been a time when she and Linda had been like magnets, each pulling him in the opposite direction. And he'd chosen Linda.

"Sorry," he said softly.

Her stomach churned, and she thought of how devastated the boys would be if Gabe left them. "We have to work this out for the boys."

"I'm not leaving *them*." He clenched his jaw and furrowed his brow.

She'd seen that expression before whenever he encountered an obstacle. And Gabriel Rose, she knew, always got what he wanted. But she couldn't worry about herself. It was the boys she had to protect. "The boys," she whispered.

"Alex, I've found an attorney who can help you, and I'll give you plenty of money for the boys while they're living with you."

She glared at him. "You really did your homework while I was busy loving you."

"Um." He shook his head.

She twisted her wedding band. "And, if you leave me—"

"I've already left, and you didn't even notice."

Rage careening through her, she yelled, "Gabe, I'm going to make sure you'll never see the boys."

"You who didn't even want children." He glanced over at her as though challenging her to refute that.

She knew it was true. Terrified she'd be like her mother, a woman capable of harming her own child, she feared having children. For years, Alex hadn't been able to become pregnant, and she knew it had been due to that fear. Finally, she became pregnant, and the boys had become her life.

"Alex, I'll make all the arrangements for—"

"For my life?" she demanded, certain without him, life as she'd planned would be gone. Nothing would ever be the same.

He eyed her. "You know what your problem is?"

"My problem? Since when did you switch from cardiology to psychiatry? Cardiology is more lucrative, and I know that's important to you."

"You never complained about all the money I make." He glared at her.

"I contribute too," she said.

"How could you even compare your chiropractic whatever to my cardiac practice?" He laughed. "I come home, and all you talk about is your patients' neck and back pains—hardly anything very serious or interesting." He shook his head in dismissal. "And then the way you are with the boys, you're so afraid to leave them for even a day. I was shocked you insisted on this weekend with your supermom schedule."

That wounded her to the edge of her soul. She was a devoted, loving mother, and he knew it. He had to know it. Anger careened through her. She couldn't listen to him belittle her, mock everything she cared for and loved. "Stop the car!" She leaned over and reached for the steering wheel.

"Alexandra, are you trying to get us killed?" He grabbed her hand and pushed her away.

"Stop now," she demanded and started to open her door.

"Alex, you can't—"

"Gabe, stop or I'll—"

He pulled onto the shoulder of the road.

She opened the door and ran. She kept running, faster and faster, deep into the desert. She ran as though that would make her pain go away. Suddenly, she tripped and fell to the ground, her outstretched leg brushing against a cactus.

Searing pain radiated from her shin to her ankle. She looked down. There were what appeared to be hundreds of tiny thorns covering her ankle, and two large thorns were deeply embedded. Blood was dripping down onto her shoe. She tried to pull the thorns out, but they were too deep.

She rolled over, curled into a ball, and sobbed. Then, she thought she heard something rustling in the brush. She looked up. Silhouetted by the sun at his back, Gabe was standing before her.

"Alex, I'm so sorry," he said softly and leaned down to her.

She sat up, put her head on his shoulder, and wept.

He put his arm around her. "We were too young when we met. Then we had the kids, the house—"

"I know," she whispered. "But, weren't we happy?"

"For a time," he said. "Then I needed more, and—"

"Why?" She pulled away. As she moved, her leg hit the ground and one of the thorns turned. She winced with pain and grabbed her leg.

Gabe looked down at her ankle. "I'll take care of it," he said as though he were still the loving man she'd married.

He rolled up her pant leg. Gently, he eased the thorns out, one then the other.

She stared at his surgeon's hands with their neatly clipped nails as he adeptly relieved her pain. Last night she'd needed to feel those hands hunger for her. But last night seemed a lifetime ago, before the secrets, lies, and, now, chasms.

As he placed his crisp white handkerchief over her bloody ankle carefully, almost lovingly, she wondered how she could have missed the signs. Gabe was always at the hospital, caring for his patients and working on his invention. Maybe there wasn't even such a project.

"Gabe, why'd you wait until now, if you've been seeing her?" she asked.

"Honey," he said.

Her heart leaped, and for a moment, she thought he was starting to apologize. Then she realized he was referring to their golden retriever.

"The boys were so upset when they lost Honey that I knew I had to wait."

"So now you're ready to leave us?" she asked, wondering what had happened to the man she'd thought she knew, the man she'd thought she could trust, the man she'd thought would never hurt her.

"We better get going," he said. "Lean on me if your leg hurts."

"Not as bad as my heart." She let him help her up, wondering which Gabriel Rose was the one she'd known all those years—the man who'd gently cared for her or the one who'd cruelly discarded her. She looked at him, now a stranger whose body had been entwined with someone else's, and wept.

They went back to the car and proceeded down the freeway.

Suddenly, a Hummer almost plowed into them. Gabe blasted the horn.

"It's amazing how we think we're in control," she said, more to herself than Gabe. "Now, like that car that almost hit us, another woman is in control and destroying my life, my family, my whole world."

28

"Alex, I told you, I'll still provide for the family."

He turned up the CD, but it didn't drown out the angry voice thundering in her head. She wondered how he could callously move the eraser back and forth across their life, ending it so easily. She prayed for numbness, numbness enough to stop worrying about the boys and numbness to stop loving Gabe.

As they approached Peggy Sue's Diner, ten miles out of Barstow, Gabe asked, "Wanna stop for a bite?"

"The hospital problem?" she asked, falling back into believing him.

"None. I couldn't continue pretending, and I thought it would be better to tell you alone, away from the boys."

Certain it was Linda who'd texted him about returning to the hospital, she imagined Gabe and Linda plotting, rehearsing his announcement for weeks, maybe months.

"I want to go home to my boys," she demanded.

"Your boys." He smirked.

Hot tears spilling down her face, she took off her wedding ring. Through her tears, she saw the white band of skin circling her finger.

Maybe what she'd called love was, in reality, only a familiarity that came from seeing each other day in, day out. Maybe what she'd thought was intimacy was just habit.

CHAPTER 4

As Gabe started to pull into their circular driveway, Alex froze. Plagued by horrific images whirling in her head, she felt an eerie disconnect with all that was familiar to her. Her hopes and dreams shattered, she no longer felt safe or anchored to the world. She pulled down the visor, flipped back the mirror, and looked at herself, wondering who she was now that she was no longer a wife, and a wife was who she was to her core. But she reminded herself, she was also a mother and had to protect her children.

She couldn't let the boys know how frightened she was. She had to be strong, hide her terror. Yes, she was familiar, all too familiar with hiding fears. As a little girl, she'd learned the only way to survive was by suppressing emotions. She kept her family secrets tightly guarded.

She touched the scar on her wrist—an accident according to her mother. Alex had never told anyone except Gabe about that scar. Only he knew all of her secrets and had promised their family would be different. But now, her home was filled with secrets, just like her childhood home.

She stared at the perfectly manicured lawn, the colorful flowerbed, and the inviting double doors. The house suddenly seemed as though it belonged to another family, a loving, happy family. She wondered how she was going to tell the boys, protect them, make sure their lives wouldn't be affected. She shivered. How could this not affect them?

Their three sons rushed out to the car with Mrs. Davis, the babysitter, trailing behind.

"How were my boys?" Alex asked and swooped Jon up in her arms. After she gave him a big kiss, she put him down and hugged Daniel, then Eric.

Mrs. Davis tousled Jon's curly hair. "Jon's smart as a whip, and Daniel's so helpful."

"Thank you." Alex reached into her purse to pay the babysitter, wondering why she hadn't said anything about Eric. Recently, he'd started to test Alex, but he was always respectful to other adults.

Jon wrapped his arms around his mother's legs. "Do I get a present on account of the babysitter told me I was the bestest boy?"

Too choked up to speak, Alex patted Jon's back.

Gabe opened the trunk of the car and reached in for their suitcases. "Maybe there's a present in these," he said just as his cell buzzed. "I've just got to take this call, then I'll bring the luggage in."

Baseball cap on backwards, Daniel patted his little brother's head. "He was a good boy and slept in the tent we made in his room."

"I wasn't going to have him in our room." Eric put his hands on his hips and looked at Alex. "And when am I getting my own room?"

"Already asked and answered," Daniel said.

"I thought you were running for president of the freshman class of Brea Junior High, not the Supreme Court." Eric smirked.

"Supreme Court justices are nominated, not elected," Daniel corrected.

"Big deal," Eric said. "Maybe if you spent more time practicing football instead of studying about the boring Supreme Court, the coach wouldn't have you sit out so much."

"Boys, you're all good at different things, and that's what makes you special," she said.

"Mommy, I thought I was the specialist." Jon looked up at her with his big brown eyes.

"I love all my wonderful boys." Alex pulled her three boys close to her, clutching them more tightly than ever before and wondering how she was going to tell them everything they knew and trusted was about to change.

Somberly, Alex walked up the long, flower-edged pathway to the front door. Unwilling to bring Gabe's impending destruction of their beautiful family into their home, she hesitated before opening the door.

When she and the boys walked into the house, their footsteps echoed on the black marble entryway, and the house felt oddly unfamiliar, suddenly void of the warmth that had been home. Honey's absence now more poignant than ever, Alex paused and looked at the living room. The L-shaped beige suede couch, the red leather chair, and the soft beige carpeting all seemed cold and sterile—no longer inviting.

Gabe tossed their bags onto the hallway floor. "Boys, come give me a big hug."

The children ran to him.

As Gabe swallowed them up in his arms, Alex's heart ached. She longed to be part of that embrace. Then she saw Gabe glance up and look at her. He seemed sad, as though painfully projecting the future, the end of the family.

She watched as Jon, already in his chicken-yellow sleeper, snuggled into his dad. As Gabe kissed Jon's little face, framed by a mass of brown Harpo Marx curls, Alex's chest tightened. She knew how much Jon, and all the boys, for that matter, needed their father.

Jon gripped his teddy bear with the missing right ear and pointed to the stuffing spilling out from the seam. "Teddy's tummy got brokened."

"Poor Teddy." Gabe kissed the bear.

Nearly as tall as his father, Eric scowled. "You guys missed my best kick at the scrimmage."

Daniel draped his arm around Eric. "When the football game was over, the guys carried him around the field. It was so cool."

"And they missed it," Eric said. Although he seemed to want his parents to watch his games, he'd grimace whenever Alex or Gabe cheered loudly.

"I'm so sorry we couldn't watch your game," Alex said.

Eric glared at her. "Mom, why did you have to go away this weekend?"

"We planned it months ago," she said, tripping on the "we."

Eric turned away from her. Then he and his brothers followed Gabe into the kitchen.

She knew Eric was angry with her for arranging the weekend, but he never seemed annoyed with Gabe. He accepted the consequences of Gabe's grueling work schedule, but he didn't tolerate the same from her. She fought back tears and tried to compose herself before joining the family in the kitchen.

Jon held his bear out to Gabe. "Daddy, what about Teddy?"

"Go upstairs and get Mommy's sewing box. We'll do an operation," Gabe said and offered to hold the bear.

Jon pressed the bear to his chest and carried it up the stairs.

While Gabe cleared the kitchen table for bear surgery, Alex tried to stay calm. She had to pretend this was an ordinary night just like any other, at least until the boys went to bed. "I'm going to make dinner," she said.

Daniel turned his cap around. "I'll help you make a family dinner."

"Family dinner," Alex repeated, trying to steady her shaking hands.

Holding Alex's red sewing box in both hands and balancing the bear on top of the box, Jon returned to the kitchen.

Gabe took the bear and placed it on the table, belly up. Then he reached into his pocket for his handkerchief, looked down at Alex's ankle, apparently realizing he'd used it to wrap her ankle. He turned to Eric, "Please go upstairs to my bureau drawer and bring down a handkerchief."

When Eric returned, Gabe took the starched white handkerchief and handed it to Jon. "Dr. Jonathan Rose, please apply the anesthesia."

Jon took the handkerchief and placed it over the bear's snout.

"Now, secure your patient's hands."

"Daddy, a bear has paws, not hands." Jon tightened his grip on the bear's outstretched fluffy limbs.

"You're right. I'm just a heart doctor, but you're a veterinarian." Gabe laughed.

"Daddy, you can fix everyone, can't you?" Jon asked.

At the irony of that, Alex's chest tightened. She turned away, pulled the spaghetti pot from the cupboard, and sent water gushing into it.

Needle threaded, Gabe placed one surgical stitch, knotted it, and looped another stitch. He repeated the process until the bear's belly was sutured.

"Teddy's gonna be fine." Gabe kissed the bear and handed it to Jon.

"Did you guys win in Las Vegas?" Daniel asked.

"I lost everything," Alex said, bursting into tears.

The boys froze.

Eric looked at Gabe. Jon and Daniel gaped at her.

Alex knew they were frightened by her tears, but she couldn't stop crying. She hurried out of the kitchen and ran up the stairs, so the boys wouldn't see how upset she was.

From the upstairs hallway, Alex heard Gabe tell the boys, "Mommy'll be fine. She just hurt her leg on a cactus."

She walked into their bedroom and stopped. There was a beautiful crystal vase with a dozen roses on top of her dresser. She gasped. *Why now? What could this mean?*

Every year since they'd been married, Gabe had sent her a dozen red roses on their anniversary. Grabbing the card, she reassured herself there might be a possibility for a reconciliation. True, Gabe had said he wanted a divorce, and it would take time for her to get over his affair, but despite her pain, she was still in love with him.

She read the card:

To my wife,

I love you.

Yours forever,

Gabe

Alex thought, no she hoped, Gabe had changed his mind about leaving. Had he telephoned the florist when she'd gone to the restroom at the gas station? This was too good to be true. A second chance was all she wished for. Then she read the note again. *Was she losing it? What was Gabe trying to do her?* Clutching the vase, she ran downstairs

Gabe looked at her and shook his head. "Jeeze, I'm so sorry. I forgot to cancel."

"Forgot?" she screamed. "Did you forget you just ruined my life?"

"Calm down." He reached for the vase.

Daniel stepped between them. "Mrs. Davis told me to take it upstairs and put it in your bedroom so you'd be surprised."

"Oh, I was." She slammed the vase onto the kitchen table.

It splintered into pieces, just like the glass Gabe had stomped on at their wedding. The broken glass, a symbol of the fragility of marriage in traditional Jewish wedding ceremonies, was now more poignant than ever.

A shard of glass hit Eric's cheek. He shrieked in pain, looked at his father, and then glared at his mother.

"What the hell are you doing?" Gabe pulled Eric to him, grabbed his handkerchief, and held it over his son's cheek.

"Mommy," Jon shrieked. "Don't you love Eric?"

"I love all my boys, but I've got to go upstairs."

"I'm scared." Jon held onto her leg and tried to stop her from going upstairs. He started to cry.

Gabe motioned for Alex to leave. "Mommy's just a little upset right now," he said.

"Fuck you," she screamed and rushed out of the kitchen. She rushed back upstairs, slammed the bedroom door, and got under the covers. Images of Gabriel flooded her mind. Their journey from college sweethearts to bride and groom had been magical, or so she'd thought until now. She'd never imagined their path would lead to this.

As she listened to the sounds of Gabe serving dinner, she knew she couldn't face the boys tonight. If she went downstairs, Daniel would put his arms around her and say, "Don't cry," and that would make her cry even more. Eric would look at her, turn to Gabe, watch his father's face for a reaction, and then mimic whatever he saw. But Jon, too young to understand the polarization of the family, would say, "I love you, Mommy," thinking that would make everything all right.

Reflexively, she reached across the bed for her beloved golden retriever, but Honey, too, was gone. She got up, walked over to the bureau, and with a sadness that took her breath away, she touched their wedding picture. Then her trembling fingers traced the other picture of their three smiling children. She reminded herself she was still their mother, and no one could take them away. No, she wasn't going to let the divorce harm her children.

She picked up the telephone to call Liz, her best friend and confidante. But distraught as she was, she knew she'd be incoherent and would melt into tears. She didn't want Gabe to hear her cry. Weakness allowed people to take advantage. She'd learned that long ago and knew the dangers.

Alex listened as Gabe instructed the older boys to shut off their lights in an hour. Then she heard Gabe reassure Jon that everything was fine. *Nothing would ever be fine again*, she thought and cried, praying for sleep.

A few minutes after she'd drifted off, she felt Gabe slip into bed beside her. Naked, he pulled her to him. "I love you," he whispered.

They kissed.

She moved close and touched his face, tentatively at first.

He smiled and then kissed her—a sweet, passionate kiss. "You know how I love when you climb on top of me," he said.

With renewed enthusiasm, she straddled him.

He traced his finger along her face, her neck, and then caressed her breasts.

She leaned toward him, and he suckled her breasts, making her nipples hard. Then she lifted her hips just enough for him to insert his erect penis into her. She moaned.

"I have to have you," he said.

They moved together, and she came.

"You having a nightmare or something?" Gabe called from the doorway, jolting her awake. She reached out to his side of the bed. The sheets were cold. She sobbed. Her mind should have been protectively insulating her from Gabe, but, instead, it had returned her to him with a dream so real she'd been certain she felt him. But it was a dream that would never come true.

"I didn't mean to wake you, but I need my surgical scrubs for tomorrow."

"Why the hell didn't you take them out of the bedroom before we left?" she asked. "You knew you were going to tell me this weekend."

"Alex, I guess I just didn't know how it was going to go, and I didn't know whether I'd have the nerve to go through with it or——"

"Or what?" she hissed at the man who was no longer hers.

He started to close the door. "I have three surgical procedures in the morning, but we'll talk tomorrow."

"Tomorrow," she whispered. He knew what he was doing tomorrow, had it all planned out. But for her, tomorrow was the beginning of a life she'd neither wanted nor expected.

CHAPTER 5

For three months, Alex was barely able to function. Aside from Liz, her best friend, and Dr. Seth Stone, her business partner, she couldn't talk to anyone about Gabe. She was fearful that, in the telling, the possibility of reconciliation would slip further away. And, she didn't want that, not with the way the boys were acting since Gabe had left.

Since the boys attended a year-round school, bedtime had always been difficult during the summer. But now it was even more so. Jon cried himself to sleep every night, insisting if his daddy didn't come back, he'd be an orphan like the girl in the movie, *Annie*. Eric constantly challenged her about everything, demanding she tell him why she sent his father away. Daniel, the gregarious one, was quiet and even refused her help with his homework, assuring her he could handle it by himself.

It was as though in Gabe's absence his presence was felt even more. There was an overbearing sense of tension, and everything seemed precarious.

Once the boys were in bed, she'd call Liz. Sometimes Liz would come over, and other times they'd just talk on the phone. Liz kept insisting Alex had to return to the First Friday Book Club, and Alex finally agreed.

Sex Happens

◆ ◆ ◆

A few minutes before noon on the first Friday in August, Alex parked her car and walked to Waters Restaurant, the First Friday Book Club's meeting place. Purse slung over her shoulder and attaché case in hand, she took the stairs down to the street-level entrance.

Despite wearing her best navy blazer, she knew she looked tired and drawn. She'd lost fifteen pounds so her clothes hung on her now-gaunt body. She had no appetite and hadn't had a peaceful night's sleep since Gabe had left.

As she walked past a man seated at the ornate mahogany bar close to the entryway, she smiled. He turned away, affirming her fear that she'd never again get another man to notice her, much less find her attractive.

She proceeded past the tables covered with pristine white tablecloths to the patio where Liz was already sitting, facing the bar. Liz wasn't beautiful. As a matter of fact, each individual feature was quite plain: her nose was a little too long for her face, her lips were a little too thin and her eyes were a non-descript brown. But there was something about her that drew people to her. Maybe it was her embracing warmth, her contagious laugh, and her quick wit.

And Liz had style. Her clothes, always in the latest fashion, perfectly accentuated her petite, toned body. Her long, glistening white strand of pearls was her trademark and a striking accessory for her classic, but contemporary outfits.

Although Liz had a busy insurance business and a fabulous husband, she was always there for Alex. Only five years older than Alex, Liz's children were away in college; therefore, she was able to, actually insisted on, the nightly talks and frequent walks with Alex.

40

Liz got up and hugged her. "Present for you." She handed Alex an elegant Christian Dior eyeglass case.

"What's this for?" Alex asked and opened the case.

"I thought you'd need a little something with pizazz for today. I mean, the First Friday women could be a little intimidating if you've been away for a while."

Alex put the sunglasses on. "They're so Audrey Hepburn. Thank you." She kissed Liz and took a seat across from her, facing the lake. Alex knew the glasses were really to hide the dark circles under her eyes, in an effort to make her look more presentable. Never judgmental, Liz always watched out for Alex, delicately providing a solution. Liz knew how to make everyone feel special, important, especially her close friends. And Alex experienced it time and again.

The waitress approached. "Haven't seen you in a while. The usual?"

"Yes," Alex said. *The usual*, she thought with irony, recalling the meeting three months ago when she'd thought her life was perfect. But that was before Las Vegas. Amazing how a few months, or even a few minutes, could change a life.

"Here comes trouble." Liz pointed to the bar.

Alex turned around and saw Meredith descending the stairway. One step, pause, and then another step: Catherine Zeta-Jones, perfectly outfitted as an attorney. Her entrance afforded the men seated at the mahogany bar a chance to gaze at her statuesque, perfectly proportioned body. Envying Meredith's confidence, Alex watched her make eye contact with a handsome gray-haired man before proceeding to the First Friday Book Club table.

Every inch the vampish attorney she was, Meredith was breathtaking in a white Prada suit, accented by her Chanel scarf and Louis Vuitton accessories.

"Oh dear, Alex, you've lost so much weight." Meredith air-kissed Alex and Liz. "Emergency shopping trip with *moi*."

"Clothing is not my priority right now," Alex said.

"Darling, it's just to cheer you up. Always does for me." Meredith took the seat next to Liz, of course, facing the bar. "And have you called any of the attorneys I recommended?"

"Lost the numbers," Alex confessed and rubbed her wrist.

"If only I practiced family law," Meredith said.

"Meredith, why don't you do family law?" Liz asked. "You'd be a killer."

"Tissues are too expensive," Meredith said and laughed. "Actually, could you imagine a soon-to-be single man looking at *moi*?" She fluffed her mane of long black hair.

Liz winked at Alex. "Meredith, now I understand why you're a real estate attorney."

"If I were Alex's attorney, I'd have the good doctor groveling, begging to pay a handsome alimony check each month."

"It's not alimony I care about," Alex said. "It's child support that I want, and he's offered that."

Meredith pursed her lips. "My motto is if he wants it, he pays. If he doesn't want it, he pays even more."

"She'll have to keep that in mind," Liz chided.

Meredith pointed to Terrie who was passing the bar. "Here comes the bag lady."

"She's your best friend," Liz reminded Meredith.

"I love her, but that doesn't mean I approve of her choice of clothes, or men for that matter."

Terrie weaved her way among tables until she got to the patio. Her pale skin and light blue eyes yearned for a touch of makeup. Her '60s outfits and blunt haircut with bangs made her look every inch the empathetic psychologist she was.

42

"New outfit?" Meredith asked, disapprovingly pointing to Terrie's white peasant blouse separated from a long flowered skirt by a silver coin belt.

Terrie twirled around, allowing the skirt to flare. "It was a birthday gift from my darling husband. Chico's is my favorite, but I'd never splurge on clothes."

"That's obvious," Meredith said. "But it kind of looks like your other outfits."

"This suits me so well," Terrie said, clearly unphased by Meredith's comment. She leaned down and hugged Alex. "I'm so glad you're back. It hasn't been the same without you."

"I missed you too, but I couldn't have concentrated on a book," Alex said.

The waitress took their orders: Chinese chicken salad for everyone except Terrie who ordered her usual hamburger and French fries. Terrie ordered for Judi since she'd spoken to her and knew she was going to be late.

Meredith motioned towards the bar. "That guy keeps staring at me."

"Maybe that's because he's never seen such a glorious creature," Liz teased.

Grabbing a sourdough roll and buttering it, Terrie nodded. "Alex, I understand why you haven't been back to the book club, but now it's time to take care of yourself."

"Yes," Meredith said and looked over at the bar. "I was just telling her Gabe owes her for every miserable year of marriage."

"Almost twenty years were good," Alex said. "It was only during the last few months that Gabe started to get volatile."

"I thought that was the way he always was." Liz gave her throaty laugh.

Alex shook her head. "Only one other time, about a year before this, Gabe was really stressed—everything seemed to annoy him. His behavior was unpredictable. He'd even forgotten about a seminar he was supposed to attend and called me from the hospital to tell me he had to leave immediately for a seminar which the hospital had arranged. He told me he couldn't even stop off at home for his luggage."

"Sounds like an affair to *moi*." Meredith tossed her head back dramatically.

"I trusted him then, definitely too much, but I thought we had the perfect marriage." Alex fought back tears.

"How could he go on a trip without luggage?" Meredith asked. "It takes *moi* weeks to pack for even a weekend trip."

"I know, Meredith, I've driven you and *all* your luggage to the airport many times," Terrie quipped.

Terrie and Meredith had condos in the same gated community. For Meredith, the condo was more of a place to change suitcases for an exotic trip to Paris, Rio, or some other destination, escorted by her boyfriend of the moment. And she was apt to point out that while the Eiffel Tower and the Louvre were great backgrounds for pictures, she'd rather spend her time shopping on the *Champs-Élysées*.

"How long was Gabe away?" Terrie asked.

"Three or four weeks, and when he came home, he was the old Gabe again," Alex said, wistfully recalling how wonderful he was after his return.

"Where was the seminar?" Terrie asked.

"I don't know," Alex said. "It was at a fishing or something place."

"Whitefish Lake," Terrie gasped. "That's Silver Cloud."

"And what could a luxurious Silver Cloud have to do with such a distasteful sport as fishing?" Meredith pursed her lips.

The waitress approached, arms laden with Chinese chicken salads and one hamburger. She placed the salads in front of the women with the exception of Terrie who got the hamburger.

Terrie explained there was a place, Silver Cloud, in Whitefish Lake, Montana, where doctors who were addicted would go for help.

"You think Gabe does drugs?" Alex asked. *Could she have missed that too? Did she even know anything about the man she was married to for twenty years? Was there anything that was real?* She started to cry.

Judi rushed to the table. She bent close to Alex and hugged her. "Oh, Sweetie." She turned to the rest. "What did you do to her?"

"I'm fine," Alex said and took a tissue from Liz. Judi was the only one with whom she didn't feel a hundred percent comfortable. It started when their husbands, both physicians at Brea Presbyterian Hospital, had a huge disagreement over a hospital issue. Judi and Alex each sided with their husband. Even though the men finally resolved their differences, the women's relationship was never the same after that.

Terrie reached out to take Alex's hand. "If he did do drugs, that's the place. There's usually an intervention. The director of the hospital confronts the doctor, and the doctor is offered one of two options: he can go to Silver Cloud and stay there until he dries out, or he can lose his license. If the doctor decides to go to Silver Cloud—and believe me, they all do—then there are no consequences, and there are absolutely no records of doctors who've attended."

"You mean there are licensed physicians who are or were addicted to drugs and still practice?" Liz asked. As the owner of one of the largest insurance agencies in Southern California, she was savvy in all areas of insurance and physicians' profiling, but she seemed surprised by this information.

"That is one of the most highly guarded secrets of the profession," Terrie said.

"Yes and evidently one of the 'most highly guarded secrets' of my marriage or what I thought was my marriage." Alex dabbed her eyes and thought about secrets. Her family was built on them. They formed the foundation of her childhood home, and now she and Gabe had built their own house of cards.

"I've sold insurance for twenty-five years, and I've heard all the dirt on providers, but I've never heard of such a place." Liz twirled her long strand of pearls.

"And I definitely would have heard about it," Judi said, smug in her role as the wife of an esteemed internist at Brea Presbyterian Hospital.

"It's intentionally off the radar," Terrie said.

Meredith blotted her lipstick. "Then how does our Terrie know about it?"

"That I can't discuss, but if Gabe spent time at Silver Cloud, then there wouldn't be any record."

"Did someone from our hospital go there?" Judi asked. Then she apparently caught herself. "I shouldn't be privy to this conversation."

"Terrie, are you going to tell us or not?" Meredith asked, obviously impatient with her best friend.

"Okay." Terrie agreed. "A physician's wife came to see me, and don't worry, Judi, he wasn't from Brea Presbyterian Hospital."

"I should hope you don't treat anyone from there," Judi said.

"Yeah, I'm sure they're all perfect," Alex said, recalling how smug some of the physicians and their wives were. Whenever they'd had conversations at hospital gatherings, their conversations frequently revolved around how much they could make from the patients, not how much they could help them.

"Get on with the story," Liz urged.

Ketchup dripping from her mouth, Terrie took a huge bit of her hamburger. "The wife, my patient, became suspicious about her husband's erratic behavior and confronted him. He adamantly denied any drug usage. He did, however, disappear for a few weeks for a 'seminar.' He wasn't allowed to pack his clothes or say good-bye to his wife and kids."

Judi tapped on her glass, her bright red nail polish and huge Marquis glistening. "I'm still not convinced there is such a place for doctors, but I'm willing to listen."

Terrie patted Alex's hand. "Like Gabe, my patient's husband was better for a while, after which he got even more abusive."

"Did the wife do something?" Alex asked and thought if only she'd done something, then, maybe, this wouldn't have happened.

Terrie continued, "My patient checked her husband's cell phone and found he'd been receiving calls from this one number. She called the number several times, but it would just ring. "The area code was in Montana, so ..."

"Montana's a big state. And are we going to get to some point that will prove helpful for Alex or not?" Liz asked, her impatience obviously motivated by her concern for her best friend.

"I'm just getting used to Gabe leaving for another woman. Now you're throwing drugs into the mix?"

"It was an affair, plain and simple," Meredith said.

"Simple?" Alex fought back tears.

Reaching for her Louis Vuitton purse and taking out a matching card case, Meredith said, "This is the simplest truth." She held out a card: *Robert Dorset, Attorney.* "Alex, you need Mr. Dorset. He *is* the devil incarnate."

"I really wasn't ready to get an attorney before when you gave me those attorneys' names, but Gabe's been acting so weird with the boys lately," Alex said. "I just might call your Mr. Dorset."

"How are the dear boys?" Terrie asked.

"The boys keep coming home with stories about how Gabe promises to take them to games and on vacations. They tell me they don't have to do chores when they're with their dad. Gabe even hired a tutor for Eric and Daniel, and they were getting perfect grades."

"Those don't sound like bad things," Meredith said. The only one without children, her comments about children were usually focused on the little monsters who didn't belong in designer stores or high-end restaurants and the parents who neglected to discipline them.

"I can't afford tutors or the stuff that he's getting the boys used to," Alex said.

"Why does he want them around so much with a new girl-friend?" Meredith asked. "I'd be jetting around the world."

"He travels plenty when it's my weekend. And when he has the boys, he and his girlfriend take them to all these great places. It kills me when the boys talk about how much fun they have with their dad and Linda."

Liz twirled her long strand of pearls. "Alex needs our support now and not a lot of delving into Gabe's stuff."

Alex decided it was time to contact an attorney, fight for what she deserved from Gabe, and, most importantly, create a life for herself and the boys instead of waiting for the possibility that Gabe would return. Hiring an attorney would push them to the point of no return, but she had to face the truth. They were adversaries, now and forever.

The waitress arrived with the check, and they passed the leatherette folder around for each to drop money into it.

"Time to discuss the book," Terrie said, holding up her copy of *The Falls.*

"I loved the way the wedding night was described, first from the wife's point of view and then from the husband's," Liz said.

"Both were believable yet contradictory," Judi agreed.

Demonstrating her ability to get to the heart of any matter, Meredith summarized, "The bride's version of the wedding night was that the groom tore her nightgown and clawed at her in the heat of passion. Whereas, the groom's version was that he tore her nightgown in an attempt to push her away in utter revulsion. I loved the intricate working of the different points of view for the same event."

"Whenever I do couple's therapy," Terrie said, "I always try to show her version, his version, and the real version."

"In my marriage, I had no idea what was real until it was too late," Alex said. Then quickly swooping up her purse and attaché case, she rushed out before succumbing to tears.

CHAPTER 6

A s her alarm clock screamed, usually dividing her night-
mares of the night from those of the day, she realized she'd
finally slept through the night without being jarred awake by the
dreams of Gabe or the chill she felt when she touched his side
of the bed.

She glanced at the open closet, registering the absence of
Gabe's business suits and surgical scrubs. Then she looked at
his tie rack, now empty of his conservative, striped neckties. This
tangible proof that he was gone confirmed her determination to
focus on the future of her new family—just her and her sons.

The sunlight burst into the uncluttered bedroom, reflecting
off of the wedding photograph on the bureau. She looked at the
photo and turned away. But like a tongue to a chipped tooth, her
mind kept returning to thoughts of Gabe. Although she'd promised herself and the women of the book club it was time to move
forward, this reality of the failure of their marriage, their family,
wrapped its tentacles around her. She got out of bed, grabbed
the picture and placed it in the drawer.

She reached for her khaki pants and a crisp white blouse, an
outfit she wore whenever she was too preoccupied to think about
her appearance. She brushed her shoulder-length brown hair,
forced her lips into a smile and left her bedroom.

On her way to the boys' bedrooms, she walked down the hall lined with family photographs. She decided she had to replace them with pictures of solid things like mountains, things one person couldn't destroy.

"Cookie Face," she called to Jon, asleep under his Spiderman quilt. Then she bent down to rub her nose against his face, smelling his still-baby-sweet breath.

Jon snuggled deeper under the covers.

"Come on," she said as she peeled back the comforter and then tickled his belly. "It's a school day."

Jon grabbed the Spiderman doll on his bed. "Mommy, Spiderman could marry you now that Daddy doesn't love you anymore."

Trying not to cry, determined to stay strong, she said, "You're so silly." Then she tickled his belly. "Let's see how you can dress yourself."

"I'll dress me tomorrow." Jon climbed out of bed.

After helping him put on his jeans and shirt, she said, "Wash your face and brush your teeth."

"Daddy told me to always ask Linda to help like a real mommy would," Jon said.

She knew he wasn't challenging her. He was just repeating what he'd heard at Gabe's, but it was painful. "I always help you with everything. Without Daddy, we have to help each other."

"It's sad without my daddy here," Jon said. Then he looked at Alex and asked, "Do you miss Daddy?"

"Yes," she whispered. She couldn't tell him how much she'd loved Gabe and how much she longed for their sweet family. She kissed his brown curls and cursed Gabe. No one had been spared, not even Jon, her carefree baby.

Alex went to open the door to the older boys' bedroom. Inhaling the sneaker smell, she surveyed the room. Eric and

Daniel had picked out the wallpaper themselves—an assortment of footballs, basketballs, and baseballs. Gabe had put up the oak shelves, now laden with trophies. Above each headboard, school certificates hung crookedly, announcing the boys' academic accomplishments. While Gabe valued their baseball and football trophies, it was their academic achievements that pleased Alex the most.

"Eric, dear, wake up." She kissed his forehead.

He climbed out of bed and went to his oak dresser. The drawer squeaked open. He had Gabe's athletic build and the same blue eyes and dark hair. Whenever she wasn't on time to pick him up, he'd get impatient, shake his head and roll his eyes, just like Gabe. She reminded herself she wasn't angry with him; he wasn't Gabe.

As she leaned over Daniel's bed, he reached up and straightened her collar. She smiled and kissed his cheek. He smiled back at her. Then he pulled his navy-and-white-checked comforter over his head, peeking out just long enough to look at the clock on the night table.

"Daniel." She gently shook his shoulder.

"Mom, you look tired," he said, voice muffled under the blanket.

Eric popped his head up from digging in the top dresser drawer. "Where's my light blue polo shirt?"

"Don't be so impatient." She went to his bureau, found the shirt and gave it to him.

"Where are my Lucky jeans?" Eric asked.

She checked his closet. "They must still be in the dryer."

"I wanted to wear them today."

"Maybe it's time you started to do your own laundry."

"I don't have to at Dad's." Eric glared at her.

Another dart to her heart, she had to ignore it. There was no point in responding, explaining how hard she was trying.

"Dad doesn't know how to do the laundry," Daniel volunteered, clearly trying to make her feel better.

"Yeah, he has a cleaning lady," Eric said.

Information about how Gabe had seamlessly settled into his new life unnerved her. She knew his move had to have been choreographed several months prior to his departure. So, before saying anything she'd regret, she rushed downstairs and restarted the dryer. Then she made her way into the kitchen. Neat and organized, with its sleek black appliances and white cabinets and countertops, the kitchen was the one room in the house where she'd always been in charge. It was her sanctuary.

She opened the refrigerator and took out the lunches she had prepared the night before. Quickly grabbing a Magic Marker and a napkin, she wrote, "I," then a heart, and then a "U." She slipped the note into Jon's red Spiderman lunchbox and wondered: *Was Gabe right about how I try too hard to be the perfect mom? Did I ignore him? Does it matter now?*

She'd finally given up her perfect-breakfast phase and placed boxes of cereal on the table. She went to retrieve the *Los Angeles Times* from the front step, brought in the newspaper and spread it out on the kitchen table. As she pulled out one of the white vinyl-cushioned chairs, she looked at the fifth chair, Gabe's chair. At every meal, she would stare at that empty chair, Gabe's absence filling the room. She decided it was time to get rid of it and lugged it out to the garage.

Jon galloped down the stairs. "I want Froot Loops."

"Only healthy cereal," Alex said, getting up to heat the water for her tea.

"We can have Froot Loops at my daddy's house," Jon said.

Eric rushed down the stairs and entered the kitchen. "I want French toast like I have at dad's."

"We're too late for that," she said, her determination slipping a notch.

Daniel put his "Daniel for Class President" sign next to his over-stuffed backpack in the corner of the entryway and took his seat at the table. He poured Cheerios into his bowl and added milk. "Mom, I've got a football game today, so I need a clean uniform."

"Dude," she said. "Would I let you down?"

He grinned and gave her a thumbs-up.

Emptying the last drop of milk into Jon's bowl, Alex realized there wasn't any left for her tea.

The kettle whistled.

"Daniel, want to go over your speech?" she asked.

"I don't want to hear his dumb speech again," Eric said.

"So don't listen." Daniel turned his baseball cap backwards. "Fellow members of the freshman class of Brea Junior High School, I need your help in order to make this the best junior high school in the county. Our school could be—"

The kettle screeched.

Alex got up, took the kettle off the stove, brought it to the table and placed it to the right of the *LA Times*.

Jon finished his cereal, walked over to her, and climbed onto her lap. She hugged him. "Go ahead, Daniel." She took her right hand from Jon's shoulder and flipped over a page of the newspaper.

"Mommy, can we go to the circus?" Jon asked, gazing down at an ad.

"Daniel's giving his speech." She picked up the kettle and pressed open the spout. Steam rose around her face. She started to pour the bubbling, spitting water over the tea bag in her "Wired for the Day" cup and glanced down at the advertisement for a circus that was coming to Brea in five days.

The black circle around the lion tamer on the Ringling Bros. and Barnum & Bailey Circus logo leaped up at her. Her mind flew back in time. *The music, the smells, the fat lady's horrible face, and her ugly warning.* Her chest tightened. Her hands went numb. She felt the kettle slip in her shaky hand.

"I said, 'Can we go to the circus?'" Jon squirmed in her lap, put his hand on her chin, and turned her face toward him.

"Um, baby?" She tried to steady the kettle.

"Yippee! We're going to the circus." Jon squealed, clapped his hands together, and then flung them out, jarring her right hand.

The kettle hit the floor, splattering boiling water onto Jon's legs. Jon wailed.

"Oh, God!" She jumped up, carried him to the counter and put his legs into the sink. As she ran cold water over his legs, he pushed the faucet away, spraying water all over the kitchen floor.

"Mommy, it hurts!" he cried.

"Cookie Face, I know, I know. Mommy's sorry."

"I'm calling Dad," Eric said, dashing to the phone.

Before she could protest, he dialed.

"Mom burned Jon," Eric said into the phone. Then he was quiet for a while, obviously listening to Gabe. He turned to her. "Dad said to come to the hospital right now."

Ignoring Eric, she said, "Daniel, get the burn cream, *now*."

"Where is it?" Daniel asked.

"In the laundry room under the cabinet." Alex unbuckled Jon's pants.

"Leave me alone." Jon pushed her hand away. "Mommy, you're hurting me."

"I'd never hurt you, Cookie Face."

"Yes, you did." Jon cried.

Running toward the sink with the first aid kit in hand, Daniel slipped in the puddle of water and fell.

"Good slide," Eric said.

"Daniel, are you okay?" Alex asked as she tried to take off Jon's pants.

Jon screamed and kicked.

The phone rang.

Eric picked it up. "Dad wants to know why we didn't leave already."

"Tell him I'm trying to put cream on Jon's legs."

"Dad said to bring him right now, and don't try to be a doctor."

"I am a doctor, and I know exactly what to do," she said, no longer willing to allow Gabe to discredit her or say disparaging things about her being a chiropractor. She clenched her jaw to keep from saying anything else. The important thing was caring for Jon, making sure he was going to be okay, even if it meant listening to Gabe and taking Jon to his hospital

She took him down from the counter, his pants soaking wet. She grabbed her keys. "Everyone in the car."

Clutching Jon to her, she hurried to the Land Cruiser.

Daniel opened the back door. She eased Jon into his seat and leaned across him to snap the seat belt.

"Ouch!" Jon kicked her. "You're hurting me again."

"Shotgun," Eric called.

"Just get in," she yelled. "One of you in the back and the other in the front. Belt yourselves in, and forget about shotgun or any-thing else except getting Jon to the hospital."

"Don't get mad at me," Eric said. "You did it."

She climbed into the car and started to drive. While listening to Jon cry, she could barely focus on the road. Whenever her baby or any of her boys got hurt, she felt their pain and needed to comfort them.

"Owww." Jon kicked at the front seat.

"Cut it out," Eric yelled.

"He's in pain," she said.

"He doesn't have to kick my seat," Eric said.

She quickly turned to look at Jon. "Cookie, if you keep your legs still, it'll hurt less."

"We'll be there soon." Daniel tried to comfort his brother. "Dad'll take care of you."

"Yes," she whispered, but the horrific reality of that statement gripped her. She knew Daniel didn't mean to discount her, but his belief in Gabe's infallibility undermined her. And she hadn't wanted Eric to call his father. She could have handled this without him. The boys had to learn that she was the parent they had to count on now.

She pulled into the semicircular entrance to Brea Presbyterian Hospital and stared at Dr. Gabriel Rose leaning on one of the marble pillars, hands on hips. He shook his head, opened the car door, and lifted Jon out of his car seat.

"I've got him now," Gabe said confidently.

Covered in a white hospital-issue laboratory coat over green scrubs, his mouth mask bunched up under his jaw, Gabe appeared taller than his five-foot-ten frame. It was difficult not to respect, even admire and trust, this man who belonged to the uniform, the hospital, the profession. But today, she saw only a man capable of destroying the serenity of her family.

Alex gave her keys to the parking attendant, and they all followed Gabe to the emergency room as he carried Jon into the hospital. She bristled at the way Gabe strode down the long corridor, confident in his domain.

Gabe turned to her. "What did you do to him?" he demanded.

"It was an accident," she said, furious at his accusation.

Two nurses walked toward them and nodded at Gabe.

"These are my boys," he said, smiling at the nurses.

My boys. Alex winced, hating his excision of her from his life.

"They're so cute," the one with the "Cindy" name tag pinned to her uniform said.

The other one made a little-girl wave and winked.

Jon cried out.

"Don't worry." Gabe kissed him. "I'm here now."

Annoyed by his arrogance and his intimation that he was the competent parent, she fought back tears.

They went through the emergency room doors. Gabe placed Jon on a gurney. As he peeled off Jon's jeans, he appeared horrified at the angry red blotches covering the boy's thighs.

Alex's heart thumped. She could barely breathe.

Gabe glared at her. "I'm going to the dermatology department to get Kaplan to look at this." He stormed out of the room.

"I'm going too." Eric approached the door.

"Wait here," she said.

Eric folded his hands across his chest. "Why?"

"Just stay put," she said.

While they waited for Dr. Kaplan, Jon whimpered. She stroked his back.

"You've gotta take me home right now," Daniel said.

"Jon is hurt," Alex said. "What's wrong with you?"

"I have to go home," Daniel repeated. "You left my campaign sign in the hallway."

She promised they'd rush home, and he'd have it before the assembly.

Five minutes later, the metal doors parted with a whoosh to reveal the imposing, six-foot-three frame of Dr. Barry Kaplan, Gabe's racquetball partner and head of the dermatology department. Usually jocular, the life of the hospital parties, Dr. Kaplan greeted them somberly. He shook Alex's hand and mumbled something resembling, "I'm sorry."

She wondered whether he was saying he was sorry about the divorce or the accidental scalding of her child.

Kaplan reached into the upper pocket of his white lab coat and took out his eyeglasses. He put them on and looked at Jon's thighs.

"Will he be okay?" Alex asked.

Ignoring her, Kaplan turned to Gabe. "Second-degree, wouldn't you agree?"

"Might blister badly," Gabe said, and then appearing as though he just had an idea, he motioned to Kaplan. "Let's go to the nurses' station and get them to prep everything."

Kaplan agreed, and then said to Jon, "Your daddy and I'll be right back to take care of you."

Kaplan walked out of the room. Gabe followed.

Alex wondered why Gabe motioned to Kaplan and why they both left the room.

Engrossed in conversation, Gabe and Kaplan returned. They stopped talking when they got within earshot of Alex.

A nurse came into the room with a sterile set-up.

As Kaplan moved to the table and reached for Jon's leg, the boy pulled away, almost kicking the doctor. "Are you going to hurt me?" he asked.

"It'll only take a second," Kaplan said and poured the sterile solution over the area.

"It's making more burns," Jon cried.

Daniel covered his eyes, and Eric watched intently.

Kaplan opened a tube of silver sulfadiazine cream, squeezed some onto a tongue depressor, and applied it. Then he placed a gauze patch over the cream on each thigh and sealed the borders with adhesive tape. He looked at Alex and said, "You'll have to make sure it stays clean."

"It'll probably blister within a few hours." Gabe shook his head. "Alex, you better be sure he doesn't pick at it."

"Absolutely," Kaplan said. "Blisters are nature's Band-Aids and, if he pops the blisters, then the area is vulnerable to bacteria and viruses. And extremely prone to scarring." Then he turned to the nurse. "The tetanus shot?"

"No," Jon screamed.

Alex went to him.

He pulled away from her. "Mommy, why did you do this?"

Gabe reached over and held his son while the nurse gave Jon the injection. Then Gabe grabbed his son's pants. "They're drenched," he said.

Annoyed at herself that in her haste to get him to the hospital, she hadn't thought about bringing a dry pair of pants. Then she looked up and saw Gabe and Kaplan nod at each other. There was something almost conspiratorial about the way they were acting, but then she decided Jon's well-being was her priority, and their reaction was inconsequential.

Kaplan tousled Jon's hair. "Buddy, you're good to go, but stay away from coffee for a while."

As soon as Kaplan left the room, Gabe pointed at Alex. "Don't you remember my rule when I brought the Wheelers' daughter here? Kaplan had to graft her arm after her father spilled coffee on her?" He shook his head in obvious disgust. "My rule has always been no hot coffee near the kids."

"It was an accident," she protested loudly. She wondered how he'd already forgotten she never drank coffee and always had tea. It was just a little detail. Maybe he'd forgotten everything about their twenty-five years together, while she was haunted by each and every detail. He seemed to have moved on seamlessly. "An accident," she repeated.

"Keep your voice down, Alexandra," he said.

"You keep your voice down," she countered. "I've had enough of your bullying."

"Just get out of here." Gabe turned away. "I'll send one of the nurses out to buy Jon a new pair of pants, and then I'll take the boys to school."

"But your patients?" she asked, surprised he'd just leave work to take the children to school.

"I've got people here who can help me," he said.

"Linda," she whispered, certain he'd go directly to Linda's office, deliver the children to her, and she'd be the one to take them to school.

"I've got to stop off home and get my sign," Daniel said.

Alex squeezed Daniel to her. "We'll run home, and then I'll drop you off at school."

"I gotta see the dead babies floating in the bathtubs," Jon said.

Eric frowned. "What's he talking about?"

Jon tugged at Gabe's sleeve. "Dad, when you and Mommy used to talk to each other, you said when the babies come out of the mommies and they're dead, then they bag 'em and send 'em to the bath."

"Path ... pathology." Gabe laughed. "That's where doctors study people who've died to determine what went wrong."

"So, there aren't any bathtubs here?" Jon touched the bandages, giving in to more tears.

Gabe took out a starched white handkerchief and wiped Jon's eyes.

"Mommy loves you," she said to Jon, her heart constricting.

"Alex, go to work." Gabe shooed her. "I've got everything under control. If Jon's better, I'll drop him off at nursery school. Right now, he needs to stay with me."

She leaned over and kissed Jon. He turned away.

She thought about the special story she'd read to him tonight. Then they'd recapture their giggly times. Blowing a kiss to Jon and Eric, she turned and left with Daniel.

As Alex drove Daniel home to pick up his sign, he practiced his speech.

"I've got my game this afternoon," Daniel reminded her as they pulled up to his school.

"Of course I remember. I'll be home early enough to take you to the game."

"Love you." He got out of the car, opened the back door, and reached in for his sign.

"Love you." Alex touched her wrist and thought about her own return from school. Fraught with fear and anxiety, she never knew what horrific torture her mother would impart on her when she returned from school or whether it would be one of the rare afternoons when her mother would be kind and loving.

CHAPTER 7

A lex rubbed the scar on her wrist, a reminder of how horrific and unpredictable her mother had always been. She recalled the time she came home from fifth grade with her little sister, Sara.

"Hi," they called to their mother who was seated in the green webbed chair that memorized the contours of her huge body and strained to support it.

Jowls jangling, her mother took a puff of her Viceroy cigarette and asked, "How was school?"

"Um," Alex said, too terrified to tell her mother that school was horrible, and it was because of her. Alex stared down at her mother's swollen feet. She knew her mother never listened to her anyway. Alex had always wanted to test her mother and say something like, "I ran with scissors at school today." But she was sure her mother would just say, "That's nice."

Sara went to her room to get her doll.

Alex's mother inhaled from her cigarette, then slowly released the smoke through her nostrils. "I asked, 'How was school?'"

"Today, there was a Mother's Day party, and you knew it," Alex said, angry at her mother for never leaving the house to do things with her like Girl Scouts, shopping, or even parent-teacher conferences.

"So?" Her mother grabbed the remote and changed the channel.

"Why didn't you come to my class today for the Mother's Day party?" Alex asked.

Her mother clicked the remote, changing the channel.

Alex approached her mother's chair. "Everyone else's mother was there."

"Um." Her mother shrugged her shoulders.

"I was the only kid in the class without a mother."

"Young lady, you have a mother, but I don't drive."

"'Cause you're too fat to fit behind the wheel," Alex said and then panicked. She knew she'd made a terrible mistake.

Her mother's face contorted with rage. She leaned over, grabbed Alex's right hand, and pulled her close.

Alex's heart pounded, and she tried to pull her arm away.

Tightening her hold on Alex's tiny wrist, her mother reached over to the ashtray with her free hand and took her lit cigarette.

There was a smell like when the English muffin was left in the toaster too long, only worse. Alex felt pain and screamed.

Sara ran into the room. "What's wrong?"

Afraid to look down at her wrist, Alex held perfectly still.

"Oh, my cigarette fell, and poor Alex was in the way." Her mother gave Alex a cautionary look and turned to Sara. "Sara, don't just stand there. Your sister hurt herself. Get her a wet towel."

Sara dashed out of the room.

Cradling her wrist, Alex said, "I'm going to tell Daddy."

"You do that, and, trust me, this won't be the last time you get hurt."

"My daddy wouldn't let anything happen to me."

Her mother laughed. "He's only home at night, but I'm here all day. Remember that, Missy."

Sara returned and put the wet cloth around Alex's wrist. "Shouldn't we take her to the pediatrician?" she asked, apparently pleased with herself for using such a grown-up word.

"No," her mother said. "Sara, you can go, and I'll take care of her." Sara didn't move.

"Come to Mommy." Her mother held out her arms to Alex.

Alex moved just a little closer to her mother's chair.

Her mother looked up at Sara standing at the door. "Sara, it was such a bad accident. Could've been you."

Sara ran out of the room.

Her mother laughed menacingly. "I'd never hurt my little girl," she said and cackled. Then she pulled Alex to her and stroked her daughter's long hair gently, lovingly.

Confused, Alex felt loved, and she wanted to believe she was.

And her mother definitely loved her—that is, if the burn on her right wrist had happened the way her mother had explained it to her father that night:

Since it had been such a bad day, her mother had to double the medication prescribed for the pain she'd had following her failed back surgery. She'd usually take enough pills to get through the day until the night, when she would take another pill and escape into sleep. But today, the pain had been intolerable, so she'd taken an extra Vicodin.

When the girls had come home from school, she'd asked Alex how school was. She always wanted to know what the girls did in school, but Alex hadn't answered. Alex had just mumbled something. In order to hear what Alex was saying, her mother had reached for the remote. But instead of pushing mute, in her Vicodin-and-Valium-induced haze, she'd pushed the channel button. Alex had gotten angry and tried to grab the remote. As Alex reached for the remote, her hand had almost knocked over the ashtray. When her mother had lunged for the cigarette, trying to prevent it from falling, it had accidentally fallen onto Alex's wrist.

If it had happened that way, then Alex's mother couldn't have burned her intentionally. It would have been Alex's fault. Even then, Alex knew that, when tested, a mother's reality was more credible than that of a child. And Alex was too afraid to say anything different; her mother could hurt her again and again.

Wondering how those childhood memories could stretch their tentacles so effortlessly into the present and make her feel like a child, Alex pulled into her underground parking spot, got out of the car, and took the elevator to her office.

CHAPTER 8

A s Alex walked through the waiting room, she started to feel calmer and knew work would soon take her away from her traumatic morning. Just looking at the way the picture window captured the second-story tree line and the sun reflected off of the cobalt blue and red in the Joan Miró print on the wall, made her relax.

Passing a handsome fireman in uniform who was sitting in the waiting room filling out the patient intake form, she started toward her private office.

"Dr. Rose, this just came in for you." Rebecca, the receptionist, handed her a fax.

Alex looked at the fax and whispered, "I need two minutes."

Rebecca nodded, her auburn hair shimmering.

Alex went to her office, shut the door, and sat down behind the desk. She looked at the fax from Robert Dorset, the attorney she'd hired at Meredith's recommendation. *Gabriel Rose vs. Alexandra Rose.* The finality of their names on a legal document nauseated her. All she wanted to do was lunge across the desk, collapse in the seat designated for patients, and have someone ask, "What's wrong? How can I help you?"

Taking a deep breath, she reminded herself that, in this office, she was not the superfluous wife whose name appeared on the divorce decree. Here, she was the doctor of chiropractic, National Board Examiner, board member of the Academy of Forensic and Industrial Chiropractic Consultants, and Qualified Medical Examiner. Although Gabe had never considered her board positions or advanced certifications of any importance, keeping up with the newest diagnostic and treatment protocols was paramount to her success.

Engrossed in the faxed divorce agreement, she was jolted by the intercom. Rebecca announced that the new patient had completed his paperwork and was ready to see her.

"Rebecca, give me five more minutes," Alex requested. She needed to clear her mind, focus on her patients, and stop worrying about Jon's burn; but she couldn't.

She punched her attorney's number into the phone. "This is Dr. Rose. I need to speak to Mr. Dorset."

"He's in court today," the receptionist said.

"He was supposed to have reviewed this agreement, but there are no corrections."

"Mrs. Rose, maybe everything's perfect."

"Perfect?" Alex wondered how anything could ever be perfect again. She'd been dealing with Dorset's receptionist who'd been blocking her access to him ever since she'd signed the papers engaging him as her attorney. At their first meeting, Mr. Dorset had assured her he'd be accessible to her at any time. But since their initial meeting, she'd only had one face-to-face meeting and two brief telephone conversations with him.

She was sorry she'd taken Meredith's advice and hired Mr. Dorset, but now, it was too late to find another attorney. And if she lost patience with his receptionist, she'd never get to speak to him. "Could you please have him call me when he breaks for lunch?"

"Mrs. Rose, he doesn't make calls at lunch. That's when he preps his clients."

"I *am* his client. He's had the draft from my husband's attorney for two weeks, and he hasn't done anything with it," Alex said, fighting to stay calm.

"Mrs. Rose, two weeks is customary for such a draft."

"He was supposed to have returned the document with his corrections," Alex repeated, her stomach churning. "It has to be ready to sign by tomorrow night."

"I'll have Mr. Dorset return your call at his earliest convenience." His gatekeeper hung up.

Alex slammed down the phone. Fearful the document wouldn't be revised by tomorrow night, she knew Gabe would be angry with her.

Just as she started to put the document in her briefcase, her partner, Dr. Seth Stone, knocked on her office door. A handsome man, his patrician features, thin lips, and aquiline nose were softened by the warmth of his blue eyes. His perfectly trimmed beard made him look professorial.

"May I?" he asked and entered her office.

She waved the papers at Seth and asked, "How could I have missed this?"

"Don't be so hard on yourself. We all think we evaluate events realistically, but the way we process is distorted by our history." He walked around the desk and put his hands on her shoulders.

"I have five patients waiting and don't have much time to talk about history," she snapped. Then she caught herself. Seth was just being kind, she realized. There was no reason to take out her frustration with her attorney's secretary on him. But sometimes, he was too pedantic.

"Alex, I have faith in you." He winked and went on to his next patient.

Alex looked up and saw Rebecca standing in the doorway with the fireman who'd been filling out the paperwork in the waiting room.

Rebecca introduced Kevin and motioned for him to sit in the chair opposite Alex. Then Rebecca placed his chart on Alex's desk.

As Kevin eased into the chair, Alex stood up and followed Rebecca out of the room, instructing her to interrupt if Mr. Dorset called.

Letting work transport her to a safe place, Alex returned to her office, sat down behind her desk, and asked Kevin about his back pain. He explained how he'd climbed up an embankment wearing a Scott Air-Pack on his back and carrying a fire hose. Alex questioned him about prior episodes of back pain, which he denied. She then escorted him to an exam room, handed him a gown, and went to adjust the next patient.

Ten minutes later, she returned to the exam room. Clad only in boxer shorts, Kevin sat on the exam table. "Didn't need the gown." He held out the folded gown for her.

She looked at him—broad-shouldered, muscular, and tanned. Suddenly, she was short of breath. She imagined him on the December page of the firemen's calendar: bare-chested with red suspenders and black rubber boots, standing on a snowdrift, holding his yellow fire hat in front of his privates. Shocked by her fantasy, she wondered if he noticed her face had reddened. She thought about how long it had been since she'd had sex. She recalled when Gabe had told her about Linda, he'd also told her to find out for herself what sex was like with another person. Although she'd said she was going to find out for herself, she hadn't even considered it.

Pulling herself back to the moment, she checked Kevin's ranges of motion and reflexes. Then she ran the pinwheel down his legs, and he reported feeling it equally. She touched his back and asked whether his pain was at that point.

"How'd you know?" he asked.

"Your back muscles are extremely tight. I can feel the spasm." Then she assured him that, after a few adjustments and therapy, he'd experience relief. For years, she'd told patients, "You'll be fine. Your pain will be gone." Today, she needed to hear those words herself.

Keeping a reassuring hand on Kevin's back, she said, "My assistant, Rebecca, will put you on the muscle stimulation machine to relax your muscles, then I'll adjust your back."

She explained how mobilizing his spine would help and hurried to Rebecca's desk and gave her instructions for Kevin. Then she proceeded to her next patient.

When she and Seth passed each other in the hallway, he paused, put his hands into the pockets of his gray woolen slacks, and studied her. "You still look terribly upset. Is it that agreement?"

"Yes," she said, not ready to talk about Jon, even with Seth.

"There's something else," he said. "I know you too well." He looked at her with concern and softly assured her, "You can tell me anything."

"I burned Jon's legs today, and he hates me," Alex said and recounted the morning's debacle.

"Jon loves you. I've seen him with you," Seth said. "All your boys adore you."

"Not today." She shook her head.

"But was he badly burned?" Seth asked with apparent concern.

"I'm sure he won't have any scars."

Seth took a breath, appearing relieved. He put his hand on her elbow and gently turned her toward him. "Alex, remember white tennis balls?"

"Yes, but ..."

"When I was a kid learning to play tennis, I was afraid of getting hit by the white tennis balls when the other kids would slam the shit out of the ball."

"Seth, where are you going with this nostalgia for tennis balls that are no longer used?"

"The tennis balls scared me until I learned to take them as they came, react, and respond as best I could. Now, when I play and my opponent is really good, I imagine the tennis balls are white. You can't be afraid of something that doesn't exist."

"True, sometimes fear overwhelms me, but this was real." She smiled at him, appreciative of how he always tried to make her feel better. "Remember, I'm leaving early for Daniel's game," she said and proceeded to the next exam room.

At 1:45 p.m., right before her last patient of the day, she reminded herself she had to leave by 2:15 p.m. in order to pick Daniel up and take him to his football game. She couldn't be late.

She studied the chart in the holder outside the exam room door: Helen Oster. Alex hadn't seen her in a year. On the intake form, Helen had indicated she had a swollen right ankle and had been under the care of a podiatrist for more than two months without improvement.

Alex opened the door. *Shit! Not today.* She moved the stool close to the exam table and probed Helen's ankle, knowing exactly what she'd feel: a fluid-filled ankle—pitting edema—a sign of congestive heart failure.

She grabbed the stethoscope and cuff from the metal cart beside the exam table and proceeded to take Ms. Oster's blood pressure.

"But it's my ankle."

"Just let me do a little extra checking." Alex wrapped the nylon cuff around Helen's left arm. The reading alarmed her: 180/105.

"I need to refer you to an internist."

"Dr. Rose, you helped me with my neck last time. The podiatrist wasn't helping much, so I thought you could adjust my ankle."

"The swelling isn't getting better because it's not caused by your ankle. It could be a sign of an internal problem. Rebecca will make an appointment for you with Dr. Feinberg."

Helen asked one question after another. Alex glanced at her watch. *Damn!* She wouldn't make it home in time to take Daniel to his game.

Seth knocked on the door. "Dr. Rose, when you've concluded the examination, could you please step into my office?"

"We've just finished." Alex resisted the urge to glance at her watch again. After assuring Helen that Dr. Feinberg was an excellent diagnostician, she excused herself and joined Seth in the hallway.

"How are you doing?" he asked.

"I've gotta go."

He nodded. "All of your boys love you, and I know nothing could have happened today to diminish that." Then sounding like the professor he'd once been, he whispered, "White tennis balls. Remember, you can't be afraid of something that isn't real."

"You convince Jon of that," she said. She'd never told Seth how her mother had burned her. She knew all too well about white tennis balls—things that no longer existed—but the terror was still tangible.

"Alex, don't worry."

"I'm late for Daniel's game," she said. "Oh, what did you want to talk about?"

"Nothing." Seth looked away.

"You're an angel," she said, appreciative of how, from the moment they'd partnered, their relationship had given her the freedom to attend all of her children's activities. He was offered the same, but he only went to Arizona to see his children once a month.

She left the office.

Once in her car, she looked at her cell phone. Three messages. Fingers shaking, she dialed the house, only to be interrupted by an incoming call.

"Helen needs to ask you one question," Rebecca said.

"Put her on," Alex said, anxious to call the boys. She repeated everything she'd previously told Helen.

At 2:35, she called home. No answer.

Terrified something could have happened, she accelerated. She sped onto the on-ramp and braked, narrowly avoiding the car in front of her.

At five minutes before three, she opened the door and called, "Eric? Daniel?"

Silence.

She ran upstairs. Daniel's uniform was gone. Fear gripped her. She rushed downstairs. There was a note on the kitchen table:

Dear Mom,

I couldn't miss the game.

Eric called Dad, and he took us.

Love you,

Danny

CHAPTER 9

Since Gabe hadn't called to tell her he still had Jon with him, she hurried to the nursery school to pick Jon up. Reluctantly, he took her hand, and they walked to the car. She secured him in his car seat and told him how sorry she was about the burns on his legs.

He put his hands over his ears.

She pulled into a parking spot at the field, got out of the car, and unbuckled Jon's seat belt. As she tried to give him a kiss, he turned his head away. The minute they reached the field, he dropped her hand and ran to Gabe.

Alex climbed up onto the top row of the bleachers as far from Gabe as possible.

Daniel spotted her in the crowd and gave her a thumbs-up. Obviously, he'd forgiven her for being late. She watched Eric and Gabe share a laugh while Jon clung to Gabe, never turning to look at her.

After a team member made the final kick, everyone ran onto the field.

Eric walked over to Alex and tugged at her arm. "I'm hungry. Let's get home."

Accustomed to Eric's demands whenever the spotlight was deflected away from him, Alex turned away and hurried to the field to join the other parents. She squeezed into place to make a victory tunnel through which the team members would run. Reluctantly, she reached across to take Gabe's hands and help form the victory bridge. As she placed her fingertips on Gabe's, connected yet distant, her chest tightened.

After the team ran through the tunnel, Alex and the boys left the field and got into her car. She looked over and saw Gabe was watching. He seemed to exude disdain, then anger. Then she saw his lower lip tighten, and a sinister look crossed his face. He had an expression she'd seen many times before—abject determination. When he wanted something, he made sure he got it.

Alex drove home for a night like every other night since Gabe had left: homework with the older boys, dinner, baths, and, finally, a bedtime story for Jon.

She entered Jon's room.

"Mommy, my legs hurt," he cried.

"I know, baby," she said.

"I need Honey to lick my tears," Jon said.

"I miss her too." Alex sat down on the blue chair near the dresser. She turned on the Spiderman lamp, and Jon climbed onto her lap. She cuddled him close and began to read. At the end of each page, she waited for him to turn to the next one.

When she finished reading *Green Eggs and Ham,* Jon closed the book and looked at her. "I'm too hurted to sleep. Tell me a real story, Mommy."

"All right, Cookie Face." Alex told him a story about a little boy who was separated from his mother in a supermarket.

"What did the boy do without his mommy?" Jon asked.

"The little boy started to cry, and the store manager went up to the boy and asked him what was wrong. And the boy answered, 'I lost my mommy.'"

Jon's eyes widened. "Did he find her?"

"The manager told the little boy, 'We'll find her, but you must tell me what she looks like.' The boy thought awhile and then said, 'My mommy is the most beautiful woman in the world.'"

"Is that true?" Jon asked.

"You'll find out." She touched his nose. "The store manager looked all over the store but couldn't find a beautiful woman. Suddenly, a lady with a hooked nose and a wart on her cheek walked up to the manager and asked if he'd seen her son. And just as the manager started to tell the ugly woman they hadn't found her son, the boy yelled, 'Mommy!'"

"Did they find the right mother?"

"Yes." Alex patted his head. "To the little boy, his mother was the most beautiful woman in the world."

"Are you the most beautiful woman in the world?" Jon asked.

She laughed, tousled his hair, and asked, "What do you think?"

"Not today." Jon climbed down from her lap and got under the Spiderman comforter.

"Sweetie, I love you." She kissed him, turned off the lamp, and went to the doorway. "Sleep tight," she said, assuring herself that, in time, he'd be her giggly Jon once again.

Jon called after her, "Mommy, I don't care what Daddy said today about how you burned me for purpose."

She gasped, ran to Jon, scooped him into her arms, and asked, "Do you know what an accident is?"

"Okay, Mommy," he said. "You're beautiful."

"Cookie Face, I love you." She closed his door and went to the older boys' room.

After kissing them good night, she went to her bedroom. *How could Gabe have said I burned Jon intentionally? Why is he trying to turn the boys against me?* Determined to keep the family unharmed, she opened her briefcase and reached for the agreement her attorney had faxed back without any changes. As she started to read the first of the twenty-five stapled pages, she stopped and stared at their names. Amid the bold black-and-white letters were two people who had loved each other. The beautiful family they'd created was proof of that.

Now, her life seemed to stop when the boys were at Gabe's twice a week and every other weekend. The nights when the boys were gone were the most difficult. The house felt so empty. Nights were proof the dream had ended.

When the boys were with Gabe, Alex tried to fill the void by playing tennis. It helped a little. The tennis club, a haven from the loneliness of the childless house, became her oasis. And she knew this Friday night could be a much-needed diversion, if she dared.

As she thought about her impending date with Luke Jackson, the man who'd become her regular tennis partner, she felt a pang of excitement. Luke had joined the club last month. Since he'd won the member–guest tournament in his division, he was given a month's membership dues as a prize. After playing at the club for the first month, insisting the whole time that he wasn't going to join since the dues were too high, he'd joined the club anyway.

Almost from the time he'd become a member, the court director had paired Alex with him in matches. They'd played together several times, winning almost every time. Subtly at first, then more brazenly, Luke had started to flirt with her.

On the tennis court, whenever it was her turn to serve, he'd hand her the ball, allowing his fingers to brush hers. She'd take the tennis ball slowly, reluctant to break the connection. Then, as they played out the point, they'd move together perfectly.

Playing tennis alongside him the past few weeks, she'd noticed how he'd prey on their opponents' weaknesses. He moved with a feline grace, wearing down their opponents with strength and speed. Tennis seemed the perfect sport for him. After they'd win the match, he'd place his hand on the small of her back ever so lightly as they'd walk to the net to shake hands with their opponents.

When he'd asked her out, she hadn't been expecting it and had agreed, partially because she was taken off guard. It had been twenty-five years since her first date with Gabe, and dating was completely foreign to her. She decided she'd talk it over with the women at the First Friday Book Club tomorrow and get some pointers from Meredith. But, she had to admit, she was attracted to Luke. He was handsome and charming, almost dangerously charming.

CHAPTER 10

Alex rushed to Waters Restaurant for the September First Friday Book Club meeting.

No one was there except Liz, thumbing through this month's novel as she twirled her glistening strand of pearls.

"Are you okay?" Alex asked, wondering why Liz hadn't returned her calls for the past two days. It was the first time she and Liz hadn't spoken in that long. And Alex had really needed to talk to Liz about Jon's burn *and* Luke Jackson. With Gabe no longer the holder of her dreams and foibles, Liz was the only one in the world she trusted with her secrets. But it wasn't like Liz to miss a check-in with her.

"I owe you a call, but things haven't been good with my dad," Liz said. "I left work early yesterday to take my dad to his doctor, get him groceries, and take him to the pharmacy to pick up his medication. When we got to the pharmacy, he realized he'd forgotten his insurance card. He's forgetting things lately. At the pharmacy, they refused to give him his medication without his card."

"What'd you do?" Alex asked, concerned about Liz's father, but even more worried about Liz.

"I told them I'm in insurance, and I know you don't have to have a card to get your prescription. But the pain-in-the-ass clerk insisted upon some form of identification such as a driver's license."

"Does he still have one?"

"No, I took it away last year when he had the accident. So, the clerk asked my dad if he had another form of ID, maybe a Costco card. I told her, 'He's eighty-six. Do really you think he buys in bulk?'"

Alex laughed. That was what she loved about Liz—she could always find the humor in any situation.

Liz checked her phone. "Then, yesterday afternoon, my father had a meltdown from the stress. I had to keep him with me for the entire day, and he even had to stay overnight with us."

"Yesterday, I called your office, and your dad answered the phone. He said now that I'm single, he'd take me out on a date." Alex took off the sunglasses which Liz had given her last month and winked.

"Alex, he didn't tell me you called. And anyway, you're way too old for my dad. He likes them at twenty or thirty, max."

"Well, maybe I'll marry him just so you'll have to call me Mom."

Liz gave a throaty laugh. "He's all yours. Take him."

Alex took a breath, preparing to tell Liz about Jon's burn. But she looked up and saw Terrie and Meredith approach. She wasn't ready to talk about the burn with all of the book club women, especially not in front of Judi, who might repeat it to some of the wives whose husbands also worked at Gabe's hospital.

"Look at the odd couple," Liz said, pointing to Terrie and Meredith.

As Alex assessed them, she agreed: Terrie wore a long jean skirt, flowered blouse, and flats. She had a macramé purse slung over her shoulder. Meredith was perfectly coiffed and tailored in a blue pinstriped Chanel suit, crisp white blouse, and stiletto heels with red soles. She carried a Prada purse in one hand and her attaché case in the other.

Terrie hugged Alex.

Meredith looked around the table. "Where's Judi?"

"She didn't call me," Liz said. "Don't know why she's always late."

The waitress took their orders—as usual, Chinese chicken salads for everyone except Terrie, who had a rare burger and fries.

"Should we order for Judi?" Terrie asked.

"I'll share with her when she gets here," Alex said. "I haven't been hungry lately."

"You need to eat," Liz said. "Your clothes are swimming on you."

"As I said last month, we need an emergency shopping trip," said Meredith. Then she extended her hand to Alex, motioning for the divorce papers.

Just touching the papers caused Alex's gut to tighten. Divorce was so much like falling in love—when you're barely able to function because the lover invades your every thought.

Liz held up the *Los Angeles Times* travel section and pointed to a picture of a sloth in a tree. "Look what I found in Sunday's paper."

"The Amazon?" Meredith glanced at the newspaper and then down at her French-manicured nails. "Any five-stars?"

"Only tents," Liz said.

"I, Meredith Blackstone, do not camp."

"It could be fun," Terrie said.

Flinging back strands of her long dark hair, Meredith said, "Terrie, obviously your hairstyle does not require the use of a blow dryer like *moi*."

"Well, I just might be too busy coiffing my hair to retrieve your mail while you're away next week." Terrie brushed her short brown bangs, shiny as a baby seal's fur, across her forehead.

"Ladies," Liz said, "the tents have mosquito netting."

Meredith shook her head. "Tents, mosquitoes, and no Neiman Marcus. I'm out."

Alex knew she'd never leave the boys for that long unless they had a trip planned with their father and the timing coincided, and she was certain that would be unlikely. She also suspected Liz might have decided a girls' trip was just what Alex needed. She was sure Liz was trying to get her to do something fun, experience a change of scenery, and, most importantly, have a respite from her divorce. And that was exactly what had motivated Alex to accept a date with the exotically handsome Luke Jackson, the man who recently joined her tennis club and surprised her by asking her out.

But Alex also wondered why Liz's husband wouldn't want to join her on such an adventure. "Liz, what about your husband?"

"Stan's arthritis wouldn't do well in the humidity," Liz said.

"Humidity?" Alex began to laugh. "This is sounding better and better."

The waitress arrived with their meals. She placed the burger in front of Terrie and distributed the salads to everyone else.

"I'm worried about Judi." Terrie dialed Judi's number. No answer.

"So you'll go?" Liz used the assumptive close that always worked when she sold insurance.

Picking up the ketchup and drowning the French fries, Terrie said, "Alex, you need some diversion."

"Divorce is enough of a diversion," Alex said, certain that diversion was the reason she'd agreed to go out with Luke. But maybe a trip to the Amazon was what she needed to take her mind off the divorce and distractions like Luke.

"Come on. You've got to decide right away so we can start the malaria medicine," Liz said.

"Malaria?" Alex said. "Bugs, heat, and malaria are supposed to cheer me up? And aren't there piranhas?"

"Piranhas are right here," Meredith said. "I've been dating 'em, except for Warren."

"Maybe she'll meet a marvelous medicine man there." Terrie's eyes widened.

"Been there, done that, remember?" Alex said.

"But maybe the Amazon medicine man won't have a receptionist to screw." Meredith pursed her lips.

"I'm thinking of dating someone," Alex said and picked at her salad.

Liz looked surprised. "Have you been holding out on your best friend?"

They all turned to Alex. Her face reddened. "Liz, I called you several times over the past two days, but you didn't call me back."

"And I told you, if you left a message at the office with my dad, you shouldn't have expected me to have gotten it," Liz reminded her.

Alex reached into her purse. "I have the tennis-club newsletter with his picture somewhere in here."

Terrie rubbed her hands together, preparing to hear a story. "Tell us all about him."

"First, I have to see if he's sexy enough." Meredith reached for the newsletter. "I mean, this will be your first time, right?"

Terrie grabbed the newsletter, looked at the front page, and squinted at the glossy photo. "I see a woman's face, but I can't see the man."

"Well, the picture is too ... um ... shiny." Alex felt her heart pound. "It's hard to see his face. He's, um, dark."

"Black?" Terrie asked incredulously.

"Bi-racial," Alex said.

Meredith dabbed her mouth with her napkin. "And he's a member of your tennis club?"

"He just joined the club," Alex said.

Liz furrowed her brow. "How long has this been going on without telling me?"

"I've only known him a few weeks. Just tennis and, um, we did dance once."

"You went to a dance without *moi*?" Meredith asked.

"Is he a doctor?" Terrie asked.

"He's a plumber."

"Seriously?" Liz furrowed her eyebrows. "As in toilets?"

"Then how did he wind up at your exclusive club?" Meredith asked.

Alex explained how there was a member–guest tournament at the club and one of the customers on his route had invited him.

"I always invite my plumber wherever I go." Liz rolled her eyes.

The picture was passed around. Terrie studied it. "Alex's dating Denzel Washington."

"I think he looks more like Danny Glover," Alex said.

Liz put on her glasses and looked at the picture. "Danny Glover's now moonlighting as a plumber."

"He owns the franchise," Alex said.

"So he doesn't actually do the dirty work?" Meredith asked.

"Well, he says he has to work if one of the plumbers calls in sick or there's a complicated job."

"Not likely," Liz said. "The owner of a franchise does not do the work. He might do the scheduling and administrative work. And what else do you know about him?"

"Not much," Alex admitted. Nervous about her date with Luke, Alex had thought about cancelling, but she'd always followed the predictable path, and where had it gotten her?

Meredith squinted at the picture. "The plumber definitely has a hard bod."

"His legs are muscular," Alex said. "And when we play tennis, he looks amazing in his white shorts. I could even see the 'V' of his jockstrap around his buttocks."

"Jockstrap?" Meredith queried. "Who wears those anymore?"

"He obviously needs one," Terrie said and rubbed her palms together. "This is so juicy! It's just like *Sex and the City.*"

"At our age, we're more like *The Mothers of Sex and the City,*" Alex said.

"Give us the details," Liz said, impatiently twirling her pearls.

"At first, Luke seemed uncomfortable at the club, but then he mixed with everyone. Maybe from being in the Marines," Alex said.

Liz almost choked. "Oh, wait, this gets better: *The Doctor and the Marine-Turned-Plumber.* Could be our next book club selection."

"Get to the dancing," Meredith said.

"One Friday night after tennis, we all went upstairs to the bar. Luke and I were standing near the dance floor. They played some song by Natalie Cole. Before I knew it, we were dancing."

"Sounds delicious." Terrie wiped a drop of ketchup from her chin. She reached for another fry. "What kind of a dancer is he?"

"Perfect." Alex smiled.

"Now we have a sexy bi-racial plumber in a jockstrap dancing with our Alex," Liz chided.

Alex shot her a withering look.

"You know what they say about dancing?" Terrie licked some ketchup.

"No," Alex said.

"Vertical sex." Terrie winked.

Meredith gave a knowing smile. "When you do have sex with him, I'll give you a little secret for some mind-blowing—"

"Why is everything with you about sex?" Liz scowled.

"What else would she be doing with a plumber?" Meredith asked.

"Actually, I'm going out with him tonight," Alex said, still not sure and nervous about dating Luke Jackson, a man she didn't really know.

"Tonight?" Liz raised her voice. "Without even discussing it with me?"

"See what happens when you don't call me back?" Alex chided, but she thought if she'd spoken to Liz about this, maybe she would've cancelled the date.

"Meredith was about to give us the latest sex techniques," Terrie said. "I might need them. After all, I'm still a newlywed, you know. Going on two years next month, and it's marvelous."

Meredith held up a tin box embossed with the Victoria's Secret logo and "Sexy Little Cinnamon Mints" printed across the top. "Warren gave me this and a few other things last night."

"I'm sure he knows a little box of mints isn't a good enough gift for Meredith," Liz said. "I'm sure Warren also gave you something else with a little more glitz."

"Of course, he knows me well enough," Meredith said and held out her wrist, flaunting her new Cartier bracelet.

"What's so special about mints?" Alex asked.

"Use your imagination," Meredith said. "You put a mint in your mouth and then go down on him."

"I'm allergic to cinnamon," Alex said and blushed. Sex with Gabe had been the missionary position with him on top. She'd occasionally climb on him, but only when he asked her. He'd seemed satisfied. But now, she knew he hadn't been. Maybe if she were more like Meredith, Gabe wouldn't have strayed.

"How else are you going to attract a man, now that you're single?" Meredith asked.

The waitress came to their table to offer coffee or tea. When they declined, as they usually did, the waitress placed the leatherette check folder on the table. Each of the women dropped money into the folder.

"Time to discuss the book," Terrie said, holding up *Dreams of Joy.*

"By the way, what kind of a car does your plumber drive, or does he just drive the company truck?" Meredith asked.

"Let's do the book," Alex said.

"Answer Meredith first," Terrie said. "What we drive is a reflection of who we are. It's how we choose to navigate the planet."

"Please." Meredith rolled her eyes. "You're into that save-the-planet shit because you drive a crappy Toyota."

"I could afford a Mercedes like you or a Jag like Judi." Terrie folded her arms across her chest. "But I know what's real."

"I loved the book." Liz tried to steer the group back to *Dreams of Joy.*

Meredith pursed her lips as only she could, demonstrating her utter revulsion. "Why would the main character, Joy, ever have left Los Angeles, especially during the reign of Mao? And then why would she marry that disgusting peasant and choose to live in squalor?"

"A dream," Alex said wistfully. "Remember when we were young and optimistic?"

"I, for one, was never optimistic enough to consider poverty," Meredith said.

"I'd have chosen love over money every day of the week," Terrie said.

"That's obvious," Meredith said. "And could you believe during the famine, Joy's husband was actually going to boil his baby girl for food?"

"I couldn't imagine a parent harming his child," Terrie said.

"No, they traded children and boiled each other's daughters," Liz corrected.

Alex rubbed her wrist. No one in the group, not even Liz, knew about the scar on her right wrist or how she definitely could imagine a parent harming a child.

Meredith reached for her purse.

Alex put out her hand. "Please don't forget. You said you'd give me your opinion on the agreement Gabe's attorney drafted. Gabe wants it signed tonight when he picks up the boys, and your Mr. Dorset hasn't returned my calls."

"Dorset will definitely come through." Meredith pulled out a lipstick and a black velvet pouch. She took a silver Brighton mirror out of the pouch, checked her face, and looked toward the bar.

"Meredith, I'm over here," Alex said.

"I know, but look at that silver fox." Meredith smiled at a man at the bar. Her cell phone rang. "Okay, I'll be right there," she promised the person at the other end of the connection. "I have to get to the office," she told Alex. "It's a huge real estate acquisition."

"Congratulations." Alex feigned a smile.

"I'll review the agreement." Meredith gave Alex an air kiss. "Don't let Gabe bully you."

CHAPTER 11

Alex rushed back to the office, saw six patients, and then picked Jon up from his nursery school. At home, she paced, waiting for a call from her attorney. She jumped when the doorbell rang, thinking it was Gabe arriving way before he was supposed to pick up the boys. But it was Ryan, their next-door neighbor. He'd come over to ask Jon to go to his house and play with a new Batman toy he'd gotten for his birthday. After Jon followed Ryan next door, Alex grabbed a pile of clothes from the dryer.

The phone rang. While holding a stack of laundry, Alex put the phone to her ear.

It was Judi. "Sorry I missed the meeting, but my mom was rushed to the hospital, and cell phones don't work in the ICU."

"Is there anything I can do?" Alex asked.

"Thanks, but everything is under control now," Judi said.

"What happened?" Alex asked.

Judi started to describe her mother's heart attack.

Alex's call waiting beeped.

"I've got to take this call," she told Judi and dumped the laundry onto the couch.

It was Meredith. "Don't sign until we talk."

"Why?" Alex asked.

"The part about the children," Meredith said.

The call waiting beeped again.

Alex looked at the phone number. "Meredith, that's my attorney. I'll call you back."

She grabbed a pencil and paper to write down the addendums or exclusions she expected from Dorset. Phone in hand, she plopped down onto the couch beside the pile of laundry.

Dorset cleared his throat. "You can't sign this piece of shit your husband's attorney drafted."

"My husband, um, I mean former, said if I didn't sign and you proceed with an investigation of his practice and subpoena his financial records, then he wouldn't make partner. He's up for partnership this year, but they'll vote him out if there are any problems."

"Why do you care?"

"If he got voted out, then he wouldn't be able to pay me anything."

"You wanna bet on that one?" Dorset said.

"No," Alex said. "He's promised to take care of me and the boys, but he said he could only do that if there was no investigation of the practice."

"I can draft a whole new agreement that'll get you what you deserve."

"What if he doesn't agree?" she asked, wondering how she could make Dorset understand. There had been hospital gossip about how one of the most successful physicians at Brea Presbyterian Hospital had diverted funds to his associates right before his divorce, and his former wife had gotten nothing. She couldn't take a chance. She had to protect the boys, and Gabe was offering to provide a substantial child support payment each month.

Eric and Daniel opened the front door, yelling, "Hi, Mom."

Alex covered the phone. "Oatmeal cookies in the kitchen. Take one, and go next door to Ryan's to get Jon."

While Eric trotted into the kitchen, Daniel stopped to kiss her cheek.

Dorset said, "Your husband's a cardiologist, big practice. You were married fifteen years, so you're entitled to half the practice, not just the house and this measly support for you for one year." He took a breath. "Although the support for the kids is decent, you're entitled to more than one year of alimony after such a long marriage."

Eric marched back into the den, munching on a cookie. "Why do I have to go get Jon? I wanna play on my computer."

Alex cupped her hand over the phone. "Your dad's picking you up in fifteen minutes. Get Jon."

As the boys closed the door, she heard Dorset ask, "Are you listening?"

"Yes. Actually, we just had our twentieth anniversary."

"Happy anniversary," Dorset said, sarcastically. "You can't sign this. We have to meet and draft a new document."

"This one gives me what I want—the house and plenty of support for the kids."

"Until he takes them."

She put down the pen and paper, fingers fumbling. "The boys would never leave me."

"The agreement states that each child can choose with whom he wants to live when he reaches the age of thirteen," Dorset said.

"Gabe hypothetically picked age thirteen, but he knows the boys have to stay with me."

"That's what you think," Dorset said. "There's gotta be a motive behind this thirteen thing. It isn't standard verbiage."

"Eric is thirteen, but ..." Alex said, but she knew Gabe would never separate the kids. He'd always had the children's best interests at heart. But, she reminded herself, she'd been thinking about the Gabe she'd known for twenty-five years, not the man he'd morphed into, and definitely not the one she no longer knew or trusted. Alex felt the phone slip in her damp hand. She gripped it more tightly.

Dorset asked, "You're a doctor too, right?"

"I'm a chiropractor."

"You know what Munchausen syndrome is?"

"Of course. So what?" She put the phone on speaker mode so she could finish folding the laundry.

"I do lots of child custody cases," Dorset said.

"This isn't a custody case," she said, trying to pry some bubble gum off of Jon's sock before putting it into his backpack.

"Yet," he said. "The parents—in these cases usually the mothers—harm the kids, put their fingers into their vaginas and break their hymens, put cigarette burns on 'em, all kinds of crap. Then the mothers take the kids to the emergency room, and doctors and nurses give the mothers the attention they crave."

"Are you accusing me?" The hairs on her arms bristled.

"I'm trying to shock some sense into you." He paused. "We ask the kids, 'What did Mommy do to you?' They say, 'Mommy didn't do it. It was an accident.'"

Alex leaned her face against the warm folded laundry. *Is Dorset warning me about something he learned from Gabe's attorney?* He couldn't possibly think Jon's burns were "for purpose," like Jon had told her Gabe had said.

As she stuffed the boys' clothes into their backpacks, her stomach churned. "Please get to the corrections."

"I hope you and your husband had a fantastic sex life," Dorset growled.

"Why are you talking about sex?"

"He's screwing you royally, and you're saying, 'I've got to give him what he wants so he won't be angry with me.' Same as those kids who think, 'if I tell on Mommy, she'll hurt me more next time, but if I keep quiet, then maybe she'll be nice to me.'"

"This isn't anything like that. I'm getting what I want." Alex knew only too well about "telling on Mommy." Her entire childhood was spent in fear of telling on her mother. Alex knew if she ever told her father what her mother did to her, there'd be horrific consequences—for her.

Jon ran into the house behind the two older boys and jumped onto her lap, his legs obviously no longer painful.

"We can't let you sign this. There are too many corrections. We have to write up a whole new agreement."

"Mr. Dorset, you keep saying that. I know attorneys often create an adversarial situation to make money. Gabe offered to pay my legal fees if I use his attorney."

"Not ethical," Dorset said. "And, that'd be the most expensive two grand you ever saved. If you won't listen to me, at least talk to someone else."

"My girlfriend, Meredith Blackstone, the attorney who referred me to you, was supposed to go over the papers with me at lunch today, but she didn't have time. She called, but your call came in just as she was going to discuss it."

"I'm faxing a substitution of attorney. Fax it back now."

"You're withdrawing?" she asked, despair careened through her. She hugged Jon tighter. "Can't we just fix a few things?"

"I can't represent you if you're thinking about signing this. You'll turn around and sue us. Any judge would say we couldn't have given you appropriate counsel if we allowed you to sign this."

She knew any other attorney would have to start from the beginning, and that would be too expensive. Also, Meredith had said Dorset was the best. She wondered whether Dorset could be right about Gabe and started to cry.

Jon touched her face. "It's okay, Mommy."

She kissed his pudgy baby fingers, took the phone off speaker mode, and put it to her ear.

"Are you listening to me?" Dorset demanded. "He'll screw you and take the boys away."

"Never!" Alex yelled. That was it. Dorset was just threatening. She'd heard about an attorney who'd represented one of the physicians and charged more than a hundred thousand dollars for the divorce. There was no way she could get that kind of money. She decided Dorset had to be bluffing because Gabe would never take the children away from her. She was a good mother. "Fax me your withdrawal."

"I'm faxing it now." He hung up.

She went to the fax machine and waited for the printout. Then she grabbed a pen and signed.

Before she could collect herself, the doorbell rang.

CHAPTER 12

G abriel Rose strode into the house as though it were still his. He pecked her on the forehead, a gesture void of love and full of loss. She pulled back.

Jon ran to Gabe and wrapped his arms around his father's legs. "Daddy, I'm still hurting."

"Tonight, I'll change the bandages, and you'll be fine." Gabe swooped his son up and kissed him.

Eric asked, "How come you didn't honk for us?"

"I have to talk to your mother," Gabe said. Then he leaned over the entry table and sifted through the mail.

Daniel looked at Alex before going over and hugging Gabe. She knew Daniel had always tried to spare her. At football games, if he stood near Gabe for a while, he'd walk over and put his arm around her for the same amount of time. He seemed to parcel out his attention as though his parents were on a perfectly balanced seesaw, and he didn't want to upset either one.

Gabe said, "Boys, go upstairs. I said, 'I need to talk to your mother.' It will only take five minutes. Then your mother and I will be finished."

The boys turned and scurried upstairs.

Alex stared at Gabe. *Finished in five minutes? After twenty years of marriage?*

Sending her a sideways glance, he said, "You look good."

"Thanks," she said, hating him for complimenting her while discounting their lives, the family they'd created, everything that was important to her.

Without separating his lips, he smiled, took a document from the breast pocket of his navy blazer, and handed it to her. "I brought the original."

She walked into the living room. Gabe followed and sat down on the beige suede couch. Since he was now a guest, she didn't want him in the family room. The family room was where they'd gathered as a family, and he no longer belonged. She watched him survey the coffee table top, sanitized of all remnants of their married life.

Leaving a gap between them, she sat down.

"See, I'll take care of everything." He pointed to a paragraph that affirmed she'd get a sizeable monthly check for each child living with her. He took out his Monte Blanc pen.

"I'm not signing it until my lawyer goes over it with yours," she said, hoping she'd be able to stall him long enough to find another attorney.

Gabe seemed to be fighting to remain calm. "You've got to sign it tonight so I can transfer the house to you."

"Why so urgent?"

"It's been four months since I moved out," he said caustically. Then he smiled at her. "Besides, I want to protect you and the boys."

"How's signing this right now going to do anything for me and the children?"

"Remember Townsend, one of the partners in the practice?"

"Gabe, I haven't forgotten everything about our life together."

"Then you recall how Townsend's divorce got ugly. His wife's attorney demanded financials from all the partners as well as all of the records pertaining to the practice."

"Gabe, I remember."

"So you know the partners would sooner fire me than go through another audit. I'm working so hard to become a partner, and I don't want to lose because of this."

"You should have thought about that before you started 'this.'"

"I'm trying to take care of you," he said.

She was no longer concerned about his success and even wished he'd experience the pain and agony he'd imparted on her, but she did need him to be solvent enough to provide for the boys. She felt a stab of fear—an investigation of his practice could uncover things like the time he'd gone to the office on a Saturday and returned home with the office mail. She recalled when she'd asked him why he'd brought home the office mail, he'd told her the partners would never find out if he cashed a few checks. Besides, he'd explained, he was the most junior associate, and he was working harder than the partners and making less.

Alex looked at him and asked, "Are you worried about the checks you took?"

"Shut up!" he yelled, then appeared to catch himself. "I did not take checks from the partners. You are to remember that."

"You cashed the checks."

"That never happened. I went in on Saturdays to work extra hours to impress the partners. There never—I repeat, *never*—were any checks."

"You bought the boat."

"Babe, I worked extra hard to give you the things you deserve. I promise I will continue to take care of you and the boys." His voice turned like a switch, from harsh to soft and caring.

She couldn't let him hoodwink her, sweet-talk her. "Why are you suddenly so concerned about me after you couldn't wait to leave?" she asked.

"Love," he said.

"Love?" She stared at him, knowing love didn't include her. Love now meant the boys and, of course, Linda.

"Yeah, I love those boys," he said.

She shifted away from him.

Again, he appeared to catch himself. "And of course, I still have feelings for you. As a matter of fact, I was going to ask you to accompany me to Kaplan's son's bar mitzvah."

"Dr. Kaplan? He was so weird when I brought Jon to the hospital for the burn the other day."

"Yeah," Gabe said. "He said if there were ever a problem in the divorce, he'd testify about the burn, but I told him it was an accident, like you said."

"Testify?" Alex asked, thinking about Dorset's warning.

"Kaplan thought we were going through a nasty divorce. He didn't know we were both so upset about Jon that we were tense," Gabe said. "But, I'd like to take you to the bar mitzvah."

"Gabe, why not take Linda? You remember her, the one you left me for."

"I'm asking you." He moved closer and stroked her back.

His familiar touch warmed her while repulsing her. She wondered aloud, "Why do you want to take me?"

"The partners can't know about Linda. If they even suspected that I've been dating one of the hospital administrators before they make me a partner, I'd be out."

She considered calling the partners to tell them the truth about Gabe and Linda or, worse, about the checks he'd cashed. She could threaten him, but she had to find an attorney first, and she couldn't jeopardize his generous child support proposal.

"Besides, you look so sexy when you wear your black evening gown." Gabe cleared his throat and moved closer to her.

Drawn to him by their history but repelled by their reality, she froze. Dizzy, she closed her eyes, and they almost kissed. Then she looked up. Eric was standing at the living room entryway. Without a word, Eric turned and ran back upstairs.

Alex stood up. "I've got to go up to him."

"You always baby them." Gabe patted her hand. "Please sign this."

"No," she said and folded her arms across her chest.

"Alex, if you don't sign, then all my money could be tied up. I wouldn't be able to pay for anything for the boys, not even their team uniforms."

"Gabe, I can afford to take care of my boys." She refused to let him coerce her.

"Maybe I wouldn't even be able to sign the boys up for football camp next weekend," he said. "You know how annoyed they'd be with you if I had to tell them they couldn't go because you lost their permission slips and didn't give them back to me."

"I gave them to you," she said.

He shrugged.

True, she could go online and print out the permission slips, but any threat to the boys' happiness, no matter how empty, scared her. She took Gabe's pen. Then she hesitated.

Gabe touched her arm. "Sweetie."

She cringed. "Don't call me Sweetie."

"Alexandra, if we go to court, you know the partners would fire me, and that would be even worse for you. I might just have to have Dr. Kaplan discuss how you burned Jon so badly he wouldn't even let you take him to nursery school." He looked at her. "Kaplan saw how I had to assure Jon you wouldn't hurt him. Now, I just don't know."

"What are you talking about?" she asked. "You know I'd never hurt the boys."

Jon clomped down the stairs and landed on the bottom with a thud. "I got 'noculars to see the elephants at the circus tomorrow."

"You won't need them. We've got great seats." Gabe drew Jon to him and then turned him around to face the stairway. "Now, leave us for a few minutes." Gabe patted Jon's bottom, and the boy scampered upstairs.

Gabe held out his pen.

Alex started to take it. She paused and sat motionless, depleted.

The phone rang.

Gabe yelled up to the boys, "Answer the phone."

"Mom," Eric called down. "It's a man for you."

She got up and rushed to the kitchen, almost colliding with Daniel as he was putting his backpack next to the stairway.

"Hi," she said into the phone.

It was Luke, and he asked whether she still wanted him to pick her up tonight, the question she'd been asking herself for two days.

Gabe walked into the kitchen, opened the refrigerator, and helped himself to a Coke.

"I gotta get to my game," Eric yelled as he came down the stairs.

She looked at Gabe and spoke into the telephone: "Eight o'clock will be fine."

After she hung up, Gabe gave her a conspiratorial wink. "I was counting on you to be my date for the bar mitzvah, but you've obviously met someone. At that tennis club, huh?"

"Yes," she said, wondering how he could've heard about Luke. It could have been from Judi. Although Judi hadn't been at today's First Friday Book Club meeting, she had to have heard about Luke from Meredith or Terrie. Alex had never trusted Judi, especially since her husband worked at Gabe's hospital.

"What does he do?" Gabe asked.

Knowing Gabe considered any profession other than a physician to be beneath him, she answered, "He's a … actually, he specializes in hydraulics."

"What's that?" Daniel asked, walking into the kitchen.

"Someone who studies water pressure." Gabe chuckled, seemingly amused by her description of Luke's profession.

Daniel scrunched up his nose. "How would anybody do that?"

"Scientists study how water flows. It flows from areas of high pressure to low," Gabe said, raising his eyebrows, an expression of superiority with which she was all too familiar. "Do you boys know what percentage of the earth is water?"

"Eighty," Daniel said. "Why is so much of the earth water?" he asked, eyes widening.

Alex watched as the boys and their father fell back into the family routine—Gabe as the authority and the boys in awe of him as he imparted his wisdom.

"My game's in ten minutes," Eric said.

Gabe held out his pen to Alex. "You wouldn't want Dr. Kaplan to talk about how our little Jon got hurt."

"I'll have to think about it," she said.

"Mom, you're making me late again." Eric glared.

She bit her lower lip. She couldn't let the children see her cry. Gabe was offering a significant amount of child support; however, his threat was quite clear. If she refused to sign or caused an investigation of his practice, he'd use the accidental burn against her. Fear deep within her made her reach out and take Gabe's pen. She signed.

Then, like a magic act happening right before her, she watched Gabe change. He snapped up the document, folded it, placed it in his jacket pocket, and hurried the boys out the door. "They'll be home late on Sunday."

The boys scrambled to kiss her good-bye.

When Gabe slammed the door shut, the echo reverberated throughout the house.

Alex wanted to run after them, to be part of them.

Suddenly, the doorbell sounded. She imagined it could have been Gabe returning to say, "Let's rip up the agreement. Let's try again." But she knew that would never be. She also hated the man Gabe had become. He wasn't the man she'd fallen in love with, or maybe he was and she'd never seen this side of him. No, she couldn't have been that naïve all these years. But love often clouds our ability to see people as they really are—that is, until it's too late.

"Jon forgot his bear," Eric said, elbowing past her to the stairway. He went upstairs and returned with the bear with the missing ear. Mimicking his father, he said, "We'll be home late."

After Eric slammed the door, the sounds of the empty house enveloped her. She wondered how she was going to get through another weekend without the boys. Weekends were for families. The family knot had been tied so easily—one string slipping over the other, then another over that one, and the knot was secure. It was the untying that was devastating.

CHAPTER 13

A lex glanced at her watch. She thought Luke had said eight, but with Gabe listening to the conversation, she'd been too anxious to pay attention.

Looking at the contents of her closet, Alex wished she'd borrowed something from Meredith. Then she'd look alluring. Pushing aside all of the professional and casual outfits, she finally decided on a white angora sweater and red skirt.

At 8:50 p.m., she opened the door and stared at Luke Jackson. This man who seemed to take such care in his selection of tennis clothes was just as fastidiously dressed now: starched white shirt, beige slacks, and preppy loafers. Although mustached, he did look like Denzel Washington and exuded sensuality.

"Wow," he said in a deep baritone as he appraised her.

She looked into his amber eyes.

"Alex, I'm sorry about being late. I would've called, but we aren't permitted to use the company cell phone unless it's an emergency."

She waved him inside. "Why can't you use the phone if you're the franchise owner?"

"Franchise rules," he said and closed the door behind him. "Even in my position, I'm obliged to obey them."

"Want a drink?" she asked, moving her hands behind her back to hide the tremble.

"A scotch would be great."

"I don't have scotch. Want a glass of wine?"

"No, that's okay." He smiled, his lips lush.

He glanced at the picture of her boys on the entryway table. A few strands of gray hair glistened through his thick black hair as he leaned over to pick up one of the photos. "How old are your boys?"

"Eric, my oldest, is thirteen. Daniel's only eleven, but he's my grown-up. Jon's just four."

"Little ones," he said.

"What about you?" she asked. At the club, he never talked about his family.

"Four girls, and there's always something." He shook his head. "Tonight, my second-to-the-oldest, Darlene, really pushed my button."

"My oldest pushes my buttons too," she said, and suddenly, they were both just parents, sharing stories.

She led him into the living room. He sat down on the beige suede couch and stretched out his legs. She watched him run his hand over his thigh.

"Can I use your phone for a second?" he asked. "Then my mind'll be at ease."

She went to the kitchen, grabbed the phone, and handed it to him.

He dialed and waited. "Darlene, just leave my truck when you're done." Without raising his voice, he sternly said, "We'll talk about it when I'm ready. Good night."

He handed the phone back to her. "After you and I talked, I was all set to go home, but then my daughter called the office. I had to switch cars with her."

"Is she okay?"

"Sure, but she told me she needed my truck right away." He shook his head. "Darlene's landlord threatened her: if she didn't move her stuff out of the apartment by tonight, it would all be donated to Goodwill in the morning."

"Why such short notice?" she asked.

"Oh, it's been coming on for a while, but she kept ignoring it. Couldn't pay the rent."

She watched him touch his tongue to a corner of his mouth, leaving a sheen of moisture on his lips. They talked about children and marriage. It was simple—their lives condensed into a few sentences. He told her how, after fifteen years of marriage, he'd fallen in love with another woman. He'd been crazed. It was like the other woman had cast a spell over him. When he'd come to his senses, his wife wouldn't take him back.

Alex understood a wife never trusting her husband again. She'd trusted Gabe, and he'd betrayed her. She also doubted she'd ever trust any man again, and certainly not one who'd had an affair.

"Believe me, I'm done with that sneaking around. I'll never do that again," he said.

Alex looked at him, wondering whether all men said that after they'd been found out. *Do men always think it's okay to destroy a woman's life? Is sex always that powerful? Does it always leave such a devastating path of destruction in its wake?*

Curious about what happens to a discarded wife, Alex asked about his former wife.

"Oh, my former, she's happier without me. She remarried," he said softly.

"Are your children okay with your former wife's remarriage?" Alex asked, the pairing of the words "former wife" with "remarriage" sounding odd to her, an oxymoron.

Then he got quiet, appearing pensive.

Alex thought maybe he was sad about the splintering of the family and the fact that he'd caused it. Trying to control her nervousness, she crossed her right leg over her left, inadvertently exposing the tops of her pantyhose. She pulled her skirt down.

Luke looked at her legs. He seemed comfortable, possibly from the physical proximity on the court for the past several weeks.

"Sure you don't want some wine?" she asked.

"Alex, we'd better be going if we want to get into the club. And thanks for putting up with me going on about my problem." He reached for her hand to help her up from the couch.

His touch felt warm and wonderful. She kept his hand in hers until they got to the entryway. Deciding to forgo a raincoat despite the forecast of rain, she reached for her purse and keys, the latter slipping free and clanging onto the black marble floor.

As Luke bent down to retrieve her keys, she stared at him. His perfectly fitted beige slacks outlined his taut buttocks. His body could have belonged to a college athlete, but considering the fact that he had an adult child, he had to be fifty or so.

After she locked the door, they walked to his car, the click-clack of her heels and the firm beat of his shoes on the pavement the only sounds. Once they got to his car, he held open the passenger door for her. While he walked around to the driver's side, she leaned back against the pristine charcoal-gray headrest and breathed in the new-car smell.

"We're going to the hottest black club in Orange County," he said.

"Are there many clubs in Orange County?" she asked, leaving out the word *black*.

"You'll love this place," Luke said.

Fifteen minutes later, they cruised down Bristol Street, five miles east of her office.

"We're here." He pointed to an orange neon outline of a couple dancing on a huge concrete wall with the "Sweets" sign above them.

"Nice, she said, nervous about her first date, especially at a club. But there was something exciting about it, almost like being another person. Since her own life wasn't working—except for the boys and her practice—she decided this was what she needed.

"Leave your purse in the car so you won't be worrying when we dance." He helped her out of the car. "Remember, you're with me."

"Sure," she said, wondering why he felt he needed to reassure her. She linked her arm through his and walked to the entrance.

He grabbed the coconut-shell handle on the wooden door and ushered her in.

At the entryway, Alex stopped and surveyed the cavernous room filled with black couples.

Two women and a man stopped dancing and stared. Alex tensed. The DJ caught her glance and held it. Her heart thumped. Tightly packed bodies, hair gel, and jasmine perfume yielded a heavy scent—like damp wool and cotton candy. She could almost feel the room sweat.

Luke took her hand and led her toward the bar.

Straightening her shoulders and feigning confidence, Alex followed him through a corridor to the right of the dance floor. Lights on the walls flashed like railroad crossings. The club exuded an electricity, which for Alex was definitely a departure from the ordinary, the boring.

At an empty table, Luke held out a purple chair painted with palm trees and coconuts and motioned for her to sit.

A waitress approached, wearing a short black skirt and fishnet stockings. "I'm Jez, what can I get you?" she said.

"Glass of wine?" Luke asked.

"Thanks, a Merlot," Alex said.

"Merlot for the lady, and I'll take a scotch and soda." Luke reached into his pocket and gave Jez a twenty. "We'll be on the floor, so just leave the drinks."

Luke took Alex's hand. "Let's dance."

They walked to the middle of the dance floor. Tentatively, Alex swayed her hips from side to side. She watched a beautiful woman in a burgundy dress with matching wedge heels dance seductively, her silver earrings glinting under the strobe light. Mesmerized by the woman's sensuality, Alex tried to mimic her moves.

Another woman dancing behind Alex gyrated her hips and pushed Alex closer to Luke. She felt him: his head, shoulders, and hips moved in perfect rhythm with the music.

After a few minutes, the pulsating music stopped and was replaced by "The Color of Love" by Boyz II Men. Luke wrapped his arms around her. Resting his chin atop her head, he sang softly. She pressed closer, feeling his heartbeat. *Vertical sex.*

Her head on his chest, she was enveloped by his wonderful scent: a blend of soap and Aqua Velva aftershave. Then she felt the hard length of his penis. She pulled away. This was too soon for her. She wasn't ready for another man to respond to her.

"Let's get our drinks." He led her back to their table.

As they left the dance floor, Alex noticed there was a special greeting Luke and the other dancers gave each other: a nod of the head, a lowering of the gaze. Luke was included. She was excluded.

Sitting together at their table, shoulders and thighs touching, they sipped their drinks. In order to be heard above the noise, they leaned close and whispered into each other's ears.

His lips brushed her ear. He took her hand and whispered, "You're a great dancer."

"I've always wanted to go dancing, but my husband, I mean former, would never go."

"We'll change that."

"I'll be right back," she whispered.

He got up and pulled out her chair. "I'll be here."

She walked through strands of red beads into a dark hallway. Feeling instead of seeing, she grabbed the coconut handle just below the wrought-iron silhouette of a woman with huge breasts.

She entered the bathroom. Three black women were cramped together, talking and laughing. Suddenly, they stopped and stared at her.

Alex froze.

One of the women at the mirror was leaning over, fixing her lipstick, her black leather skirt hiking up above her buttocks. Alex's gaze landed on the butterfly tattoo nestled to the right of the thong strap that divided the woman's firm buttocks.

"Girl, what you looking at?" The woman at the mirror turned around and tugged at the hem of her leather skirt.

"Uh, nothing." Alex looked away.

The two other black women standing in the tiny bathroom moved together, blocking the door to the one stall.

The butterfly-tattooed woman placed two fingers on Alex's shoulder and pushed. "Girl, what you doin' here?"

Alex steadied herself to keep from falling back into the second woman with the hot pink skirt that matched her nail polish.

The hot-pink-skirted woman put her hands on her hips and asked, "You here with a date?"

"Yes," Alex answered.

"Black or white?" the butterfly-tattooed woman asked, her voice too loud for the tiny bathroom.

"Um." Alex stared at the butterfly lady.

The third woman, dressed in black pants and a bird-of-paradise blouse, asked, "'Ya don't know?"

"Black," Alex said. "Actually, he's bi-racial," she corrected.

"Aren't there enough white dicks for you?" the butterfly-tattoo lady asked.

White men don't have white dicks, Alex thought. Not a good time for an anatomy lesson, she decided. She tried to squeeze past the women, but the hot-pink-skirted woman wouldn't move. Instead, she pointed a hot-pink nail at Alex.

"What are *you* doing here?" the hot-pink-skirted woman asked.

Alex didn't answer.

The hot-pink-skirted woman picked at Alex's white angora sweater as if she were removing a piece of lint. Then she reached out, touched Alex's pearl necklace, and hooked her fingers around the strand of pearls. "You a teacha or something?"

"Nah, she's a nurse," the butterfly woman answered. "Look at those stockings."

Laughter echoed in the tiny bathroom.

Alex's knees weakened.

The hot-pink-skirted woman tugged at Alex's necklace. Two pearls broke apart, and the necklace pinged to the floor.

Laughing, the three women walked out of the bathroom.

Alex picked up the glistening white pearls, cringing as her knees touched the dirty bathroom floor. When she stood up, she stared at her reflection in the mirror. She did look like a nurse or a teacher with her little white angora sweater and red skirt hemmed to just above her knees, and stockings! She shimmied out of her stockings and threw them in the trash. Too nervous to go into the stall, she pushed open the bathroom door.

"Oh." She jumped back, surprised to see Luke standing outside the bathroom.

"What happened?" he asked.

Without answering, Alex buried her face in his chest.

"Did they hurt you?"

"No," she said and opened her hand to show him her pearl necklace.

"I should've followed you and then waited outside," he said. "It won't happen again."

He kissed her, scotch and soda sweet, like nothing she'd ever tasted before.

"Let's go." He took her hand, and they walked out of Sweets Club. "I'll take you to a nicer place next time."

"Okay," she said, uncertain whether she wanted to venture further into his world.

CHAPTER 14

A s Alex and Luke left Sweets, she vowed she'd never go to a place where she didn't belong. Her children needed her, and she couldn't take chances like that.

"Are you okay?" Luke asked before opening the car door for her.

"Fine," she said. True, she needed to move on with her life, but she had to be sensible, cautious.

Luke turned the ignition on and looked over at her. Then he glanced down at her legs.

Alex met his gaze.

"Great legs." He reached over and stroked her thigh, his touch so light she almost wondered whether it was his hand or her need.

She didn't pull away. He moved his hand up her thigh. His soft, feathery touch made her moisten, and she let out a low moan. She imagined him running his finger along the top of her lacy bra, turning down the cup, and licking her nipples. When he pulled his hand away to turn off the car, she gasped, realizing how her body responded to him.

He got out, walked around to the passenger side, and took her hand to help her out of the car. "I'll walk you to the door and be outta here," he said.

Wondering whether she was supposed to object or agree, she said nothing.

As they lingered under the post light, she stared up at the angry scar above his right eyebrow. Beneath those eyebrows were the lightest brown eyes she'd ever seen. She reached into her purse and took out her key. When she gave him the key, their hands met—her tiny hand covered by his large calloused one. Incongruous, how their hands seamlessly fit together. His lips brushed hers, and she tingled.

He opened the front door for her. "Could I get a CD from my car and have one last dance?"

"Okay," she said. As she stood in the doorway and waited for him to retrieve the CD, rain started to pelt onto the overhang. She stared at Luke's car in her driveway and wondered whether she wanted him to return or she wanted to bolt the door shut, run to her bed, and imagine making love to Gabe, the only lover she'd ever had.

Within a few minutes, Luke was back at her doorstep, CD in hand. His soaked shirt clung to his chest, revealing his muscular body, defined and full of power. He was gorgeous.

"Would you like a towel?" she asked, throat dry.

"Nah," he said. "I'll only stay for one dance."

They walked to the family room, and she pointed to the CD player.

He put the Ray Charles CD into the machine, forwarded it, and beckoned to her.

She moved into his arms, unaware of the prophecy of the song, "I Can't Stop Loving You."

As Luke hummed, she relaxed against him. She looked up at him, and their faces touched. She felt his smooth, shaved face against her cheek. Their lips a whisper away, she moved closer, and they kissed. She needed him to take away the bitter taste of Gabe still lingering on her lips.

They clasped hands, and their entwined hands played a duet to the music. Luke's thigh pressed against hers. Then he stroked the scooped neckline of her sweater, lingering at the deepest part. She felt the heaviness of her breasts straining against her bra, her nipples begging for his touch. They kissed again.

Letting the longing take over, she turned and led him upstairs. Since she hadn't planned on inviting a man into her bedroom tonight, or ever, she hadn't thought about candles or soft lights. With Gabe, it hadn't mattered whether they took each other when the lights were out or in the bright sunlight. His body had become as familiar to her as her own. *That's the past,* she reminded herself, *and it's over.*

They undressed, each keeping pace with the other. She unfastened her skirt button and then her zipper. Her skirt fell to the floor.

Luke unbuckled his belt and then guided his zipper down, tooth by tooth. He stepped out of his pants, the jangle of keys jarring her. He slipped his hands on the sides of his light-blue boxer shorts and pushed them down.

She unfastened her lacy white bra, releasing her breasts.

He looked at her. "Alex," he whispered. "All the times we've played tennis together, I've wanted to see you naked, touch you, kiss you."

Surprised by his confession, she wondered whether she, too, had been as attracted to him. Her heart beat faster as she climbed atop the light-blue-and-white sateen coverlet.

Naked, they lay facing each other. He reached out to her. She trailed her fingers along his chest. Then, unable to trespass farther on his flesh, she stopped and started to get up.

115

He gently pulled her back to bed.

Tense, she looked at him.

He lifted her face to his and kissed her. Then he lowered his head and sucked on her erect nipple. With each stroke of his tongue, she moaned.

He rolled her onto her back and slowly caressed her body. She arched her body up to him and was shocked by her hunger.

He licked his finger and then slid it into her, his touch soft yet urgent. She felt a throbbing to her core and reached down and stroked his penis. With each rhythmic movement of her hand up and down his velvety shaft, she felt his excitement. As she feathered the shaft of his penis, then the crown, his deep, primal moans excited her.

Suddenly, invaded by thoughts of Gabe, she looked at the man who wasn't Gabe on Gabe's side of the bed. Or was it that Gabe had been on Luke's side? Images from the past jumbled in her mind, yanking her away from pleasure. She pulled back, longing for the familiarity that was Gabe. Sex was Gabe, not this stranger. "I can't," she said.

"Don't be scared," he whispered. "I'll be gentle."

She believed him for now, just for now. She relaxed. He moved her on top of him and cupped her buttocks with his hands, pressing her to him.

Suddenly, the pelting rain seemed to quiet down so as not to disturb their delighted moans. Touch became the conductor in their symphony of pleasure, with the other senses—sight, smell, sound, and taste—all playing their parts in building to a crescendo of passion.

He rolled her onto her back and climbed on her as gracefully as though he were dancing again. Her legs wrapped around him as his hips moved from side to side, carrying her with him.

"Tell me what you feel," he urged.

"I feel you," she said.

"Take me. I'm all yours," he said.

Each time he thrust into her, she shuddered with excitement. She couldn't tell where her body ended and his began. "I'm coming!" she yelled, shocked at the sound of her own pleasure.

Arms and legs entwined, they fit together.

They drew away from each other, but hunger made her press close to him. Her desire hadn't been sated, and they made love again. This time they were gentler—the exploration just as exciting as the orgasm. Maybe their lives possessed no shared symmetries, but tonight their bodies resonated as sex bridged the chasm between them.

He took her hand in his.

She looked at their entwined fingers: black, white, black, white. She started to drift off.

He nuzzled her neck. "I'd better be going," he murmured.

As though awakened too early from a dream, she watched him dress. Then, wondering why she had given herself to him, she belted on her red velour bathrobe and followed him downstairs.

At the door, they kissed briefly, strangers once again.

She bolted the door behind him. The quick flight from distance to intimacy and back left her disoriented. What had happened wasn't just parts entering parts, his penis into her vagina. For her, it had been him plunging into her soul.

At two in the morning, Alex changed her semen-and-sweat-soaked sheets. She put them into the washer and thought about sex, the counterfeit of love with all the excitement but none of the entanglements. Entanglements were what gave life meaning and bound lovers together. And it was the entanglements she craved most.

CHAPTER 15

In the morning, Alex felt like a stranger in the bed that had once been her cocoon, an embrace that protected her from the world. As she snuggled between the down quilt and the sheets, she wondered whether she should buy another bed—one without the depression on the left side—one that no longer held the memories of life that was Gabe.

Then her thoughts turned to Luke Jackson: *Why had she let him into her bed and allowed him to rekindle a lust she'd thought was lost to her forever?* She decided she needed the validation of her sexuality which Luke offered, and, although it was sex and not love, that was all she needed at this point.

The phone rang, jarring her.

"What happened last night when Gabe came over?" Liz asked.

"I signed." Alex felt her gut twist and a sour taste invade her mouth.

"Why?" Liz asked.

"Gabe insisted the partners would fire him if the divorce triggered an audit. Then he wouldn't be able to pay for the children."

"He's lying."

Alex choked back tears, recalling how the truth could destroy a life, a home. "Gabe also said Dr. Kaplan from Brea Presbyterian Hospital would testify that I intentionally burned Jon."

"He's bluffing," Liz said. "My husband's signaling me to hurry up and invite you out for breakfast."

"I'm not up to it."

"We're taking you out. Pick you up in fifteen."

"Okay," Alex agreed. It would be good to see Liz and Stan, and having breakfast with them would be better than standing over the kitchen sink and eating a toasted bagel without even bothering with a plate.

She reached for her white shirt and khaki pants, then she pulled a comb through her hair and brushed her lips with peach lip gloss. Draping her apricot cashmere sweater over her shoulders, she went outside, sat on the bench in front of the house, and waited for Liz and her husband. After sex with a man who wasn't Gabe, she felt like an intruder in her own home.

Liz and Stan pulled up in their new Lexus, and Alex climbed into the backseat. While Liz and Stan talked about their construction mishaps, Alex tried to pay attention, feigning interest in their problems with contractors: chipped tiles, cracked cement, and warped wood.

Ten minutes later, Stan dropped Alex and Liz off and went to park.

Liz slipped her arm through Alex's arm, and they walked to the tiny restaurant hidden in an alleyway between a children's shoe store and a dentist's office.

"Why'd you sign?" Liz asked. "What's up with Gabe's power over you?"

Alex felt her eyes tear. "The family was everything to me. I believed nothing could happen to our perfect family. I thought Gabe was just too tired from working so hard, and I didn't even notice that we hadn't had sex for months."

"Wait," Liz said. "Is this conversation leading to you having sex with the first person who asked you out?"

"How did you know I had sex with Luke last night?" Alex asked, guilt making her face flush.

"You had sex?" Liz shouted.

The man in front of them in the line turned around.

Alex shot him a mind-your-own-business look. "Liz, I wasn't planning on doing anything with Luke. We went dancing. When we got back to my house, he asked for one more dance, and sex just happened."

"Just happened? What do you have in common with a plumber?"

"He owns the company, remember? And Gabe and I had everything in common, but it didn't make a difference."

"What'd you ever see in Gabe, anyway?"

"Gabe and I met in my first year of college. Before we knew it, life happened—marriage, children. Life was perfect, or so I thought. I never expected to lose everything."

"What about your practice, your life? And the boys are your children too."

"Liz, do you really think women are respected for their careers? It's whether they have a husband, a family, children—that's how a woman is valued."

"What'll it be?" the man behind the counter asked.

Alex ordered a short stack of pancakes, which she didn't feel like eating, and coffee, which she needed. Liz decided on two vegetable omelets and insisted on treating. They took the coffee cups from the clerk, filled them at the dispenser in the center aisle, and ferreted out a table in the crowded restaurant.

Liz put down her coffee cup and looked at Alex. "Why are you so attracted to this guy?"

"He's so different from Gabe, and he makes me feel sexy, feminine."

Liz shook her head. "I don't get it."

"When Gabe told me he was leaving me, he said sex with me was 'like scratching an itch.' I started to doubt whether any man would ever be attracted to me."

"Alex, you're beautiful. You can't let any man do this."

"Gabe wasn't any man; he was my husband. Now I'm done with him."

"Doesn't sound like you're done."

"I needed to be reassured. It wasn't just sex. It was validation."

"I'm here for you," Liz said.

"Liz, I know, but I needed a little proof that my life isn't over just because Gabe left me."

"Whatever it takes." Liz leaned over hugged her. "You can count on me."

Stan pulled out a chair at their table. "May I join you two gorgeous chicks?"

The server delivered their orders, and Alex moved aside for her to put down the plates.

"Liz told me you had a date last night," Stan said. "Better than when we invited you over to the house to meet Rob, I'm sure."

"Much better," Alex said and pushed the pancakes around on her plate, trying to take enough bites to make it appear as though she was eating.

"Tell us what you really said to Rob to make him reach for the Viagra." Stan winked.

"I agreed to go for a walk to his boat after dinner. Then he pulled out a tissue from his pocket, unwrapped a pill, and dropped it."

"I still laugh when I think about Rob crawling around on our dining room floor, trying to find his Viagra, yelling, 'The dogs will eat my pill.'" Liz transferred a few home-fried potatoes from her plate to Stan's, a small wifely gesture that made Alex's heart ache.

"He does have a fabulous boat," Stan said, as though that should be enough of a reason for a woman to date a man.

Alex's cell phone rang.

"Hi," she said, motioning an apology to Liz and Stan.

"Ever been boating?" Luke asked, his question almost an appendage to the conversation she was having with Liz and Stan.

"Wait a minute." She excused herself and took the call outside.

"I just bought a boat, and I'd like to take you out."

"Luke, I need to talk to you about last night first."

"Last night was great. I thought about asking if you wanted to go out on the boat in the morning, but I'm on the ocean by six with my buddy. I didn't think you'd be up to it, but how about tomorrow?"

"I can't," she said, wishing she could. "My boys'll be home by five."

"We'll be back way before then."

"I'd be too nervous about getting back on time," she said.

"You have my word," he said. "You're safe with me."

She didn't know why she agreed to go out with him again. Maybe it was the word "safe."

CHAPTER 16

At seven on Sunday morning, Luke arrived at Alex's house dressed in jeans and an old gray sweatshirt. When he put his arms around her, she moved close with an ease that surprised her.

He looked at his watch. "We gotta get going now. The ocean's perfect at this hour."

She grabbed her navy windbreaker from the hall closet and locked the door.

He took her hand, and they walked to a black Toyota truck. After he opened the passenger door, she stretched one leg onto the runner and hoisted herself up. Pushing aside the debris and trying to clear a place, she sat on the edge of the seat. "Weren't you driving a Honda on Friday night?" she asked.

"I told you that my daughter needed to use my truck, so we traded." He closed the door and went around to the driver's side.

Alex glanced at the backseat, littered with CDs, discarded paper cups, dirty socks, an open toiletry bag, two empty Snapple bottles, and a small plastic container with orange Tic Tacs. She thought it was amazing he could emerge so fastidious from such a disheveled vehicle.

He got behind the wheel. As he turned the ignition key, an Aretha Franklin CD blared through the speakers. Reaching his right hand back, he pushed some of the things that were scattered across the backseat into a pile. "I was gonna clean it up for you." He glanced at her. "It's a mess 'cause, in addition to all of my responsibilities for Southern California Plumbing Company, I have another business on the side."

"What's that?" she asked.

Proudly, he held out a card. The logo—a picture of a toilet—was in the top left corner, and "SNAP" was written in big red letters across the middle of the card.

"See, S-N-A-P. 'Service Not Attitude Plumbing.' Designed it myself."

She took the card. "Um, I have a question for you."

"Fire away. I can answer anything you need to know about drains and toilets."

Alex decided that a discourse on toilets was all she was going to get, so she mentally shelved her question about Friday night. She thought it odd that he'd have another business on the side if he owned the franchise.

Twenty minutes later, they arrived at the parking lot of Southern California Plumbing Company, a division of VIP, Victory International Plumbing. "Because I own the franchise, I'm allowed to park my boat in the lot," he said.

"Nice." She stared at the rows of parked neon-yellow trucks, each painted with a white toilet and black wrench under letters denoting the Southern California Plumbing Company. Then she watched as this rugged, un-Gabe-like man hitched his boat to the truck.

After securing the boat, he climbed back into the truck. "It's only five miles from the office to the Dana Point Marina. You ready to fish?"

"We're fishing?" She crinkled her nose. "I thought we were just taking the boat out for a ride. I've never fished."

"You'll love it," Luke said.

"Maybe," she said, doubtful fishing would interest her.

He pulled up to the launch pad. "I'm going into the office to pay for the boat lift, and then I'll park the truck."

She got out of the truck and watched as the two dockworkers wrapped chains around the boat, hoisted it, and then deposited it into the water.

Luke returned to the launch, climbed aboard the boat, and helped her onto it. She glanced at the cabin below and noticed the same kind of disheveled mess she'd seen in the truck.

Touching the boat's stern, he said, "Just bought my boat two weeks ago. Came into some cash and couldn't resist this beauty. It's meant for fishing, not like those fancy ones that just sit in the harbor."

The one that Gabe bought, the ones their friends had, she thought. No, this wasn't familiar, but maybe that was good. The familiar had disappointed, even devastated.

Luke got behind the wheel and deftly negotiated the channel, the engine gurgling. When they approached the ocean, he increased the speed. "Duck behind the windshield with me so you don't get sprayed."

"The ocean's beautiful." She inhaled the salt air, recalling how much she loved being on the ocean and how long it had been since she'd done something like this. With the exception of tennis, and that was only because Gabe had paid for membership for the entire year, she'd never spend any time away from the boys or work.

"That's why I love it here." He wrapped his arms around her.

Basking in the sparkle of the shimmering water, she smiled up at him. The sunlight caught his face, highlighting the cleft in his chin. She loved the feel of his body against hers, familiar yet foreign.

"I hope there's bait left at the station," he said.

"Bait?" she asked, wondering where one would purchase bait in the ocean.

When they pulled up to the bait station, the stench of dead fish on the platform overtook her. She fought the rising bile in her throat.

A woman in yellow plastic rain gear and black rubber knee boots approached their boat. "How much bait?"

"Just half a scoop." Luke paid and turned the boat south toward San Diego.

After adeptly guiding the boat, he shut off the engine and then went down to the cabin to retrieve the fishing poles. He returned with two poles, reached into the bait tank, and took out two wiggly, slimy eels. Fishing poles in his left hand, he slid the bait onto the hooks of the two poles and handed her a baited pole. She took it tentatively.

Studying the GPS, Luke maneuvered the boat until the screen burst into fireworks. Each dot, he explained, confirmed the presence of fish. He dropped his line, and instructed her to do the same. Methodically, he reeled in one bass after another and measured them against the ruler decaled onto the ledge of the boat. He threw back the ones that were less than sixteen inches, the minimum length for keeping fish.

With each tug on her line, Alex struggled for a few seconds then lost the fish. After several attempts, Luke moved behind her, slipped his hands around her waist, and then placed his hands over hers on the fishing pole. With his help, she reeled in two bass.

When Luke's twelfth bass filled the tank, he smiled. "That's enough for today." His hands were covered with blood, and the deck was littered with bits of bait and blood.

Luke went below deck and returned with a board and knife. "Now the fun begins." He placed the board into the holder on the side of the boat, retrieved the first fish from the bait tank, and gutted it.

Surprised by the speed and skill with which he wielded the knife, she thought he could've been an excellent surgeon. Then she looked down at the fish and realized she'd dropped Luke into Gabe's world. "How'd you learn to do that?" she asked.

"I can teach myself anything I put a mind to," he answered.

"Anything?" she teased, thinking about his sexual prowess.

"Yep. That's how I taught myself tennis and played all over the world for the Marines."

He was an incredible athlete. That's what had first attracted her to him, and now she was enjoying this foray into his world, a world as far away from Gabe as possible.

Luke returned the poles to the lower deck and then took the wheel.

"Move behind the window, near me," he said.

She leaned into him. After years of living in her white-collar world, this Marlboro man enticed her. She felt like she'd sneaked into another life and didn't want to leave. And maybe this man wouldn't leave her. Maybe he really had learned his lesson with his former wife.

When they reached the launch pad, Luke told her to wait while they hoisted the boat out of the ocean. He went to get his truck from the parking lot. Fifteen minutes later, with the boat in tow, they drove back to his office.

"Only need about twenty minutes to wash down the boat. You wanna rest in the truck while I clean?"

"I'll help," she offered.

"If you insist, you could wash down the deck." Luke gave her a mop and liquid soap.

While he walked around the boat to hose and wash the exterior, she soaped up the bait tank and then the deck. By the time he returned, she'd lathered up everything.

"I'll hose down the deck," he said.

"No." She reached out her hand. "Give me the hose." She watered the deck but, unaware of how the soap residuals would kill the fish, decided it would be best to leave the soapy water in the bait tank to let it soak.

Luke washed off his fishing poles, leaned them against the railing, and surveyed the scrubbed deck. "You really took to fishing. We'll get in several more times before the weather turns."

Needing clarity before proceeding with him, she summoned her nerve. "Um, about Friday night? You left right after we, um ..."

"I had to check on my daughter, make sure she moved all of her stuff out of the apartment and into my house. Hey, would you go out with me again next weekend?"

"I'll think about it," Alex said.

While they were driving back to her house, she weighed Luke's abrupt departure on Friday night with his parental responsibility. She agreed to go out with him again—not next weekend, since she had the boys—but another time, maybe one more time. Maybe he'd fill the hunger raging in the pit of her stomach. But right now, she needed to get home before the boys returned.

When they got to her house, Luke said, "I'll help you repack the fish, 'cause it can be messy."

She looked at her watch.

After he parceled the fish into small bags and placed the last bag in the refrigerator, he bent down to kiss her. She felt his eyelashes brush her cheek. Her lips met his. The tips of their tongues touched. He caressed her hair. His hand trailed down the nape of her neck and then rested on the small of her back.

She wanted him but pulled away. "The boys'll be home soon."

"I want you." Luke pressed closer to her.

She looked up into his amber eyes and felt a stirring she couldn't resist.

They slipped off their shoes and raced upstairs, laughing, touching, and leaving a trail of clothes.

When they reached the top step, Luke put his hand on her shoulder. "Alex, after fishing, I gotta wash up."

"You can use the shower first."

"It'd be better if we showered together." He kissed the back of her neck.

Leading him to the master bathroom, she unfastened her bra and tossed it aside. Then she took off her watch and placed it on the sink. They only had a half hour before the boys would be home.

She got into the shower and let the water caress her face. Luke opened the glass shower door and stepped in behind her. Gently reaching in front of her, he took the bar of soap. He lathered his hands and then smoothed the soap onto her breasts, lingering on her nipples.

Moaning as he massaged soap over her body, she leaned back into him. *Magical how he knows how to touch me*, she thought and turned around to kiss him.

"Hold on to me and let me lift you."

"I'll fall."

"I won't let you," he promised. "Wrap your legs around me."

Water pelting onto her back, she let him lift her. He slid his penis into her. Draped against him, she surrendered to him. As he drove her to ecstasy, she shuddered. A few moments later, she felt chilled. She left the shower, grabbed a towel for him, and then wrapped herself in another.

He went to the bedroom and pulled back the covers. "Get in for a few minutes."

"Luke, the boys'll be home soon."

"Just let me feel you on top of me."

"No." She glanced at the clock on the night table. "We've got to get dressed."

As she dressed, Luke playfully tugged at her panties. "When can I have you next?"

"Never, if you don't get out of here." She bent down, picked up his jeans, and threw them at him.

He dressed and then followed her downstairs.

"Go now." Alex kissed him.

CHAPTER 17

The headlights from Gabe's silver Mercedes sliced through the living room window. Alex heard the slamming of car doors, the boys laughing, and then pounding on the front door. As she opened the door, Gabe's car pulled away.

Each clutching a balloon adorned with the Barnum & Bailey logo, Jon and Daniel ran to Alex. But Eric, also holding a balloon, lingered at the doorway.

"Hi, guys." She bent down to kiss Jon's cheek. He cuddled into her, and Daniel leaned over and kissed her.

"How was the circus?" She straightened Jon's collar and then ran her hand along his chocolate-stained white shirt.

"Fun, but the elephants stinked." Jon crinkled his nose.

Eric stood at the entryway, his hands behind his back. Wearing his blue-and-white Oxford shirt and jeans, he looked preppy. He held out a red balloon. "Here. It's for you."

"Thanks." She started to kiss his cheek.

He turned his head from her.

Wondering why he'd pulled away, she decided it had to be "teenage behavior," but it wasn't like him to be that cold, almost rejecting, to her. She decided she'd talk to him tonight. Maybe his father upset him—that had to be the reason. "Boys," she called to Daniel and Jon as they started towards

131

the stairs, "I caught some fish on a boat today. I'll cook it for you guys."

"Did it died?" Jon turned around.

"Cookie Face, of course it's dead." She laughed. "You can tell me all about the circus while I fix dinner."

"We already ate," Eric said.

"At the circus?" she asked.

Eric somberly studied the black marble floor. "I'm going to live with Dad."

"Eric, shut up." Daniel's eyes flashed. "Dad said not to say anything yet."

"Me too," Jon said.

"What?" Alex stared at her sons. This had to be a terrible nightmare from which she would soon awaken.

"Well, Dad told us it would be better with him." Eric took a step further into the foyer.

"No!" Alex screamed.

"He's moving into a big house with a swimming pool." Jon held out his arms. "This big."

Eric's eyes lit up. "Dad said that he'd get us another dog, just like Honey."

"Honey," she whispered. Trying to stay calm, she took a steadying breath. "Let's not talk about it now. You've got to get ready for school tomorrow."

Daniel looked at her with sad eyes. "Dad said the school there's better."

"Nonsense." Alex knew he was being Daniel, trying to protect her by giving her a reason that, in his mind, would not hurt her as much. It did. Devastated, she picked Jon up and held him tight. Certainly her baby couldn't leave. None of them were going to leave her, she decided. She'd been a good mother.

As though reading her mind, Daniel put his arms around her waist and looked up at her. "Love you," he said reassuringly.

"Your dad has to discuss this with me first," she said, sorry she hadn't taken her attorney's advice. That was definitely a mistake, a weak moment. There'd be no more of those. There couldn't be. She was going to keep her boys. She had to.

"I'm going to call your father to clear this up." She went to the telephone and dialed Gabe, fingers shaking.

No answer. Direct to voice mail. *What a bastard!*

Somehow, she managed to help the older boys with their homework, read Jon a story, and kiss them all good-night.

She dialed Gabe again. Voice mail. She hung up.

She tried again.

Finally, he answered.

"Gabriel, what the hell did you tell the boys?"

"You signed the agreement giving Eric permission to live with me." He exhaled into the phone. "Eric and I were talking about it, and the other boys asked why they couldn't live with me too. They didn't want you to separate them."

"Me?" she screamed. "And why'd you pretend to protect me? How could you?"

"I've already told you that Townsend lost everything," he said. "And because his former wife's attorney subpoenaed the practice's records, the partners fired him. I couldn't take that chance."

"Don't compare this to Townsend. You pressured me to sign because you wanted your name off the deed so you could buy yourself a new house." She wasn't going to let him lie to her again. "The boys are not leaving," she screamed. Then, realizing she might wake the children, she lowered her voice. "Why did you show the boys a new house you're buying for them?"

"I'm not buying a house," he said.

Trembling, trying to keep her rage to a whisper, she asked, "If you're not buying a house, how could you have shown the boys a house with a pool?"

"It's Linda's house."

"Right," she said. "The boys said it was a new house."

"Actually, the boys had never seen Linda's house before today," he said. "We've been living in a rental while the house was being renovated for the boys."

"For the boys?" she repeated. Shocked, she wondered how he'd been able to sail so effortlessly from one life to another while her life had been turning inside out from the minute he'd told her he was leaving. She demanded, "Why'd you tell the boys they could live with you?"

"It's all in the agreement. As you recall, since Eric is thirteen, he can choose where he wants to live."

"Gabe, you said the kids would stay with me."

He sighed loudly. "I'm sure you'd never want to separate the boys and ruin the family."

"The family's ruined, Gabe. You're the one who ruined it. I won't let the boys go."

"You've got no choice on Eric. He's thirteen." His voice sounded calm, measured. "You can let 'em go now, or you'll lose them one by one, like ripping a bandage off hair by hair."

"You fucking shit." She threw down the phone, almost wishing she had grabbed his steering wheel on the trip home from Vegas. If they'd both died, she'd be spared this agony.

She needed to call Liz, but first she poured herself a glass of Merlot. Hands shaking too much to walk into the carpeted living room or family room while holding a glass of red wine, she sat at the kitchen table and stared at the balloons. Jon's blue balloon dropped to the floor next to Daniel's green one. Eric's red one stuck to the ceiling.

She looked at her watch: 11:08 p.m. It was too late to call Liz. She called anyway. "Gabe's taking the boys."

"I'm coming over," Liz said. "I'll be there in a half hour."

Alex went upstairs. As she looked at each of her sleeping boys, her heart hurt.

Twenty minutes later, she heard a knock at the front door and rushed downstairs. "I can't lose the boys." She collapsed into Liz.

Liz decided they had to call Meredith. They went into the kitchen. Liz picked up the half-empty glass of Merlot and looked at Alex. "You're drinking?"

"No, I haven't been drinking." She gulped. "Yet."

Liz picked up the phone and handed it to Alex. "Call Meredith."

"She's a real estate attorney." Alex hesitated before dialing.

"She's shrewd, and she's the best we can do at midnight," Liz said.

"Hello." Meredith yawned into the phone.

Alex explained.

Meredith said, "I tried to warn you, but you had to get off the phone to talk to Dorset."

"He quit."

"Oh, God, no."

"Wrong answer," Alex said. "What do I do?"

"I don't usually call family law attorneys at midnight." Meredith lowered her voice. "Warren's here, but I'm going to get up and review the agreement again."

"It's too late for that," Alex said. "Just go back to sleep."

"I'm awake now. You just hired Meredith Blackstone, attorney extraordinaire, whether you want her or not. I'll call as soon as I review everything."

"Thanks." Alex hung up and nodded at Liz.

"Meredith can be bitchy, but she always comes through." Liz handed Alex a tissue. "You'll keep the boys."

"But the boys said they're going," Alex sobbed.

"What do the boys really want?" Liz asked.

"Eric said he wants to live in Gabe's new house." Alex took a breath. "Jon talked about his father's fabulous swimming pool. Daniel said something about the school there being better."

Liz studied Alex, shook her head, and softly said, "Maybe you should let him take the children."

"Why would you even think that?" Alex asked.

"I don't want to see you get hurt." Liz looked apologetic. "You could go through a custody battle and then lose."

"I'm their mother," Alex said. "How could you think I'd lose my children?"

"Money," Liz said and hugged Alex.

Alex pulled away. "How could you think money would prevail?"

"It always does," Liz said. "It's who buys the best attorney."

Alex agreed. "There's no way I could afford a Beverly Hills attorney like the one Gabe hired."

"But why do you think Gabe wants the boys?" Liz asked.

Alex looked at Liz. "I'm sure he loves them, but I think this is more about control."

"Control?" Liz asked.

Alex explained how Gabe was always talking about Townsend, one of the doctors in the practice who got a divorce and was thrown out of the practice because his former wife had the practice audited. But the worst part was that Townsend's wife had a boyfriend who was one of the children's coaches. The kids adored the boyfriend who poisoned them against their father. The kids decided to live with the mother, and Townsend was completely ostracized from his children.

Alex also recounted how Gabe had told her if they ever got a divorce, which he'd said would never happen, there was no way anyone would prevent him from seeing his kids whenever he wanted, and he'd said he would never let another man bring up his kids. She'd ignored that, certain a divorce would never happen to them—until it did.

CHAPTER 18

It was midnight by the time Liz left, and Alex was appreciative of every minute Liz spent with her. There was nothing like a caring friend, and, at this moment, that was the only thing of which she was certain.

She walked upstairs. As she approached the landing, she thought she heard a sound and turned.

Daniel stood in the hallway. "Mom, I'm sorry."

"What's wrong?" She reached out and hugged him. With her arm wrapped around his waist, they walked into her bedroom. She turned on the light.

Wiping his eyes with the sleeve of his blue pajamas, Daniel said, "I told Dad we could stay with you one night and then with him another night."

"That's a great idea. You're so smart." She sat down on the bed. "What'd your dad say?"

"Dad said it would be too disruptive. So I said we could stay with you one week and him another." He got on her bed.

"That would work," Alex said, fighting back tears.

"Dad said it wouldn't be a good idea, and Eric said our friends would be too confused."

"Your friends would figure it out." Alex pulled him close. "Everything will be fine, but we've got to take care of Jon."

Daniel took a deep breath, and she could feel herself breathe with him. "Jon did say he needed to be with his mommy."

"What did your father say to that?"

"Dad said, 'Your brothers and I are men. We've got to stick together.' Then Dad asked Jon if he was a baby."

Alex fought back tears. "Jon *is* a baby." Gripped by a sense of disbelief, she could hardly think. "Jon has to stay with me."

"Mom, don't be mad at Jon."

"I'm not mad at any of you. I know it's best for you guys to be together, but I've got an idea."

She moved her hands, pretended to sew her heart, touched Daniel's chest, and then made an imaginary stitch.

"What're you doing?" Daniel asked.

"I'm making a connection between us that can never be broken, no matter what."

"I won't tell Dad about this."

"It's our secret." Alex kissed him.

"That's not why." He shook his head. "Dad said you're going to be upset, and you might do weird things. He said to tell him about the stuff you do. He said he'd explain it all to us. He said he couldn't protect us unless he knew everything."

"Bastard." Alex put her hand over her mouth. She didn't mean to curse in front of Daniel, but she couldn't help herself. Her anger was visceral. "I can protect you," she promised, fearful Gabe might even have told them they'd be safer with him. He might have warned them that a mother who had burned her child once might do it again, on purpose.

"Mom, do you still love Dad?"

"Um," she said, unable to tell him she used to love Gabe so much it made her heart ache, and now she hated him with the same intensity. It would be too confusing for him. He had to learn to live with this new reality, and so did she.

"I love you," he said and looked up at her, tears spilling down his cheeks.

She kissed his cheek and pulled him to her. "Sweetie, go back to bed."

As soon as Daniel left her room, she went downstairs to pack their school lunches. She was going to do it in the morning, but now, she had to do something, something that would affirm that she hadn't lost her boys. And routines had always saved her whenever reality was too cruel to face.

After she picked up the deflated blue and green balloons up from the kitchen floor, Eric's red one popped. She jumped, dropped into a chair, and was swept back to the day at the circus when her father had bought her a red balloon.

Seven-year-old Alexandra looked up from under her navy bowler hat with the blue satin bow, her wavy chestnut hair cascading down her back and dancing around her tiny waist. She saw the fat lady in the circus with her pancaked face, orangey-colored hair, and rotted teeth. The fat lady crinkled her gnarled index finger and beckoned Alexandra to her. Scared, Alexandra squeezed her dad's hand and smiled up at his gentle, handsome face, hoping he wouldn't ever let go of her hand.

"Babe, go ahead." Her dad nudged her toward the fat lady.

Staring at the grotesque mountain of flesh draped in a pink floral muumuu, Alexandra shrank back into her dad. Until that moment, her new hat, black patent leather shoes, and white stockings had made her feel magical, like Alice in Wonderland.

Her dad patted her bowler hat. Then, moving closer to the bulging figure on the platform, Alexandra stared at the fat lady's dull brown eyes peeking out from her pillow of a face. The mixture of sweat and pancake makeup streaking the woman's face made Alexandra's tummy turn.

Her dad nudged her to within inches of the fat lady's ruby lips. Alexandra stared at the deep pockmarks on the woman's face. She felt the fat lady's hot, sour breath and quickly turned her face away.

The fat lady pushed her face close to Alexandra and hissed, "It's the scrawny little girls like you who always grow up to be like me—alone and miserable."

"Me?" Alexandra asked, wondering how the fat lady could have known how intensely she feared she'd grow up to be fat just like her mother. She used to think her mother never left the house because she was too fat. Now, she feared if her mother did leave the house, this would be where they'd take her.

"Hee hee!" the fat lady shrieked and then whispered, "You don't believe me, but you'll see." Shifting her fat cheeks into a smirk, the fat lady held out a signed photo of herself.

Alexandra grabbed the black-and-white picture and stepped back against her dad's legs.

"What'd she say to you?" he asked.

"Nothing." Alexandra folded the picture and shoved it into her jacket pocket. Terrified, she asked, "Daddy, when I grow up, will I be like you?"

"Of course not." Her dad laughed. "You'll be just like your mommy."

Horrified by the fat lady's warning and her father's confirmation, Alexandra thought of her mother. She wondered how the fat lady in the circus could have known about her balloon of a mother at home, the woman Alexandra sometimes wished would fly away.

Then, to the background of Igor Stravinsky's "Circus Polka," Alexandra and her dad walked past the sideshow to their seats at the Ringling Bros. and Barnum & Bailey Circus. She watched the fire-eater, the midget, the giant, and the bearded lady, but none frightened her more than the fat lady. The farther away they got from the fat lady, the more Alexandra savored the circus: the music, the colors, and the smells of sawdust mingling with the cotton candy.

Years later, when Alex had married Gabriel, she'd thought she'd be safe forever. But tonight, her hopes and dreams were like balloons, floating off to distant places without her.

CHAPTER 19

On Monday morning, she sat at her desk and reviewed her first patient's chart, feeling the sense of security the office always provided.

There was a knock on her office door, and without waiting for her to invite him in, Seth walked into her office. "Alex, don't panic, but you need to come to the waiting room with me." He went to her desk, moved behind her, and put his hands on her shoulders.

She looked up at him.

"There's a process server here to see you," he said.

Terrified that Gabe's plan to take the children was coming to fruition and was moving faster than she'd imagined, she started to cry. She tried to stand up, but her legs buckled. "Seth, there are patients in the waiting room. Please tell him to come back here."

The process server entered her office, asked if she was Dr. Alexandra Rose, and handed her an envelope. She tore it open. Shocked, she stared at the legal document from Gabe's attorney: Form FL-300, "Request for Order." It was a court order for her to appear at the Lamoreaux Justice Center in Orange, California. The boxes labeled "Modification" and "Child Custody" were checked.

Seth looked on as she read the form. There was a case number, which she recognized as her divorce case number. Gabe was requesting legal *and* physical custody. Expecting to see only Eric named, she was shocked. Daniel and Jonathan Rose were also included. Panic gripped her as she touched each name on the page.

She turned the pages and read the section entitled "Facts in Support." Gabe had alleged she'd committed one irresponsible act after another. No, she wasn't the woman who'd intentionally burned her child. She wasn't a careless mother. She hadn't been habitually late to transport the children to and from their practices and games.

Devastated at how their love had turned from soft and gentle to harsh and ugly with the stroke of a pen, she called Meredith.

Meredith told Alex to stay calm.

"Too late," Alex said. "I'm a wreck. What do I do?"

Meredith promised to find her an attorney immediately, and within an hour, Joshua Leventhal called. He explained they had to file a response within twenty-one days. He recommended they meet within the next few days and assured her he'd draft a formal reply.

Alex called to thank Meredith for the referral and asked why an attorney of the caliber she'd described would've been available on such short notice.

"He's in love with *moi*," Meredith said.

"Please," Alex begged. "No time for humor."

"He's fabulous, the valedictorian of our class, and I called in a marker. I'll probably have to have sex with him for this."

"I'll have sex with him too if he gets me custody of the boys." Alex laughed through her tears.

Meredith recounted Joshua Leventhal's credentials and described several extremely difficult cases in which he'd prevailed.

Alex felt a modicum of relief. There was no way Gabe could convince a judge to take her children away from her.

◆◆◆

Four days later, Alex went to Leventhal's office, and, within one hour, he'd completed the draft of the respondent's pleading. Leventhal explained the process: They'd serve their response on Gabe and the court. Then she and Gabe would have to go to mediation; however, in Orange County, which is different from most other counties, the mediator isn't permitted to provide any recommendations to the court. Mediation is just to give the parties an opportunity to resolve the issues.

"Not likely," Alex said and rushed out of Leventhal's office to get to the October First Friday Book Club meeting.

She thought it amazing how time had moved forward so effortlessly while she was slipping backward, losing the life she had built. She walked down the stairway to the main entrance to Waters Restaurant and then to their usual table on the patio. As she passed the ornate mahogany bar, a man in a navy blazer looked up at her. Then he quickly returned his attention to his martini. She decided she had to learn how to enter a room like Meredith, commanding everyone's attention.

Passing the pristine fish tank, she saw her First Friday friends already seated on the patio. Earth mother Terrie was clad in a black peasant blouse. Judi wore a beige ultraconservative suit. Meredith was seductively tailored in Chanel, and Liz wore a classic cashmere sweater with her long strand of glistening white pearls to accentuate her outfit. Alex tied the red sweater she'd draped over her shoulders.

She pulled out the chair between Liz and Meredith and sat down with her back to the lake.

Their food had already been delivered, and they were halfway through with their lunch.

"I ordered Chinese chicken salad for you." Liz pointed to the plate of salad.

"Um, you smell good. Are you wearing Angel?" Terrie asked.

"No," Alex said. "Pink Sugar."

"Same cotton-candy smell." Meredith grimaced. "And how does the new perfume mix with our plumber's eau de toilette?"

"Owner of a franchise," Alex corrected.

"Whatever," Meredith said.

This was the first time all of the members of the First Friday Book Club had assembled since Alex had received the petition from Gabe. True, she'd seen Liz every day, Meredith had found her another attorney, and Terrie had called numerous times to make sure Alex maintained her sanity. But none of them had said anything about this month's book selection prior to today's meeting. They had all seemed to be avoiding it, even Terrie, who usually glommed onto emotionally charged subjects. And there appeared to be some collective tension that, Alex knew, was due to the sensitive nature of this month's novel.

Sophie's Choice, the story of a woman who had to decide which child—her daughter or son—would survive the Holocaust, ironically mimicked Alex's life. She knew the women were uncomfortable about discussing the loss of a child in front of her.

Judi wrapped her Million Dollar Red fingernails around her glass, her huge marquis ring glinting in the sun. "What'd everyone think of *Sophie's Choice?*"

No one spoke.

Finally, Alex asked, "Who picked this depressing book, and why this month?"

"You know we select the books at the beginning of the year." Terrie looked at Alex apologetically.

Alex burst into tears. "I couldn't finish it. I'm living it."

"No one could've predicted there'd be custody issues," Judi said. "I, for one, couldn't have added another book to my busy schedule."

"If you really were my friends, then substituting a book wouldn't have been an issue," Alex said.

"We *are* your friends," Judi snapped.

Alex knew Judi was right. After Gabe had left, the other physicians' wives had shunned her. Gabe had consistently sent numerous referrals from his cardiac practice to other physicians at the hospital, but Alex had nothing to offer them. Her small chiropractic partnership could never provide the lucrative referral base Gabe's busy cardiac practice offered.

Judi seemed uncomfortable whenever Alex talked about Gabe. Hospital gossip, after all, was supposed to stay within the hospital walls. From the moment Alex had told the First Friday women about Gabe leaving, Judi had stopped talking about the hospital. Alex also suspected Judi had probably known about Gabe's affair for a long time, even before he'd told her.

"Let's talk about the book and get it over with," Liz said, once again trying to protect her friend.

Alex looked at the women and realized how much she appreciated each and every one of them. "I'm so sorry. You're more than friends. You're my family, and I appreciate and love you all."

Terrie got up, walked around the table, and put her arms around Alex.

Liz reached over and rubbed Alex's back. "I could never make a decision like Sophie and choose whether my son or daughter would live. It's inhumane."

"I can't relate to that, but if my little Paws were taken," Meredith said, referring to her Siamese, "I'd go absolutely crazy."

"This is ripping my heart out." Alex fought back tears.

"You'll be fine," Meredith said, softening. "I've been talking to Josh Leventhal, your new attorney, and we've got some ideas."

"Now I wish I had listened to Dorset, the first attorney, when he told me Gabe might try to take the boys. But I couldn't believe it would ever become a possibility."

"Actually, the agreement states that the children don't have the right to choose where they want to live until they reach the age of thirteen; therefore, technically, only Eric, since he's thirteen, could have chosen." Meredith pursed her lips. "However, the pleading presents the issue of change of custody for all the boys."

"I know," Alex agreed. "But I can't separate the boys. That would be worse than losing them, because they'd lose each other."

"That's the true test of a mother's love," Terrie said.

"Was there any question?" Alex asked.

"Are you really going to fight Gabe?" Judi asked. Then she apparently caught herself. "I mean, he—"

"Wouldn't you fight if your husband left and tried to take your children?" Alex asked.

Judi looked away. "I just mean Gabe has so much money to spend."

"Wait a minute," Liz said. "Judi, how do you know how much Gabe has to spend?"

Judi picked up her purse. "Linda, his fiancée, is—"

"Fiancée?" Alex screamed.

"If you don't stay calm, you'll definitely lose in court." Meredith said. "Judi, tell us what you know."

"Linda came into this incredible wealth. Some bachelor uncle left her and her sister tons of money." Judi tapped her glass with her shiny red nails.

"How do you know?" Alex asked.

"Nothing stays a secret in the hospital," Judi said. "Anyway, Linda and her family had no idea their uncle had so much money. I mean, he was a mailman. He invested very wisely, and since he had no children of his own, he left all his money to Linda and her sister. Linda's former husband, who, as Alex knows, is also on staff at Brea Presbyterian Hospital, is pissed because he still has to pay her alimony and child support."

"Alex, make sure your attorney is advised of that," Meredith said.

The waitress put the leatherette folder on the table.

"This has been fascinating, as usual," Judi said, dropping a twenty into the folder. "I gotta get to the wedding planner. My daughter's meeting me there in fifteen minutes."

"I can't believe your daughter's getting married," Liz said. "I remember her bat mitzvah. It seems like only yesterday."

"Gotta go," Judi said. "You should all be getting your invitations soon."

After Judi left, Meredith turned to Alex. "You'd better get rid of your boy toy."

"Why?" Alex asked.

Meredith stopped applying her lipstick and held the Pink Icing tube in the air. "A black plumber might have deleterious effects on your case, now that it's a custody case."

"No one judges anyone by color anymore, and he's bi-racial," Terrie said.

"Any opposing attorney would jump on it. Come on, a plumber compared to a doctor." Meredith laughed.

"Maybe Meredith is right." Liz put her arm around Alex. "What's the attraction?"

"Sex is great," Alex said.

"I got that loud and clear," Liz said. "But once or twice, then get over it."

"I don't agree," Terrie said. "Women need the validation that only comes from a man, and besides, good sex is ..."

"Great sex." Alex flushed.

"Get a vibrator," Meredith retorted.

"When I'm with Luke, I relax."

"Drink wine while you're vibrating," Liz said.

"Actually," Alex said, "I invited him over for dinner this Saturday."

Meredith winced. "Not with the boys. They'll tell Gabe, and it doesn't matter how nice he is to the boys, Gabe's attorney will twist everything and have you married to a plumber who's using you for your money."

"The boys kept asking about the guy who calls. I don't want them to think I'm hiding anything from them." Alex rubbed her wrist, recalling the secrets her parents had kept from her. She knew how a child's imagination could distort reality.

"That's important," Terrie agreed. "Children need to feel included."

"Terr, give me a break. Alex can't chance it." Meredith pushed her half-eaten salad away, put money in the leatherette folder, and gave everyone an exaggerated air kiss as she rushed off.

Alex looked at Terrie and Liz. "Do you think I should get rid of him, like Meredith said? Or would it be better to let them meet him?" She burst into tears. "I can't lose the boys over this—or anything"

"How do you think they'll react to Luke?" Liz asked.

"I know Daniel and Jon'll be fine, but Eric ..." Alex shook her head. "He's so Gabe."

"Then I say you should cancel," Liz said.

"And I say you need to let them meet him," Terrie said.

CHAPTER 20

After Eric's football game on Saturday afternoon, Alex opened the back door of her Land Cruiser for Jon to climb into his car seat. She fastened his seat belt.

"I get the front," Eric shouted, annoyed after losing.

"No, it's my turn," Daniel retorted.

"Pick a number." Alex took out a pen and paper. They waited for her to write down a number. Daniel guessed the correct number, seven, on the second try. She opened the front passenger door for him. *If only all arguments could be settled this easily,* she thought.

Alex got behind the wheel, fumbled with the keys, and turned on the ignition. "Um, I invited one of my tennis partners over for dinner tonight." She looked in the rearview mirror, checking for Eric's reaction. Her palms started to sweat.

"Bet it's that Luke guy who keeps calling." Eric smirked.

"As a matter of fact, it is," she replied.

"I knew it," Eric said.

"Can I go too?" Jon asked.

"Duh, Doofus, she's invited him to our house." Eric punched Jon's arm. "But Mom, I want to play my new computer game, and I've got homework."

"You never worry about your homework," Daniel, the family peacemaker, said and turned to look at Eric in the backseat.

"As soon as we get home, you guys take a shower and get ready." Alex quickly turned back, checking Eric's expression.

"Do I have to?" Eric asked.

"It'll be fun," Alex said. "He's nice."

As soon as they got home, she and Jon prepared the chicken while the older boys showered. Then she went to the garage for the fifth chair, Gabe's chair, the one she'd removed from the family table. She lugged it back into the kitchen, placed it at the head of the table, and surveyed the room. Now the room looked so right.

When the doorbell rang, the boys, clad in jeans and polo shirts, ran downstairs.

Before opening the front door, Alex said, "I want you on your best behavior."

"I always do behaving good." Jon looked up at her, his big brown eyes warming her.

"I know, Cookie Face." She leaned down to kiss him and then opened the door.

Luke handed Alex a tiny bouquet. "Hey, guys," he said and smiled at the boys.

She reached for the bouquet of daisies and baby's breath. "Thanks," she said, pleased to have the boys see that she was worthy of flowers. These flowers were not a mistake like those Gabe had forgotten to cancel the day he'd announced his plans to leave her.

Alex smiled approvingly at Luke. His short-sleeved white polo shirt cut into his powerful biceps, his perfectly fitted jeans were neatly ironed, and his cordovan loafers gleamed.

"Wow," Jon said and clapped his hands. "It's Roosevelt Franklin in our house."

"What are you talking about?" Eric asked Jon.

"Are you Roosevelt Franklin?" Jon put his hands on his hips and looked up at Luke.

"Who's that, buddy?" Luke patted Jon's head.

"No, he's not," Alex said, worried that she'd made a mistake by inviting Luke and nervous that Jon might insult him.

"You're Roosevelt," Jon insisted. "Right?"

"Doofus." Eric scowled. "Roosevelt Franklin is a Muppet on *Sesame Street*. He's not real."

"Mommy, why's Eric teasing me?" Jon pointed to Luke. "Look at him."

Daniel put out his hand and said, "Nice to meet you." Then he turned to his brother. "Jon, come upstairs to get Teddy to introduce him to Mr. Luke."

"No." Jon stared at Luke. "I wanna stay here."

"Cookie Face, come to the kitchen and help me for a minute." Alex took Jon's hand, hoping Luke wasn't upset by Jon's assumption that he was a black Muppet from *Sesame Street*.

"I hear you guys play tennis," Luke said to Eric and Daniel.

"Can we play now?" Jon dropped Alex's hand and turned back to his brothers and Luke.

"If your mother lets you," Luke said.

"Sure, but where?" Alex asked.

"Come on outside while your mom finishes making dinner," Luke said. "I'll show you boys how to make a tennis court right here."

"I'm not going with ... um ..." Eric said.

Alex looked at Eric, cautioning him not to be rude.

"I'll get our racquets," Daniel said.

Reluctantly, Eric agreed. "I'll play for a few minutes."

While Daniel went to open the garage and got the racquets, Luke took Jon with him to his truck for his racquet and then to the garage to get supplies for the makeshift tennis court.

Fifteen minutes later, Alex went outside to watch. Luke had improvised a tennis court on the cul-de-sac in front of the house. Three folding chairs comprised the net, chalk lines marked the borders, and a Coleman lantern lit the makeshift court. Eric and Daniel were on one side of the "net," Luke and Jon on the other. She watched for several minutes, convinced that it was good to have invited him. Maybe now Eric wouldn't get as annoyed when he answered the phone, and it was Luke.

"Mommy, I'm winning," Jon said, holding his racquet up in the air.

"He's cheating," Eric said.

"Dinner's ready," Alex called.

While Luke folded the chairs, the boys picked up the tennis balls and went into the house for dinner. They gathered around the kitchen table and took out their usual seats.

Luke started to pull out the remaining chair at the head of the table.

"No." Jon jumped up. "That's my daddy's chair."

"Dad's not coming back." Eric shook his head and whispered under his breath, "I wish my dad were here instead of ..."

"I want Daddy," Jon cried.

"Boys, be polite." Alex put her hand on Jon's arm, reminding him to remain in his seat.

"Oh, they're fine." Luke winked.

"Sorry," Alex said and went to the oven to take out the chicken. Luke followed.

"Don't worry," he said and smiled. "I know how to read people, and your boys are doing great, under the circumstances."

154

"Thanks." She almost kissed him but turned and saw the boys watching them.

Luke carried the chicken platter to the table.

Jon turned to Luke. "Will you read me a people story?"

"What are you talking about?" Eric asked.

Jon scrunched his lips. "I heard him say he 'reads people,' and I wanna hear him read a story."

Alex laughed and placed a chicken leg, a stalk of broccoli, and a scoop of rice onto Jon's plate. "Luke means he understands people." She stretched out her hand for Eric's plate, then Daniel's.

"I still don't get how he reads people." Eric smirked.

Alex prepared a plate for Luke and handed it to him.

"Thanks," Luke said. Then he looked at Eric. "Let me explain. It's like this: For a flashing second, a person truly looks at you—unguarded, from the gut. After that, the person becomes aware of his true reaction and guards against it. I can always tell when people are genuine or when they're trying to hide their feelings."

"Am I hiding something?" Eric challenged.

"All you boys looked at me with kindness." Luke tapped his finger over his heart. "Comes from here."

Eric rolled his eyes, but Daniel nodded.

Luke smiled. "Tell me about your Little League teams."

"Now it's football," Eric said. Then he and Daniel competed with tales of the season's games.

After dinner, Luke asked, "Wanna pile into my truck and go for ice cream?"

"Can we, please, Mommy?" Jon looked at her.

"Sure, but we have to take my car since I have Jon's seat in there," Alex said. "Help me clean off the table, and we'll all go."

They cleared the table, jostling into one another in their hurry.

"Take jackets," Alex said.

"It's not cold." Eric looked to Luke, a new ally.

Luke said, "I always used to tell my girls, 'You gotta do what your mother says.'"

"How much girls did you get?" Jon asked.

"Four," Luke said and helped Jon with his jacket. "They're all grown now."

"You got a lot of girls." Jon turned around to Alex, and she zipped his jacket.

"What's everyone's favorite flavor?" Luke asked, and the boys called out flavors as they climbed into the Land Cruiser.

During the car ride to Farrell's Ice Cream Parlor, Luke questioned the boys about their favorite sport, favorite athlete, all the while engaging them.

When Luke ordered bubble-gum ice cream, the boys giggled.

"That's a kid's flavor," Eric said, his tone lighter.

On the short drive home, Jon fell asleep. Luke carried him up to his bed, and then said goodbye to the older boys.

Alex walked Luke to the door and thanked him for a delightful evening. Yes, the charisma that had attracted her to Luke was definitely palpable. At the tennis club, everyone sought a match with Luke, not only because he was an excellent athlete but also because he was charismatic and charming.

◆◆◆

The next morning, Jon cuddled in bed with Alex. Suddenly, he pulled away, looked worried, and said, "I got a question, Mommy."

"Just ask." She kissed his curly hair.

"When do we go home?" Jon asked.

"This is home."

"Not for real." He pursed his lips. "I got my G.I. Joes at home."

Funny—for Jon, life was simple: home was where his G.I. Joes live. Alex kissed him again. "For Hanukah, I'm going to buy you a set of G.I. Joes to keep here."

"But isn't Hanukah long ago?" Jon asked.

"It's coming in December," she said.

"So is 'ember soon?"

"I'll get you one tomorrow. Then we'll have the whole collection by Hanukah."

"Thank you, Mommy." Jon put his arms around her and snuggled closer. "Then this'll be home too."

She kissed Jon, wishing it really could be that simple.

CHAPTER 21

Alex's stomach was in knots. In an hour, she would have to face Gabriel Rose at the mediation. She was doubtful they would resolve the custody issue with the mediator, but she was willing to try anything. Leventhal, her attorney, had explained that only the parents were allowed at the mediation; therefore, he couldn't attend. Leventhal also told her there were no consequences for failure to reach an agreement at the mediation.

She walked into the room, looked at Gabe, and had to turn away, amazed at how her body reacted just as powerfully to the hate as it had to the love.

The mediator introduced herself. "Today we are going to discuss issues of custody. The goal of the California courts is to encourage frequent contact with both parents. I'm here to help you devise a parenting plan that will allow your children to spend time with both parents. I'm also here to help you learn how to deal with your anger and resentment."

"And your credentials are?" Gabe asked smugly.

"I'm a psychologist, and I've been a mediator for twenty-two years."

"Sounds fine, but we're not going to reach an agreement." Gabe looked at the mediator sternly.

The mediator made it clear this was voluntary. She stated if they could not reach an agreement, then the matter would have to go before a judge. She explained going before a judge was second best because the judge is a stranger, but the parents are more familiar with the children's needs. Therefore, mediation was in the best interests of the children.

Alex agreed. Then she looked at Gabe and knew it was futile. Gabe stood up.

The mediator said, "I understand how emotional this is for both of you, but if you could think about the best interest of the children. As I stated, California's policy is that children should have as much time with each parent as—"

"I really don't have time to listen to you tell me about California's policy. I have patients and more important things to do." Gabe looked at the mediator dismissively. "We're done here."

"I'll advise the court that the mediation was unsuccessful, and the case will proceed on the scheduled date."

Alex watched Gabe stride out of the room. Determined to do whatever it took to maintain custody of her children, she gathered her things and left. This time, she decided, she was going to listen to her attorney. And whether it took selling the house or working more hours, she was going to pay for whatever legal proceedings were required. Gabe's hold on her was finally over.

◆◆◆

Two weeks after their failure to reach an agreement at mediation, the day Alex feared the most arrived. Her neck tightened, threatening to morph into a headache that could short-circuit her ability to think rationally in case the judge asked her any questions. Even though Leventhal had told her it was rare for attorneys to cross-examine the parents at the hearing, she was nervous.

She entered the courthouse, passed through security, headed down the corridor, and took the elevator to the sixth floor of the Lamoreaux Justice Center. On the sheets of paper stapled together and tacked onto the board outside the courtroom, she saw her name and Gabe's name and felt sick to her stomach.

She heard footsteps and turned around.

Joshua Leventhal, her attorney, shook her hand.

Assessing his red-and-navy tie, his impeccable navy suit, and his starched white shirt, she decided he looked professional. And that was exactly what she needed—professional, impersonal, unemotional. She was determined she wasn't going to allow the sight of Gabriel Rose to unnerve her, make her appear anything like the woman he'd described in his pleading.

"Don't worry," Leventhal reassured her. "We've addressed everything your former husband presented in the petitioner's pleading." He smiled, then turned and opened the courtroom door for her.

As Alex and Leventhal walked into the courtroom, she felt swallowed up by the masculine oak that was everywhere—the judge's desk was on a platform, and there was a long table facing the judge's desk with the four now-empty chairs reserved for the attorneys and their clients. Behind the long table, there were four rows of seats for those who were waiting to go before the judge.

Alex turned to the right and looked at Gabe seated amongst the other couples and their attorneys. Impressive in his tailored gray pin-striped Armani suit and light-blue tie, Gabe appeared confident, but she wasn't going to let that influence her. He was her enemy, the man who wanted to take her children from her. She took a seat in the last row and focused on the little stuffed animals on the judge's desk.

The judge entered the room, took his seat behind the desk on the podium, and studied his computer. He announced, "*Rodriguez vs. Santos.*"

The first couple and their attorneys walked to the long table. The woman sat in the chair behind the petitioner's placard, the man sat in the chair behind the respondent's placard, and their lawyers took the two remaining seats between the couple. After only fifteen minutes, the judge made his determination and then called another case.

Waiting for their case to be heard, Alex watched as each group took their prescribed seats, the attorneys presented their positions, and the judge either made a decision or scheduled a hearing. Then the couples got up and vacated the courtroom— their lives completely altered by the judge's proclamation.

Finally, *Rose vs. Rose* was announced.

In the now-familiar arrangement, Alex proceeded to the seat behind the placard for the respondent. Leventhal sat next to her, then Gabe's attorney, and finally, behind the placard for the petitioner, Gabe took his seat.

The attorney for the petitioner, Mr. Wright, spoke first. He introduced himself to the judge and then introduced his client. He reiterated all of the accusations, a litany of lies.

Then it was Leventhal's turn to speak. After address-ing each accusation, Leventhal looked at Gabe. "It is our opinion that Dr. Gabriel Rose couldn't have been worried about the safety of the children. If he were that concerned, he wouldn't have waited twenty-one days. He would have demanded an emergency hearing." Leventhal then requested that the judge ask Dr. Gabriel Rose why he hadn't called for an emergency hearing.

The judge agreed it was a viable question and asked Gabe.

Gabe shook his head and looked down at his hands. "Your Honor, I wasn't there, so I believed what Alex said about the incident. I wanted to give her the benefit of the doubt. But three days ago, the boys told me she's been so ... weird. Frankly, I'm terrified for them."

"Can you explain?" the judge asked.

"They've told me that whenever she lights the oven, she stares at the flames and warns them to be good or she'll do what her mother did to her. The boys can't be left with her until she gets help."

"That's not true!" she exclaimed.

The judge looked at Leventhal. "You'll have to restrain your client."

The bailiff walked up to Alex and motioned for her to calm down.

Ignoring them, Alex continued in rapid fire: "I was reading the newspaper. Jon climbed onto my lap, and he knocked over the teakettle. There was no other—"

The bailiff moved closer to Alex. Standing right in front of her, he put his finger to his lips and narrowed his eyes.

Gabe smirked. "That's exactly what I was referring to. She can't control her emotions."

Alex started to stand, but Leventhal pulled her down.

Gabe shook his head. "As I was trying to explain, after she burned our son, he had to be treated at *my* hospital. The dermatologist was considering a debridement for my little boy, and she just went off to work." Gabe held his hands out, palms up, as though to show how useless she was.

"Yes, all that is in the petitioner's pleadings," Leventhal concurred, "but ..."

After listening to Gabe twist the truth, tears welled in her eyes. She wasn't this horrific woman he was describing, the one who was careless enough to burn her baby. And there wasn't any mention of debridement.

"… as I was saying," Leventhal continued, "we responded to each of the allegations."

Alex started to defend herself but stopped, fearful she'd confirm Gabe's allegations if she tried to tell the truth.

The judge took off his glasses, folded them, and looked at Alex. "I've reviewed the father's allegations and the mother's explanations. Wherein the father noted that the mother is 'prone to rages,' and the mother denies it, I feel it's in the best interests of the children to go forward with a full hearing on this matter. We'll schedule the hearing as soon as my calendar permits, but with the holidays—"

"Holidays!" Alex hissed. "It's only October."

"Shh," Leventhal cautioned.

"I'm making this matter a priority." The judge gave Alex a cautionary look.

"I'll need to grant a temporary custody order. Will the mother agree to the temporary custody order providing for the children to reside with their father?"

Alex started to get up again, but Leventhal placed his hand on her arm.

The judge continued, "If we can't come to an agreement, we'll have to refer the children to Social Services for a dependency hearing. Therefore, will you, Dr. Alexandra Rose, submit to the tentative ruling?"

"Social Services," Alex echoed. Her mind was whirling. Fear and anger gripped her as she faced the horrific fate that was unfolding before her eyes.

Leventhal moved the water bottle toward her and motioned for her to take a sip.

The judge continued to speak. Alex could barely make sense of his words. She was crazed with fear of losing the children forever. "Do something." Alex wrote on a piece of paper and pushed the note to Leventhal.

The judge looked at Alex. "I'm issuing a restrictive custody order. Dr. Alexandra Rose will have monitored, supervised visitation. The visitations will be in the presence of a sister or brother or any other family member or friend. If you cannot agree on the individual, then the court will provide a monitor whose salary will be paid for by the noncustodial parent."

"I don't want anyone with me," Alex whispered to Leventhal.

The bailiff ran over to her, looked at her sternly, and shook his head.

"Shh," Leventhal cautioned.

Gabe gave the judge a conciliatory nod.

"Please have your client present a list of monitors." The judge nodded at Leventhal.

"This can't be happening," Alex moaned.

Leventhal called for a break to confer with Alex. They went to the hallway, and he presented her options: "If we don't agree on a monitor, the court will appoint one. If they select an independent court-appointed monitor, then the children and the 'supervised parent' are required to have their meetings at the agency's facility."

She couldn't think.

"Pick someone you trust," Leventhal urged, "or they'll appoint someone."

Alex thought of her girlfriends. Except for Meredith, who was always traveling, the other First Friday women had husbands and families. Their lives couldn't be interrupted. Then she thought of Seth. He'd promised to help her if she needed him.

"Seth," she whispered.

They returned to the courtroom and presented her choice.

Gabe conferred with his attorney.

"My client agrees, Your Honor," Wright said.

"Dr. Alexandra Rose, what are your current business hours of operation?" The judge took off his smudged glasses and looked at Alex.

"I can alter my schedule however I see fit," she said.

The judge looked down at some papers on his desk. "Well, let's do Saturday and Wednesday afternoons from noon to seven. How does that sound?"

"Why can't I see the boys more?" Alex whispered to Leventhal, who turned away from her to agree with the judge.

"Now, Dr. Gabriel Rose, you are to understand that the order is temporary. That means the children are not to take all of their possessions. Do not consider this a permanent custody ruling. It's only a precaution for the children."

"A precaution?" Alex repeated and moaned.

The judge folded his arms across his chest. "You're both to remember this is not about you. It's about your children. I hope you act in a civil manner, even if you have to fake it. I'm ordering both parents to refrain from discussing the matter with the children. You're not to give the children any written or oral instructions about how to act while with the other parent. Your relatives, should the children spend time with them, cannot ask questions about this matter."

Alex put her head in her hands.

The judge turned to his computer. "The trial will commence on January—

"Why?" Alex whispered to Leventhal, who put his finger to his lips, cautioning her to be quiet.

"Mr. Leventhal, if you cannot restrain your client, I will have to hold her in contempt." The judge looked sternly at Alex and proceeded, "Now, I'll need a Seven-Thirty evaluation in order to help me decide on the issue of permanent custody."

"Seven-Thirty?" Alex wrote and pushed the note to Leventhal.

"A report from a psychiatrist, psychologist, or social worker," Leventhal wrote on a piece of paper and handed it to Alex.

She couldn't breathe, she started to sweat, and she felt as though the room was spinning. She grabbed on to the table to steady herself.

"Your Honor, we've taken care of the evaluation. With the permission of the court, we've spoken to the office of Dr. Weisbarth, just in case it came to this." Wright smiled confidently. "I do believe he's on your appointed list."

The judge riffled through a stack of papers, pulled out a sheet, and reviewed it. "Dr. Weisbarth is acceptable."

"Your Honor, we have a tentative appointment scheduled in three weeks with Dr. Weisbarth. My client has already advanced his portion of the fees and will proceed if agreed."

"If the other party agrees, we will use Dr. Weisbarth," the judge stated.

"Agreed," Leventhal said.

"Why does Gabe choose?" she wrote.

"It's fine," Leventhal wrote.

"Nothing is fine," she whispered.

"The temporary custody order is in effect until we reconvene." The judge restacked his papers, preparing to hear the next case.

"How did Gabe already make an appointment with a psychiatrist?" Alex asked.

"I'll explain later," Leventhal said.

Gabe and his attorney got up and left the courtroom.

Unable to move, Alex looked up at Leventhal. "How did this happen?"

"It usually takes months to obtain an appointment with a forensic psychologist," Leventhal said. "But I'm glad it's

Weisbarth. His reports are solid, and his recommendations often favor the mother."

"Why didn't you make an appointment with him for me?" Alex asked.

"I didn't know it would come to this," Leventhal said.

CHAPTER 22

On Saturday afternoon, the boys went to Alex's house to pack up their things. Although the judge mandated her visits were to be limited to Wednesday and Saturday afternoons, Gabe conceded and agreed to let the boys stay with her until 9:00 p.m. in order to pack everything they'd need—that is, as long as Seth was there to supervise.

In his new role as court-appointed monitor, Seth was supportive without being intrusive. After dinner, he insisted on doing the dishes and told Alex to go up to the boys. As she walked upstairs to help the boys pack up the last few remnants of their lives in her home, her heart pounded.

On her way down the hall to Jon's room, she heard Eric and Jon shouting at each other.

"Gimme it," Jon demanded. "Ahh."

"They're mine," Eric said.

"Give!" Jon shrieked.

Alex entered the older boys' bedroom. Glancing down at the floor, she saw, between shredded wads of packing paper, the miniature figurines on the beige carpet. She picked up the two-inch porcelain cow that stood upright, holding flowers in its hooves. Then she looked at the one-inch telephone with a dial that moved.

"Mom, can't I have them?" Jon asked, a glass unicorn disappearing within his tiny hand.

"No one takes these." Alex cupped her hands over Jon's clenched fist. "They belonged to my father's sister, and they're very special to me. That's why I put them in the hall closet. Why did you take them out?"

"Why can't I have 'em?" Eric asked.

"Because something like this could happen, and they might break. My dad waited until I was old enough before he gave them to me."

"Mom, I'm old enough." Eric scowled at Jon. "I'll be careful to keep them away from him."

"I'm keeping these figurines until you boys are old enough and won't fight over them," she said, recalling the day her father had given them to her. That was the day she'd discovered the truth about her father. When he'd taken her downstairs to the basement to show her the figurines, that was when she'd found the box of books. And that was when she'd turned over the photograph that was tucked inside a book, the inscription revealing all the secrets of his life. From that photograph, she'd learned how he'd had to choose between a "normal life" and love. And it was love that had lost.

"Why can't I play with them?" Jon whined.

Quickly, before the memory ghosts once again held her within their grasp, she scooped up the figurines.

"Don't worry, Mom." Daniel leaned over and hugged her. "It's not forever."

"What are you talking about?" Eric scowled at Daniel. "You wanted to go to Dad's too."

"Shut up," Daniel said.

"Like you didn't want to move too." Eric gave him the finger. "You know what Dad told you."

"Be quiet," Daniel said.

Wanting to ask what Gabe had said but fearing that the telling would give his story more credence, she said, "I love you guys."

"Love you, Mom," Daniel called out.

As she went to Jon's room to finish putting his stuff in cartons, she paused. Paralyzed, she stared into the one picture of Gabe with the boys that still remained on the hallway wall. Although she knew Gabe had said he'd never let any stepdad raise his boys, she wondered why his vengeance had pushed him to this point. She'd trusted him with her secrets, trusted him with her fears, and this was how he guarded them! He'd probably continue to convince the boys they shouldn't trust her. She also knew the boys had to be confused, and they were too young and powerless to stand up to a father like Gabe.

Seth came upstairs and put his arm around her. "How are you holding up?"

"I'm fine," she said.

"You were lost in thought," he said. "Want to talk?"

"I can't," she said, tears welling. She went to Jon's room and continued to pack. As she picked up Jon's last toy, she thought maybe he'd start crying and refuse to go with Gabe. He needed to be with his mother, but then she had to face the reality—the court order had to be obeyed.

The chiming of the doorbell jarred her.

She ran downstairs and opened the front door. Stunned by the presence of a U-Haul truck, she scowled at Gabe. "How much stuff do you think the boys will need until the hearing, and don't you remember what the judge said about the boys taking just enough for school and sports?"

170

Overly cheerful, Gabe said, "Never can tell. I thought the boys might need the truck." He walked past her and followed the boys to their rooms. They carried cartons and suitcases downstairs and hoisted them into the truck.

Alex's chest tightened. She loathed Gabe for creating this carnage, but she bit back her rage. She would vent, but not in front of her children.

As they were taking the last few boxes, she turned to Gabe. "I have one question for you."

He looked at her as he'd look at a fly that landed on his shoulder right before he flicked it off. "What is it?"

"Why?"

"Townsend," he said and started to walk out.

"I'm not Townsend's wife. I'd never turn the boys against you," Alex said.

"I couldn't take that chance."

She reached out to touch his arm. "I'd never ..."

He turned and walked away.

Alex forced herself to breathe.

Daniel ran back to hug her. Jon followed. She embraced them.

Gabe shouted, "Let's go home!"

She turned to Seth. "I really need to be alone."

"Alex, you don't have to be strong with me." He hugged her.

"I certainly wasn't strong," she said. "I just let Gabe walk all over me."

"No one demeans you," he corrected.

"That's at work. That's different. There, I'm in control."

"Alex, you believe people are going to do the right thing, and when they don't, you're shocked."

"I can't do a lecture right now. I'm hurting and need to cry—alone."

He kissed her forehead and left.

After shutting the door, she climbed the stairs to Jon's room in a state of shock and collapsed onto his bed. Pressing her nose to Jon's pillow, she inhaled his baby-powder scent. Then she rolled over and stared down at the carpet. She saw the white plaster-of-Paris cast of Jon's little hand that he'd brought home from nursery school just the other day. She reached down, grabbed the cast, and flung it across the room. Then she cried as the silence in the house enveloped her with its ghostly screams.

CHAPTER 23

As Alex wandered from empty room to empty room, the home she'd loved suddenly seemed cold and uninviting. Jarred by the phone, she ran to pick it up. "Seth, I'm doing fine," she said.

"It's Luke, and just how much does Seth call you?"

"I thought it was Seth because he saw how upset I was when the boys left."

"You need me there with you," he said. "I'll be right over."

"No," she said. Usually willing to do whatever anyone asked of her, she was firm. The only one she needed to talk to right now was Liz. She hung up the phone and dialed her best friend.

Thirty minutes later, Alex opened the door and folded into Liz's arms. "My world just collapsed."

"You're going to be okay," Liz said.

"There was nothing I wanted more than this family, this life. Gabe was my world. I believed in him. All I wanted to do was please him."

"Why?" Liz asked.

"Does it matter?" Alex sobbed. "Look what happened, and he was the only person to ever tell me he loved me."

"I don't get it. I need a glass of wine for this one." Liz pulled out a bottle of Merlot from her purse and handed it to Alex. "What about your parents? They must have told you they loved you."

"My father was wonderful, but if he ever showed affection, my mother would ..." Alex looked at Liz. "My mother abused me." There, she said it.

"How?" Liz asked.

Alex held out her wrist.

Liz gasped. "You never said anything about that. I just assumed it was some childhood accident. Are there more?"

"Yes."

"Where?"

"My butt. I think she burned me there so no one could see. She knew if she burned me there, I'd never show my father."

"Alex, I'm so sorry. Why didn't you tell me?"

"I've never told anyone—except Gabe. I was so ashamed."

"Ashamed of what?"

"At first, I thought maybe I deserved it. I thought I needed to try harder to please my mother." Alex looked at Liz. "I kept trying, but she'd just get more and more angry. I felt there had to be something wrong with me if I couldn't get my mother to love me."

"Amazing how a parent can scar a child—not just physically." Liz hugged her.

"I believed I was broken, screwed up. I believed my mother would never have hurt me unless I'd done something terrible. I'd even cover up for her. The first time a teacher asked me what had happened, I told her the iron fell on me. Then it became easier. When I couldn't sit down because my mother burned me, I told my teacher I had a bad fall from my bicycle."

"Why'd you protect your mother?"

"She threatened me. She said if I ever told anyone, especially my father, then she'd hurt me more. I was terrified."

"Did Gabe ever abuse you?"

174

"Of course not. He promised me our family would be different. He told me he understood why I was so insecure, and ..."

"What?"

"When we were just freshmen in college, I thought he was so understanding, and I had sex with him." Alex cried. "I felt loved for the first time. I wanted to do whatever it took to please him."

"Oh my God." Liz hugged her.

"What?"

"Stockholm syndrome," Liz said.

"No," Alex said. Her heart pounded, her hands started to shake, and tears flowed.

"Alex, you were abused, and then Gabe rescued you. You even said you'd do anything to please him."

"This has nothing to do with Stockholm syndrome," Alex said, tears filling her eyes.

"Alex, don't you remember Manson would have sex with the women, and that was how he controlled them?"

"Right," Alex said, uncomfortable with the possibility Liz's insight was accurate. "The women all fell in love with him and would do anything. I ..."

"Gabe was your rescuer," Liz said.

Alex looked at her best friend and admitted: "In a sense, he did control me. And whenever he'd get distant or angry, I'd always think it was something I had done—my fault."

"Why did you put up with it?" Liz asked.

"He was just like my mother. He'd be so nice for a while, loving and ..."

"Alex, it's classic."

"That isn't the kind of classic I was striving for."

"You chose someone just like your mother." Liz shook her head.

"I didn't choose him. He choose me. I ..."

"Alex, what do you want? Really want?"

"My children."

"You'll get them. I promise. You have the First Friday Book Club behind you."

"I'm so sorry I didn't stay with that first attorney, Mr. Dorset."

"I remember asking you why, and all you did was defend Gabe."

"I didn't think I could go through litigation. I didn't have the money for a protracted divorce. One doctor paid a hundred thousand for his divorce."

"But Alex, your practice is going well. I don't get it."

"While we were married, Gabe took care of all the finances. I'll never be this naïve again. I believed Gabe when he told me that the partners would fire him if there were an investigation of the practice. Then, he said, he wouldn't be able to pay me anything."

"Bluffing!"

"I finally see him for who he really is. Why did I allow him to walk all over me?"

"You don't have to be a victim anymore," Liz said.

"Victim?" Alex looked at her friend and knew she was right. She'd really been a victim as a child, but as an adult, she no longer had to be.

"You have too much to offer, and your children need a strong mother."

"Liz, I want the boys to love me, but I also want them to respect me. Gabe has been trying to destroy me in their eyes. I'm not going to let him do it."

"You allowed him to walk all over you when you were young and vulnerable, but you're not the person he married."

"And he definitely isn't the man I married. Now, I'm going to take care of my boys. They might not live with me—for the time being—but whenever I see them, I'm going to do whatever is needed. I am still their mother."

"I can feel your resolve, and I love it." Liz hugged her and left.

Alex went upstairs to her room, wondering how love had brought her to this. Tossing and turning, she thought about the night in the Bellagio when she went to bed waiting for her husband—her lover and best friend—only to wake and find that he was none of those. Yes, she'd thought she was secure in Gabe's world until it was too late—until his heart found another home. Armed with a new determination, she decided she was going to build a home for herself and, eventually, the boys.

CHAPTER 24

Monday morning. Alex knew work would save her. She had a reason to abandon her bed, brush her teeth, and comb her hair. Her patients needed her.

She pulled into Starbucks and waited in the long line, absently humming Jon's favorite song, "The Wheels on the Bus." She purchased lattes for Seth and herself and got into the car.

Lattes secured in the holders in the Land Cruiser, she drove out of the shopping center. Almost missing a red light, she slammed on the brakes. Reflexively, she reached across the passenger seat, her right hand outstretched to protect whichever one of the boys was sitting in the front seat. But the boys were gone. She thought it amazing how such an ordinary act could remind her she'd lost her place in the novel that had been her life.

As she pulled into her parking space at the office, she noticed Seth hadn't arrived yet. She threw her purse over her shoulder, grabbed the three patient charts she'd taken home to work on, and climbed out of her car. Balancing the lattes and charts, she took the elevator to her office. When she opened the office door, Rebecca took the charts from her.

Seth arrived a few minutes later, pristine in a starched powder-blue shirt and perfectly pressed tan slacks. "Hello, ladies." He reached for his latte. "Thanks, Alex," he said, even more softly than usual.

"You're welcome," she said, comforted by their ritual. It reassured her that some things were going to remain the same even if her world had completely changed this weekend.

"Nice outfit," he said, looking at her light-blue blouse and tan slacks that mirrored his own. They often arrived at the office in similar attire. Whenever patients saw them dressed alike, they'd ask if they were a couple. She'd laugh, but Seth would get quiet and turn away.

Alex and Seth moved to the end of the hallway to the spot where Rebecca posted their daily patient schedule. While reviewing the list of patients, they sipped coffee together—their ritual. Standing close to him, Alex inhaled his scent: clean, fresh, like the color yellow.

Seth cleared his throat. "On Sunday, I checked out your tennis club." A compact man with the body of a runner, he was a seasoned tennis player.

"Did you like it?" She hoped he didn't. Luke became possessive whenever other men approached her. Luke probably—no, definitely—wouldn't accept the fact that she and Seth had a purely platonic relationship.

"Alex, I'm not sure if you're ready to lose to me at tennis," Seth teased.

"Dream on," she said and followed him to his office. "Seth, could you cover for me on Friday morning?"

"Sure. What's going on?" he asked.

"I'm going to a concert Thursday night, and it'll run late." Except for the First Friday Book Club meetings and the boys' events, she'd never asked Seth to cover for her.

She didn't want to explain that Luke might stay over on Thursday night, and she was looking forward to it. Ever since the boys had moved out, he would usually come over after tennis and stay for just a few hours. After he'd leave, she'd walk from empty room to empty room, determined the boys would soon return.

Although he'd never stay the night, he did mention that the concert would be a special night. She imagined spending the night with Luke, curled up next to him in bed, his muscular thighs against the backs of her legs and his long, sensitive fingers trailing over her body. Then, during the night, he'd brush against her, and they'd take each other with an urgency that defied the spent passion of just a few hours earlier.

"I'm jealous," Seth said, interrupting her fantasy.

"Why?" she asked, wondering why he'd be jealous about her going out with Luke.

"St. Clair's conducting Beethoven's Ninth, and I really wanted to go, but it's sold out."

"Um, that's not the performance I'm attending." Alex knew how much Seth loved classical music and wanted to see Carl St. Clair, the renowned conductor of the Orange County Pacific Symphony Orchestra.

"Then who are you seeing?" he asked.

"Kirk Franklin."

"Never heard of him."

"He's a gospel singer."

"Oh, that. What else from that Luke guy?" Seth slammed his empty coffee cup on the counter and strode away.

Shocked at his uncharacteristic display of anger, Alex followed him down the hallway, almost colliding with Rebecca.

"I'm putting Mr. Tully in your office," Rebecca said.

Seth stopped, turned back to Alex, and asked, "Don't you realize?"

Before she could answer, Rebecca stood between them and said, "Dr. Rose, the patient's chart is on your desk."

Neither Alex nor Seth moved.

"I'm sorry." Seth patted her shoulder. "I'll cover for you on Friday morning."

"Thanks," she said.

She entered her office, walked to her desk, and introduced herself to Robert Tully, the first patient of the day. Before she could review his chart, there was a knock on her office door.

"There's a call for you," Rebecca said.

Since Rebecca had been instructed never to disturb her unless there was a call from the boys or her attorney, Alex tensed. "What's wrong?"

"It's Barbara from some flying group," Rebecca said. "She said it was extremely urgent."

Alex apologized to the patient and picked up the phone. The woman explained that the chiropractor who was scheduled to go to Clinica Jesus Maria with the Flying Samaritans that weekend had had an emergency, and the patients needed chiropractic services.

"Count on me," Alex said. Gabe had told her he was taking the boys on a trip this weekend; therefore, she'd be able to go. It was so important to her to devote time to the indigent villagers. She wished she could do even more.

"Dr. Rose, thanks so much," the woman said. "I'll e-mail the pilot and get back to you with the particulars."

"Sure," Alex agreed. She hung up the phone and turned to her patient. "Now, Mr. Tully, tell me about your back pain." And, for the rest of the workday, she only thought about her patients and their pain.

At four o'clock, Mr. Jamison, an attorney who referred patients to the practice, called the office requesting appointments for five clients who'd been involved in an auto accident. He wanted to send the patients over within an hour.

Like hands on a clock crossing over each other without inter-fering, Alex and Seth worked in complete harmony. They con-sulted, examined, and x-rayed all five patients. Fitting into the perfectly choreographed triage, Alex reviewed the intake forms with each patient and performed the examinations. Seth took the x-rays and explained the results to each patient. Rebecca put the patients on the therapy beds. After the patients had therapy, Alex adjusted two of the patients and Seth adjusted the other three. Then Alex went over the home-care instructions with each patient.

At 7:30 p.m., Alex collapsed in the waiting room chair. "Seth, you're such a great partner," she said appreciatively.

"This is just like tennis because you have to depend on your partner." He looked at her and paused, as though preparing to deliver a deep sentiment. Then he looked away. "You know, your game is as good as your partner."

"That's why I play with Luke so much."

Suddenly, Seth appeared upset. "What do you know about this guy who just showed up at your tennis club?"

"He's a great tennis partner," she said, but she could tell this was not about tennis. When she and Seth had decided to work together years ago, they'd promised they wouldn't allow anything to interfere with their business relationship. But she'd been married then, and he'd had a girlfriend.

"Sorry," he said. "It's none of my business."

"Seth, speaking of the business, this is the first time we've ever had five new patients at the same time."

"Let me take you out for a celebratory dinner," he said.

"I'm a mess after working all day."

"You've no idea how attractive you are," he said, voice quiet.

She smiled at him, appreciative of his compliment but certain he wasn't professing his attraction to her. Their agreement about keeping their relationship professional and not personal was paramount. And, as honorable as Seth was in everything he did, she knew he'd never renege on a promise.

"Let's get out of here, but just for a quick dinner, since it's so late," she said.

They put away the patients' charts and went to El Pollo Loco. After dinner, Alex was reluctant to leave the warmth she always felt with Seth.

CHAPTER 25

On the day of the Kirk Franklin concert, Seth seemed unusually distracted and distant. When she reminded him about covering the practice the next morning, he snapped at her. Alex refused to allow his behavior to dampen her excitement. She finished treating her patients, thanked Seth again for covering, and left the office to prepare for the evening.

Recalling the Bruce Springsteen concert she and Gabe had gone to last year, she grabbed her jeans and a white shirt. Then she threw her raspberry cashmere sweater over her shoulders and waited for Luke.

A few minutes later, Luke arrived, gorgeous in a tan suit and black silk T-shirt. He kissed her and then pulled back and looked at her jeans. "My people really get decked out for these concerts."

"I'll go up and change."

"Want me to come up with you?"

"Wait right here or else we'll never get to the concert." She turned and went upstairs. She selected a floral-print dress then slipped her feet into her black high heels.

Allowing him to take in her long sleeveless dress with tiny red roses on a black background, she slowly walked down the stairs.

"You look perfect." He pulled her close and embraced her.

She moved into him, thigh against thigh, longing to feel skin on skin. "Let me get a jacket," she said, pulling away.

After locking the door, they walked to his truck. During the hour-long drive to Los Angeles, he told her about the last Kirk Franklin concert he'd attended and how Franklin had electrified the audience.

"This weekend I'll bring over some of his CDs," he said.

"Wait until I see if I like his music," she said.

"You will." He grabbed a CD from a pile in the console. "Oh, speaking of the weekend, wanna go fishing?"

"I'm going to Mexico on Saturday and Sunday with the Flying Samaritans."

"What's that?"

"Physicians fly to a remote Mexican village, Jesus Maria, and work on people who can't afford medical, dental, or chiropractic care."

"Why go to the middle of Mexico to do that?"

"It's near Baja, not in the middle," she said. "We leave here at five in the morning and get there by ten to start the clinic."

"Sounds like a big trip for nothing."

"It's important to help the villagers," Alex said, explaining her desire to make a difference in the world. When she'd been married to Gabe, he'd argue with her every time she'd wanted to go. He'd say it was important for hospitals to take care of the poor, but only so that doctors could practice on them before treating the real patients—the ones who paid. She hated that about Gabe and decided now she could volunteer more, especially on the weekends when she didn't get to see the boys.

Considering what Luke had told her about his upbringing—albeit extremely limited information and only when she asked—she'd been certain he would understand her desire to help those who were less fortunate. "Aren't you into helping others?" she asked.

"Oh, I help people plenty." He patted her hand. "You'd be amazed how thankful they are when I show them the clogs I collected from their toilets or drains."

"You do understand," she said sarcastically.

He shook his head. "Aren't there enough poor people to help here?"

She had to agree, but traveling to Mexico was the least she could do to contribute. She now knew he didn't share her values. Sexually, they had synergy, but otherwise, they were worlds apart.

"You're going to be flat-out amazed by this concert." He let go of her hand and turned the wheel.

As Luke pulled into a parking spot, she stared at the continuous line of people walking toward the Gibson Amphitheatre at Universal City Walk.

Luke laughed. "Bet you never saw so many black people in your life."

"No," Alex agreed. Recalling her experience in the bathroom at Sweets, she gripped Luke's hand, climbed out of the truck, and walked to the amphitheater.

Exploding with a carnival's vivacity, the amphitheater was filled to capacity. The women wore vibrant, ruffled dresses in lipstick-red, neon-blue, or sun-yellow, many adorned with rhinestones. The men strutted in suits with large shoulder pads. Little girls wore organdy dresses with bows and sashes, and little boys sported suits and ties.

Alex and Luke squeezed through the throngs of people to their seats. She was enjoying this escape into Luke's world, traveling far away from her own. Then she heard the first few bars of "Jesus Took Me to the River" and marveled at the distance from her Jewish roots.

Energized, everyone jumped up, linked arms, and swayed to the music. As the lights scanned the audience, the cacophony of colors and ribbons of rhinestones glistened.

Luke sang along softly, familiar with the words. He wrapped his arm around her. She followed his lead, moving with the music.

Too quickly, "Hallelujah" reverberated through the amphitheater, signaling the end of the concert. Then, as though a veil had fallen over the audience, everyone became somber, reluctant to leave this foray into faith.

On the drive back to Orange County, Luke seemed different, nostalgic. He told her, "Momma was a preacher."

"A woman preacher?"

"Yep. I was the eldest of five, so I *had* to be at church every Sunday."

"Were her sermons good?" she asked, pleased he was sharing his past.

"Guess so. Got some to go slithering down the aisles, yelling out, 'I seen Him.' Some kinda craziness."

"What'd you do?"

"I was in the choir." He smiled and tapped the right side of his forehead, a habit she'd come to expect on the rare occasions when he'd reveal something from his past. "Never missed a Sunday."

"Was your dad a preacher too?"

Luke laughed. "He never went to her church. They'd never accept him there 'cause he was white. Besides, he was a drinker."

"An alcoholic? That must have been hard for you." She wondered whether Luke could also be an alcoholic, but he seemed so removed from his roots. *Or was he?*

Luke nodded. "My daddy'd hide his booze in his tool chest. He'd be drunk by early evening."

"I think it's amazing any one of us survives our childhood," Alex said, more to herself than him. He'd never asked about her childhood, and she wondered whether it was his lack of interest or respect for her privacy.

He turned up the CD and hummed along until they arrived at her house. Helping her out of the truck, he asked, "Alex, you too tired for me to come in?"

"No. I want you to."

He walked her to the front door and waited for her to hand him the key. After he opened the door, they stood at the entryway. His hand entwined with hers, he pressed his lips to her forehead. She looked up at his amber eyes and smiled. Then she got up on tiptoes and kissed his neck, sure she could taste his need. Excited by his clean, masculine scent, she pressed close and felt his heartbeat against her own.

His fingers traced her chin, then her face, and he kissed her hungrily.

She turned to make her way upstairs.

He followed, caressing her buttocks. "I love the way you move in that dress."

She lit the vanilla candle on the dresser, softening the bedroom. Then she turned the CD to "I Can't Stop Loving You," a background for their dialogue without words. As he unbuttoned the front of her dress and cupped her breast, she felt herself moisten.

He nudged her dress straps off her shoulders, and her dress fell to the floor in a soft heap near the white lounge chair. Sitting down on the lounge chair, he beckoned her onto his lap. As he embraced her, her breath quickened.

He unfastened her bra, took her nipple between his fingertips, and whispered, "I want you."

"So good," she moaned, longing for his warmth, his strength, his lust.

"I love touching you." His fingers lingered on her breast and then down her belly.

"C'mon. Let's see what I can do to you when you're naked," she said, easing up from his lap. She took his hand and walked across the room to the bed, her toes sinking into the plush beige carpet. As she got into bed, she thought of how she was going to make him hunger for her now, later tonight, and again in the morning. On other nights, his impending departure would give their lovemaking a sad urgency, but now they had all night.

Slowly, he undressed, throwing his clothes on the floor. He got into bed beside her. "Touch me," he whispered, his voice raw with desire.

She moved her hand along his firm abdomen, and he arched his back, thrusting his erect penis at her. Her hand moved up and down his silky shaft, his erection becoming tauter with each stroke. When she fingered the head of his penis, he moaned with delight.

His tongue teased her nipples, and he slipped his hand between her thighs and touched her with feather-soft strokes until she begged, "I need to feel you in me."

He mounted her, and she lifted her pelvis to him. They almost came together, but he stopped, rolled off her, and looked into her eyes. "I want to kiss every part of you," he said and caressed her with his tongue.

She touched his hair, his skin, and whispered his name.

He eased away. Looking deeply into her eyes, he asked, "Would you do me a favor?"

"If I can." She held her breath, her gaze locked on his.

"Alex, I'd like you to walk across the room so I can see your body."

She slid out of bed, stopping at the foot. She stood in front of him and trailed her fingers across her breast and then down her belly, giving him a seductive smile.

"You're beautiful."

Gabe was the only other person who'd ever called her beautiful, and she no longer trusted him. Now she trusted Luke's lust but not his love. Illusions gone, she decided lust would do.

"I want to keep your body fixed in my mind like I keep your smell when I'm not with you," he said.

"My smell?"

"Alex, it's on my clothes when I leave: sweet, flowery." He smiled. "Now I want to fix a picture of you in my mind." He stretched out his hand to her. "Come back to bed. I want you."

He entered her. "Give it to me," he whispered, his breath heavy, raspy.

Engulfed by him—his scent, his strength, his touch—she came.

"I'd love to take you again," he said a few minutes later.

"Sounds like a plan," she said, savoring the feel of him.

He chuckled. "I'm not that young."

"Sleep," she said, preparing to drift off wrapped in his arms.

He sighed and sat up. "I'd best be going."

"I thought you'd spend the night."

"I'd love to, but my work truck's parked at home." He kissed her forehead.

"So?" she said, pulling away. "You could get it in the morning."

"I've got to be at the office by six thirty—company rules—and I wouldn't want to wake you."

"If you own the franchise, then why do the rules apply to you?"

"A franchise owner has to keep with the rules of the parent company. If we don't, then they won't insure us." He tousled her hair. "I've got to be on the road at six, no matter what."

While he retrieved his clothes from the floor, she slipped into her robe and followed him to the door. After a quick kiss, he left and she returned to her bed. Fatigue pulling at her, she thought about her Mexico trip on Saturday. Then she'd have time to think and decide whether or not Luke belonged in her life.

CHAPTER 26

In the semidarkness of early Saturday morning, Alex opened the front door and walked a few steps to retrieve the newspaper. She stumbled to a halt when she spotted Luke. "What're you doing here?" she asked, wondering if he was checking up on her.

"You said you were leaving at five." Luke bent down to get the newspaper for her. "I'll give you a ride."

"Actually, I'm fine driving," she said.

"Suit yourself." He turned to walk back to his truck.

"Wait," she called. It would be easier if he dropped her off, and he'd already driven over. "Sure, I'll take a ride."

He took her backpack, threw it in the truck, and helped her get in. "Alex, how much do you get paid for this Mexico thing?"

"Actually, we all pay for our own hotel rooms, and the pilots donate their planes." She didn't think it was any of his business how she spent her money, and she definitely had some thinking to do about their relationship.

"I just don't get it," he pressed.

"I told you, 'This is my way of giving back, doing as much as I can to help those in need.'"

Apparently realizing this was important to her, he said, "It's great you're doing this."

She hoped he meant it. Their relationship seemed to make sense only when she projected her values, ideas, and hopes onto him. And, she had to admit, maybe it didn't even make sense then.

Once they arrived at the airport, she pointed to the hangar. "You can let me off, and I'll walk to the entrance."

"No. I'll park and walk you in."

"Luke, I'm fine."

"What's the matter?" he asked, an edge to his voice. "Are you ashamed of me?"

She stared at him. "Of course not."

After Luke parked his truck, he took her backpack and then they walked toward the private terminal adjacent to John Wayne Airport.

Alex approached a tall mustached man at the counter. "Are you Ed?"

Ed looked up and smiled. "Yes. And you are ...?"

"Dr. Alex Rose, the chiropractor."

"Can I ask you a personal question?" Ed asked.

She saw Luke clench his jaw. "One hundred and ten pounds," she said. "And my backpack weighs eight."

"Thanks, Doc." Ed continued with the calculations in order to distribute the weight evenly on each of the three airplanes.

Alex reached for her backpack from Luke, took it, and thanked him for the ride.

"Call when you get back. I'll be here in twenty minutes," Luke said but didn't leave. He pressed her to him and looked over her shoulder, surveying the group.

Engaged in animated conversation, three women entered the airport and approached the counter. They greeted Ed, and he put his arm around the one with the ponytail, announcing, "We're ready to roll."

"Be careful." Luke kissed her and left the terminal.

As she turned to proceed to the plane, she felt a jolt, then stumbled and fell. A man bent down, gripped her arm, and helped her up.

"Are you okay?" he asked in a gentle, deep voice.

"I'm fine," she said and looked toward the window. With all the people milling around in front of the window, she couldn't see whether Luke was still watching.

"I don't usually walk around with a backpack full of medical supplies and then bump into a pretty woman." He smiled, a kind, gentle smile.

She smiled back at him.

"The least I can do is carry your backpack." He reached for her backpack.

She turned and saw Luke was still watching through the window. "I've got it. I don't want to give you another weapon," she teased and then walked to the tarmac and boarded the six-seat Cessna.

The man who'd accidentally knocked her over took the seat next to her. "My backpack's stowed away, so you're not in any danger." He winked and extended his hand. "I'm David."

"Alex," she said and looked up into his warm green eyes, the color of old-fashioned Coca-Cola bottles.

They shook hands.

As the engine roared, the plane vibrated. Alex clicked her seat belt and then clutched the arms of her seat.

"Nervous?" David asked, noticing her white-knuckled grip on the armrest.

She eased her hold on the armrests. "I'm always a little tense during the first few minutes in a small plane. You?"

"I'm used to every plane there is." He described some of the encounters he'd faced in his native Israel. Then he told her he was a gynecologist and had been with the Flying Sams for several years.

As they talked for the first hour of the flight, Alex ignored the horrific turbulence. She was amazed at how she and David spoke so effortlessly. When she'd first seen him in the terminal—or rather, had felt him grasp her arm to help her up—she'd thought he was ruggedly good looking. Now, sitting next to him, she had to admit she was attracted to him and thought he'd be the perfect escort to accompany her to Judi's daughter's upcoming wedding instead of Luke.

◆◆◆

Finally, their plane landed.

After Ed parked on the strip of dirt a quarter mile from the clinic, Alex looked at the barren fields interrupted by tiny white stucco houses. The rustic doors revealed a pallet of peeling yellows and greens peeking through more recent applications of paint.

Five volunteers exited from each of the three planes and started to walk down the dirt road toward the small village. Like the characters in the *Canterbury Tales*, each volunteer carried items particular to his profession: the dentist carried extraction tools and cold-water sterilization equipment, Alex had her adjusting board and a roll of headrest paper, and David's backpack was overflowing with speculums and Pap smear kits.

To keep the weight of the plane down, the volunteers had been instructed to bring as few toiletries and clothes as possible. The women had also been asked to donate old underwear for the village women. While packing, Alex had thought about poverty so bleak that one would appreciate the gift of someone else's used bras and panties.

She surveyed the school-turned-clinic. Unlike Jon's nursery school, there was no playground with swings or monkey bars with rubber mats covering the concrete. The five classrooms lacked everything considered standard for children in Alex's world. She decided she had to help the village children. They deserved the same chance her children had. After her custody case was over, she would find sponsors to help create a scholastic program for this school. And given Seth's love for education and his kindness, he'd probably help.

Twenty or thirty patients were already lined up outside the schoolhouse. Mismatched clothing seemed standard attire, as were huaraches, the sandals with soles made from old tires.

Since there wasn't any waiting room, the patients stood, fanning themselves with the manila folders that housed their medical records.

Alex bent down, opened her backpack, and pulled out a plastic bag brimming with underwear. She handed the bag to Carmen, the school's headmistress and clinic director.

"Gracias," Carmen said and led Alex to a tiny classroom.

Hanging from a wire, a solitary light bulb covered in dust gave off a sickly yellow glow. Folding chairs lined one of the walls. On the opposite wall, a near-empty bookshelf stood beside a section of chipped paint. A pencil sharpener jutted from the wall at waist height, and broken crayons occupied an open wooden box on the shelf. The six-inch globe on the lone desk announced the existence of a world beyond this village.

Alex placed a sheet of headrest paper onto the adjusting bench. The green vinyl covering on the bench was cracked in so many spots that it looked like a mosaic. Her first patient, Hector, a cherubic-faced toddler with straight black hair still wet from bathing, entered the room with his mother.

"Hola," Alex said in greeting.

"Hola," the mother replied, pointing to her son's feet.

Alex examined the pigeon-toed child and then adjusted his hips. In Spanish, she instructed the mother to take her son to an orthopedist.

"Ya fuimos." The mother explained how she'd already taken Hector to an orthopedist who'd prescribed a special brace, which she couldn't afford.

Alex told the mother to take a pair of shoes, put them on a wooden plank at a 45-degree angle, and then nail the shoes to the plank of wood. Hector would have to wear them every night.

"Gracias, gracias," the mother said.

Patting Hector's head, Alex thought about how happy he'd be with just one of the toys her boys left lying on the floor, tired of them after only a short while. She was definitely going to find a way to help the children of this village. *If everyone who could afford it dedicated himself to just one person in a village, the world would be so much better,* she thought and placed the next piece of headrest paper on the adjusting table.

As patients streamed into Alex's room for the next two hours, she worked tirelessly.

"Doctora," Carmen called out from the kitchen directly across the hallway from Alex's room. "Por favor, venga por su almuerzo."

Alex squeezed into the tiny kitchen where four women were crowded near the oven preparing lunch for the volunteers. With a little girl clutching her legs, a thick-waisted woman in a print polyester dress with a zigzag pattern was stirring a pot of beans. Another woman with shiny black hair flowing down her back was rinsing plates. A third woman was drying the plates and handing them to Carmen, who doled out tamales.

"For you." Carmen handed Alex a plate filled with tamales smelling of sweet corn.

"*Gracias.*" Alex took the plate, turned, and saw David.

"This is the real reason we come here," he teased, pointing to his plate overflowing with tamales and beans. He winked at her.

She smiled. He seemed nice, but Alex was certain that a handsome, professional man like David would never stay with her. Instead, he'd be lured away by someone like Linda, the woman who'd taken Gabe from her. Then she caught herself. Gabe had destroyed her life, but she couldn't let the sting of his rejection continue even in his absence.

She wondered whether David had seen Luke kiss her at the airport. Alex knew that, to the casual observer, she and Luke were an unlikely pair. But for her, their attraction was as tangible as paper clips to a magnet. With Luke, she was sensual and uninhibited. Luke equaled sex, pure and simple. It was the smell of his spicy shaving lotion, his minty hair cream, even his musky scent after tennis that had attracted her. But most of all, she loved the sweet taste of scotch and soda on his lips.

Nights after tennis, when they'd go back to her house, he'd take a shower. She'd delight in the way the water would glisten on his chocolate chest when he walked from the shower to the bedroom, ready to have her.

"Doctora," Carmen called to her, interrupting her thoughts. "Many patients."

"Gracias," Alex said and went back to her classroom-turned-examination room.

Everything was going smoothly until Sofia, a little girl with the saddest face Alex had ever seen, walked into the room. After Sofia's dad explained how his daughter had fallen and injured her arm, Alex gently touched the girl's hot, swollen arm.

"No tocame!" Sofia shrank back against her father, obviously in pain.

"It could be fractured." Alex shook her head. "You need to take her to a hospital for x-rays."

The father held out his hands, palms up and lowered his head. "No tengo dinero."

Alex explained how important it was for his daughter to see an orthopedist. Alex knew if Sofia went unattended, her arm wouldn't heal properly. The growth plate could be affected, causing her arm to become deformed. She could even develop osteomyelitis, a bone infection.

The little girl tugged at her dad's hand. He bent down to her, and she whispered in his ear.

Avoiding eye contact with Alex, the father said, "Sofia say it no hurt."

But Alex saw something in Sofia's eyes—a plea for help. Alex understood the little girl had probably learned she should never ask her father for more than he could give her. Alex recalled how she had trusted her own father and how she'd never betray him even after discovering his life had been a lie.

"Let me see what I can do," Alex said and went to the pharmacy, where she grabbed a spool of tape and several tongue depressors. She returned to the room and splinted Sofia's arm. After Alex finished, Sofia gazed up at her with a sweet, sad face that made her trip worthwhile. But Alex also knew that setting the child's arm in this manner wasn't a guarantee that the bone would mesh properly. The little girl really needed to see an orthopedist and have x-rays taken. For now, this was the best Alex could offer, and the on-site pediatrician would have to give Sofia antibiotics—that was, if they had any left in the pharmacy.

Treating children whose parents were unable to pay for the medical treatment they needed made Alex ache. She yearned for her own children. Gabe's portrayal of her as a danger to the boys was wrong. She was capable of taking care of them.

Pushing herself to forget, Alex worked zealously until just before sunset, when Carmen announced the clinic was closed. As the grateful villagers started their journey home, the volunteers returned to their planes for the ten-minute flight to El Sueño Dulce—"The Sweet Dream"—the only hotel in Guerrero, Mexico.

CHAPTER 27

Ensconced in her seat on the flight to the hotel, Alex glanced at David and then looked down at his left hand. There was neither a ring nor the telltale band of white where a ring no longer rested.

Ed landed the plane on a tiny patch of concrete and maneuvered it down the rock-strewn runway. He pulled into a spot between the two other Flying Samaritan planes on the strip of concrete that served as the Guerrero Airport.

The volunteers deplaned and made the five-minute trek across the sandy, tumbleweed-covered field to the hotel. Looking like the Bates Motel in *Psycho*, the rundown, one-story structure was right on the Sea of Cortez.

As the pilots, doctors, nurses, and interpreters entered the dark lobby of El Sueño Dulce, two stray dogs wandered between them, sniffing at them. To the right, a warped wooden table which was collapsing in the middle, served as the registration desk. Two weathered wicker chairs completed the lobby.

Dropping their luggage on the concrete floor, the tired volunteers leaned against the soiled wall across from the makeshift reception desk. Except for the whir of the high ceiling fan, everyone was quiet while they waited for Zeke, the internist and volunteer coordinator, to speak to the clerk.

Zeke shook his shaved head several times before returning to the group. "They gave away our rooms. We'll have to sleep on the beach," he told the volunteers.

"Nights get pretty cold," David said.

"I'm sure they'll give us some blankets," Zeke promised.

Alex had stayed at El Sueño Dulce before and was familiar with the now-much-coveted Spartan rooms with mismatched, scratchy linen.

Zeke tried to quiet the group. "We can complain all we want. They said they're sorry, but they didn't receive my reservation request this month. There's a fishing excursion in town, and every room is taken. So we'll just have to improvise on the beach."

"I don't camp," one of the dental hygienists said.

Thomas, a pilot who kept his trailer parked near the hotel, said, "You can all wash up in my trailer, but my wife and kids are here this weekend, so we don't have any sleeping room."

"Not working for me," the other dental hygienist said, agreeing with her colleague.

Zeke thanked Thomas and asked about supplies. Thomas assured the group that he had enough blankets, chaise lounges, and drinks for everyone. The doctors, interpreters, and two other pilots smiled in appreciation.

The pharmacist insisted, "Zeke, you have to tell them we book the rooms every month. Go and demand they give us our rooms."

Zeke went back to the clerk. After negotiating, he returned to the group and told them the clerk had offered to give them a free dinner, but that was all the clerk could do.

Resigned to camping on the beach, everyone followed Thomas to his trailer amid good-hearted jeering about the reservation mix-up. Walking along the pristine aquamarine Sea of Cortez, Alex was at peace, calmed by the sand sifting through her toes and the water lapping at her ankles.

When they finally arrived at Thomas's trailer, he unlocked the storage unit and took out folding chairs. Everyone grabbed chairs and placed them in a circle around Zeke.

Thomas introduced his wife and children, and then his wife went back inside to make drinks for everyone.

Margaritas in hand, the volunteers listened to Zeke read the clinic statistics: "The pilots put up ten shelves and fixed two lights, the dentist performed fourteen extractions, the gynecologist examined eighteen women, the pediatrician treated twenty-one children, and the chiropractor adjusted thirty-eight."

Everyone applauded after each tally, and Alex felt appreciated, a real team member.

After a review of the clinic's statistics, the group went back to the hotel and took their seats at the tables assembled on the concrete platform. Alex faced the ocean, and David selected the seat directly opposite her.

They feasted on oysters and shrimp encrusted in a golden covering—an amazing meal for the broken-down hotel with the makeshift reception desk that was caving in. The village fishermen delivered seafood daily, and the cook prepared it to perfection. The group used to stay at another rundown hotel that was also a fifteen-minute plane ride from the clinic, but now El Sueño Dulce was the only remaining hotel in the area.

While they were enjoying the seafood, the hotel clerk came over to the table and announced that the hotel now had one vacancy. Everyone agreed to give it to Frank, one of the pilots and the most seasoned volunteer.

"Does anyone else want the room?" Frank asked.

Everyone protested.

"The least I can do is share it with someone," Frank offered. No one answered.

Alex longed for a room, a shower, and a bed. "Do you snore?" she asked, feeling bold.

"Don't think so." Frank moved his glasses up the bridge of his nose, his wrinkled face a reminder of the handsome man he'd once been.

"I'm in," she heard herself say.

"You go, girl," the dental hygienist said. "If I had the nerve, I'd be in his shower right now."

After saying good night to her fellow volunteers, Alex followed Frank to their room. When he opened the door, the smell of cleaning fluids assaulted her. She surveyed the two single beds with mismatched floral pillowcases and sheets topped with checked blankets.

She dropped her backpack on the nearest bed and asked, "Mind if I shower?"

"Help yourself."

She entered the bathroom and pushed the shower curtain aside. When she turned on the hot-water faucet, cold water pelted out. She showered quickly and then dressed in her long gray jersey nightgown, sorry she'd obeyed instructions to bring bare essentials and hadn't packed a robe.

"That was fast," Frank said.

"No hot water," she said, knowing there was no possibility of asking the hotel clerk to send someone to fix it. She looked at Frank standing beside the bed near the wall and asked, "Is it okay if I keep the overhead light on and read?"

"It's fine," he said, tugging at the collar of his pale-blue pajamas. "Light never bothered me when my wife would read until all hours of the night. But that was before she ..."

"What happened to her?" Alex moved her fingers across her pearl pendant.

"Left me twenty-two years ago."

"How long did it take to get over it?" Alex asked with an intimacy fostered by the hour, the small hotel room, or perhaps the close proximity of the two single beds.

"Wasted my life," he whispered. "Never got over the hate, the anger. It was like *I* kept taking poison, hoping *she'd* die."

Alex stared at him like one used to do with a Polaroid photo, waiting for it to develop, but he didn't say another word.

Since there were no lamps in the room, she decided it would be rude to keep the overhead light on. "I'll just go to sleep. Good night, and thanks for letting me share the room."

"Good night," he said.

She shut off the overhead light, crawled into bed, and thought about the magical intimacy within hotel rooms. She recalled the Bellagio Hotel with its pristine white feather comforter and lavender-scented pillows. That hotel room was where she had had everything and then nothing. Then she thought of this seedy hotel room and Frank's words. Determined there would only be one wasted life in this room, she decided it was time to silence her memory ghosts. She was no longer going to carry the poison from Gabe into her future. No man, not even Gabriel Rose, was going to destroy her life.

◆◆◆

On the plane ride back, David took a seat next to her.

"I could blackmail you," David teased.

"What are you talking about?" she asked.

"I know who you slept with last night," he said.

"Promise you won't tell my husband." Alex laughed. She wondered whether she should tell David she was kidding about being married, so she turned the conversation to the accommodations: "There was no hot water in the shower, but the room was fine."

"The beach was freezing. You were smart to have shared the room with Frank."

"It was nice of him to have offered to share his room," she said.

"Frank's a good man," David said. "I knew you'd be safe."

"Safe?" she repeated. "Why would you even think about that?"

"You're a woman, and I ..."

"Yes?" she said, giving him permission to proceed.

"A man in a room with such a beautiful woman, I don't know if I'd be able to be a gentleman."

Beautiful. He called me beautiful. She smiled. "He wasn't such a gentleman when I attacked him."

"Lucky guy," he said. "But I don't know if I would have waited for you to make the first move in that situation."

"Are you implying that you're not a gentleman?"

"Find out for yourself." He winked.

Her heart pounded. She felt that elevator feeling. There were flutters, good flutters. She remembered when Gabe had challenged her to find out for herself whether sex was that different with someone else—and she did. Sex definitely was different with Luke. She wondered what it would be like with David, then stopped herself. Her life was already too complicated with the custody battle.

"A peso for your thoughts," David said.

"Aren't they worth more than that?"

"Depends on what you're thinking." He laughed. "Seriously, I didn't mean to imply anything. I guess being a gynecologist, I see so much, and—"

"I bet you do." She smiled.

"No, I mean men not treating women appropriately," he said. "Have you heard about Women's Options?"

"No, what's that?"

He explained that Women's Options was a charitable organization that sponsors women who are unable to care for themselves and their children for one reason or another. He told her Women's Options also helps train women for the workplace.

"Do you give the women free gynecological care?" she asked, assuming that was his role in the organization.

"Well, of course, but I'm one of the founders, so I also have the fundraising and administrative responsibilities."

"How'd you get into that?" she asked.

"I saw a need," he said. "I wish I could do more, but my practice is so busy." He paused. "I hate to leave my daughter at night. She needs me, and I—"

She was going to ask about his daughter, but one of the dental hygienists in the front row turned around and said, "David, your group helped one of our patients. She came in with three broken teeth and refused to tell us how she fractured them. Finally, she told us her husband had beaten her, and she was so afraid. We called your group, and they took her right in."

"I remember her," David said. "What ever happened to her?"

"She moved to Ohio," the dental hygienist said. "We lost contact with her, but she sent us a Christmas card thanking us for referring her to Women's Options."

The dental hygienist and David talked about the organization.

"Helping one woman is wonderful, but it's not enough," David said. "Men think they have a right to treat women like that. It sickens me."

Alex listened to David talk with such passion. He appeared so caring, concerned.

She thought about Sofia, the little girl with the fractured arm and sad face. She wondered whether the little girl trusted her dad as much as Alex had trusted hers. Then she recalled the day she'd discovered her dad's secret: how he hadn't chosen love.

As she sat in the den watching the rain-spattered window, her father playfully teased, "Too old for cartoons and too young for boys, huh?"

She'd just turned twelve and wanted to tell him how her mother would torment her and her sister during the day when he was gone, but she didn't. She was too afraid of her mother's vengeance.

Her father tapped her shoulder. "Alexandra, I've got a surprise for you if you come with me."

Eager for the surprise and time alone with her dad, she followed him downstairs to the basement. They passed her mother's old Nancy Drew books in the wrought-iron bookcase, her record collection—mostly Elvis—and the old Victrola with the small spindle for the 78s and the larger holder for the 45s.

Passing the leather-bound Encyclopedia Britannica *in the wooden shelves, purchased from the door-to-door salesman who guaranteed it would ensure the children's admittance to the colleges of their choice, her dad walked farther back in the basement.*

As she followed him, lightning cracked and the rain hammered the tiny slats of the basement windows. Her dad turned on the lights. Then he opened the door to the closet opposite the pantry. He pulled out three large boxes, taped up and marked "Sally 1," "Sally 2," and "Sally 3." Alex knew her father had a sister named Sally who'd died, but her father never talked about her.

Her dad opened the first box. "This isn't the one."

Alex glanced into the box and saw hardbound books with titles that looked intriguing: The Good Earth, How Babies Are Born, *and* The Fountainhead. *Each book smelled like the library. "May I take one?" she asked, picking up* The Fountainhead *by Ayn Rand.*

"Sure, but that's not why I brought you down here." He opened the next box and withdrew a wooden cigar case filled with miniature figurines. He unwrapped a three-inch replica of a whimsical cow in black-and-white milky glass holding a bouquet of flowers. Then he unwrapped a miniature telephone that actually dialed, a glass slipper, and two-inch wooden dogs of all breeds. All the figurines were perfect.

"Where'd you get these?" Alex asked. Although she sensed the collection was something to be treasured, she cared more about the box of books.

He looked sad, nostalgic. "They were my sister's. I practically raised her, and she died so young. She would have wanted you to have them, but they're so fragile I was afraid you'd break them. You're old enough now."

"I'll be careful with them." She kissed her dad and went upstairs, carrying the box of figurines and the book.

That night, right after dinner, she went to her bedroom and started to read The Fountainhead. As she turned to page forty-two, a picture fell onto the floor. She picked up the black-and-white photograph of two handsome men. One of them she immediately recognized as her dad, and she wondered if the other man might have been her Aunt Sally's husband. Studying the faces, she felt a sudden sense of panic. The men looked at each other in a very odd way.

Walking into the den to ask her father about the photo, she distractedly turned the picture over. On the back, she found a note addressed to her dad:

Dear Hal,

I'm so sorry, but I just couldn't attend your wedding. So, I've asked Sally to give you this picture of us when we thought our love would continue through eternity. Even though you've decided you can't live the life we planned, I'll always love you.

Yours forever,

Robert

She stuffed the picture back into the book and slammed it shut just as her father looked away from the television. "What is it, Alexandra?" he asked.

"Nothing." She clutched the book to her chest and hurried back to her bedroom, her heart racing.

Once she'd unlocked the mystery of her father, her world had changed and become a place where mothers were incapable of love and fathers lived a lie.

CHAPTER 28

As their plane landed at Orange County Airport, David gently patted her shoulder and whispered, "Sleeping Beauty, you can wake up now."

Alex smiled up at him.

"Will I see you next time?" David asked.

"Sure," Alex agreed.

They deplaned, and while they waited for the pilot to unload their bags, David told her a joke. She laughed. Then she collected her backpack and walked to the building.

Luke was standing there, hands parked on his hips.

"Hi," she called to him. "I thought you were going to wait for me to call before coming to the airport."

"That's a fine greeting," Luke said sarcastically.

"I'm beat." Alex waved toward the group. "We worked our butts off."

Luke gestured toward David. "Did you work with him?"

"No," Alex said, annoyed at Luke's suspicion.

He took her backpack. As they walked to the parking lot, he asked, "What about at night? What did you do?"

"We sat around the beach and then went to our rooms," she said. There was no need to tell him about sharing a room with a man. He'd never understand that nothing had happened.

He pulled her to him for a hug. Then he tossed her backpack into the truck, helped her into her seat, and went around to the driver's side.

Alex glanced at the backseat and saw a rifle nestled between the seats. "What's that doing there?"

He laughed, seemingly amused by the alarm in her voice. "Went hunting this morning. Just had time to put the dogs in their run and take a shower. I forgot to put the gun back in the safe."

"You killed something?" she asked.

"That's the goal of hunting, and I have a surprise for you. My number's been drawn for the annual deer hunt in Utah!"

"Luke, are there actually so many people who want to hunt deer they have a drawing?"

"Yep, and they picked my number and two of my hunting buddies' numbers." He smiled at her. "And I'd like you to join us."

While the fishing was tolerable, she knew hunting wasn't something she could handle. She shook her head and told him, "Hunting's definitely not my thing."

He took his right hand off the steering wheel and reached for her hand. "We'll spend the entire weekend together."

"I have the boys every Saturday, and I'm going to start with the forensic psychologist on Fridays." She wasn't sure a weekend with Luke would resolve anything, especially not a weekend involving a deer hunt.

A menacing look crossed his face. "It's that guy in the airport. I saw the way you and he were laughing together."

"Don't be ridiculous."

Abruptly, he released her hand, cut the wheel, and turned into her driveway. He got out of the truck and slammed the door. As she climbed out of the truck, he grabbed her backpack and they walked to her front door.

"I'm tired," she said. "We'll talk tomorrow."

"I want to talk now." He stood in the doorway, hands folded across his chest. "Alex, something's going on. You know, I don't even have to be around you, and I can feel you."

Unlocking the door, she assured him, "Nothing is going on."

"I'm coming in to talk," he insisted.

"Only for a few minutes. I need to get ready for work tomorrow."

He followed her into the house, dropped her backpack just inside the front door, and walked into the den. "Could you fix me a drink?"

"Just one," she said and went into the kitchen. She poured a glass of wine for herself and a scotch and soda for him. Then she carried the drinks into the den and sat down on the couch.

"I have an idea that'll work," he said.

"What?" she asked.

"Alex, as I recall, you invited me to a wedding, right?"

"Yes, Judi's in the First Friday Book Club, and her daughter's getting married." Alex said and picked pieces of cork out of her wine. Uncertain about whether or not she wanted him to accompany her to a wedding where Gabe would be, she said, "I'll go alone."

"Now I'm not good enough for your fancy friends?"

"You're overreacting." She kept her tone mild, fearful of agitating him. There was a gun in his truck.

"I don't want you going alone," he said, an edge to his voice. "And why do you have to go, anyway?"

"I told you, Judi's in my book club, and my closest friends will be there." Then, more to herself than him, she added, "And Gabe will be there because Judi's husband works with him."

"Since when did Gabe become your best friend?" He shook his head and then laughed. "You two have a damn strange relationship."

"You're right, we do, but then divorce makes for a damn strange relationship." She gave him a probing look. "You probably don't know about divorce."

"What are you saying?" Anger overtook his face, contorting it to near ugliness.

"Luke, for all I know, you're still married."

"That's it." As though in slow motion, his glass moved from his hand through the room until it hit the wall, the crash resounding.

Staring at the scotch-and-soda-splattered wall, she froze in shock. A man who would hurl a glass at a wall was terrifying. As a child, she'd learned it was better to keep quiet than to provoke, and she knew she could get hurt if she said the wrong thing.

"Why would you think I'm married?" he demanded.

She didn't say anything.

"Tell me," he insisted.

She looked at him.

He grabbed her shoulder and shook it. "Talk."

Fear short-circuited her brain. She couldn't think.

His fingers dug into her shoulder.

She looked at the pieces of glass glistening on the floor, and strength emerged from deep within. She decided it was time to stand up for herself. Although she'd been blindsided by Gabe's betrayal, she wasn't going to let Luke do the same. Without wavering, she said, "This isn't the relationship I want. You never stay over, and you've never introduced me to your friends, your family, or anyone in your life."

"My work truck is only insured when it's either parked at the office or my house or when I'm en route to a customer's house." He released her shoulder and clenched his fist.

"What about the weekends?" she asked.

"I'm on the ocean too early." His amber eyes darted back and forth like a cornered animal. "I'll tell you the truth."

"The truth?" She hated that word. Her stomach churned. She knew about the truth all too well. In Gabe's Mercedes on the return trip from Las Vegas, his truth had destroyed the family. The truth was like an airbag: once deployed, everything changes, and there's no going back.

She bent down and picked up a few pieces of fractured glass, careful not to cut her trembling fingers.

"I'll do that." Luke leaned down beside her and took the glass from her hand.

"Tell me your truth and then get out," she said.

He explained how Cherie, his twenty-year-old daughter, wasn't right: "Ever since her mother and I got a divorce, Cherie gets upset if she suspects I've been with another woman. Since she lives with me, she gets agitated whenever I come home late. And, if I didn't come home, she'd go ballistic."

"At twenty?" Alex asked. Then she remembered the danger of challenging someone who was volatile. After seeing Luke fling the glass at the wall, she was convinced his anger could cause great harm. There was something familiar, although unsettling, about his volatility.

"Alex, let me explain. Up until now, my daughter hasn't been able to take care of herself. She was finally at the point where she was going to work. Then her sister moved in, as you know. She'd had her own room up until then, and she isn't fond of sharing a room with her sister."

"If you're really divorced, why would your daughter get angry about you being with another woman?" Embracing the strength she felt within her, she said, "We're done, Luke."

"There's more." He looked at her beseechingly. "Several months ago, actually a month before we started dating, I got custody of my oldest daughter's thirteen-year-old son, Mark. Before she died, my daughter made me my grandson's legal guardian."

"Your daughter died?" she asked, shocked. "You've got your two daughters and a grandson living with you now, and you take care of them all? And you didn't tell me any of this, except for the one who moved in when we first started dating?"

"I'm used to taking care of everyone. I can handle more than you can imagine."

"Like what?" she asked, hoping to unpeel some of his mystery. But then she recalled how it had been months until she'd been able to tell anyone Gabe had moved out. Maybe, she decided, it was too painful for him to talk about his loss.

"Alex, I believe the man should protect his woman, his family. I'm the person my family depends on." He stroked her leg.

"Don't," she said. "And how could you have a thirteen-year-old grandson?"

"My daughter had him when she was only fifteen."

"That's really young," Alex said, certain he was telling her the truth. No one would ever makeup a story like that.

"My daughter was ... I can't discuss it."

She decided he probably wasn't going to tell her any more, but the glimpses of violence—the gun, the shattered glass—this was a part of Luke she'd never seen before. And he'd always been so gentle with her when they made love. *Which was real?*

He drew her close.

She pulled away.

"Alex, you know you get the best part of me." He smiled at her. "I've got another idea that will make everything better for you."

"Right now I need you to leave." She went to the door and opened it.

"I'm leaving, but you're going to be surprised at how I'm going to change." He winked at her and left.

◆ ◆ ◆

At five thirty the next morning, Luke rang her doorbell.

She stared at Luke Jackson, the man who'd been her lover, now standing there—a stranger dressed in green work pants and a matching green jacket. He put his hands in his pockets, and his jacket opened to reveal a too-yellow shirt with "LUKE" sewn on it in cursive writing. Then she looked up at his yellow cap with the white toilet-bowl logo and "LUKE" embossed over the rim.

Suddenly, she felt disconnected from this man standing on her doorstep in a uniform that announced his name not once but twice. "What are you doing here?" she asked and tied the sash on her red velour bathrobe.

"You think I could have a cup of coffee?" he asked.

Confused by his casual request, his uniform, and his unexpected appearance at her door at five thirty, she asked, "If you own the franchise, why do you wear a uniform?"

"If one of the technicians calls in sick, I'm ready."

It doesn't make sense, she thought as she went to the kitchen to make coffee.

Luke followed her.

She measured the coffee.

After putting his cap down on the counter, Luke took a seat at the kitchen table. "Do you think you could make me a slice of toast?"

"One slice or two?" Alex asked. Recently, she'd become accustomed to her solitary breakfasts. Now her own morning voice surprised her.

They buttered their toast, drank their coffee, and talked about nothing.

He winked at her and asked, "Like to go up to the bedroom for a while before I leave for work?"

"No," she said. Then, slipping back into her usual desire to please him, she said, "I've got to get ready for work."

"It won't take that long." He got up, leaned over her, slid his arms around her, and kissed her neck.

"No," she repeated, wondering how she was going to untangle herself from the gravitational pull he exerted upon her.

"Give me just one more chance. You'll never see anything from me but love."

"Love?" she repeated. Their relationship had been what she'd thought she needed right after Gabe, but she wasn't certain she'd ever fall in love again. And, it certainly wasn't now.

"Let me at least prove it to you. I want to go to the wedding with you and show you how I can be there for you."

She folded her arms across her chest. "But if I see one more demonstration of temper, I will not tolerate it."

"You'll see." He kissed her forehead.

"Right now I just don't know." She walked to the door and signaled for him to leave.

CHAPTER 29

A s Alex dressed for Judi's daughter's wedding, she was nervous about whether it was appropriate to have invited Luke. Although she'd promised herself Gabe was no longer going to invade her life, she didn't want to go to a formal event alone, especially if he was going to be there. She thought about David, the gynecologist from the Flying Samaritans, and decided he would have been the perfect escort for the wedding. She imagined him in a tuxedo—his tall, svelte physique, twinkly green eyes, and thick gray hair. Most of all, she recalled his smile—so warm and inviting. She closed her eyes, imagined dancing with David, and wondered whether she'd be able to join him next month in Mexico.

Since the First Friday Book Club women had all decided on formal attire, Alex took out her long red evening gown. She pulled it over her head and looked in the mirror. The three bands of rhinestones across the top sparkled in the light. The dress fit perfectly, but she wasn't certain she was confident enough to survive an evening where she'd be surrounded by physicians and their wives, all of whom had to know Gabriel Rose had left her.

When the doorbell rang, she grabbed her heels and rushed to open the door.

Luke smiled at her. "You look nice."

"Thanks." Alex stared nervously at his light-gray suit, inappropriate for the black-tie-optional wedding.

"You okay?" he asked.

"Sure, why?" She knew it was too late for him to go home and change, and he probably had no suit that was better. At least he was wearing a tie.

"You seem edgy," he said.

"I promised myself I wouldn't let Gabe get to me, but I'm anxious about seeing him at the wedding with Linda, his fiancée," Alex admitted. Also, Judi had told her Gabe and Linda's relationship was now out in the open, which meant Gabe had probably been made a partner.

Luke put his arm around her. "You'll be fine."

Longing to believe him, she nodded.

He kissed her cheek. "Can we take your car? Mine's a mess, and with your fancy dress and all ..."

She handed him her car keys and pushed the button for the garage. He helped her into the car and walked around to the driver's side. He got in, adjusted the seat, and inserted the key. Reaching into his jacket pocket, he winked at her. "Here." He handed her a tiny box.

Alex opened the box and was shocked. There was a ring with two gold hearts entwined. She wondered why he was giving her a gift, much less a ring.

"Put it on your finger." He smiled. "I was going to wait for your birthday, but I thought you might want to wear it tonight."

She slipped the ring with the two tiny hearts onto her right ring finger. "It fits perfectly."

"Alex, you *could* wear it on the other hand."

"I like it on the right, and I'll wear it there," she said. Then she saw his disappointment and moved it to her left ring finger. "The ring is beautiful."

"You're beautiful." He kissed her hand. "I told you I'd be making changes, and I have another surprise for you."

Wondering how he was going to change, or for that matter, if she really wanted more from a relationship with him, she asked, "What's the surprised?"

"You'll see." He turned up the CD player and hummed to "I Can't Stop Loving You," the same CD he'd brought to her the first time they'd made love.

As Luke pulled into the parking lot of the Beverly Hills Jewish Center, he reassured her, "Don't worry."

She looped her arm through his, and they walked into the synagogue. An imposing chandelier like the one in *Phantom of the Opera* dominated the entryway and spotlighted some familiar faces of couples with whom Alex and Gabe had socialized, couples they knew from the hospital. As she walked farther into the chapel, she took a deep breath and nodded at some of the physicians and their wives. They appeared to glare at her, or she was just imagining it? She wondered what Gabe had told them about their divorce.

Luke took her hand, and they followed the crowd into the chapel. A tuxedoed young man shepherded them to seats on the bride's side of the white-ribboned aisle. Alex sat beside Luke, fingering the diamond hearts on the ring he'd just given to her.

Radiant in a midnight-blue backless gown with a slit up the right side, Meredith slipped in next to Alex. "Your Denzel's gorgeous," she whispered to Alex and then put out her hand to Luke. "And you are?"

"Luke," he said and reached across Alex to shake Meredith's hand. "Glad to meet you."

Meredith took a loud, deep breath and whispered, "Even sexier than I imagined." She winked at Alex and then introduced her boyfriend, Warren, to Luke.

The music started. Everyone turned to face the back to watch the wedding procession—first the groom, followed by the attendants.

There was a hush.

Upon hearing the first few bars of Pachelbel's "Canon in D Major," everyone stood up.

Luke seemed surprised. "Why don't they play, 'Here Comes the Bride' when she walks down the aisle?" he whispered.

"Wagner was anti-Semitic, and they don't play it at Jewish weddings," she explained.

Suddenly, the back wall of the synagogue parted, revealing a beaming bride flanked by her parents, Judi and Gary. The groom walked back down the aisle toward his bride.

Luke chuckled and whispered to Alex, "He's backing out, huh?"

"No," she said. "The groom's supposed to take the bride from her parents and ask for their blessing. It's customary for the groom to escort the bride to the *chuppah*."

"Coopa?" he repeated.

"It's that canopy covering the bride and groom. It's where they take their vows, and it's a symbol of the home they'll build together," she said.

"That little piece of cloth?"

"That's the way it's supposed to be: open on all sides, symbolizing how family and friends will always be welcomed at the new couple's home."

"Well, maybe my family should be Jewish with all the people I got camped out at my house," Luke said and laughed.

Alex watched as the bride and groom clasped hands and walked toward the rabbi. During the ceremony, she pretended to listen but replayed her own wedding instead. *How did we travel so far away from those promises? And how did those promises morph into lies?*

When the groom stomped on the glass, the pop reverberated throughout the chapel, bringing Alex back to the moment.

Everyone yelled, "Mazel tov!" and applauded.

"Why'd the groom stamp his foot?" Luke asked. "Last time he'll do that, I'm sure."

"They wrap a light bulb in cloth, and the groom stomps on it, symbolizing the destruction of the first temple and the fragility of Jewish life all over the world."

"That's kind of depressing."

"No, it also reminds us that relationships are as fragile as glass," she said and for the first time in her life, she understood how true that was.

"Whatever." Luke shrugged.

Alex looked down at the ring he'd given her. The two entwined hearts on the ring definitely did not represent their shared future. She wanted more from a relationship than momentary pleasure, but she had to heal first. She had to wait until the sight of Gabe didn't make her heart pound the way it had when they were young and in love. She turned to watch the bridal procession leave the chapel.

As the other guests followed the wedding party to the foyer, Alex and Luke waited for their row to exit. They moved into the foyer where people crowded around white-gloved waiters carrying trays of artfully arranged kebabs, stuffed mushroom caps, and miniature knishes. Then they negotiated a path to the table with place cards denoting their seat assignments. As she reached for the card with her name, her hand collided with Gabe's. Their glances locked.

Gabe stared at her right wrist as though seeing the scar for the first time. His expression exuding disdain, he asked, "Alexandra, what're *you* doing here?"

"I was invited," she said calmly, confidently.

Luke moved closer to her, his left hand on the small of her back as he extended his right hand to Gabe. "Luke Jackson. Pleased to make your acquaintance."

Alex watched Gabe stare at his own hand, now swallowed up within Luke's huge, powerful grasp. Then she looked down. Gabe was standing on his tiptoes, as if trying to equal Luke's imposing frame. There seemed an odd sense of familiarity between the two men. *Could it be because I've slept with them both?* No, there was something else; they had an eerie connection.

Luke released Gabe's hand and settled his own on Alex's bare shoulder. Reflexively, she placed her left hand atop Luke's. Appearing shocked at the appearance of a ring on the finger that had once held the diamond wedding band he had given her, Gabe gaped at her, turned, and walked away.

As Gabe proceeded to his table, Alex studied Linda. Statuesque with long frosted hair, Linda wore a light-pink dress with a plunging neckline that provided the perfect backdrop for her dazzling garnet necklace.

"You're better looking," Luke said, as though reading her mind. "Hot."

Why can't I take my eyes off Linda? Why am I measuring myself against my ex-husband's paramour, and why do I feel inadequate? Does every woman who has been left by a man give her ego over to the woman who replaced her? Alex slipped her hand through Luke's arm and walked to the First Friday Book Club women's table. She decided neither Linda nor any woman was ever going to make her feel inadequate. The past was over and, with this incredible group of women to support her, she'd be fine—she hoped.

Sophisticated in a black handkerchief skirt and pale-blue satin blouse, Liz motioned to two empty chairs. "Alex, Luke, sit here," Liz said.

"Helloooo!" Terrie approached with her husband, Lawrence. Her maroon velvet dress and matching hat were classic Terrie—romantic, soft, pale, with a touch of Bohemia. Taking their seats, Terrie introduced herself and her husband to Luke.

The bandleader announced, "The couple's first dance as husband and wife will be to 'I Will Always Love You.'"

Alex was overcome by emotion. She didn't want to hear her own wedding song—not now, not with Gabe within her peripheral vision.

Then the bandleader invited everyone to join the bride and groom on the dance floor.

As though on cue, with a familiarity that comes from years of knowing on which side of the bed to sleep, couples throughout the room flowed onto the dance floor.

"Shall we dance?" Alex asked.

Luke shook his head. "Not my kind of music."

"I danced at your club," she said softly.

Reluctantly, Luke stood up and escorted Alex to the dance floor. He took her in his arms with an unexpected reserve—until Gabe and Linda joined them on the dance floor. Suddenly, Luke transformed into the provocative dancer who'd first taken her to the club.

Luke twirled her around as though to showcase her. Exuding blatant sensuality, he held her close. Couples next to them stopped and stared. He became the music—sexy, seductive. Alex glanced over at Gabe dancing stiffly. She felt confident within Luke's graceful embrace.

When the song ended, Luke slid his arm around her waist, assuring her, "I can hold my own with any man. When you're with me, I'll make sure you do too."

"Yummy," Terrie said as she walked past Alex.

They took their seats.

Meredith winked at Alex from across the table.

Luke picked up his fork and pushed the endive salad around his plate.

"Now, this is a good salad," Terrie said as she ate the candied walnuts with the gusto usually reserved for the hamburgers she regularly consumed at the First Friday Book Club meetings.

"I'm not much for rabbit food." Luke put down his fork.

The waiter cleared the salad plates and proceeded to put the next course down in front of each of them.

Terrie gestured at Luke's plate of smoked salmon and whitefish dressed with a dollop of sour cream, capers, and a lemon wedge. "Luke, what fish do you catch?"

"Well, actually, Alex is getting good at fishing. If you ladies like bass, she'll fill your freezers." Luke nodded approvingly at Alex.

"Speaking of fish and, of course, water, Luke, I hear you *own* a plumbing company," Meredith said.

Alex knew Meredith was checking to see if he'd been truthful about owning the company.

"And I have another company on the side," Luke said. "SNAP, Service Not Attitude Plumbing."

"Very clever," Meredith said with apparent disdain.

Warren, her boyfriend, reached across the table and handed Luke a card. "Well, Meredith, my girlfriend, is an attorney. If you're ever looking for a real shark."

"Meredith's in corporate real estate," Alex said, thinking Luke's need for a real estate attorney was improbable.

"Excuse me." The waiter presented their dinner choices: chicken wrapped in a pastry shell layered with asparagus or a thick cut of roast beef with scalloped potatoes. Luke selected the beef and Alex opted for chicken.

The evening was going even better than Alex had expected.

CHAPTER 30

While they ate dinner, children and pets dominated the conversation as the First Friday Book Club women and their men exchanged stories. The soft violin music provided the perfect background for their conversation, filling in some of the awkward pauses that occurred whenever Luke was asked a question about his family.

After the dinner plates were cleared, the band played the Hora, the traditional Jewish folk dance. Judi signaled everyone to gather around, clasp hands, and form a circle.

"Let's dance." Luke reached for Alex's hand.

"You don't know how to do the Hora, do you?" she asked.

"I can learn any dance by following. Come on. It looks like line dancing." Luke took her hand, and they walked to the dance floor and entered the circle. Right foot crossed over the left, then a half turn, and the circle moved on. Luke followed, not missing a step.

Four men left the circle and grabbed a chair. Positioning the bride on it, they broke through and proceeded to the center of the circle. Then four other men grabbed another chair, placed the groom on it, and they, too, went to the center of the circle. Hoisting both chairs in unison, the men bounced the chairs up and down to the music. The guests all danced in the circle surrounding the bride and groom until the band finally stopped playing.

The emcee announced, "With the exception of the single women, everyone is invited to return to their tables."

As the bride prepared to toss her bouquet, Gary, her father, took the microphone and called to Gabe's fiancée, "Linda, come on out here, and no sneaking away."

Then Stan, Liz's husband, joined in: "Go on, Alex."

"Meredith, come with me," Alex said and returned to the dance floor.

Linda was standing to Alex's left with her arms up, ready for the bouquet to land in her outstretched hands. After the toss, Alex leaped up like a phoenix.

Meredith caught the bouquet.

Alex crashed into Linda on the way down.

Linda hit the floor. Sprawled on her back, she didn't appear able to move.

Alex offered to help her up, but Linda pushed her hand away.

The crowd gathered. Gabe and Luke rushed to the dance floor.

"Sorry," Alex said to Linda, who lay on the dance floor, belly up.

Gabe tried to lift Linda but failed. "I can't lift her," he barked and then demanded, "Someone help me get her up."

Effortlessly, Luke leaned down, swooped Linda up, and carried her to a chair as Gabe watched, shaking his head in obvious disgust.

Alex and Luke returned to their table and received conspiratorial nods from her friends.

Victorious, Meredith placed her bouquet on the table. "Guess Warren's going to have to make good on this one."

"We're all coming to the wedding," Liz said.

Warren winked at Meredith.

"Oh, I love weddings," Terrie cooed. "They are so delicious."

The band played the first few bars of "That's What Friends Are For," and Judi signaled to Terrie, Meredith, Liz, and Alex. They put their arms around one another. Alex was between Terrie and Liz and across from Judi and Meredith. Alex looked across and saw Judi smile and wink at her. Although she'd always been sure of where she stood with Liz, Terrie, and Meredith; Judi was an enigma. Now, for the first time since she'd joined the First Friday Book Club, Alex felt Judi genuinely accepted her.

◆◆◆

Later, in the privacy of her car, Alex asked, "Do you think Linda got hurt when she fell?"

"Why would you care?" Luke asked. "You gotta level your enemy in order to win."

"Why are you calling Linda my enemy?"

"Don't you want what she has?" Luke asked.

"Not anymore," she said, surprised by Luke's insight. She had to admit she had enjoyed seeing Linda on the floor, flailing around with her feet up. And she had to admit seeing Gabe struggle to lift Linda had also pleased her.

"Alex, I see everyone who prevents me from winning as an adversary."

She looked at him quizzically. "But you always seem so jovial and friendly on the court."

"You know what we say in the Marines?"

"No."

"Hold your friends close and your enemies closer." He stroked his chin as one does when imparting indisputable wisdom.

"No one's your enemy at the club," she insisted.

"That's what you think. Those people only play with me because I'm better than they are. I know that. And they feel all macho if they beat me."

Luke had an expression she'd seen many times before, usually in a competitive tennis match. Upon decisively smashing the ball into the opponents' court to win the point, his eyes would widen and his face would exude satisfaction and power. After their tennis matches, he'd dissect each point. He'd tell her how they could've done better if only she were more aggressive. He'd explain how important it was to take control, show strength.

Luke pulled her car into the garage. "Alex, go on in. I need something from my truck."

She walked into the house and waited by the door.

He returned with a plastic grocery bag.

"What's in the bag?" she asked.

"Toiletries and clothes for fishing." He winked. "I'm staying the night."

"What about your daughter?" she asked, surprised he intended to stay.

"I told them all that I had a bachelor party for one of the men in my company, and we'd be going out on my boat in the morning."

"Them all?" She looked at him quizzically.

"The kids and ..."

"And?" she pressed.

"My two daughters who are living at the house and my grandson." He kissed her, short-circuiting her brain as only he could. Scooping her up in his arms, he mimicked the way he'd lifted Linda at the reception.

She surrendered to his power and snuggled against him as he carried her upstairs, willing herself to feel instead of think. *For now*, she promised herself. *Just for now.*

He carried her to the bed and placed her atop the blue-and-white comforter. He gently kissed her forehead, then her eyelids. She reached for him.

Standing at the side of the bed, he took off his slacks. He unbuttoned his shirt, tossed it aside, and then removed his boxer shorts. Naked, he reached for her.

He took her hand and helped her up from the bed. Twirling her around, he smiled approvingly and kissed her neck. As he unzipped the back of her dress, her legs trembled. She stepped out of the dress and bent forward to drape it over the lounge chair. He moved behind her and leaned close, his breath on her spine. Delighting in the touch of his curly chest hairs, his taut stomach, and already-erect penis, she ached to have him inside her.

They moved to the bed and took each other.

Afterward, she rested her head on his shoulder and listened to him breathe. Enjoying the feel of his body, she started to fall asleep. Suddenly, her mind was filled with thoughts of the wedding, the synagogue, and the ornate entryway with the unsmiling guests glaring at her under the huge chandelier.

Then she wondered what had happened to the twinkly crystal chandelier that had hung in the dining room of her childhood home. She recalled how the light from the chandelier's glistening glass rectangles, ovals, and teardrops would reflect a rainbow of colors onto the mahogany dining room table. The shades of reds and browns within the mahogany seemed to pirouette beneath the light.

Alex would often turn on the chandelier just to watch the glistening glass reflect on the silky table. She could almost smell the ammonia her dad had used whenever he took the chandelier apart to clean each crystal.

As a little girl, there were many nights when she'd been awakened by the clinking of the chandelier in the dining room. She'd hear the groan of the floor straining to support her mother's weight as she sneaked from her bedroom, through the dining room, to the kitchen. There'd be a rattle of plastic and, finally, the crunch of cookies being devoured.

Alone in her bed, little Alexandra would wonder how many more cookies it would take and how many more pounds her mother could add before her dad would be so repulsed that he'd leave. But he never did. Instead, he stayed with his wife and daughters, living a lie. And now, because of Gabe's lies, she was living without her boys.

CHAPTER 31

Toward the end of October, the First Friday Book Club women gathered for a "nonintellectual, non-monthly" lunch. At the wedding, they'd had so much fun they decided they had to meet more than just once a month.

By the time Alex arrived at Waters Restaurant, everyone had already complimented Judi on the lovely ceremony, fabulous food, perfect venue, and, of course, her beautiful daughter.

"And when did Gary learn to dance like that?" Meredith asked Judi.

"You know what dancing is," Terrie said and smiled. "Vertical—"

"I know," Judi said. "Gary and I took lessons from an incredible instructor, Eric, at the Starlight Ballroom Studio."

"If this Eric person got Gary to look that good, I'm sending Warren to him, and speaking of dancing, Luke's definitely a sexy specimen," Meredith said.

"And wasn't it amazing how he embarrassed Gabe by helping Linda get up after she fell?" Liz laughed.

"I couldn't believe how all the doctors and their wives were watching Luke dance," Judi said. "Alex, could you imagine if anyone in your *havurah* was at the wedding and saw you with him?"

Alex's face reddened, recalling the weekend after the wedding when her *havurah* had met Luke.

"I never did understand who decided on that *havurah* thing at your synagogue." Meredith flipped back her mane of long black hair.

"Tell us why Gabe didn't choose to stay in your *havurah*," Terrie said.

"Gabe told me he didn't need them as much as I did," Alex said.

Liz gave a throaty laugh. "What a martyr."

"I had the *havurah* at my house last Saturday night," Alex said. She decided she might as well tell them before they'd hear it from some of the other women that they know who were there.

"Your *havurah* is all couples." Judi looked surprised. "I know a few of the couples in your *havurah* from the synagogue, although I'm not friendly with them. They are ... um ... quite nice, and I think it's wonderful that you have continued to be affiliated with them. I mean now that you're ... um ... single."

Obviously trying to deflect the conversation, always watching Alex's back, Liz said, "I've met some of the members of her *havurah*, and . . . "

"Georgina and I are in another book club, and she's really bright," Terrie said.

"I bet that book club doesn't discuss books as critically as we do," Liz teased.

Meredith nodded. "I'm sure no other group is as committed to literature as we are."

"Of course not," Terrie said. "But Georgina makes the yummiest desserts. Did she bring her Death by Chocolate?"

Taking a bite of her salad, Alex explained that she and Georgina had coordinated the event and had decided the group could use a surprise, some excitement. They hadn't told anyone about the dancing until after dinner.

"Dancing?" Terrie lathered ketchup on her hamburger. "I know Georgina, and dancing would not be something she'd suggest."

Meredith pursed her lips. "A group of old married people dancing isn't my idea of a lively evening."

"Luke and I aren't married," Alex reminded her.

"He was there?" Meredith barked. "Why did you invite him with *them?*"

"I told her she was taking a chance," Liz said.

"They aren't the easiest group for an outsider," Terrie said.

Judi raised her eyebrows. "And Luke is quite the outsider."

"Why did you invite him?" Meredith repeated.

"I was tired of being a fifth wheel and always going to couple things alone. So, since the dinner part was at my house, I invited Luke. I wanted him to be comfortable with the group, and I knew he'd be the most at ease if it was at my house." Part of that was true. After the wedding, Alex felt better about Luke and wanted to have him join her more often. She decided he fit in so well with the First Friday women at the wedding; therefore, she wanted to see whether he'd be just as at ease with her *havurah.*

"How'd they respond to Luke?" Terrie asked, eyes wide.

"Well," Alex said, stifling a laugh. "He refused to join us for dinner. He said he wasn't much for small talk. So, since I didn't know if he'd even show up, I didn't tell the *havurah* he might be coming later."

"Isn't he inappropriate for your group?" Judi asked.

"Interracial dating is quite acceptable," Terrie said. "It's actually in vogue. Who's that model who married Seal?"

"Alex is *not* a model." Meredith stabbed at her salad.

Liz winked at Alex. "She looked like one at the wedding."

"Get on with the story," Meredith said, dismissing Liz's compliment.

"At nine o'clock, Luke showed up, gorgeous in his tan suit and black shirt. I was excited ... and nervous."

"I'd be excited by Luke too." Meredith pushed aside her plate. "The plumber would be my Death by Chocolate."

Ignoring Meredith's reference to Luke as "the plumber," Alex continued. "At first, no one said a word. There was absolute silence, which is unusual with that group. Then Bradley, one of the guys, said, 'Oh, I get the surprise: Alex hired a stripper.'"

They all burst out laughing.

"It gets worse," Alex said. "Georgina held up a five-dollar bill."

The women couldn't stop laughing.

"Tell them what Luke said," Liz prompted with a knowing grin, since Alex had called her the morning after and recounted the entire evening.

"Luke said, 'I don't strip for that,' and everyone laughed. He broke the ice, sort of. Then we went to the tennis club, because they had a DJ."

Terrie wiped away tears of laughter. "Did your yummy guy do his vertical sex?"

The waitress put the leatherette folder on the table.

The women started to take out their wallets.

"Wait, I have an important question," Meredith said. "I need to know if anyone has a good cleaning lady for me. Mine is moving back to Mexico. I never thought they ever actually went back."

"Do you remember when we read *The Tortilla Curtain*, the way those rich people treated the poor darling Mexican couple?" Terrie dipped a French fry into the glob of ketchup. "I was quite ill over that."

"It's real life," Meredith said. "How else could we get our houses cleaned?"

"That's a terrible thing to say," Terrie said.

Alex agreed. She knew Meredith didn't understand why she wasted her time doing volunteer work with the Flying Samaritans when she could be earning money for things like designer purses and shoes, neither of which Alex had any interest.

"There was nothing new in *The Tortilla Curtain*. I mean, slavery, castes, hired help, and abuse of the underprivileged have been around forever." Meredith took out her Brighton lipstick holder and opened it. Then she waved her Chanel lipstick and applied it, studying the tiny mirror in the lipstick case.

"I thought this was going to be a 'nonintellectual' lunch. I guess we're so devoted to literature that we just can't help referencing literary works." Liz laughed.

"You try keeping up with your house, working, traveling, and men ... actually, now it's Warren exclusively." Meredith smiled coyly.

"I gotta run," Judi said.

Alex looked at her watch. "Oh, God, the forensic psychiatrist is at three today. I've got to get back to the office for at least an hour before closing up early to get to the first appointment with the court-appointed psychiatrist—handpicked by Gabe, I might add. And Seth has been so generous with his time. This monitoring thing has to be such an inconvenience for him, but he's been great."

Liz folded her arms across her chest. "Alex, tell us why you're not dating Seth?"

"He's my business partner," Alex said dismissively.

"Right, dating your business partner isn't appropriate." Meredith laughed. "And we all know how appropriate the plumber is."

"It works for now." Alex grabbed her purse and left.

CHAPTER 32

In preparation for the meeting with the forensic psychiatrist, Alex and Seth closed the office two hours earlier than usual.

"Seth, I really appreciate what you're doing more than you can imagine," Alex said.

"You know I think the requirement of a monitor is ridiculous." Seth stroked his trim beard and then took a small notepad from his pocket. "I'll continue to document your interactions. When I testify as to your competent mothering skills, I'll deluge them with details."

"You're the best," she said and smiled at him. He was so conscientious about writing everything down when she had the children. The first time he'd let her read his notes, she'd cried. Her love for the boys was captured on every page. She was sure when he testified, the judge would be convinced she was a loving mother.

"Don't worry, Alex." He put his arm around her. "I know it'll all be worth it."

They walked downstairs to their cars.

In an effort to prove that her work schedule was flexible, she was able to care for the children, and, above all, she was an attentive mother, Alex had called Gabe and offered to pick the boys up at school for their first family session with the forensic psychiatrist.

Although her visitation schedule was limited to Wednesday nights and Saturday afternoons, Gabe had agreed to allow her to pick the boys up for their appointment, cautioning her this was not going to be a routine. It was just for the first session. Then Gabe called to tell her he'd forgotten about the monitor rule and reminded her that Seth had to accompany her. She knew Gabe was probably testing her. He must have assumed she and Seth would never leave the office unattended during working hours. Gabe probably planned to use her initial offer to pick the boys up and then her inability to follow through as evidence that she put the practice before the children. But Seth insisted her children were reason enough to close the practice earlier than usual.

"Alex, you're too tense to drive," Seth said. "Do you want me to transfer Jon's car seat to my car or take yours?"

"Good idea," Alex said, appreciative of his compassion.

They got into her car and talked about a few patients' histories and treatment plans until they arrived at the older boys' middle school.

Daniel rushed to the car, leaned forward, and kissed Alex's cheek.

Eric glanced around, then gave Alex a peck on the cheek. "Why's he driving your car?"

"My car has Jon's car seat," Alex said, deflecting the fact that she was too tense to drive. "How was school?"

"Fine," Eric said.

Daniel launched into an animated overview of the student council meeting.

A few minutes later, they stopped to pick Jon up from his nursery school. Before Alex could sign him out, she had to show her driver's license to the teacher's aide. Then Seth had to co-sign. This "security measure," at the court's insistence, felt intrusive and demeaning.

Jon's eyes twinkled when he saw her. He wrapped his arms around her legs, and then he took her hand as they walked to the car.

She belted Jon into his car seat.

"Why do we have to go to this psycho thing?" Eric asked.

"Your dad arranged it," she said, although she wished she could drive home with the boys and pretend they were a normal family. "Saturday, we'll pick you guys up, and it'll be fun. We'll have a real family day."

"How can it be, without the dad?" Jon asked quizzically, head tilted to one side and eyebrows elevated, as though his expression would help him solve grown-up issues.

"Jon, when you go to your dad's house, there's no mom," Alex reminded him.

"Unh-unh." Jon shook his head. "Dad said Linda's the mom of his house."

She felt a sharp jab in her gut. *How could Gabe have dared to tell the children that?*

"I told you, Linda's not our mom." Daniel turned to Jon and gently put his finger on Jon's lips, but it was too late.

Alex had heard Jon say Linda was "the mom." That was enough to bring tears to her eyes, but she had to stay focused for the meeting with the forensic psychiatrist. "We're at the doctor's office," she said. "Everybody out."

"I don't want a shot," Jon whimpered.

Alex tousled Jon's curly hair. "Don't worry. Dr. Weisbarth is a talking doctor, so no shots."

"Chin up." Seth leaned close, pressing a quick kiss on her cheek. "I'm here for you."

They all trooped into the building and approached the elevator.

"I wanna push all the numbers," Jon announced.

"Here." Seth gently took Jon's hand and guided his fingers to number three.

When they reached Dr. Weisbarth's office, Daniel studied the nameplate on the door. "What's a forensic psychiatrist?"

"He analyzes people and tells the lawyers what he thinks is in the best interests of the parties," Alex explained, although she really wanted to tell him she thought Dr. Weisbarth was, in reality, someone Gabe had paid to document her incompetence as a mother.

Seth opened the door for them, nodded at Gabe, and waited for Alex and the boys to enter. Then he shut the office door and took a seat in the reception area.

Jon ran and jumped onto Gabe's lap.

"Just got here myself." Gabe hugged Jon and motioned for Eric to sit beside him.

Daniel glanced at Alex before he sat down on the other side of his father.

Watching the boys surround Gabe, she wanted to lash out and chastise him for making the family crumble to the point where they needed a psychiatrist to assess their love. Instead, she fought to stay calm. She looked away and saw the window to the receptionist area was closed and, surprisingly, there was no receptionist.

Dr. Weisbarth emerged from his private office and stepped into the waiting room. Elegant—an odd description for a man, but that was how he appeared—he was tall and lithe, with wavy silver hair.

"Gabriel," Dr. Weisbarth said, shaking hands with a familiarity that shocked Alex.

"Norm," Gabe said, returning the greeting.

The forensic psychiatrist shook Eric's hand, then Daniel's. "Hi, little fellow," he said, smiling down at Jon. He turned to

Alex. "And you must be Mrs. Rose." As he extended his right hand, the monogrammed shirt cuff peeked out from his perfectly tailored navy-blue, double-breasted jacket.

Determined to appear confident, Alex greeted the doctor. She stared at the "NRW" on his shirt cuff and then looked up and met Dr. Norman R. Weisbarth's gaze.

He took her right hand in his and covered it with his left, a solicitous gesture that made her stomach churn. "This way, please," he said, leading them to his office. "My office girls get Friday afternoons off since I only see a few cases then. Gabe, as you know, some days, I'm so booked they can't even take a lunch break."

They all walked down the hallway.

Dr. Weisbarth stopped, turned, and looked at Seth. "I'm assuming you're the monitor." Without waiting for an answer, he instructed: "You can wait outside until we're finished."

Dr. Weisbarth continued to his office, and the boys followed, single file.

Alex and Gabe paused at the doorway, glared at each other, and then went into the room.

"Why don't you boys sit there?" Dr. Weisbarth directed the three boys to the couch and strode behind his desk. Then he motioned to the lone overstuffed chair positioned diagonally opposite his desk. "Gabe, you can sit there."

Gabe nodded.

Dr. Weisbarth glanced around the office and asked, "Mrs. Rose, where would you like to sit?"

Feeling like an appendage in this otherwise perfect arrangement of males, Alex joined her sons on the couch. Crooking her neck, she looked at the photos adorning the doctor's huge mahogany desk: a glamour shot of a woman who resembled

Gabe's fiancée, Linda, was framed in Waterford crystal. The other framed photos displayed smiling children.

Was it possible that Dr. Weisbarth was married to Linda's sister? Her attorney had told her Gabe's attorney played golf with the judge every Sunday at Rancho Santa Margarita, but she didn't think Gabe would do anything as risky as hiring a psychiatrist who was related to his fiancée.

The doctor cleared his throat. "Let's talk about the last time you were together as a family."

"It was when she brought Jon to the hospital with the burn." Gabe glowered at her.

"No, Gabe, we were at Eric's football game a few days ago," Alex corrected.

Ignoring her, the doctor said, "Let's discuss that burn incident."

"I was reading the paper, and Jon was sitting on my lap." Alex rubbed the scar on her right wrist.

"What drew your attention away from Jon?" the doctor asked.

"I didn't ignore him," she said. "I just glanced down at a circus ad."

"Did the ad trigger any particular memory for you, Mrs. Rose?" he asked.

"My memories have nothing to do with the boys," she said, determined to make him understand she was a responsible, loving mother who would never harm her child.

"I'll be the judge of that," Dr. Weisbarth said and smiled without separating his lips, a Gabriel trait which she hated.

Alex leaned over and hugged Jon. As she looked back, she saw Gabe make eye contact with the doctor. They appeared oddly conspiratorial, which increased Alex's anxiety about the possibility—no, probability—that they were working together to discredit her. *Stay calm,* she told herself as she watched the doctor jot down a note on his legal pad.

"Please continue," Dr. Weisbarth instructed.

"There was an advertisement for Ringling Brothers, the circus, and—"

"When she was my age, the fat lady scared Mommy this much," Jon interrupted, stretching out his arms, obviously proud of himself for remembering a story she'd told him about how the fat lady in the circus had frightened her when she was little.

The doctor nodded. "How did that make you feel, Mrs. Rose?"

"It's Dr. Rose," Alex said.

Eric tapped his foot on the sea-foam-green carpet. "Why do we have to be here?"

"I'm sorry, gentlemen. I didn't explain." Dr. Weisbarth rested his palms together. "Boys, as you know, your father examines people's hearts and fixes them. Well, my job is to examine how people think and ..."

"Can you see in my brain?" Jon asked.

Eric scowled. "I'd rather be at my game is what I'm thinking."

"My mother fixes people's backs," Daniel offered.

"Eric, I do believe you acted responsibly and called your father at the hospital," the doctor said, dismissing Daniel's comment about Alex's profession.

Eric nodded.

Alex bit back a protest.

In minute detail, they reviewed the day she'd spilled the boiling water. By the end of the hour-long session, Jon's second-degree burn which barely blistered had become a near-death experience which he'd survived only due to Gabe's intervention.

"Time to schedule our next appointments," Dr. Weisbarth said and explained he wanted to meet with Alex the next week, Gabe the week after that, and then with each child alone during the subsequent weeks. Then they would finally meet as a family the week after that.

"But that's six more sessions. Your report probably won't be ready within sixty days," Alex said.

"I can always request a slight extension due to my schedule," the doctor said with mock apology and turned to Alex. "What about three o'clock next Friday for you?"

"I'll be out of town next week. I'm leaving on Thursday." She glanced at the boys, praying that Jon would be quiet and not say anything about her plans to go hunting. He'd been sitting on her lap when she'd been on the phone with Liz, and he'd definitely heard her tell Liz she was going hunting with Luke. She hadn't thought he'd been paying attention to the call, but after she'd hung up, he hadn't stopped asking questions about shooting animals.

With his usual enthusiasm, Jon blurted out, "Mommy's going to shoot a deer."

Her throat tightened. "I can reschedule my patients and come in any other afternoon next week."

Dr. Weisbarth feigned sympathy and explained, "I only have time at three each Friday afternoon for this particular case. As I've stated, I'm completely booked."

"Gabe could switch with me." She glanced over at him.

"Sorry, Alex, but I've already changed my surgical schedule for my meeting with Dr. Weisbarth in two weeks."

She wondered how he could have known his appointment would be in two weeks but decided it wouldn't be prudent to interrogate Gabe in front of the doctor. She couldn't do anything that might cause Dr. Weisbarth to label her as paranoid. It didn't matter. She wasn't going to go hunting and miss her meeting. Although Luke would be disappointed by her inability to accompany him on the hunting trip, the boys were her first priority.

The doctor pressed his palms together, a gesture that increased her annoyance with the man. "As you yourself stated, Mrs. Rose, we really need to implement this schedule in order to get the report to the judge within a reasonable time frame."

"I'll be here," she said.

"Perfect," Dr. Weisbarth said.

Gabe stood up and walked to the door. "Boys, let's go home."

Exiting the waiting room, Daniel leaned close to Alex. "Mom, I love you."

"See you tomorrow," Eric said.

"Mommy, don't go." Jon grabbed her legs. "I wanna see you for soup bizitation now."

"Supervised visitation is tomorrow." Alex kissed him.

"Boys, we're late," Gabe said sternly as they crowded into the tiny elevator, the tension so thick even Jon remained silent until the elevator doors opened.

As she watched the boys sprint to Gabe's Mercedes, her heart thumped with longing.

Seth opened the car door, looked at her, and asked, "Can I do anything?"

Fighting back tears, she shook her head.

"How about dinner tonight?" he asked.

"I'm playing tennis tonight."

"Of course." Seth frowned. "That Luke fellow. Well, I'm joining your club."

CHAPTER 33

Late, Alex rushed to the club locker room, hurriedly changed into her tennis outfit, and ran to the court. Luke was already there, warming up against their opponents. She took her place beside him on the court and started to play. Dreading the fact that she'd have to tell him she wouldn't be able to go hunting with him, her concentration wavered. She made numerous errors. The other couple won the first set.

She sensed Luke's growing anger about losing. That was a part of their relationship she loathed. Whenever she didn't play well, he took it personally. And since his shots were often dependent upon how she hit the ball and set him up, he was critical of her. Whenever he was caught off balance, out of control, he'd glare at her. For him, tennis was clearly more than a game. It seemed he had to demonstrate his prowess, continually prove he could hold his own with other men—especially wealthy, professional men.

After a grueling duel at the net, the ball ricocheting back and forth with lightning speed, she turned to Luke and said, "That was a great rally, almost worth losing the point."

"Nothing's worth losing," he snapped. Then he caught himself, as though realizing he needed her to focus in order to win. He patted her back. "Set me up, and I'll put the ball away."

She served. When their opponent returned the ball, Luke slammed it, bouncing it high into the opponents' court. A return was impossible. They won the second set.

As they approached the net to shake their opponents' hands, Alex whispered, "I don't want to go up for drinks. I need to talk to you."

"What's wrong?" he asked.

"Later," she said.

"You both played well," their opponent said. "Going up for a drink?"

Alex smiled tensely. "Another time."

Luke stayed to arrange a rematch and then caught up to her in the parking lot.

"It's not like you to run off," he said. "What's going on?"

"I can't go hunting with you."

"Why the hell not? I already told my hunting buddies. I even made arrangements for us to have the largest bedroom," he said, the veins in his forehead visibly throbbing.

"I have the meeting with the forensic psychiatrist next Friday."

As though weighing her words, her truthfulness, he studied her through a narrow-eyed gaze. "Then reschedule. How tough would that be?"

Alex shook her head. "I could lose my boys if I miss the appointment. I can't go."

There was no way she was going to back down. In the past, she would have capitulated. *Shades of Gabe,* she realized. *Being measured, being found inadequate.*

"I can't imagine one meeting could be that critical," he said.

"It definitely is," she said, firmly, refusing to back down.

"Alex, think about changing the appointment." He held the door for her as she got into her car. "Please."

"I'll start dinner," she said, enjoying the routine they'd established: he'd come over each night after tennis, and they'd have dinner together. Preparing dinner for him made the pain of being in the house without the happy sound of children and Honey more bearable. When Luke came over after tennis, she was distracted and didn't dwell on the empty chairs surrounding the dinner table.

"No, I gotta get home, call my buddies, and tell them about the changes."

"You're not coming over?"

"I hate when things change after I set my mind to one way." He opened his truck door. "I'll call you tomorrow."

She went home, turned on her computer, and started to write a report on one of her patients. There was an e-mail from Gabe: "Linda made plans for a trip in two weeks. I need to take your appointment next week."

In Dr. Weisbarth's office, Gabe had said his surgery schedule, "couldn't be changed." But this meant she could now go hunting with Luke. Excitedly, she e-mailed Gabe, agreeing to the schedule change. Then she phoned Luke. It went to his voice mail. She left a message.

Whenever she called Luke's home phone, it would go directly to voice mail. He'd always call her back within a few minutes or, at most, an hour. She left two more messages.

When Luke hadn't called back by 9:00 p.m., she decided to go to his house to tell him in person. Although he'd told her one of his daughters was "difficult" and got upset about him dating, Alex was certain he'd be so excited she could go hunting with him that he probably wouldn't mind if she came to his house.

She called information to get his address. Unlisted.

Two weeks ago he'd had to take his work truck to be repaired, and she'd met him at the auto mechanic. She'd given him a ride to the entrance of his development. He'd insisted it would have been impossible for her to wind her way back out of the development if she had driven all the way to his house. She remembered the street where she'd dropped him off.

Confident she'd be able to find his truck since his development seemed relatively small, she got into her car and drove. As she got closer, she vacillated about the probability of him welcoming her to his house. Heart pounding, she thought about turning around. *What if he gets angry with me for showing up unannounced?* Then she decided since he'd made himself so comfortable in her home, it was her right to see his house.

Following the route they'd taken when she'd dropped him off, she drove up to the two faux-marble pillars at the entrance to the development. She followed the main street through the complex. Neither his Toyota Tacoma nor his work truck was in front of any of the houses or in any driveway of the main street. She decided to take the first side street. After several turns, she thought she'd spotted his truck. She pulled up next to it and realized the truck had a lockbox attached to the cab and a sign that read, "Lawn and Gardening."

Disappointed, she took the next street, San Sebastian, until it dead-ended. She turned around and drove for ten minutes, landing in one cul-de-sac after another. She feared there was no way out of the maze-like development.

Then she saw his yellow work truck with the white toilet logo was parked in a driveway and his black Toyota Tacoma with the "SNAP" sign on the side panel was parked across the street. She pulled up behind the work truck and got out of her car. Closing her car door, she turned and stared at the tiny single-story house. She walked toward the aqua doorframe with the crisp new paint and looked in the front window. Blinds raised, the place appeared to be exploding with people.

Luke, bare-chested, sexy as ever, was pointing his finger at—no, he was shoving a man who appeared to be thirty or so. There was a young woman standing behind the thirty-year-old guy. Luke and the younger man seemed to be arguing. Then the younger man moved toward Luke. She heard Luke yell, "You won't treat my daughter like that!"

Too scared to ring the doorbell, she rushed back to her car, climbed behind the wheel, and watched. Mesmerized, she saw a third male, a teenager wearing a baseball cap, grab Luke. The teenager appeared to be trying to restrain Luke. The three males closed in on one another, overpowering the tiny house. Alex saw Luke raise his hand. Then Luke turned and started to walk toward the front door. She had to leave before he saw her spying on him.

She drove back to her house, relieved he'd told her the truth about his daughters and grandson living with him. She was also certain Luke had told her the truth about being divorced. If his wife were there, she would have rushed in and insisted they stop arguing, and then she would have pulled her grandson to her protectively—or, maybe, she would've learned not to intervene?

◆◆◆

The next morning, a few minutes before her alarm sounded, her phone rang.

"Why'd you call four times last night?" Luke asked. "You okay?"

"I wanted to tell you I could go hunting with you. As a matter of fact, I was going to go to your house last night, but—"

"You were going to come here?" Luke raised his voice. "Didn't I tell you about my daughter?"

"I thought you'd be excited that I could go with you."

"You're gonna love the hunt," he said.

CHAPTER 34

Dreading a Saturday afternoon without the boys, Alex decided to cancel the hunting trip. She called Gabe to tell him she'd changed her mind about going away and would pick up the boys at noon as scheduled. He said it was too late. He'd already bought tickets for some sporting event and told her how excited the boys were about it.

Alex knew if she insisted on seeing the boys, then Gabe would definitely tell them he'd bought the tickets, but their mother wouldn't let them go. She decided there was no point in staying home if she couldn't spend the day with the boys. She might as well go hunting.

Right after she finished throwing the last few toiletries into her suitcase and loading the ice chest, the doorbell sounded. She opened the door and greeted Luke.

"Did you pack an orange hat like I said?" he asked, and without waiting for an answer, he held out an orange cap with a brown grease stain around the inside rim.

Alex frowned. "It clashes with my pink ski jacket."

"This is about safety, not style." He picked up the cooler and suitcase.

She put the hat in her jacket pocket, surprised at how easily he transformed himself from the sensual dancer and accomplished tennis player to hunter. He was the perfect chameleon.

After loading up his truck, they buckled themselves in and were on their way.

He yawned. "Excuse me."

"Tired?" she asked.

"Yeah. Did too many service calls today."

"Luke, why don't the technicians cover for you?"

He cleared his throat. "Oh, I meant I had to inspect everything. Can't trust some of the guys with the more complicated jobs. If you want something done right, sometimes you gotta do it—I mean check it—yourself."

"Luckily, I can trust Seth with my patients."

"You can trust Seth," he repeated with a smirk. "You seem to spend a lot of time with that fella. Why'd you pick him to be your whatever-they-call-it for the kids?"

"Court-appointed monitor."

"Yeah. Why'd you pick him?"

"I couldn't have asked Liz to give up time with her husband."

"So, this Seth has all the time in the world to spend with you?"

"It's not like that," she said, knowing how possessive Luke was. But there was no reason for him to be jealous of Seth. He was her partner, and they had a business relationship and nothing more.

"Whatever," he said and then changed the subject. "Alex, wait until you see this place."

"How often do you go there?" she asked.

"Yearly, when my number gets picked in the lottery. It's the only vacation I ever take."

"Why only once a year, if you love it?"

"Did enough traveling in the Marines: Germany for three years, 'Nam for two tours of duty, and Korea for two years."

"Why two tours of Vietnam?" she asked.

"It was my duty."

"What about your wife and family?"

"Alex, that's the past. You know you've got to me like no other woman. I think about you whenever we're not together."

She hated how he was so reluctant to talk about his family, but it felt good to hear him compliment her. She tried to remember the last time Gabe had told her something nice. It had been a long time ago, and she hungered for it. For the time being, she decided she would settle for lust masquerading as love.

Luke smiled at her. "When I come to your house at night, it's like a sanctuary for me. I have no worries there."

"Why haven't you ever invited me to your house to meet your family?" she asked, recalling the frenetic scene within his house.

"You'll meet my family in due time." He took a deep breath. "And I wish you could have met my daughter who passed. Besides, I've told you about my other daughter. She'll be fine with you, but it will take time."

"You could bring them to the club," she offered.

"Um," he said and turned up the CD, signaling the end of the conversation. As he hummed along with the music, she drifted off to sleep.

Several hours later, Luke pulled into the semicircular driveway of the Panguitch Lake Lodge and stopped the truck. He slid close, wrapped his right arm around her, and pointed with his left to the row of cabins. "Amazing, huh?"

"Beautiful." Alex gazed at the snowcapped mountains thrusting into the peacock-blue sky. Then she looked down at the row of six grungy gray clapboard cabins.

"That one's ours, the second from the end." He gave her a peck on the cheek. "I'll be right back. I'm going to get the key from the manager."

She climbed out of the truck, walked to their porch, and peered through the window. In the sparsely furnished room, a blue-and-green-plaid couch—probably there since the place had opened—faced the window. The other side of the tiny room housed the kitchen alcove with a long wooden table and two benches.

Luke tapped her on the back. She jumped and turned around. "Nice, huh?" he asked.

"Cozy," Alex said and returned to the truck for her purse. As she turned back toward the cabin, she looked across the alleyway at the neighboring cabins. Two white men were standing on their porch. She nodded to them. They didn't respond.

She walked into the living room and was assaulted by the smell of Pine-Sol. "We should leave some windows open," she said.

"It'll be cold, but whatever you want," he said. "I'll bring in our stuff."

Alex placed her purse on the wooden table and inspected the galley kitchen with the bottom-of-the-line appliances. She walked down the dark, narrow hallway to the bathroom. Awful—the only word to describe the yellowed plastic shower curtain caked with green mold along the bottom. She grimaced. When showering tonight, she'd have to remember to maneuver herself into the stall without touching the curtain.

She closed the door to the bathroom and made her way to the master bedroom. As she sat down on the double bed, it sagged and creaked. She considered the paper-thin walls and the squeaky bed and decided they'd have to be especially quiet when they made love tonight.

Returning to the living room, she saw Luke had dumped his hunting gear onto the floor—clothes and boots sprawled everywhere. "Luke, where's everyone going to sleep?"

"We get the master bedroom with the door." He winked. "Clay and his wife will get the loft."

"And the other one?"

"Thomas." Luke hesitated and then looked around as though he hadn't considered that. "The sofa," he finally said.

She glanced at the threadbare couch. "Does it open?"

"Why do you care? You thinking of sleeping with Thomas?" he asked and laughed. "Let's check out the hunting grounds before it gets dark."

♦♦♦

Silent except for the crunch of the snow beneath their boots, they traversed the snowy embankment around Panguitch Lake. The descending sun made the greens and golds of the treetops disappear into blackness. He reached over and tucked a strand of her hair back beneath her pink cap.

"Tomorrow, you'll have to wear the orange cap I gave you." He took her gloved hand in his bare hand, and they walked deeper into the woods, their shadows blending together in the dusk.

After what seemed like only a few minutes, Luke said, "It's getting dark, so we'd better head back."

They turned back, and just as they approached the road to their cabin, Luke's called out, "There's my man."

Under the post light, Alex saw two black men standing in front of a Chevy Blazer. And she also saw their neighbors were watching them.

Clay, a handsome man neatly dressed in jeans, a black turtleneck sweater, and a jean jacket, greeted Luke. "Great to see you, my man."

Thomas, the other man, turned to her. "You must be Luke's woman." He put his hands on her shoulders, pulled her to him, and bear-hugged her. Alex's nose pressed against a gasoline stain on his olive-green overcoat. Repulsed, she drew back.

Clay extended his hand. "Alex, pleasure to meet you," he said, his voice strong. Leaving the perfect amount of space between them, he shook her hand. She liked him but could do without Thomas. Then she realized Clay's wife was not with them.

"Clay, wasn't your wife supposed to come?" she asked.

"Wife?" Clay looked at Luke and then said, "Oh, she got sick at the last minute."

"Is she okay?" Alex asked, feeling the balance suddenly shift. She was now the lone woman with three men in a cabin in the woods.

"Are we gonna bag a deer or what?" Luke asked and high-fived Clay.

Laden with duffle bags, an ice chest, and rifles, Clay and Thomas walked into the cabin.

"Cleaned out my freezer to make room for the venison," Clay said as he put his gear in the far corner of the living room, out of the way. He hung his jacket up on one of the wall hooks.

Thomas dropped his duffle bag on the floor, threw his coat onto the sofa, and parked his rifle in a corner of the room.

"Hey, we gotta use the living room," Clay said. "Don't crap it up." He removed his orange wool cap, revealing thick hair slightly graying at the temples.

Thomas retrieved his jacket from the floor and put it on a hook. "Mr. Clean here hasn't stopped criticizing since we started. Let's eat."

Luke nodded toward Alex. "She was up all night cooking."

"I always appreciate home cooking." Clay took a soap dish from his bag and went into the bathroom.

Wondering why Clay's wife hadn't sent any food and why he'd made the remark about home cooking, Alex went to the kitchen.

She heated the soup on the stovetop and slid the pot roast and potatoes into the oven.

"The soup looks great." Clay said and reached above her to take several plates down from the shelf.

She smelled his aftershave—fresh and spicy.

They all took turns washing up in the one sparse bathroom.

Clay set the table. Thomas plopped the bucket of chicken on the table and sat down on one of the benches. Luke sat on the other bench, leaving room for Alex.

As soon as the soup was warmed, Alex ladled it into bowls for Clay to take to the table.

After the soup was served, Alex sat down beside Luke and watched the men as they stared at the matzoh balls dancing in their bowls. Then, as though an orchestra conductor had signaled a concert to commence, they brought their spoons to their lips.

Silence.

"Excellent," Clay finally said.

Alex smiled at the irony of the three black hunters feasting on her "killer matzoh ball soup," a revered family recipe from Bubbe Yetta, a tiny woman who'd never left her Romanian village until she'd followed her husband to America.

His mouth full, Thomas asked, "When you guys were growing up in New York, did you ever have this Jewish soup?" He wiped his mouth with the back of his hand.

"No," Clay said and then asked, "But Alex, has Luke told you about the crazy stuff we did as kids?"

Luke shook his head. "I don't think she needs to know about any stupid stuff we did."

"I'd love to hear." Alex glanced over at Luke as he was signaling Clay to stop.

Clay looked mischievous. "This one time, we were with our friend Spud, and—"

"She doesn't need to hear that," Luke said.

"Sure I do," she encouraged, curious about his past.

Thomas scraped his spoon along the bottom of the bowl, leaned back, and waited for Alex to clear the bowls from the table. Then he took out a cigarette.

Clay snarled. "Go outside with that."

"Come on." Thomas lit his cigarette. "It's not like we're in your truck."

"Not in here." Clay glared at Thomas.

"You guys sound like the odd couple," Luke said and laughed.

Thomas grabbed his coat and left.

"He went ballistic when I stopped the truck and made him go outside to smoke." Clay shook his head. "You should see his work truck."

"You work with Thomas?" Alex asked.

"For now," Clay said. "California Pool and Spa Cleaning pays my tuition, and that's all I care about."

She took the pot roast from the oven with towels since there were no potholders.

Thomas burst into the room, slamming the door behind him. "Don't know what's up with the guys next door."

Luke went to the window. "They're standing outside and looking over here."

"Ignore them," Clay said.

"Yeah," Luke agreed. "We got a whole bucket of chicken and her pot roast to go through."

Clay reached for a piece of chicken. He looked up at Alex and said, "Luke tells me you're a doctor."

"I'm a chiropractor," she said.

"Don't you need physical strength for that?" Thomas asked.

Before she could respond, Luke said, "You should see how strong she is."

She knew he was referring to her prowess at tennis and had no knowledge of her work. She listened as they talked, telling stories about the rich people on their routes—the men who treated them as though they were invisible, the housewives who assured them the snarling dogs don't bite the people who work at the house, and the scantily clad teenage girls who came to the door and gave them dirty looks if they so much as glanced at them.

"Well, we'd better get to sleep if we're hunting at four," Clay said.

Alex began to stack the dishes and silverware.

Luke put his hand on hers. "I'll take care of the dishes. You've got bathroom priority."

"Thanks," she said and went to the bedroom to grab her robe before proceeding to the bathroom.

Careful not to touch the grungy shower curtain, she showered, donned her bathrobe, and walked from the bathroom to the bedroom. Then she closed the bedroom door, got between the cold sheets, and waited for Luke.

He showered and crawled into bed next to her.

"You won't believe how exciting your first hunt will be." He kissed her forehead and rolled over.

"Did you know all along that Clay's wife wasn't coming?"

"I really wanted you to come. Let's not discuss that now. We need our strength for hunting."

"Are you going to sleep?" she asked.

"That's the idea." He laughed. "I can't have any smell on me. You wouldn't believe how a deer can track a human by smell, especially if there's a trace of sex."

Sure that he was teasing her, she reached over and stroked his back.

"Alex, it's bad luck to have sex, and we're here for you to see your first deer kill."

CHAPTER 35

Unable to sleep, Alex turned over and stared at Luke, sound asleep beside her. Without sex to blur her vision and short-circuit her brain, she thought about their relationship. Their differences were too vast. She and Luke weren't right for each other. But a cabin in the woods with two other hunters was definitely not the time to end the relationship.

She tossed and turned and then decided to get up and go to the kitchen. Maybe a cup of herbal tea would help her fall asleep. As she approached the kitchen, she came to a halt.

Wearing only boxer shorts, Clay quickly turned away from her.

Uncomfortable in the tiny kitchen with Luke's best friend clad in his underwear, she started to turn back to her room.

"Didn't think anyone would be awake, but give me a minute," Clay said and went upstairs.

Alex put the bowl of soup Clay had filled into the microwave and placed the teakettle on the stove.

Wearing jeans and a plaid shirt, Clay returned to the kitchen. He took the soup out of the microwave and offered to pour her a cup of tea. Then he took a spoonful of soup. "This is even better than the first bowl."

"It's a family recipe."

"Yeah. Food is culture," he said. His face had a soft, faraway look. "I remember when my Pappie'd bring home a watermelon. He'd throw it on the sidewalk. We'd watch it split into chunks, and then my dad would pick up the middle section and take a bite. We'd wait. He'd nod. Then we would grab the chunks of watermelon scattered on the ground."

"Wasn't it dirty?" she asked.

"It was sweet." He smiled. "I sure miss family."

"Don't you have a wife?" she asked.

"No," he said. "Luke didn't think you'd come if you were going to be the only woman in the cabin."

Her suspicion confirmed, she said, "You're right on that, but why would he have lied to me?"

"He's the most principled man." Clay put down his spoon, looked at Alex and started to recount a story about Luke. "There was this girl, Jocelyn, from our projects. She offered to show Spud, one of our friends, a 'good time' for five bucks."

"How old was she?" Alex asked.

"Twelve." Clay hesitated and then continued. "Spud could only get his hands on two bucks, so he convinced Luke and me to go in on it with him. We each gave Spud two bucks, and we headed to Jocelyn's apartment. When she saw all of us, she slammed the door in Spud's face. Then, after several minutes, he persuaded her to let us in."

"What happened?" Alex's eyes widened, certain he was going to tell her something about Luke that was unsavory.

"Jocelyn went back with Spud, and Luke and I looked through the crack in the door." Clay pushed the bowl away. "Never mind."

"You're not going to stop now." She needed to hear his story. Maybe then she could put some of the pieces of the puzzle that was Luke together.

Clay nodded. "Okay, Luke and I were in the living room waiting. We heard these weird sounds and tried to see what was going on, but all we could see was Spud's butt moving and gyrating. Then it was Luke's turn. He walked into Jocelyn's room, saw her wrists tied to the headboard, and untied her."

"Good," she said.

"Well, I got so angry with him." Clay looked down at his calloused hands. "I pulled my knife out of its cradle, grabbed Luke, and slashed him in the face."

"The scar over his right eye?" she asked.

"I just missed his eye." Clay pointed at her. "You know what Luke did?"

Fearful he would tell her something she didn't want to hear about Luke's temper, she whispered, "What?"

"He took Jocelyn out for a Coke."

"She must have been relieved." And so was Alex upon hearing the story, an affirmation of the gentle side of Luke.

"Yes. Luke was always a gentleman; that is, until—"

"Until what?" she asked.

"'Nam. He's been different ever since, and I'm sure he has PTS ..."

"D," she said. "PTSD—Post Traumatic Stress Disorder." Her heart pounded. *That explained some of his behavior.*

"I should never have said that." Clay lowered his head. "Luke was the bravest of them all. He was a tunnel rat."

"What's that?" she asked.

Clay explained how the "tunnel rats" were the Marines who'd go into the Vietcongs' tunnels before they'd toss the grenades in. The "rat" was sent in to see if there were any dead Americans in the tunnels so they could take them out. Sometimes if a Vietcong was still in the tunnel, he'd wait for the American to drop down, and then he'd shove his rifle into the American just as he was entering the tunnel. Other times, the Vietcong would capture the tunnel rat and torture him. Clay explained how most of the Marines wouldn't even think of doing that, but Luke had volunteered.

"Amazing he survived," Alex said, but wondered what would have possessed him to have volunteered for such a dangerous task. Maybe, he really was a hunter to his core and craved the challenge, even if it could have cost him his life.

Clay got up and took the soup bowl to the sink. He looked at her and said, "Luke's a great guy, but he can be volatile. I mean, he'd never hurt you, but ..."

"But what?" she asked, fearing his answer.

"Just be careful," Clay said and looked toward the loft, where Thomas was snoring so loudly that it almost shook the house. "Well, I'm off to see the music man upstairs."

Alex returned to bed and thought about Jocelyn, a child who'd been willing to sell her body for five dollars. Then she thought about Luke. As a teenager, he'd been ethical and hadn't taken advantage of the young girl. He was a good man. Clay had said it, but he also cautioned her. Too tired to think right now, she turned away from Luke and fell asleep.

◆◆◆

Suddenly, blood was everywhere. There were bodies covering the ground. Luke's eyes glinted with delight, blood dripped from his hands, and then he licked his fingers.

Terrified, she woke with a start. Her heart was pounding and she was sweating. Unable to sleep, she lay wide awake, watching Luke sleeping peacefully.

Finally, she dozed again.

Within what seemed like a few minutes, Luke shook her. "Get up or we'll be late."

"I can't go," she said and buried her head in the pillow.

"What do you mean?" he exclaimed. Before she could answer, he grabbed her wrist and demanded, "Why else would you have come all this way?"

"I just had a horrific dream."

"This isn't the time to start that," he said.

"Luke," she said, looking into his angry eyes, "I'll go out in the afternoon with you when I calm down."

"Chances are greater in the morning. If you knew you couldn't take it, why would you have come?"

"I really didn't want to see a deer killed. You said we'd be together, so I came to be with you."

"This is me," he yelled.

She stared at him. He was right; he was a hunter first. "No, I can't," she said.

"You're not going to embarrass me in front of my friends." He grabbed her wrist. "You will get up now."

There was a knock on the door.

"We gotta leave now before it gets too light," Clay said.

"I told you I can't have bad luck." Luke let go of her wrist, turned, and went to his duffle bag. He pulled out his worn green work pants, flannel shirt, and orange hunting vest. He dressed and slammed the door.

She listened to the men in the kitchen—a loud jumble of male voices, challenging, cajoling, giddy with the excitement of the hunt.

There was an eerie familiarity to Luke's behavior—threats and love. She knew that behavior all too well. It was predictable, almost comfortable. It was home, her childhood home.

CHAPTER 36

A s Alex sat on the porch and waited for the men to return from their morning hunt, she thought about Luke, the man who'd been kind to the little girl, and Luke, the man who'd grabbed her wrist this morning. He could be charming, but there was a dark side. *Maybe*, she thought, *everyone has a dark side, and it's just a matter of time before it surfaces.*

She opened this month's First Friday Book Club selection, *The Pilot's Wife,* and just as she started to read, the neighbors' Eddie Bauer Limited Edition British-racing-green truck veered into the driveway next door. Two men got out, slammed the truck's doors, and walked toward their cabin.

From her perch on the porch, she heard one of the men agitatedly complain, "Did you see the way he smirked at us when he hoisted the deer onto his fuckin' Toyota?"

There was laughter, and the other man said, "Let's puncture his tires tonight. Then we'll see what he does with a dead deer rotting on top of his truck."

"Better yet, let's steal the deer," the first man said.

"Yeah. Those black guys fuck our women, and now they're baggin' our deer," the second growled, shutting the cabin door.

She closed the book and thought about the neighbors' vengeance. Dealing with prejudice like that could cause anyone to become cynical and distrustful. Luke probably had to battle for, and then defend, everything he achieved.

Suddenly, to the accompaniment of much hooting and horn blowing, Luke pulled up. He jumped out of his truck, ran to the porch, and grabbed Alex's hand. Proudly pointing to the dead deer atop his truck, he described how he'd shot the buck, trailed after it until it collapsed, and then dragged the carcass through the forest.

"Alex, you would have been so impressed," Clay said and gave Luke a congratulatory slap on the back.

"We're gonna gut it right now," Thomas said.

"Don't you need a butcher to do that?" Alex asked.

Luke shook his head. "We can't wait for that. We have to remove the innards right away or else decay will seep into the meat. That way, we can get a good night's sleep and then leave in the morning."

Alex didn't know what to do. If she told Luke about the men next door, there'd be a horrific confrontation. If they stayed, Luke would lose his deer. She hesitated.

"Let's get the deer off the roof and start gutting," Luke said.

Standing on opposite sides of the truck, Luke and Clay struggled to haul the deer off the roof. Then Thomas guided it down.

"Alex, you don't want to see this," Clay said.

"I'm not squeamish. We dissected cadavers when I was in anatomy, but I just wasn't up to a kill this morning."

"That's the best part," Luke said.

While the three men carried the carcass to the yard behind the cabin, she went to the kitchen and retrieved garbage bags.

Then Thomas and Clay held open the first garbage bag while Luke slit the deer's abdomen, pulled out several feet of intestines, and dropped them into the bag. Then Luke plunged his ungloved hand deep into the slit in the deer's abdomen and removed the liver.

Watching Luke gut the deer was so different from the way he cleaned and filleted the fish on his boat. The fish gutting appeared to be just a task to be accomplished at the end of fishing. Here, as he reached his hand into the deer's abdominal cavity, his eyes narrowed in sinister determination, his brow furrowed in concentration, and his breath appeared to quicken in excitement. It was chilling how he seemed to be salivating over his prey.

Alex was repulsed, and it had nothing to do with the exposed innards. She was comfortable with that, but she was unnerved by the sadistic delight Luke appeared to take in disemboweling the deer. She wondered whether this was reminiscent of the way he'd stood over his victims in Vietnam. And why would he have volunteered for a second tour of duty if he hadn't derived satisfaction from killing? Unable to watch the hunter in Luke gloat over his prey, she turned away. But after seeing that side of him, she knew she'd always view him through that prism.

"Let's get ice and wrap the deer so it'll keep 'til tomorrow," Luke said. "I want to take Alex out on the hunt this afternoon."

"I'm fine with leaving," she said. Tense, she knew if they stayed, then the neighbors would steal the deer the minute it was left unguarded.

Clay shook his head in disapproval. "If you ice it and wrap it, then tomorrow, when you put it on top of your truck and drive, it'll drip all over and make a mess."

"Don't listen to him," Thomas said. "He's always worried about the mess. The deer'll be fine."

"Clay, can you call that guy in Vernon, the butcher we used last time when you got the kill? See when he can open his shop to put the carcass in the freezer?" Luke asked.

Clay nodded. "He's in my church, and I'm sure he'll do it for us, especially if we give my portion to the church for a dinner."

"I thought you cleaned your freezer for the venison," Thomas said, teasing Clay about his proclivity for cleanliness.

Ignoring Thomas's remark, Clay said, "The butcher did a great job the last time we got a kill. I also remember how perfectly he divided and wrapped it for each of us." Then he called the butcher and left a message.

Alex decided she'd seen and heard enough. While it was clear Luke was a good man, he did have a sinister side that, she decided, could be dangerous. And if they stayed, he'd definitely lose his deer. "I'm fine with leaving now," she repeated.

"Are you trying to spoil my victory?" he asked, and before she answered, he said, "I wanted you to experience a real hunt."

"I ..." She started to speak, but he turned away.

The cell phone rang. Clay handed his phone to Luke.

Luke told the butcher about his kill. Then he seemed to be agreeing with the man on the other end.

"What'd he say?" Clay asked.

"The butcher said it was best to get the deer to him as soon as possible, but he really didn't want to open on Sunday morning because of church. Then he agreed 'cause he said if there was too much time, then the meat wouldn't be good."

"Luke, you'll still owe for the entire weekend if you leave early," Thomas said.

"Let me think it over. I really want to take her out on a hunt, but if I do, then it would be too late to drive home tonight," Luke said, as though she weren't standing right there.

"I told you that I'm fine without going on a hunt."

"Well, this isn't my first kill, and there will be other hunts," Luke said smugly. "I'm showering, and then I'll decide."

She followed him to the bedroom. She knew if she told him what she'd overheard, there'd be a horrific confrontation. Instead, she decided she had to convince him it was okay to leave. She smiled at him. "I'm so proud of you for shooting the deer, and I'm going to find out how to cook it."

"It was amazing," he said. "I'll tell you all about it."

"I'd rather hear you describe it than see it," she said.

"I get it," he said. "I thought you'd be into it, but I guess there was no point in bringing you."

He showered, dressed, and threw his bloodied hunting clothes into the bag with his clean clothes. Then he grabbed his bag and went out to help Clay and Thomas position the deer atop his truck and tie it down.

Alex finished packing, checked the bathroom and bedroom, and offered the leftovers to Clay and Thomas.

"Alex, we'll see you next year," Thomas said.

"Right," Clay said, seemingly aware of the improbability.

While they drove, Luke recounted the hunt in minute detail. He looked over at her triumphantly. "How much venison do you want?"

"I'd rather have a hamburger about now," she said.

"I was going to drive straight through to get to the butcher," he said.

"It's a twelve-hour drive," she said. "Is the butcher going to open in the middle of the night?"

"He said to call the minute I get in, and I want my daughters and grandson to see the deer before I take it to be butchered."

"Luke, you're going to wake them up to see the dead deer?"

"Of course. Some people are more appreciative of the skill it takes." He pulled up to Rocky's Diner and circled the parking lot twice.

"There's a spot." Alex pointed to an empty space.

"I need to be in front," he said. "I gotta keep an eye on the deer."

"Luke, it's dead. It's not going anywhere."

"You'd be flat-out amazed at what hunters do when they don't get their own deer," he said.

She knew he was right.

Finally, he found a spot near the front. They entered the diner and made their way to a booth with a good view of the truck.

A waitress followed, handed them menus, and said she'd be back in a few minutes.

Alex looked at the menu and then absently glanced at their reflection in the window of the diner. She and Luke were in the foreground and the dead deer, strapped to the truck, was in the background. She stared at this picture of herself with the hunter and his kill and wondered, *into whose life have I trespassed?*

CHAPTER 37

Ever since the trip, she'd been reluctant to see Luke. She hadn't even gone to the tennis club. He'd called repeatedly and insisted on coming over, but she put him off. She promised to see him tonight, after discussing the trip with her First Friday Book Club women. Then she'd decide what she wanted to do about their relationship.

Several minutes late for the November First Friday Book Club meeting, Alex rushed to their usual table at Waters Restaurant. She sank into the chair between Judi and Terrie.

"It's Annie Oakley," Meredith said, quickly setting aside a stack of papers.

Wearing her usual sixties outfit: peasant blouse, macramé belt, and black skirt that was probably too long, Terrie smiled at Alex. "I ordered for you, dear."

"So, how was the hunting trip?" Judi asked, seemingly uninterested.

Alex decided she'd give them as little information as possible about the deer hunt. They certainly wouldn't be interested in such a masculine sport. "Luke bagged a deer," she said.

"What's bagging a deer?" Judi asked with apparent disdain.

"He killed a deer," Alex said, trying to sound blasé in front of her friends.

273

Terrie tugged at the right sleeve of her peasant blouse, as though insulating herself from the prospect of killing. "He actually shot something?"

"That's the general idea of hunting," Alex said, repeating Luke's words.

Tapping her Million Dollar Red nails against her water glass, Judi said, "That must have been fun. I mean, alone in a cabin in the woods. Romantic?"

"Luke's two friends were really nice—well, one was," Alex said.

"You stayed in a cabin with three men?" Meredith flipped back her mane of black hair.

"We had two bedrooms," Alex said.

"Oh, that makes everything perfect." Meredith pursed her lips. "Who'd want to go with a group of hunters? It's the Ritz or nothing for *moi.*"

"I don't think he asked you," Terrie said, obviously unable to resist a dig at Meredith.

"Where's Liz?" Judi interrupted.

"Liz said she was going to be late," Alex said, suddenly sensing an undercurrent of tension that was clearly directed at her. She and Liz had already discussed the hunting trip. Liz said it had been an interesting experience for Alex but it was time to move on.

Their waitress delivered several plates of Chinese chicken salad for everyone, even Terrie.

Terrie reached for *The Pilot's Wife.* "Let's discuss the book."

Looking from one to the other, Alex said, "We never actually talk about the book. I mean, we usually wait until after lunch."

Meredith folded her arms across her chest. "Let's have Terrie, our resident psychologist, give us her opinion on how the pilot could have had one family in the U.S. and another one in

England. And please tell us how both of the women could have been so naïve that they didn't suspect anything."

"The pilot was able to compartmentalize so well that his behavior didn't arouse suspicion in either woman." Terrie glanced down at her salad, a deviation from her usual hamburger. "I've seen it often."

"One of the wives had to have sensed something." Judi raised her eyebrows.

"Without a doubt," Alex said, studying Judi. Now she was certain Judi had known about Gabe's affair all along but had never said anything to her. Alex had always vacillated about whether she could trust Judi. She'd always known Judi's loyalty was to the physicians at the hospital where both her husband and Gabe practiced, but at her daughter's wedding, she'd seemed so inclusive, accepting of Alex.

"Most women intuit their husbands are having an affair," Terrie said.

Meredith pursed her lips. "And they get rid of the bastards."

"Women don't always want to admit the truth," Terrie said. "If they face the truth, then their lives change. People are usually more terrified of the unknown than the known, no matter how awful it might be."

Alex rubbed her wrist. "I didn't suspect anything with Gabe until Las Vegas."

"We're not talking about Gabe." Meredith picked up the stack of stapled papers and handed them to Alex. "You need to see these."

Alex accepted the documents from Meredith and read: *The Trust Deed for 5 Calle Santa Maria, Fountain Valley, California, Cora and Luke Jackson, a married couple.* Her stomach bottomed out. The room whirled. "What's going on?" she asked in a faint voice.

"I was worried about some of the things you said about Luke." Meredith took a deep breath then blotted her lips. "As I was reading *The Pilot's Wife,* I was struck by similarities between the pilot and Luke."

"What do you mean?" Alex rubbed her wrist again.

"Meredith is explaining how Luke seemed like the pilot," Terrie said. "You know, compartmentalized and able to move between diverse environments with ease."

Judi nodded. "I thought it odd how Luke seemed comfortable at the wedding; I mean a plumber with all of the physicians."

Meredith pointed to the trust deed. "Luke seemed as though he was playing a role. There was something off. So I decided to do a little research."

Rushing to the table, Liz almost bumped into the waitress. "Sorry, I had a CE course, and it ran over."

"CE?" Judi asked.

"Continuing education," Liz said. "What are we talking about?"

"Meredith just gave us a document that proves Luke's married. He *and* his wife bought the house a year ago." Alex looked at the property deed again. "Apparently, they were still married one year ago, and Luke told me they'd been divorced for years."

"The perks of having a real estate attorney for a friend," Liz said, giving Alex a hug and then sitting down opposite her.

"How could he have lied?" Alex asked.

"I have trouble keeping up with my one life, let alone juggling two," Liz said.

"Tennis, hunting, and sex—those activities put him in the moment. He didn't have to think about anything except the target," Terrie said. "The adrenaline kept him going."

"All the evidence was there." Judi tapped her glass.

"I guess I wasn't looking," Alex admitted.

"If you think about it, I'm sure Luke gave you just enough information about his life to keep you from suspecting anything," Terrie said. "A pathological liar is usually very clever."

"Luke did give me bits and pieces about his family," Alex said, anger rising.

Terrie shook her head. "With pathological liars, all the pieces of the puzzle are a jumble of unconnected images, but if you take the time to assemble enough of the pieces, a picture emerges. If you look carefully enough, you see that the lies are sometimes contradictory."

Anger overtook Alex. "Well, Luke's history."

"Not so fast, Alex. You'll need to be very, very careful. When controlling men don't get what they want, they can be unpredictable—even dangerous." Terrie stabbed at the last two chunks of lettuce on her plate with obvious disdain, clearly missing her usual hamburger. "I've seen it too many times. The women get restraining orders, but the orders are meaningless." She took a breath. "The women are often ... um ... harmed."

Recalling Clay's story about how kind Luke was to the teenage girl and how he refused to take advantage of her, Alex shook her head. "I don't think Luke would hurt me."

"Don't be foolish," Meredith warned.

Liz scowled and crossed her arms. "Alex, don't you get what Terrie is cautioning you about?"

Alex pushed aside her nearly full plate, her mind whirling. She thought of the way Luke gutted that deer and had to admit there was a side of him that could be dangerous. She had to end the relationship, but Clay had warned her about disappointing Luke. She was going to careful, very careful.

"I also checked on Mr. Luke Jackson's franchise," Meredith said. "He's a lowly technician—I mean journeyman. They work under the men in the company, the ones who have the licenses."

"No," Alex shouted.

"Come on," Judi said. "Did you really think he was more than that?"

"He could have been the owner of a company," Terrie said. "Just because he is black doesn't mean that—"

"Bi-racial," Alex whispered, tears filling her eyes.

"Luke's lying about being married is a little more critical than his lying about owning a company." Liz reached across the table and touched Alex's hand.

Alex grabbed her purse and took out money for lunch and a tip. "Thank you for finding this out about Luke. I've gotta run to the office and treat patients before my appointment with Dr. Weisbarth, the forensic sleaze who Gabe hired. And today—well, on every visit—I have to convince him that I'm normal!" She laughed. "This really hasn't helped."

"Not true," Terrie said. "Look at the way you reacted to Luke's betrayal. You're ready to break up right away, but with Gabe, you were submissive."

"Maybe Luke's just for practice," Meredith said. "You know, learning until the right one comes along."

"Meredith, men are not just stepping stones," Terrie said.

"Wanna bet?" Meredith smirked. "'Trade up' is my motto."

"I'll keep that in mind," Alex said. "Let's see, what's the next step in a relationship with a married man?"

"This isn't about men." Terrie leaned over and hugged Alex. "This is about you. You have grown, and we're not going to let you go back to the Alex who allowed Gabe, and then Luke, to walk all over you."

Alex looked appreciatively at her First Friday Book Club women. "I'm so lucky to have you all in my life."

"Gotta stop before I mess my makeup." Meredith blotted her eyes, makeup still perfect.

Alex looked at each of the women seated at the table and felt safe, safer than she'd ever felt in her life. These women were her family. Her mother had died years ago. After her mother's death, her father had moved to Florida to be with Robert, his lover. She and her father had spoken every few days until he'd passed away two years ago. Her sister had her own struggles as a single woman in New York. It was Alex who initiated contact with her sister, and that was infrequent and strained. She'd never discuss any of her problems with her sister, who had enough problems of her own.

Terrie motioned for everyone to join hands.

Alex thought the joining of hands was a little much, but she reluctantly grasped hands with Judi and Terrie and waited for Terrie's pronouncement.

"We, the First Friday Book Club women, vow to not only read a novel a month, but also to be each other's mirror," Terrie said and triumphantly held up her hand that was clasped to Alex's.

Meredith pursed her lips. "A lot of good that does when I keep holding up a mirror to you, and you refuse to let me help with makeup."

"You know it's not about looks," Liz said as they let go of each other's hands.

"It was levity," Meredith said. "I get that way when things get really heavy."

Liz pointed a finger at Alex. "And, I repeat, you are not going to allow any man to overpower you. Not just Luke, but Gabe, also."

Alex felt her heart swell with gratitude. With this incredible community behind her, she knew she could do anything.

CHAPTER 38

A s Alex approached Dr. Weisbarth's office, her stomach churned. She was determined to convince him she was not the woman Gabe had portrayed in his attempt to steal their children. She was certain Dr. Weisbarth couldn't really think she posed a danger to the children. But she still wondered why Gabe wanted the boys so desperately. She wondered whether Gabe really thought she'd turn the boys against him, just like Dr. Townsend's wife had done.

There was also the possibility that Gabe didn't want to give her the agreed-upon monthly child support and had decided he'd rather have control of the boys' financial and other needs. But it could also be due to his desire to assuage his guilt about his infidelity. If he proved she was unstable, an unfit mother, then he'd be the one who was the perfect parent, the one who saved the children from their imperfect mother.

She decided Gabe's motivation wasn't important. She had to show Dr. Weisbarth how much her children needed her and how much she loved them. And after the First Friday Book Club meeting, she felt strong. She settled into a chair and stared at the sky-blue swirls on the sea-foam-green carpet, perfectly coordinated with the green-and-blue-tweed chairs.

The tall, imposing psychiatrist stepped into the waiting room. "Ms. Rose, how are you?"

"Fine, thank you," Alex said. "How are you?"

Without responding, he led the way to his office. She followed and sat down in the chair opposite his desk.

"Ms. Rose, tell me a little about yourself, please." He looked down at his desk.

"It's still Dr. Rose," she said softly. "Some things don't change in two weeks."

"Of course. Now, let's talk about your childhood."

"It was normal," she said.

"How so?"

"My mother stayed home, and my father worked as a contractor." *As normal a household as a homosexual dad and an obese, agoraphobic mother could create,* she thought.

"Parents aren't always perfect," Dr. Weisbarth said. "They have quirks that we overlook, but those quirks can severely impact a child." He shook his head and wrote a note.

Alex waited.

"Any siblings?" he asked.

"A sister."

"Do you have a good relationship with her?"

"Yes," she said, hoping he wouldn't probe. Then she'd have to tell him her sister was a recluse. She had a menial job at a call center where she sat in a cubicle and never had any face-to-face interactions with the customers. And as far as Alex knew, her sister didn't even socialize with any of her co-workers. She just went home after work and read romance novels. Alex feared any information about her sister would fortify Gabe's picture of her family as unstable. But then again, Gabe had probably told Dr. Weisbarth every detail about her unsavory upbringing.

"I see." He made another note. "And what else can you tell me about yourself?"

"I want my boys," Alex said.

"Why?" he asked, meeting her gaze. *That*, she thought, *is a stupid question*, but she remained calm and explained, "I'm their mother, and I want my boys more than life."

"We don't have to go over the incident with Jonathan," Dr. Weisbarth said. "Alexandra ... may I call you Alexandra?"

"I prefer Alex." She didn't want to be called Alexandra. Alexandra was the little girl who was terrified of her mother and feared people who threatened her. Most of all, Alexandra was the little girl who'd been taught she was unworthy of love unless it was wrapped in anger. For that little girl, love only came as a reward for enduring pain at the hands of her mother and keeping family secrets. Alex was a strong name, and that was the woman she needed to be.

"And how will you manage to take care of the boys with your work schedule?"

"Like any single mother."

"I see," Dr. Weisbarth said with what she was sure was sarcasm.

"The bottom line is my boys come first. I've always balanced work with their schedules. If I need to hire a housekeeper, then I will."

"What about a significant other?" he asked and waited.

"I had a boyfriend, but I've ended the relationship." *Well*, she thought, *not quite, but before the day ends, Luke will be history.*

"Really?" Dr. Weisbarth seemed surprised. "You're no longer with him?"

She shook her head, wondering what Gabe had told him about Luke.

"Tell me about him anyway."

"He never stays overnight," she said, sounding defensive.

"Why do you consider that an issue? I mean, the boys aren't there at night, are they?"

"The boys don't stay over," Alex agreed.

Dr. Weisbarth pressed his palms together. "Why don't you tell me about that relationship?"

She hesitated, uncertain about what to say. *Talking about Luke is pointless. This is about my competence as a mother,* she thought with renewed fury.

"Alexandra ... Alex ... sorry, are you okay?"

"Yes. I was thinking."

"I see." He wrote on his pad.

"Gabe shocked me with the divorce. He moved out of our home and went to live with his girlfriend. Obviously, they'd been having an affair. Then he transformed my accidental spilling of water into a legal debacle in order to claim custody of our children."

"I believe it was boiling water," he said, his expression remaining enigmatic.

"I never harmed my children. I'm a good mother. That is what you need to know," she said and thought she saw Dr. Weisbarth nod empathetically. She was also sure she saw him give her an understanding wink. *Did it happen? Or am I just wishing this man who will determine my fate is showing compassion?*

He looked at his watch. "Yes, that's all I need from you. If I have to schedule another private session with you, I'll let you know." He stood up. "And how was your trip? Hunting, I believe."

"Good," she said.

"I'll see you in four weeks for the family session."

The words "family session" made her hungry—hungry for her old life. Her reality could never be meaningless sex with a man who tied a dead deer to the top of his truck. Her reality was children, PTA meetings, football practices, and helping patients. Initially, she'd been drawn to Luke because he'd reassured her of the sexuality she thought she'd lost forever. The touch of his body was like a medicinal herb: she'd feel relief for a while, but after they'd had each other, her emptiness would return.

Fortified by the camaraderie of a group of loving women, Alex was no longer willing to accept the morsels Luke, Gabe, or any other man offered. She would make it on her own with the love of her children and the support of the women of the First Friday Book Club.

CHAPTER 39

A lex entered the house, threw the property deed on the coffee table in the family room, and ran upstairs to shower and change into jeans.

Luke rang the doorbell, and she reluctantly unlocked the top bolt and opened the door.

"This is for going with me on the hunt," he said and handed her a bouquet of pink roses.

She looked at the flowers and refused to accept them. "I don't want anything from you. We're done."

"Why?" he demanded. Then, without waiting for her to answer, he shook her. "I get it. It's that doctor from your Mexico thing, isn't it? Did he contact you?" He let go of her, slammed the door closed behind him with his free hand, and walked past her. "I should never have let you go. I should've stood guard, protected my property."

"It has nothing to do with David," she said.

"David," he said and glared at her. "I knew it was another man!"

Cognizant of Terrie's cautionary words, Alex softly protested, "I haven't even spoken to him since the trip to Mexico. The woman who does the scheduling called and asked me to go, but I refused."

"The minute I saw the look in your eyes when you opened the door, I knew." He clutched the flowers, choking the stems. "I can stand up to any man."

"There's no other man," she said, determined to stay strong. She had to end the relationship, now.

He hurled the bouquet onto the floor. "You're lying."

Alex folded her hands across her chest, straightened her back defiantly, and said, "I don't lie."

He laughed, an ugly laugh that echoed in the vestibule. "In my next life, I'm going to be a rich white man. Maybe even a doctor."

"This has nothing to do with how you earn a living," Alex insisted.

"It has everything to do with who I am!" he shouted. "Alex, I had hoped you were different, but I always suspected you'd betray me."

"Stop yelling! You're the one who is guilty of betrayal, not me." She strode into the family room, scooped up the property deed, and then returned to the vestibule. "Here." She slapped the stapled pages into his hand. "It has to do with this."

He took the document, glanced down, and then tossed it onto the vestibule table. "My ex-wife co-signed on the house for me. What's the issue?"

"Look at the date. It says, 'a married man and a married woman.' I will not date a married man. And if Gabe's attorney finds out, it'll discredit me."

"Gabe, Gabe, Gabe. Do I care?" He reached out, grabbed her, and pulled her to him.

"I do." She freed herself and rushed to the door. She reached for the doorknob and flung open the front door. "Leave, and don't come back."

"Alex, you're making a mistake." He put his hands on her shoulders and tightened his grip.

With his fingers digging into her and his tone threatening, she was terrified. She steadied herself. "You lied about everything. Gabe's attorney could twist this too."

"Gabe wouldn't care," he said.

"Right." She looked at him. "How could you possibly know what Gabe would do?" She almost laughed at the absurdity of Luke giving her advice about Gabe. They were worlds apart.

He pushed her chin up and looked into her eyes. "Why are you fixated on that piece of paper? I'm telling you the truth."

She backed away and grabbed the property deed. "This is the truth: print on a page, the truth in black and white."

He glared at her. "Where'd you get it?" he demanded.

"Meredith."

"Bitch," he hissed.

She felt his anger blossom into a living, breathing thing. She stood her ground. "Please leave."

"I don't intend on losing you," he said, his words those of a man capable of doing great harm to an adversary. Then he smiled, and the light played on his face.

Repulsed, she stared at his bright, too-pink bridge that clashed with the purple-pink of his gums as though seeing it for the first time. "Luke, you've already lost me."

"You're all the same. My hunting friends weren't high-class enough for you. And your friends think they're so high and mighty just because they have money. Your friend Meredith is whacked-out. With her shopping crap and her Siamese, she's one strange lady. Her boyfriend—Warren, or whatever his name is—he's in for it. I couldn't believe the way he looked at her at the wedding, like she's something special."

"Men love Meredith," she said, reflexively defending her friend.

"Not this one. And the other one—what was her name? Liz, yeah. She was studying me. Don't cross her. I'll tell you that."

"Liz is my best friend."

"Alex, you're just like your friends, with the exception of Terrie and her husband—they're good people. I could tell that. And Judi. Oh, she smiles and couldn't be more polite, but I'm sure she had a lot to say about me."

"This has nothing to do with my friends," she said, staying focused, holding her ground.

"It has everything to do with what your precious friends said about me. I could just hear them say, 'Poor Alex couldn't get a date, so she had to take that Luke guy.'"

"No, they didn't say anything about you," she lied.

As though not hearing her, he continued. "My friends are solid men."

"Luke, you've been lying to me. You don't even own the company."

"Why did you check on my company? Tell me right now."

"Meredith found that information. You lied about that too. I'm done."

"This isn't over," he said, his face contorting into the same expression she'd seen when he'd gutted the deer—that glint in his eyes. He strode past her and out the front door.

Alex had been certain he'd look at the mortgage papers, ask her not to say anything at the club, and then just leave. But Terrie was right: a hunter wouldn't leave his prey until the kill. She clutched the doorframe, feeling almost paralyzed. Then she locked the door, went to the family room, and slumped down onto the couch.

After what seemed like hours, she got up and checked every door and window. She crawled into bed but was unable to sleep. There'd been something eerie in Luke's expression when he'd left. As she watched the numbers change on the clock, she feared he might return.

At 3:00 a.m., the sound of the doorbell sliced through the silence of her bedroom.

She didn't answer.

Her heart raced as the chiming continued.

Then the ringing abruptly stopped. She sank back against the pillows, her gaze sweeping over the closed blinds that covered the sliding glass doors to her balcony. She often left them open, but tonight, she'd closed them and secured the bolt into the slider.

A few minutes later, there was a clank outside on the balcony, then a thud, followed by a fist pounding on the glass door.

"Let me in," Luke demanded, his voice a raspy whisper.

Alex slipped out of bed and went to the glass doors. "How'd you get up there?" she asked.

"My ladder's always in my truck. Now, open up!" he shouted. "We need to talk."

"It's after three o'clock in the morning. Go away." She panicked. If her backyard neighbors saw a man on her balcony trying to open the door, they'd summon the police. She couldn't take a chance on a police report before the custody hearing.

"I'll wait here until you open the door," he said.

Heart thumping, she slid back the security bolt on the glass door, raised the blinds, and unlocked the slider, all the while praying she wasn't making a fatal mistake.

He walked into her bedroom, turned, and locked the door behind him.

Smelling liquor on his breath, she backed away. She sat down on the edge of her bed and stared at the man who'd been her lover, unsure of the next step in their turbulent dance.

"Get me a drink," he demanded, his presence overpowering her bedroom.

"You've had enough booze tonight."

He surged forward and grabbed her, jerking her to her feet. "You're the one I want."

"No!" She tried to move away, but his grasp tightened.

"You don't know what love is." He pulled her to him.

"Yes, I do, and this isn't it. We're finished."

"You're wrong. It's you who'll be finished if ..." He looked at her with raw anger and then grabbed her. She lost her balance. Wondering whether he'd pushed her or she'd fallen, she landed hard on her back. Reality, she knew, always twisted events like that. She got up.

As she scrambled away, Luke caught her. "You're mine, so get used to it," he shouted.

"Never!" She pulled away.

He jerked up her nightgown. "I want what's mine."

"I'm not yours." She spat out the words as she fought his overpowering strength.

"I will have you." He raised his hand to her and then stopped just short of delivering an open-handed blow to her face.

Alex waited, too terrified to move.

"I'm going to let you off this one time, but ... I'm warning you." He twisted her arm, then let go. "This time," he said. Then he turned, walked out of her bedroom, and went back to the balcony.

Alex rushed to lock it.

"Alexandra, listen to me very carefully," he yelled to her from outside the closed balcony door. "If I can't have you, no one will."

CHAPTER 40

At 4:00 a.m., Alex called Liz. Within fifteen minutes, Liz arrived at her house and insisted they go directly to the Brea Police Department. Alex refused, explaining she'd lose the custody battle if Gabe found out. She was certain he'd use the information as fodder and claim a woman who couldn't take care of herself certainly couldn't take care of her children.

"We're talking about someone threatening your life," Liz insisted.

"My children are more important. Without them, I have no life."

"Alex, we'll just go to the police and talk to them."

They went to the Brea Police Department, a sterile public building. As Liz pressed the buzzer, Alex cringed. She was certain this was a mistake.

The officer on duty asked what they wanted. Liz looked directly into the screen and explained they had an incident to report. The police officer buzzed, and the door unlocked.

Alex and Liz walked into the station and up to the reception desk.

"How can I help you?" the officer asked.

Alex stared at his badge—Sergeant John Collins—and said, "I'm here to discuss an incident, but I don't want to file a report. My boyfriend—I mean, former..." She sobbed.

Sergeant Collins looked at her and asked, "Was there a rape or any other act of physical violence?" Before she could answer, he asked, "And were you hurt?"

"He made horrible threats," Alex said.

And within an instant, the sergeant's expression changed from empathy to apathy. "Threats are just that," he said and leaned down and produced a piece of paper. He handed the paper to Alex. "Take it home and fill it out, or fill it out now," he said. "Then I'll look at it and give it to the officer in charge."

"Can't we talk to the officer in charge?" Liz asked.

"First, you have to go over everything with me," Sergeant Collins said. "And then I'll talk to him."

Upon Liz's prompting, Alex explained how Luke had threatened her and told her, "If I can't have you, no one will."

"That's from a movie, *Enough.*" Sergeant Collins rolled his eyes. "It was just on television."

Annoyed at the sergeant's dismissal, Alex was certain Luke's threats were real. She'd seen the glint in his eyes. He wasn't just mimicking a movie. "Aren't you going to let us talk to the officer in charge?" she asked.

"I'll go check." Sergeant Collins got up and went to the back.

Alex took a seat in the waiting room, which was just a row of chairs facing the reception desk. She started to fill out the paper. Liz put on her glasses, leaned over Alex's shoulder, and read the form along with her.

Sergeant Collins returned. "You can fill out the paperwork. After the officer in charge reviews the report, he'll dispatch an officer to the perpetrator's house to talk to him."

"If he talks to Luke, then he could hurt me. I'll need a restraining order, but ..."

"Why don't you just take the form home and think about it. Bring it back when you're ready," Sergeant Collins said, his lack of interest apparent.

"No, you're filling it out now," Liz said.

"But if the police go to Luke's house, he'll definitely come after me."

"Alex, you can stay with us. You can't let him get away with this."

The sergeant interceded. "It's usually a good idea to have an initial complaint. That way, if he does anything else, we have the record. Also, when a police officer talks to the perpetrator, the guy often gets scared and stops. Unless ..."

"Unless what?" Alex asked.

"You've got to protect yourself," Liz said.

The police officer started to explain, "But sometimes—"

"Fill it out," Liz repeated.

As soon as Alex completed the report and handed it to Sergeant Collins, she knew it would only be a matter of time before Luke would confront her; however, she had to make sure he faced the consequences of his threats.

◆◆◆

At ten o'clock the next night, her phone rang.

"What the hell did you do?" Luke yelled over the telephone. "An officer came to my house. I was embarrassed in front of my daughters and grandson."

"Luke, you terrified me," she said, trying to steady her voice.

"You will pay for this. Don't you know police officers stick together? It's like the Marines. I called my nephew who is a police officer."

"If you were embarrassed in front of your daughters and grandson, why would you then call your nephew?"

"He's a police officer in Compton, where, believe me, they have more to worry about than a little white lady who concocted a story about a black guy she dated a few times. She wanted to have sex with him, but he refused. And because he refused, she made up a story and reported him to the police."

"That's not what happened," she said.

"You try explaining that while you're involved in a custody case because you burned your son."

"I didn't burn my son—intentionally, I mean." She couldn't let this—or anything—destroy her credibility, make her look incapable of protecting her children.

"Well, now my nephew is going to help me. He's already spoken to the officer in Brea, and believe me, the police won't be bothering me anymore." He slammed the phone down.

She tossed and turned the entire night, fearful of his anger. Anger, she knew, always had wings.

CHAPTER 41

"Alex, what's the matter with you?" Seth asked when he picked her up for Eric's football game.

"Nothing," she lied. She wasn't ready to tell him about the other night—about how she'd seen the underbelly of love and lust and feared them both.

"Come on," he prompted. "You can talk to me."

"I will, but not right now." She knew he'd want to protect her, but he was no match for a powerful hunter like Luke. She'd never do anything to harm Seth, and she couldn't risk any interference with the practice—her only safe haven.

"Alex, remember you asked me if I knew about Silver Cloud? Well, there is such a place, and it's in Whitefish Lake."

"No." Alex gasped. The probability that Gabe had gone there was spinning closer to reality. *Had she been so in love with Gabe that she didn't question anything he said or did?*

Seth touched her arm, gently, caringly. "It's amazing how the files are organized by the date of the patients' initial evaluations. When the patients arrive, they each select a pseudonym. No one uses his real name."

"Seth, who cares about how they operate? You're always into the details. I want to know whether Gabe went there." That was the one thing about Seth that irked her: everything had to be in order. That was the way he insisted on running the practice, but it worked there.

"As I said, they use pseudonyms only, and the file numbers are the dates when the physicians enter the clinic. Very clever system."

"What if more than one person enters on a given day?" Alex asked, trying to grasp onto the facts. Maybe if she found inconsistencies, impossibilities, then she wouldn't have to accept the truth, and it was the truth she feared.

"They only accept one person a day, so we have to find out the exact date Gabe entered."

"I might be able to go to the bank and get the cancelled checks," Alex said.

"Cash." Seth shook his head.

"How do you know?"

"My brother, the gastroenterologist, has been investigating this from the moment you asked whether I knew about Silver Cloud."

Disappointed that Seth hadn't found anything, she knew he always tried to help her. That's why she couldn't tell him about all the terrible things Luke had done. He would ferret out everything about Luke and then want to confront him. Seth wouldn't understand how the policemen's brotherhood took precedence over the truth. He always acted as though honesty and justice would prevail, but Alex knew it was money and power that prevailed.

"Honesty can be bought," she said.

Seth didn't agree. She knew his belief was from his life as a university professor before becoming a chiropractor. He'd refused to face the fact that, outside of the university environment, life was real, and people rarely played fair.

As they got out of his car, Alex thanked Seth for trying. They walked to the bleachers and took their seats.

"Alex, are you okay about the Silver Cloud thing?" he asked.

"Now I'm sure Gabe did—or is doing—drugs. And drugs can make people do crazy things. They even think they can get away with anything." She rubbed her wrist. "I can't believe I never even suspected anything with Gabe."

"You couldn't have known." Seth put his arm around her.

"Of course I could have. I mean, he went away for several weeks, and I believed it was a seminar. He was in a detox program. Now, I'm sure of that." She fought back tears. "Before he went, he was irritable, but when he came home, he was a changed person. Oh, how could I have ignored everything?"

"Don't be so hard on yourself. You were in love."

"And blind," Alex said. Suddenly, she looked to the right and saw Gabe. "Is he coming over here?" she asked as her gut tensed.

"Looks like it to me," Seth said.

Gabe walked up to her, hands folded across his chest, his beige suede jacket gaping open over his stomach. He smiled, that Gabe smile, the one without parting his lips, the one he used when he really didn't mean to smile. "Alex, can I talk to you alone?" he asked.

"I have no secrets from Seth," she said. She wasn't going to let Gabe bully her again. Accustomed as she'd been to reflexively responding to his requests in the past, now she was going to tell him what she wanted and act on it—even if it was something as insignificant as insisting he talk to her in front of Seth. It was a start.

"Thanksgiving's coming up." Gabe tugged at his jacket, trying to close it.

"So?" she said, marveling at how easily the calendar continued uninterrupted, even after their marriage had ended.

"I've decided to allow you to see the boys during the holiday."

How magnanimous, she thought sourly. "Great. I'll take them for the Thanksgiving weekend."

"No, just Thanksgiving day," Gabe said in a harsh voice.

"Why not the entire weekend?"

He arched his eyebrows. "Don't push it, Alexandra, or you won't see them at all. This is an act of kindness."

"Why?" she asked, uncharacteristically challenging him.

"Linda's family is having dinner at her mother's, and I thought, for your sake, it would be nice to allow you to have them."

"Doesn't Linda's family want them?" she asked.

"Forget it," Gabe said and started to turn away.

"Wait," Seth interjected. "Alex and the boys will be my guests for Thanksgiving."

"Someone has to keep an eye on her." Gabe turned and made his way down the bleachers.

"Don't." Seth gently put his hand on her arm as she started to get up. "Thanksgiving will be perfect."

◆ ◆ ◆

Spatula in hand, Seth opened the door and welcomed her into his pristine condo overlooking the ocean. With the sun streaming into the condo and the smell of turkey baking, she felt tranquil for the first time in months. She walked to the balcony.

Seth turned her around to face him. "I'm worried about you."

"No need, I'm fine," she said, attempting to reassure him, even though he probably knew she was lying. "We have to pick up the boys in a half hour."

"Let me check the turkey, and then we'll leave," Seth said.

She followed him to the granite island in his stainless-steel-and-white kitchen. From the kitchen, she surveyed the artfully set dining table: silverware placed in perfect order, dishes and napkins beautiful. Norman Rockwell America beautiful.

Seth insisted on driving, stating that she was his guest and had to relax today. He transferred Jon's car seat to his car, and they went to pick up the boys. As soon as Alex and Seth pulled up to Gabe's house, the boys stopped kicking the soccer ball across the manicured lawn and climbed into the car.

On the way back to Seth's house, Eric and Daniel argued over who kicked the ball farther. Alex tried to erase the picture of the boys' perfect home, perfect family, perfect life.

"Be good," she whispered as they boys got out of the car and started to run to Seth's condominium. Once inside, they immediately rushed to the patio to look at the ocean.

"We can walk on the beach after dinner," Seth promised. "Dinner's ready."

As Alex looked at her boys seated around the table in Seth's high-back caramel leather chairs and smelled the fragrant turkey wafting through the air, her heart swelled with love. The boys were the most wonderful part of her. She smiled and was transported back to a time when her identity as a good mother remained unquestioned.

"Does anyone know why we celebrate Thanksgiving?" Seth asked, his tone soft yet professorial.

"I do," Daniel said. "In 1620, the Pilgrims came to America to escape religious tyranny. We're thankful they landed in the colonies."

Seth smiled kindly.

"Can I have the money for my shoes?" Jon asked.

Eric rolled his eyes. "What's he talking about now?"

"Mommy told me about the colony days." Jon glanced at her. "You know, the right foot and the left."

"Doofus," Eric said.

"He's correct," Seth said. "In colonial times, both the right and left shoes were the same, and, until the shoes molded to their feet, they'd put a penny in the right shoe to differentiate it from the left."

"See," Jon said. "I remembered."

Seth winked at Jon. "Here's a quarter. Be sure to put it in the right one."

"Thanks." Jon took the quarter and smirked at Eric.

Alex nodded and smiled, appreciative of how adeptly Seth interacted with her boys.

"Can I get money for the other shoe?" Jon asked.

They all laughed—a warm laugh, thanks to Seth's lead.

After devouring the turkey, mashed potatoes, creamed spinach, and cranberry sauce, they walked along the beach. Pant cuffs drenched, they threw a Frisbee until it grew dark. Then all three boys climbed into the backseat of Seth's Volvo.

As Seth passed the pillars at the entryway to Gabe's, or rather Linda's, circular driveway, the sensor lights came on. *Gabe is living our dream without me,* she thought as she stared at the pillars of perfection at the front of the house.

Seth went up to the door, rang the bell, and waited for the housekeeper to open the imposing, sixteen-foot-high door.

"All out," Alex said and opened the back door.

"My belly hurts 'cause I eated too much," Jon announced, a crooked grin on his face.

"Let me kiss it." She lifted his shirt and planted a noisy tummy kiss.

Throwing his arms around her, Jon said, "Mommy, I wanna stay with you."

"I know, Cookie Face, but this is the way it is now." She didn't trust herself to say much more without dissolving into tears.

Then she hugged each of the boys. "Love you," she called after the boys as she watched them enter the house.

Alex and Seth returned to his condo.

"Like to come up for an aperitif?" he asked.

Unwilling to let go of the day, Alex nodded. "Sounds good, but then I have to head home."

He reached for her hand to help her out of the car. She took it, savoring the gentle power of his grasp.

While he poured some peach schnapps, she settled into the plush black couch beside the warm fireplace. He handed her a long-stemmed cordial glass, his fingers brushing against hers. Suddenly, she felt the setting change before her eyes from a comfortable family gathering to something else, something romantic.

He sat beside her on the couch, their shoulders touching. "Alex, we need to talk."

She turned to him and studied his face. He looked at her softly, kindly, his sky-blue eyes twinkling. In her gut, she felt he was different from every man she'd ever known, but then again, that could just have been due to the fact that he was her partner, and business had always been an easier terrain for her to navigate.

Seth glanced down at his drink. "I'm moving to Arizona to be with my children."

Stunned by the possibility that he, too, would leave her, Alex felt the familiar ache of loss. Until now, she'd never thought about his needs. "The practice needs you," she said. She really wanted to tell him *she* needed him but didn't.

"That's the reason I have to go." He spoke with care, as though placing a porcelain doll on a shelf. "The practice is the only aspect of your life where you see me."

"You're my court-appointed monitor."

"I'll wait until the custody issue is resolved." He brushed a strand of her hair back, his fingers lingering along the curve of her cheek. "I need to leave."

"Why?" she whispered. She couldn't handle the practice without him. Maybe she couldn't handle her life without him.

"Alex, I need more. The practice isn't enough."

"But we're doing so well."

"You'll have the entire practice," he said.

Shocked, she looked deep into his blue eyes. She'd thought of him only as the classmate with whom she'd gone to chiropractic college years ago and then her trustworthy business partner. But, in all the years, she'd never thought about her feelings for Seth, the man. Instead, she'd been consumed by Gabe and then Luke. She looked up at him. "Seth, I need you."

He moved close and kissed her lips.

She liked it.

He took her hand and brought it to his lips. "Let me take you out for a farewell dinner."

She withdrew her hand. "I can't."

"Alex, I don't mean to pressure you."

"That's not it," she stammered, unable to reveal the truth about Luke and the danger he posed to everyone around her.

"What is it?" Seth rubbed her back.

She looked at her watch, fearful that Luke might call. "I've got to go home."

Seth followed her to her car, transferred Jon's car seat, and opened the door for her.

As she started to slip into the driver's seat, she stopped and turned to him. He drew her into his arms, embracing her with more tenderness than she'd ever experienced. "Alex, even when I leave Orange County, I'll always be here for you. Always."

CHAPTER 42

A lex pressed the garage door opener and pulled into the garage. As she entered the house, she saw a dim light flicker within the family room. She headed in that direction, trying to remember whether she'd left the lamp on. Then she heard rustling. Suddenly, the springs of the big white chair in the family room squeaked.

She froze.

Luke grabbed her. "I know where you've been."

She stepped back. "I was with my boys," she said in the calmest voice she could manage, heeding Terrie's warning.

"At this hour?"

"How'd you get into my house?" she asked.

"Wouldn't you like to know?" He laughed. "After you started to get all uppity, I did a little research on your locks. I can get a duplicate key made very easily." He pulled her closer.

Smelling booze, she decided she had to stay one step ahead of him. He could harm her. She recalled Clay's warning about PTSD and knew that could account for his irrational behavior. "It's Thanksgiving, and I spent the afternoon and evening with my children."

"You were with Seth." He glared at her, rage in his eyes. "Did he fuck you after the boys went home?"

Stay calm, Alex told herself. "Nothing happened between us."

"Don't even think of lying." Luke shook her.

She understood his warning: *mock me or lie to me, and you'll suffer.* Ever since Luke had morphed into this monster, she'd been counting the minutes until the judge ruled on the custody case. As soon as she gained custody of the boys, she'd go to the police and proceed with a restraining order. Then she'd be finished with Luke, brotherhood or not. She'd even hire a bodyguard if necessary. Now, she needed to placate him so that nothing could besmirch her character. If she reported Luke to the police again, there was a chance Gabe's attorney would find out.

"I'll tell you how it's going to be." He pushed her down on the couch and sat next to her, not even a hair between them. "You're the one I want." He gritted his teeth and narrowed his eyes. "Now, I discover that you were out all night with him."

"It's only midnight." She wondered if she'd ever be able to make him understand the most he'd ever get from her was a pyrrhic victory, taking her without having her.

He twisted her wrist, fragile under his enormous calloused fingers. "I'm as attuned to you as a hunting dog is to his prey."

"Nothing happened," she repeated, fearful the wrong word would push her closer to danger.

"Alex, I've never let a woman reject me."

She knew he meant he wouldn't allow her to leave him. Terrified, she longed for the rhythm of life where every day was a mirror image of the preceding day—not this horrific roller coaster, first with Gabe and now with Luke. She whispered, "Please, we can work everything out in time."

He put his arm around her and pulled her to him. "Alex, I'm not a toy you can play with for a while and then toss away." He let go of her. "Pour me a drink. I need time to think. Do I help Alexandra or destroy her?"

"Alex," she whispered. She wasn't Alexandra anymore—or was she? Terrified, she went to the kitchen, picked up the phone, and started to punch in 911. She thought she heard him walk toward the kitchen. She quickly put down the phone. Trying to collect herself and plan her next move, she slowly pressed the ice button on the refrigerator door and let the ice clunk into the glass.

"What's taking you so long to mix my drink?" he called from the family room.

"One second," she said. She poured scotch and soda into the glass, returned to the den, and put his glass on the coffee table.

He grabbed the glass, drank it in two gulps, and demanded, "Let's go to the bedroom."

She remained perfectly still.

"Alex, what are you thinking of doing? Calling the police? Response time's twenty minutes. I'll be done by then. Remember, my nephew's in the force, and he knows how irrational you are. My nephew told his buddies how you sometimes get violent and force me to have sex."

"That's a lie," she said. No, she couldn't tolerate the feel of his body on hers, not tonight, not ever again. She ran to the vestibule, grabbed her keys and purse, and dashed into the garage. She got into her car and pressed the button to open the garage door. As she backed out, she caught a glimpse of Luke running out the front door to his truck. She stomped on the gas. Her car careened backward into the street, and she sped away, tires squealing.

She started to drive to Seth's but stopped. Luke would look for her there. After driving for an hour, certain Luke had not followed her, she realized she was near Knott's Berry Farm. She spotted a motel with a vacancy sign flashing in neon lights. She got a room.

She washed her face with the harsh soap, brushed her teeth with her finger, and climbed into bed. The sheets were coarse, so unlike the silk–cotton blend at the Bellagio Hotel, the place where her life had unraveled. This stark room, void of the stuff people thought defined a person, felt safe.

◆◆◆

The next morning, Alex called a security specialist to have an alarm system installed. Even though it was the Friday after Thanksgiving, when she told them she was in danger, they agreed to send out a technician immediately.

By the end of the day, the technician had installed the alarm, placed the signs on all of her doors and windows, and explained how safe she'd be with the alarm that went directly to the police station.

"Safe," she repeated. Wanting to believe him, she closed all the doors and windows and waited. Luke didn't call, nor did he come to her house.

Saturday afternoon, Alex and Seth picked up the boys for their supervised visitation. Since the boys didn't have any football games scheduled on the Saturday after Thanksgiving, Alex and Seth took them to the park with the tennis courts. She couldn't chance taking them to the tennis club. The possibility of seeing Luke at the club was too terrifying.

After the park and a trip to McDonald's, it was time for the boys to return to Gabe's house. They all got into the car. With his usual ability to engage the boys, Seth asked them to come up with two rules about playing tennis that they should obey.

Daniel and Eric called out, "If you hit the other person with the ball, even by accident, then the person who hit the ball gets the point."

"Right," Seth said. "And the other one?"

"No talking," Jon said.

"Right, but it's a little more complicated than that," Seth said. "Hint: when the ball is ..."

"Yellow." Jon grinned.

"You can't talk while the ball is on the other side of the net," Daniel said.

"Excellent," Seth commended Daniel.

Alex recalled the time when Seth had told her about being afraid of the white tennis balls—the ones that don't exist anymore—and how he overcame his fears. But now it seemed she was afraid of everything, especially things that hadn't yet happened.

As they drove up the long driveway to Gabe's house, the automatic lights went on. Gabe came out to greet them.

On the ride back to Alex's house, Seth told her how much he enjoyed spending time with the boys, but it made him yearn for his children in Arizona. He told her now that his son was in little league and his daughter in ballet, it was too difficult to remain in California.

"Seth, please don't make a final decision without talking to me one more time."

He squeezed her hand. "How about dinner tomorrow?"

She agreed.

CHAPTER 43

While dressing for dinner with Seth, she reassured herself there'd be no problem going out with him. If Luke saw the signs from the alarm company on the doors and windows, it was unlikely he'd take a chance breaking in.

Just as the doorbell rang, she finished spraying her hair.

She opened the door and smiled at Seth standing on her doorstep, pristine in a pressed, light blue shirt and tan trousers. His beard was perfectly trimmed, and he looked even more well-groomed than usual—actually quite handsome.

He handed her a yellow rose. "Ready for Chat Noir?"

"Of course." She put the rose in a glass vase, locked the door, and she and Seth went to his car.

She sank into the soft leather seat and inhaled the mint-clean scent. Glancing around, she saw no sign of Luke and started to relax. They talked about the practice: how it had grown and how they'd nurtured it together. Before she could ask him to reconsider leaving, Seth immediately found a spot in front of the restaurant and parked.

They walked up to the hostess, and he announced himself. The hostess led them to a corner booth. Seth smiled approvingly, waited as she slid into the booth, and then sat down beside her.

The wine steward approached. While the steward and Seth discussed the wine selection, Alex started to panic. She knew Luke was capable of anything and wondered, *What if Luke followed us here? Would he harm us?* Assuring herself they were safe, she took the red velvet menu folder from Seth.

The waitress placed a basket of bread on the table and offered olive oil and balsamic vinegar.

"Order anything you'd like," Seth said.

Alex smiled and looked at him, almost boyish despite his sophisticated demeanor. She broke off a piece of bread and dipped it in the olive oil. "Seth, you can have a bigger percentage of the practice."

"That's not important to me. This is not a ploy to get you to offer me more. I told you, I'm going to give you the whole practice when I leave."

"Why?" she asked.

"Maybe one day you'll trust me."

"Please wait." She needed him, but before she could make any promises to him, she had to break the bonds that chained her, first to Gabe and now to Luke.

Seth reached over, took her hand, and kissed it. "Actually, I don't know how I'll be able to leave your kids."

"I'm sorry you've had to spend so much time with them with this monitoring," she said, appreciative of the way he brought out the best in them.

"Alex, I've loved it. I'll miss them terribly, and Jonathan has me wrapped around his little finger."

The waiter approached, and they both ordered.

The steak with the mushroom garnish was perfect. The soufflé was pure heaven. Conversation flowed from memories of the years they shared studying and then building their practice to her children and, finally, to how much Seth enjoyed getting to know them. Then, almost too quickly, the curtain fell on their magical evening.

Seth opened the car door for her and then went around to the driver's side. "Damn," he said.

"What happened?" She got out of the car and stood near him.

He assessed the slashed tire. "Some kids, I'm sure," he said.

"Probably," she agreed but knew it had to have been Luke.

"I've got the auto club, but I can change the tire in a few minutes."

As Seth started to remove the knife-damaged tire, she cast nervous glances up and down the street, expecting Luke's truck to round the corner.

"Alex, please go into the restaurant and wait," he said.

She agreed and went into the restaurant. Twenty-five minutes later, the spare tire securely in place, she and Seth drove away. When they reached her house, she was too afraid to let him come in, not with the metronome that was Luke threatening to destroy her with every dissonant beat.

Obviously sensing her reluctance, Seth kissed her good night and left.

She looked around the house and checked her phone. No calls from Luke. She waited. No pounding on the door. She finally fell asleep, only to be awakened by the phone ringing well before dawn.

She fumbled for the receiver and then pressed it to her ear.

"So you made it home from your date at the Chat Noir exclusive dinner establishment," Luke said.

"How do you know where I went?" she asked, confirming her suspicion that Luke had followed them and punctured Seth's tire.

"I was on my way to pay you a visit when I saw my enemy's car in front of your house. And I'll be damned, but then I saw you. You were all gussied up when you got into his car. My curiosity was up, so I just had to follow him for a little while."

"Leave me alone," she yelled. "I'll call the police."

"Do that and you'll pay. Seth has already started to pay."

"Why were you at my house?"

"Alex, Alex, don't you get it? I was outside of your house, getting ready to come in to see how you were doing with your new alarm. You know, help you out with the codes." He laughed. "Then I watched you get in his car. I can't have you going on dates."

She slammed the phone and sank back against the pillows, tasting the anger within his words.

CHAPTER 44

As Thanksgiving flowed into Christmas, Alex marked off each day on the calendar, desperate for the resolution of her custody battle. The boys went to Hawaii with Gabe and Linda, Seth was heading east to visit his children in Arizona, and the First Friday Book Club women cancelled their December meeting.

The new alarm system worked perfectly, but she still feared Luke. It had been three weeks since he'd called. His eerie silence haunted her. Strange how she felt a modicum of safety only when Luke was within view. It was like holding a live grenade for security.

After finishing her over-the-sink tuna fish dinner, she heard the doorbell ring. Certain it was Luke, she called out, "I'm not opening the door."

"Do as I say," Luke demanded, loudly enough for her to hear him through the closed front door. "Or would you rather I go to Seth's house?"

She opened the peephole and spoke through it. "Why are you involving him?"

"Seth's my enemy," he said. "I have the codes to his exclusive condo. Even *they* have plumbing problems, and they're on service with my company."

She knew Seth wasn't leaving until the morning, and she feared Luke would confront him. "Luke, you can't use business information like codes for personal reasons."

"The codes are office knowledge. I think I'll just enter Seth's complex and chat with him for a while. I want him to be scared about his fate if he continues with you."

"He has nothing to do with this," she said.

"Or maybe I should just visit Jon, your little boy."

"Gabe wouldn't let you near him."

He laughed, a harsh menacing laugh. "I'm sure I could find out where his little nursery school is located."

"No," she begged, terror short-circuiting her brain.

"Alex, I came to give you your Christmas present. I'll leave, but please open it. I'll call when I get home to see if you like it."

"I don't want any presents from you." She walked away from the door.

Relieved, she heard his truck pull away. Then she went to the door. Through the peephole, she looked down and saw a beautifully wrapped box with a huge pink ribbon.

She started to go upstairs but stopped. She decided it would be safe to retrieve the gift. She looked through the peephole again. His truck wasn't in the driveway or in front of the house. Relieved, she punched in the code to shut off the alarm, opened the door, and picked up the gift. Before unwrapping it, she shut the door and started to reset the alarm.

After she programmed the alarm, the system wouldn't turn on. The code wasn't accepted. She tried again but still couldn't turn the alarm on. Her fingers were shaking so much she thought maybe she'd gotten the code jumbled. After fumbling with the phone, she managed to dial the alarm service.

The technician on duty told her maybe a door or window was open.

She assured him that she had closed everything and checked it. She also insisted she would have heard the alarm ring if anything had been opened after she set it.

The technician said he would check her system from his computer.

She waited, wondering whether she should call the police. But she was certain, just like before, the sergeant would tell her it was just a threat. Maybe he wouldn't even believe her.

The technician returned and told her the side door, the one from the garage to the backyard, was open.

"It was closed."

"Dr. Rose, my system shows it's the side door that's open."

"But the alarm was on only a few minutes ago," Alex said.

Impatiently, the technician insisted, "It needs to be shut in order to turn the alarm back on. Please check it, now."

She walked to the door leading from the house to the garage. It was locked. Then she walked through the garage to the side door, the one from the garage to the backyard. It was open. She knew she had closed it this morning, but maybe she hadn't locked it, and the wind blew it open. She wasn't sure. Lately, she wasn't sure of anything.

But if the door had been opened, then Luke could be in the garage. Panic gripping her, she looked around, expecting him to reach out and grab her at any second. Quickly, she locked the side door, then went into the house and locked the door from the garage to the house. She tried the code again. This time, it was accepted.

"Are you there?" the technician asked. "Everything's clear from this end."

Still uncertain about how the door had opened, she went to the family room, sank into the couch, and placed the present on her lap. Wondering whether his gift was another malevolent warning wrapped in a pink bow, she pulled off the ribbon and opened the box. She stared at the pink-and-white tennis outfit. Presents and threats—the chaotic reality from her childhood reborn in Luke.

She left the present on the couch, checked the deadbolt, and went upstairs.

She turned on the bedroom light and gasped.

Luke grabbed her.

Her heart started to race, and she tried to pull away from him. "What are you doing here?" she screamed.

"Wouldn't you like to know? I'm smarter than you, even with your high-priced alarm."

"Luke," she said, the name burning her throat. "How did you get in here?"

"I've told you, I can read a person and gain more knowledge than any intellectual could from any book."

"Yes, you told the kids that, but how did you get up here?"

"Carefully planned," he said. "I was sure you wouldn't open the door for me tonight. So earlier today, I set up the ladder leading to your balcony. You were so busy you didn't even notice me walking around your precious house. You probably felt so safe in your new 'a-larm,' you didn't even think about me. You didn't think I could outsmart you and your 'a-larm.'"

"But your truck was gone," she said, terrified, shocked at the sight of him, here in her bedroom.

"I backed my truck out of your driveway and drove just out of sight. Then I quickly ran back to your house, hid by the bushes, and waited for you to open the front door to get the present. After you opened the front door, I had to run fast to get to the side yard and open the door to the garage so you wouldn't be able to put the alarm back on. That gave me time to climb the ladder, get on your balcony, and open the sliding glass door to your bedroom."

"Why?" she asked, too terrified to think.

"By the way, I knew you'd forget to put the bolt into the slider."

"Luke, you can't just come into my house, my bedroom."

"Getting into your house without triggering the alarm was a piece of cake. I was trained in 'Nam."

"For this?" she asked.

As though he didn't even hear her, he continued. "Vietnam, now that was a challenge. If you weren't very clever, you'd fall through the traps—the rolling traps or the window traps."

"I've heard about—"

"You people heard about it, but I lived it. I had a buddy who fell into a rolling trap. Twenty-four bamboo sticks lacerated him. When I tried to pull him out, the sticks rolled and shredded him."

She was afraid to say anything. It could trigger a horrific memory and set him off. She smelled alcohol and knew the synergistic effect of PTSD and alcohol; it could make an already volatile man commit horrific acts. Terrified, she knew she had to let him talk.

"I was selected to be the one to go into the tunnels to check and see if any of our dead were in the tunnels before we'd throw in the grenades. We had to retrieve our dead. The Vietcong laughed at us for caring, but we did."

So he's been trying to prove his prowess ever since—first the fishing, then the hunting, and now me, she thought and knew she had to extricate herself from him. "Luke, I need you to leave—now."

"It's me who will make the demands. And I'm here to give you my terms for your peace, or rather Seth's—I mean Jon's—peace."

"Jon?" she whispered. Unwilling to allow him to bully her any more but fearful of any harm he might do to her son. "I can't keep doing this with you."

"You can't, huh? Listen to me. You will give me the new code. And you will have sex with me when I tell you." Then like a scratched CD that kept replaying the same line, he repeated his demands.

She stood there, too scared to move.

He put his hands on her shoulders and turned her around to face him. "Now, get your ass into bed, or your friend Seth won't be able to work again. Trust me."

Fearful but resolute, she'd decided she wasn't going to let him coerce her into sex. The touch of his body once so enticing, now repulsed her with the same intensity. She looked at him and said, "I will not have sex with you."

He laughed. "People like to think they're smarter than animals."

"They are," she said, recalling how he delighted in vetting himself against his prey. It didn't matter the sport; he was a hunter, and, tonight, she was his prey.

"Yeah, the richer they are, the further away from animals they think they are. But I can smell when they're afraid. I can smell you now." He glowered at her. "I'm a trained hunter."

"I'm calling the police. Your ladder is on my balcony, and they'll know you broke in."

"Alex, there's no broken window or door. And don't you remember, you asked me to fix the light on the balcony. I took out the light earlier this evening so it wouldn't turn on when I got on the balcony. I put the old balcony light in my truck and left a new one on the table on the balcony. You know, like I was getting ready to replace it for you."

She dashed to the door. He jerked her back. Then he grabbed her wrist and squeezed it forcefully.

She struggled, trying to free herself. "I won't have sex with you tonight or ever again."

317

"You won't, huh?" he asked and glared at her. "You're very brave, very brave." He pulled her hair, turned her, and pushed her onto the bed.

"How long do I have to do what you want?" she asked. Repulsed by his strength—the strength that had attracted her to him—she shook with disgust.

"Undress," he demanded.

As though in a trance, separating herself from reality—a trick that had always worked for her as a child—she undressed. Exposed, she turned onto her back. *What had happened to the man who had untied the teenage girl's hands from the bedpost years ago? How had his kindness turned to rage?*

As Luke took off his jeans, she started to get up.

"Don't even try anything," he warned and leaned over her, his penis above her face. He reached for a pillow.

She stared up at him and felt as though, once again, she was watching the delighted hunter.

"Turn over, lie face down, and put this under your belly." He pushed the pillow at her.

She took the pillow, turned over, and adjusted her body to allow him the perfect angle to thrust into her, denigrate her by doing it doggie style. It was better facedown, she thought. Then she wouldn't have to look at his face and watch him overpower her.

He climbed on top of her, stopped, and stood up.

Suddenly, she felt much more weight than his one hundred and eighty pounds being lifted off her.

"I don't know what got into me," he said, as he put his pants on, ran to the bathroom, and then left.

She lay motionless until she heard the door shut. She staggered to the bathroom. There, on the mirror, was a message scribbled in bright red lipstick: "Tell anyone +Seth dies/Jon cries." It was smeared. Luke had probably written it before she came upstairs and then tried to hastily erase it right before he ran out. She also knew Luke had no fear she'd go to the police because that could destroy her custody case; therefore, he'd become more brazen.

If she reported him to the police, she knew Gabe's attorney could use it to discredit her. She knew how easily the truth could be twisted. But she decided she couldn't let Luke get away with this. She had to go to the police station—they had to believe her this time.

As she distractedly drove to the station, she realized she'd missed the exit for the station, but she kept driving. When she reached the two gilded, winged angels at the gates of the Brea Cemetery, she didn't know how or why she drove there. But she did know the sometimes fear guides us to the place we need to be no matter how much we resist.

She parked and shut off the engine. Staring through her car window at the names on the headstones, she finally saw her mother's grave. Her mother had died of a stroke at fifty-four, freeing Alex's father to reunite with his lover, Robert. Although her father had never said anything, Alex was certain he knew what really had happened at home while he was at work. But a man whose wife kept his secret would keep hers until the end.

CHAPTER 45

Suddenly, lights were shining into Alex's car. Another car door slammed. Alex gripped the steering wheel. *Luke?*

The lights were too bright for her to see the vehicle.

A security guard tapped on her window. "Everything okay, ma'am?"

"Just thinking," she said.

"Can't you think at home?" he asked.

Alex stared at the security guard, aware of the futility of trying to explain the divorce, custody problems, sexual assault, and memories of a mother who'd threatened to inflict horrific pain upon her if she ever told anyone the truth.

"You need to get going," the guard said.

When she didn't answer, he lowered his flashlight and stared at her quizzically. "Why are you here in the middle of the night?"

"I needed to put a pebble on the headstone."

"And what made you think the headstone needed a pebble at three in the morning?" The security guard shook his head.

"I'm here to honor the Jewish tradition of placing a pebble on the headstone when you visit the grave. It's out of respect for the dead." She took a breath. Tonight she needed to touch the headstone in row five. It was the woman below that stone who'd made

320

her believe she was unworthy of respect. Tonight was going to be the last time she would ever allow anyone to debase her. And this was the last time she was going to be prey for a weak person who needed to trample another person in order to demonstrate his power.

"Yeah, whatever," the guard said. "You still have to leave."

"I'll leave in a minute." She got out of the car, grabbed a smooth white pebble, and walked to row five. She placed the white pebble on top of the black granite headstone and spoke to the cold corpse beneath that stone: "Mom, I once read that many people go to the grave with their song within. Maybe there were so many lies in your life that you had no song. But I'm not going to die without living and sharing my song."

Depleted, too tired to talk about what happened, Alex decided to forgo the police department. It would just complicate everything, and they probably wouldn't even listen to her. She left the cemetery and drove to Liz and Stan's house.

Stan answered the door.

Alex recoiled from the scent of a man.

Liz took in Alex's tension and stepped in front of Stan. "Girls only, Stan. Go back to bed."

Alex whispered to Liz, "Luke almost raped me."

From the far end of the foyer, Stan yelled, "I'll call the cops."

"No!" Alex took a steadying breath.

"Why not?" Liz asked as she guided Alex inside and closed the door.

"I was going to the station, but his nephew works for the Compton department, and Luke told me the police, no matter which precinct, protect their own. I vacillated about going, but I decided I can't chance filing a police report."

"You're staying here," Liz said.

Alex agreed. She couldn't go home. She couldn't sleep in a bed where love and lust had both turned to hate. "And you have to promise you won't call the police. I can't lose my boys."

"You really should contact the police," Liz said.

"No! Too much is at stake." Alex exhaled shakily. "I can't chance this."

Liz drew her close and held her until she stopped shaking. "Alex, none of this is your fault."

Alex thought for a minute and then nodded wearily.

Liz led her to the spare room. "Get some sleep."

"Thanks," Alex said and collapsed onto the bed.

♦♦♦

When Alex opened her eyes, she saw Terrie, Meredith, and Liz. Registering Judi's absence, she sat up and accepted a mug of tea from Liz.

"Tell us what happened," Terrie said gently. "All of it, Alex, every detail exactly as you remember."

"Terr, you can do better than that," Meredith said.

"This is the way to process." Terrie started to tap Alex's hand.

Alex felt like a daughter receiving the comfort only a loving mother could give: love laced with acceptance, even now, at the ugliest moment of her life. Then, feeling oddly detached, she began to speak. As she revealed each and every detail of Luke's horrific debasement, sweat beaded on her forehead.

Terrie kept tapping on Alex's hand. "Did you leave anything out?"

"What's the deal with the tapping?" Meredith interrupted.

"EMDR is a process to—"

"Just do it and get her better," Liz said.

"I told you every sordid detail." Alex trembled.

"Let me explain," Terrie said. "Sexual abuse isn't about sex."

"Wanna bet?" Alex said.

Terrie shook her head. "It's about control. Luke feared he couldn't control you any longer. He lost power over you and had to do something to claim you, so he escalated.

Alex rubbed the scar on her right wrist.

"Let's go over it again," Terrie said. "It's the best way to process. Trust me."

Alex began anew. It was as though each detail in the retelling made the pain and ugliness float away. When she completed the tale for the third time, she felt both exhausted and unexpectedly strong. She looked at her friends, more grateful for their support than she could ever express.

"Enough psychoanalyzing. What about drugs?" Meredith smoothed back her mane of long black hair with her left hand.

Alex stared at Meredith's ring finger. "You?"

"Warren gave it to me last night." Meredith flashed her ring.

Alex smiled faintly. "You said marriage was pedestrian."

"For others, but not for *moi*." Meredith winked.

"What are all the guys at Waters' bar going to do?" Alex asked, sinking back in bed.

"They can dream, can't they?" Meredith said. "And Jon will be my adorable ring bearer."

"If I have custody of him by then."

"You will," Liz said. "It's only a matter of time."

"Time," Alex repeated. Time used to be clocks and calendars. Now, time was measured by before Gabe took the boys and then after they left. And after was also the chaotic reality that was Luke. Time, real time, didn't matter. Now, the only thing that mattered was time with her children. She looked at her friends and wondered aloud, "Do we ever appreciate anything until it's taken from us?"

"I appreciate you all so much that I'm having you in my wedding party," Meredith said.

"Yes, tell Alex about your absurd idea for the wedding," Terrie said.

"Warren doesn't want to wait, so we're doing the deed in six months. I have this perfect vision: the bridal party, composed of the fabulous women of my First Friday Book Club, will all wear black tuxedos, and I'll be in white. Oh, the drama of it."

"That's ridiculous. Meredith, you'll look beautiful without all of us looking like shit in tuxedos," Liz said.

"For one night, I want everything to be focused on *moi*."

"It always is," Terrie said.

Alex looked up as Judi entered the room.

"A patient died in the hospital this morning," Judi said, her gaze on Alex.

"Death happens in hospitals," Alex said, "Just like sex happens...never mind." The mere mention of Gabe's hospital took her mind to its unsavory, destructive place.

"Judi, after being married to a physician for so long, you can't be surprised by that," Liz said.

"Twenty-five years. Silver anniversary party's coming up. You should be getting your invitations soon," Judi said. "But listen to me. Someone died in the hospital, and—"

"Is there a correlation between the patient who died and Gabe?" Meredith asked.

Judi somberly looked at the women. "The patient had chest x-rays two days ago, and then she died. Her lungs were filled with fluid. The radiologist recommended sending the patient to a pulmonologist, but—"

"Then it wouldn't be Gabe's responsibility. He's a cardiologist, not a pulmonologist," Alex said, reflexively defending Gabe.

Judi shook her head. "He was her primary care physician, the one who admitted her. His entries for two days prior to the patient's death were: 'Patient stable. Doing well.' The note was signed by Gabe, but he hadn't even examined the patient."

"How'd they find out he didn't examine her?" Meredith asked.

"Easy," Judi said. "The patient's son told the nurse either he or his sister had been with their mother around the clock, and it wasn't until they were about to take the patient to the morgue that Dr. Gabriel Rose raced into the room, yelling, 'I need her chart.'"

Alex's eyes widened. "Are they going to sue Gabe?"

"Since the patient was seventy-five and on Medicare, it's considered a federal offense when a physician documents chart notes and doesn't actually perform the service," Judi said.

"Yep," Liz said, "And in all my years in insurance, I've never seen a case where Medicare doesn't investigate. Then the secondary, let's say Blue Cross, also files a criminal charge."

"Criminal?" Alex gasped. Even though Gabe was now her enemy, "criminal" was not a word fit for the father of her children.

"Gabe's chart notes indicated he'd examined the patient every single day and had reviewed all of the diagnostics," Judi said.

"It's definitely a federal offense," Liz said.

"Judi, your husband has to give Alex the patient's name," Meredith ordered.

"Don't really need it," Liz said. "If a physician is accused of Medicare fraud, all the medical records are seized by federal agents. Then they conduct a thorough investigation."

"But Gabe could cover it up," Alex said, slipping back into the past when Gabe had been successful, infallible, strong.

Liz shook her head. "Medicare fraud is serious. Why would Gabe chance it?"

"He's a gambler," Alex said, images of their last night at the Bellagio Hotel flashing before her.

"I guess he kept getting away with it," Terrie said. "Remember, I told you, people escalate until they're caught."

"Cut the psychoanalyzing," Meredith said and impatiently returned to the issue. "Let's focus on how we're going to destroy the good doctor."

"Meredith, go call Alex's attorney now," Liz instructed.

"Good idea," Meredith agreed and left the room. She spoke to Mr. Leventhal for several minutes, and when she returned, she was smiling.

"What did Leventhal say?" Alex asked.

"Leventhal said you've got nothing to worry about. He has it all handled."

CHAPTER 46

The week after the Christmas vacation, Alex left the office early on Friday and rushed to the final and most critical meeting with Dr. Weisbarth for his "unbiased" forensic evaluation.

A tanned Dr. Weisbarth walked into the waiting room and greeted her. "Could you please wait for the family?"

She stared at him, wondering whether that meant he'd already made his decision to exclude her from the family. Before she could answer, he turned and went back to his office.

Gabe and the boys arrived a short while later.

"Mommy," Jon yelled as he dashed to her and hurled himself into her arms.

Eric and Daniel followed Gabe to a seat in the waiting room.

The doctor opened the waiting room door, and, with a wave of his hand, he urged them to follow him to his office. Alex took her seat in the now-familiar arrangement.

"Boys," Dr. Weisbarth said and smiled cordially, "I need you to tell me where you're the most comfortable. I mean with your dad or ... um ... with your mother."

Daniel looked at his mother, then turned away. "I'm good with both parents," he said.

Eric nodded at Gabe, and then said, "I kinda feel better at—"

"Can you do that cork trick for my mommy?" Jon interrupted.

"Eric, please elaborate," Dr. Weisbarth said, ignoring Jon's question and appearing anxious, a departure from his previously composed demeanor.

"A cork trick?" Alex prodded, taking a cue from Dr. Weisbarth's discomfort.

"Yeah, Mommy, a cork from a wine bottle," Jon said. "It was funny, and you'd like it."

"Just a silly trick I did during one of our prior sessions." Dr. Weisbarth smiled without parting his lips.

"You showeded everybody at the beach," Jon said.

"Jon-a-than," Gabe said, his voice stern and impatient.

Jon's lips began to quiver and tears welled in his eyes.

A tense expression on his face, Dr. Weisbarth said, "Since this is our last session, I need you boys to really think about where you'd like to live. Actually, I think it's best to talk to each one of you separately." He dismissed them all with the exception of Eric, his first interviewee.

Alex could barely draw a breath. *Hadn't Daniel already answered the question that would determine her fate?* As her gaze swept over her vacation-tanned children, she despaired. *Will Dr. Weisbarth make certain my sons remain in their father's world?* It took every ounce of strength she possessed to say nothing. She wanted to ask Dr. Weisbarth when he'd shown Jonathan a cork trick on a beach. *Could Gabe have invited him on a vacation? A bribe?*

"Jonathan, come with me," Gabe said and forcefully took Jon's hand.

Silently, they sat in the waiting room. One by one, they were called back to talk to Dr. Weisbarth. When it was Jon's turn, he refused to go, even after the older boys told him they'd each gotten a piece of chocolate. Finally, he reluctantly agreed to talk to the doctor.

As soon as Jon came out of the doctor's private office, Gabe rushed to him, obviously making sure he didn't say anything else about the cork trick. Then Gabe instructed the boys to follow him to the car.

It was finally Alex's turn to speak to Dr. Weisbarth. Fearful she'd say something the doctor would construe as evidence she was an unfit mother, her heart was beating so quickly, she thought she'd faint.

"What else can you tell me about this family?" Dr. Weisbarth asked.

"This isn't a family anymore, and although I'm no longer a wife, I am a good mother."

"I know," he said softly.

Alex wondered whether he said it because he feared the repercussions of the cork trick or he finally believed her.

After asking a few more questions, Dr. Weisbarth told her his report would be completed within a week. He dismissed her without even smiling, without even giving her the perfunctory smile, the one where he didn't part his lips.

She left the office and walked to her car, reassuring herself the meeting had gone as well as she could have hoped. As she started to drive back to Liz's house, she thought about the boys. She missed them so much now that they were living at Gabe's. She missed Daniel's gentle reassurances and his thumbs-up at just the right time. She missed Jon's snuggles. She even missed the way Eric would mimic Gabe.

She looked over at the empty front seat, the boys' shotgun seat. She didn't remember moving it back that far, nor did she remember the boys reclining the seat at such an angle. Suddenly, she felt a firm grip on her right shoulder. She knew the touch but was sure she was just imagining it.

The grip tightened.

"Keep driving," he said. It wasn't harsh; it was more a plea.

Terrified, she turned to look at Luke in the backseat. She hadn't seen him when she opened the door. He had to have been lying on the backseat floor. "How did you get into my car?"

"Gabe gave me the key," he said.

"What?" Fear and anger overtaking her, she couldn't unscramble his words—*Gabe, key?* It made no sense.

"Alex, I'm here to help you. I've got to talk to you."

"I don't want to hear anything you have to say," she said and thought about stepping on the gas and speeding to the police station.

Suddenly, Luke slid across the backseat. He was directly behind her. Then he catapulted himself over the console, inadvertently kicking her as he moved to the front passenger seat. He was right next to her.

She put her hand on the door and thought about jumping out.

"I promise I can help you win in court," he said.

Moving her hand from the door, she clutched the steering wheel. She realized she'd almost forgotten about pressing her foot on the gas. Confused and disoriented, she tried to focus on the road but couldn't. "Why would Gabe have given you the key?"

"Stop the car." He reached for her arm and held it tightly.

She pulled over.

"Do you have a gun?" she asked, fearful he was going to kill her.

"I'm here to help you," he said.

"You have a strange way of helping," she said.

"Gabe wanted me to—"

"What are you talking about?" she asked. "You don't know Gabe."

"Oh, I know Gabe. I was at his house doing some plumbing, and I saw that he had tennis racquets in the garage. That's how the conversation got started."

"You had a conversation with Gabe?"

"Yes, he actually talked to me while I was fixing a plumbing problem at his house. Even rich people have to shit." He laughed, then appeared to catch himself. "I'm sorry—I shouldn't have said that. I'm just so tired of them thinking they can buy people, and I'm ashamed I fell for it."

"What are you talking about?" She was sweating and trembling. *There couldn't be any connection between Luke and Gabe. It wasn't possible.*

"Gabe paid me to date you."

"He would never do that," she said, horrified.

"I'm here telling you the truth about what Gabe wanted me to do, and you defend him."

She didn't believe Gabe would have stooped to that. Sure, he'd left her and was fighting—an ugly, dirty fight—for the children, but she had to believe he'd loved her at one time and wouldn't do something like that."I don't get it," she said. "Why?"

"Alex, I'm so sorry, but I needed money for my daughter's funeral. I was so broke after paying for her surgery and caregivers, and I was going to lose my house. Just at the exact time I was stressing, Gabe offered me more money than you can imagine."

"No, that can't be the truth." Her stomach tightened. "Why are you tormenting me? You've done enough. Gabe started to destroy me, and now you're trying to finish."

"Alex, please listen."

"Why would Gabe have thought I'd go out with you?" she asked. Head throbbing, she recalled the car ride home from Las Vegas. After Gabe had told her he was leaving her, she'd asked him whether sex was that different with someone else, and he'd told her to find out for herself. She wondered whether he'd thought she'd fall for the first guy who asked her out.

Then she also recalled that there was a time when she and Gabe were at a party, and there was a heated discussion about interracial dating. When they left the party, Gabe had asked her whether she'd ever date a black man. She'd told him it would never happen because she was in love with him. But she did tell him that race would never be a factor, and she'd definitely date a black man. Gabe had said he would never consider dating a black woman because people think less of you when you date like that. At that time, she was so in love with Gabe that she overlooked everything negative, even his prejudicial statements.

"Gabe wouldn't have paid you to date me," she repeated, but, in her heart, she knew it was possible. Gabriel Rose was capable of more, much more, than she'd ever imagined. There was also the possibility that Gabe wanted to keep her away from a man who might engage the kids and, in his opinion, Luke was so inappropriate that the boys would be alienated.

No. She couldn't believe Gabe had had to continue to control her even after leaving. Refusing to believe the truth, even when it was before her, was the way she'd survived her childhood. It was the only way to explain how her mother would torment her and how her father would believe her mother.

"I'm so sorry, but I needed to pay for burying my daughter."

"You said that already." She looked at him. The death of a child was an unfathomable horror, and she couldn't even imagine how painful that had to have been. But she couldn't trust him. He had to be lying. "What about the tennis club? Huh? How can you have afforded the dues if you have no money?"

"Gabe offered to pay for my membership to your tennis club. He wanted me to meet you. Then you were just a stranger—a means to pay back my debts."

"You used me." She started to cry.

He looked at her and lowered his head. "Have you ever wanted something so much that you could taste it?"

"Wanting doesn't give you the right to abuse people like you abused me." She knew about want—wanting to be loved so badly that she had believed her mother when she'd say she was sorry for burning her. Yes, she knew about want—wanting to be loved so badly that she hadn't seen Gabriel wasn't hers until it was too late. Want!

"I worked two jobs my entire adult life, barely making it each month, and then this guy offers me more money than I've ever seen just to play tennis with a certain lady and take her out for a few drinks—that is until he demanded I do more."

"I don't believe you needed the money." She rubbed her wrist. "You have a house, a boat."

"True, I bought the boat after Gabe gave me enough for the down payment, but it was only because I thought I'd get my grandson into it. He was so distraught after my daughter—his mother—died, he had no interest in anything."

"You could have sold the boat and stopped taking money from Gabe, and you could have just left me alone."

"I told Gabe I didn't want to do it anymore 'cause my wife and I—"

"Wife?" she yelled, shocked he'd just admitted what he'd been denying since they'd met. "What did your wife say about you taking me out?" she asked sarcastically, trying to stay calm enough to unscramble the truth from all the lies.

"With all our expenses, my wife was sure we'd lose our house. We'd never owed anything to anyone before. My wife knew about Gabe's deal, but she didn't know about the sex. There wasn't supposed to be any."

"So you had sex with me for free, and Gabe didn't have to pay for it?" she asked, too angry to think clearly. Who was to blame for this—Gabe, Luke, herself? True, Gabe devised a plan, Luke executed it, but she fell for it.

"Sounds ridiculous to someone who could afford a club, but to me, being able to play tennis at a club was the epitome. I never did anything for myself. I've been putting my two younger daughters through college. My oldest daughter got pregnant in high school, so she never had a chance, and then she ..."

"With all your lies, I don't know if I even believe your story about your daughter dying." But she looked at him and knew she was wrong. The sadness in his eyes confirmed the depth of his loss.

"My daughter died a long, horrible death. Now, we have her son—my grandson—to put through school."

"What about your daughter, the one who couldn't handle it if you were with another woman, which I understand with you being married?"

"That daughter's been difficult. We've sent her to cosmetology school, then secretarial school, but she can't hold a job. But this isn't about my children, my family; it's about how I fell in love with you. For the first time in thirty years, I betrayed my wife."

"You lied from the first date, when you told me you got a divorce because you fell in love with another woman."

"It was an innocent fib then, but—"

"Innocent," she repeated. "Nothing about what happened was innocent." *Amazing how we really think there's such a thing as innocence. Everything we do has a domino effect—one person can hurt so many, maybe not intentionally, but we damage each other.*

"Alex, I did fall in love with you."

"Don't tell me that you love me. You don't treat people you love the way you treated me." His debasement was beyond anything she could forgive. "Love doesn't act like that."

"No, but anger and alcohol do. Something happened to me after Vietnam. Whenever I have too much to drink, I get—"

"Are you drunk now too?" Alex asked.

"I'm stone sober and ashamed of myself. I guess I let myself fall for easy money, first because I needed it and then because I just wanted it. I was so disgusted with myself that I drank more and more. After Vietnam, I—"

"Alcohol isn't an excuse for the things you did to me."

"No, but it does get you to where you can't think straight. I thought maybe my daughter's death was some punishment for things that happened in 'Nam and for surviving. I know I hurt you, and you never deserved it. And when you wanted to end the relationship, Gabe wouldn't let me. I had to continue seeing you because I was afraid."

"Or because you liked the money," she said.

"Please let me finish. Gabe—rather, his wife, or whatever she is—told me they owned me, and I had to do whatever they said. His wife threatened to have me arrested if I didn't do what she said. She said she was going to go to the police and tell them I stole her diamond ring."

"Did you?" she asked, her chest tightening and almost too weak to take a breath.

"Alex, of course not. I never stole a thing."

"So why would you be afraid?"

"You really don't get racism. I'm black."

"I know you're black, or bi-racial, whatever, but what does racism have to do with this?" she asked. His whining about bigotry wasn't going to convince her to forgive him.

"I couldn't defend myself against a rich doctor and his wife. Their word or mine—which do you think the police would believe?"

"You told me the police were like the Marines, and your nephew is a police officer who would make sure the police would believe you, not me."

"He did call in some markers at Brea, but he also told me I wouldn't stand a chance against a man like Gabe."

She knew what money and power could do. She'd seen it first-hand in her own case. "So you kept dating me due to fear?"

"Yes." He looked down at his hands, palms up, imploring her. "I told you the deal was a few drinks for funeral money and tennis club membership for a year. Then Gabe escalated. Tonight, I was supposed to—"

"What?" she demanded.

"Gabe and his wife asked how many guns I had. I was supposed to beat you badly with a gun or do whatever I wanted to you, but they said I had to use a gun. Then I was supposed to leave you as far away as possible." Luke started to cry.

"I don't believe that," she said, vacillating between anger and shock. There wasn't enough air in the car. She opened the window and tried to breathe.

"Last night, I called to tell Gabe I couldn't hurt you. He said he understood, but then I heard his wife in the background. She asked him what he was talking about. He covered the phone and talked to her. I couldn't hear, but when he came back to the phone, he was like a new man. He demanded I come to his house right away."

"Did you go?" she asked, afraid to hear the answer—certain that in the telling she'd learn Gabe was a man who was not only capable of destroying her emotionally, but also of hiring someone to inflict great harm.

"I had to go. Gabe told me if I didn't come to his house to discuss things, he'd have me put away for the rest of my life."

"He could never do that," she said.

"Alex, he could. He said his wife would claim I not only stole her diamond but that I also raped her when I was alone in the house with her."

She couldn't believe Gabe could be that malevolent. She turned to Luke. "You've got to be lying. Get out of my car."

"Alex, I need to help you," he pleaded. "Listen to me."

"I can't," she cried out. "You're telling me Gabe, my children's father, wanted you to kill or physically harm me?" She gasped. *Drugs—that was the only explanation. Gabe had to be on drugs like Terrie said months ago.* She knew how crazed drugs could make a person. It could have made Gabe feel omnipotent, as though he could get away with anything.

"When I went to their house, I set up my cell phone to record so I'd have proof. Here. Listen." He pressed the play button:

First she heard Linda tell Luke she was going to report him for stealing her ring and raping her. Then she heard Gabe's voice: "You've been dating and stalking Alex for months now, and nothing has come of it. This has to end. I want this over. I want it done."

Reflexively, Alex grabbed her throat. Unable to believe Gabe would harm her—even when there could be no doubt—she hesitated. "It's Gabe's voice, but—"

"Here, take it to court,' Luke said.

"Let me hear it again," she demanded.

He played it again.

Alex listened. "The part with Linda—she didn't say she was threatening you. She said she was going to report you to the police for rape. That sort of sounded like it happened. They could use it against you because you didn't deny any of it."

"I couldn't answer her back. She'd call the police right on the spot if I started to argue with her."

"Why would they do it?"

"Rich people don't have to worry. They know they can get away with things."

Then she realized the brilliance of Gabe's plan: He hired Luke to do the dirty work, date her and make her look distracted, irresponsible, even miss important meetings. But when she continued to try to regain custody, Gabe had come up with another plan to harm her. And with his plan, the blame would fall on Luke. Gabe would be extricated.

"Luke, I think he was going to pin the whole thing on you and walk away. There would be no connection between him and you. They set you up."

"Alex, I'm so ashamed of the way I treated you. I should never have laid a finger on you when you refused me. I don't know what came over me."

Tears filling her eyes, she looked at him. "You did a horrible thing to me, but Gabe trying to have me killed, that's ..."

"Take it to court tomorrow." He handed her the phone.

"No," she said. "I doubt it will help." Confused, distraught, she wept. She knew the taped conversation could easily be manipulated by the right attorney. "Gabe and his attorney took the time I accidentally burned Jon and twisted it to show I was irresponsible. This could be turned into another example of my craziness for dating you. It might discredit me even more."

"I couldn't live with myself if you lost the kids because of me," he said.

She handed the phone back to him. "It's too dangerous for you. In addition to the accusation that you stole jewelry and raped Linda, it also sounded like you were stalking me, and Gabe wanted you to stop. I heard Gabe say, 'Luke, make it end.' That could be misinterpreted. I know first-hand just what Gabe and his attorney are capable of. The truth doesn't matter."

"I'm going to help you." He took the phone. "Please take me back to the psychiatrist's office so I can get my truck."

While she drove him back, she tried to convince him of the futility for her and danger for him of playing the recording. He told her he'd think about it and got out of the car.

Depleted, she sat in the car and cried.

CHAPTER 47

Alex kept driving until she reached the beach. She stopped and parked her car. The winter sun was setting, and the waves were grey, angry. It was cold. Even though she hadn't brought a jacket, she had to get out of her car and walk.

She had to clear her mind, try to comprehend Luke's horrific confession, and grasp onto the truth—if there was any. She'd listened to Luke's taped conversation and heard Linda threaten him. She'd also heard Gabe and knew it could all be misconstrued in the capable hands of the right attorney.

Luke hadn't been truthful from the moment they met at the tennis club. Their whole relationship—if she could call it that—had been based upon deception. But then again, the taped conversation was real, surreal actually.

Alex kept walking. She had to reconstruct each and every detail. Then, and only then, could she be convinced of the truth. Maybe she'd find inconsistencies, holes, and contradictions in Luke's story.

If she believed Luke, then Gabe was even more malevolent than her heart would allow, and that negated twenty-five years of trusting and loving a man who was capable of inflicting—or paying someone else to harm her. She didn't know whose truth to believe.

Then she thought about the car ride from Las Vegas when Gabe said he had to tell her the truth. When he'd told her his truth, confessed his love for Linda, Alex was devastated. But then she had no idea how dangerous the truth could be.

And exactly two months after Gabe had left, Luke had joined the tennis club, right after the August member-guest tournament. Then a month later, that was when it happened: That was when she accidentally burned Jon. Yes, it was accidental—that was important to keep reminding herself. She wondered whether that was the reason Gabe had decided he had to gain custody of the children. Could he really have believed she was unstable? Could that have been why Gabe hired Luke to make her look irresponsible? Could that have been why Gabe insisted Luke make sure she wasn't at the final court date? The timing was right.

Then Alex thought about her first date with Luke, exactly a month after he'd joined the tennis club. She recalled when Luke had called her, Gabe was at the house picking up the boys and trying to get her to sign the divorce agreement. After she got off of the telephone with Luke, Gabe asked if she'd met a man at the tennis club. She'd been so preoccupied with the divorce agreement that his apparent knowledge about where she met Luke hadn't registered.

Gabe also had asked her what the guy on the telephone did for a living, and when she'd told him Luke worked in hydraulics, he laughed. But she'd just thought Gabe was exhibiting his disdain for any profession which he'd thought was beneath him—and there were many. She hadn't thought anything about his interest in the man who'd telephoned her, the man he'd hired to carry out his plan.

She tried to recall all of the details of the night she signed the divorce agreement, which was also the night of her first date with

Luke. And, she had sex with Luke on that very night. How stupid! It was a setup, and she fell for it—a diversion delivered by Gabe.

She also wondered whether there was any truth to Luke's confession about it being the first time he cheated on his wife. Did it matter? It wasn't about her having sex with Luke or him betraying his wife; she had to decide whether or not to believe his story.

Forcing herself to think as clearly as possible, she kept walking briskly. It was getting dark, but she couldn't stop walking. She looked up and saw boats coming into shore. Thinking about Luke's boat and how he'd told her he'd bought it with the money from Gabe, she had to admit there could be validity to that. Without Gabe's help, it was improbable Luke could've afforded such a luxury.

Then there was the wedding, Judi's daughter's wedding. She remembered the way Luke and Gabe looked at each other, almost as if they knew each other. She'd thought she was imagining it just because she'd had sex with both of them. She never fathomed their sinister plot had already taken wings.

She stopped and sat down on the sand. She had to recount every facet of her relationship with Luke from the time she met him to right now. It was the only way to confirm or refute his confession. She gasped, recalling the time she went hunting with Luke. When she'd first told him she couldn't go with him due to her appointment with the forensic psychiatrist, he'd gotten very angry. Of course, now it all made sense: Luke was supposed to make sure she missed her first private session with the forensic psychiatrist.

It was on the hunt that Luke's friend, Clay, had told her about Luke's PTSD. Clay had warned her to be careful. She'd thought Luke's PTSD explained his irrational behavior. Now, she wondered whether Clay had known Luke had been bought and was trying to warn her.

Then she recalled the first time she tried to break up with Luke. After Meredith had given her the trust deed to his house, proving he was married, she decided to end the relationship. And when she'd told Luke she didn't want to see him ever again, he refused to accept her decision. He'd acted as thought his life depended on keeping her, and now she realized it did.

And the keys. Luke had the key to her car, and he told her Gabe had given it to him. But what about the other keys? There was the time the alarm wouldn't turn on, and he'd opened both the side door and the balcony door, claiming he had all these master keys due to his plumbing jobs. No, it had to have been Gabe who'd given him the keys. Certain he'd never need them again, Gabe probably handed all of the keys from his life with Alex over to Luke.

Yes, the pieces were coming together, but she still needed proof, more proof. She had to hear Luke's story again. She dialed his number.

"I need to see you," she said.

"Where are you?" he asked.

She explained how she'd walked from Newport Beach towards the pier in Huntington Beach and was at Fiftieth Street.

"Wait there," he said.

"Luke, I will not see you if you've had so much as one drink. I need total clarity."

"I promise," he said. "I'll be there in twenty minutes."

She found a bench and waited. Once he arrived, she insisted he repeat everything he'd told her before.

He explained each and every detail, held nothing back, and apologized over and over.

After processing as much as she could possibly remember, Alex had to admit there was absolute accuracy to Luke's confession. Everything fit together seamlessly.

"Alex, did you ever do something that seemed so right, so easy, only to find it was the opposite? It was wrong, evil, and malicious. I did that to you."

She started to cry. "You hurt me terribly."

"I told you I used to think my daughter's death was punishment for the things I did in 'Nam, but now I know hurting you was worse than anything I did in 'Nam. If I didn't have my grandson, I'd..."

"You can't go there," she said quietly, touching his arm.

There was sincerity in his voice. The lies and truths all fit together, woven into an ugly tapestry of evil.

"Luke," she said with resolve. "Please drive me to my car. I need to compose myself for court tomorrow."

CHAPTER 48

T wo hours before the court hearing, Seth picked Alex up at Liz's house.

"We'll all be there," Liz said and hugged Alex.

Seth put his arm around her and led her to his car. "You're going to do fine."

"Gabe paid Luke to harm me," she said.

"Harm you?" Seth asked.

She repeated the entire story.

"Alex, why didn't you go to the police the minute he told you?"

"The police would have arrested him," she said.

"That's exactly as it should be, and why do you care?" Seth asked, obviously unable to comprehend her refusal to report Luke.

"On the tape, Linda said, 'I'm going to go to the police and report you for raping me and stealing my diamond.' Luke didn't respond to that. It sounded like a real accusation." She started to cry. "I can't believe Gabe paid him to date me."

Seth stroked his beard. "Yes, I knew all about Luke."

"You did?" Alex asked.

"I decided to check him out. Since I wondered how he could've afforded the membership dues, I went to the club to inquire about membership. While I was talking to the membership director, I glanced over and saw a file cabinet that was labeled 'Membership.'"

"Seth, why didn't you tell me all of this before?"

"You wouldn't have believed me, and I didn't succeed in getting the proof I wanted." He looked at her. "I was the odd man out, and Luke had some spell over you."

"Sex," she said. "But why did you decide to check on his club membership?"

"A plumber—excuse me, supposed owner of a plumbing company?" Seth shook his head. "There is no way he could have paid those dues."

"Of course not, and I didn't even wonder about that," she said. "So I went back to the club with Rebecca."

"Rebecca? Our office manager? Why would you go back with her?"

"I decided that someone, maybe even Gabe, must have paid for Luke's membership."

"Wow, you *are* smart," she said.

"Is this the first time you realized that?" He smiled. "If Gabriel had paid by check or credit card, I would have had proof that he bribed Luke. So Rebecca and I went to the club. Rebecca asked the membership director for a tour of the club, and I said I'd just wait in the office. And, I might add, the membership director thought Rebecca and I were a couple. Pretty impressive, since she's only twenty-five."

"Seth, this is Orange County. Of course they'd think you were a couple. Get on with the story."

"I opened the file cabinet and saw that all of Luke Jackson's dues were paid in cash."

"Why would you have taken a chance on opening the file cabinet in the director's office?" she asked. "You could have been arrested."

"Love," he said.

"Love?" she repeated, no longer trusting the word.

"I'm in love with you," he said.

She had always known and appreciated how protective he was of her. She'd also known he cared for her, even loved her, but he'd never acted or told her he was in love with her. "What if you just moved to Arizona without saying anything?" she asked.

"Alex, I tried to tell you, but it never seemed to be the right time."

"It could have ended without even ..." Tears welled in her eyes. She realized she'd missed all of the overtures from this wonderful man, and the possibility could have ended before it began.

He touched her face. "We all choose the consequences of our lives, whether we are aware of it or not. We do one thing, and the next follows in a logical sequence. When you hit the tennis ball, the next move is the direct result of that shot. I had to stop trying and give up on you for my sanity."

"You ..." She stopped and forced herself to breathe as she spotted Gabe's silver Mercedes.

"We'll get through this," Seth said. "The main thing is that you aren't hurt, but it's critical that you stay focused."

They passed through security and made their way inside. Alex came to a halt. Shocked, she saw Jon positioned between Gabe and Linda, holding their hands as they walked down the hallway. She couldn't fathom why Gabe had brought the children.

"You're their mother, not her," Seth whispered.

She took calming breaths and stared. Eric stood as tall as his father, looking grown-up in his blue oxford shirt and tan slacks. Daniel, preppy in a white shirt and navy chinos, seemed tense and uncomfortable. *Wishful thinking?*

Dr. Gabriel Rose, clad in his Republican-red tie and navy suit, gave her a smug look and turned his back to her.

Alex longed to scoop Jon up into her arms, reach out to Daniel, and connect with Eric. Then Linda's perfume—some lavender sachet—enveloped Alex, almost making her gag. She couldn't allow this fortress of family strength to weaken her.

Linda pulled Jon close.

As Alex studied Linda's perfectly tailored maroon suit and matching leather heels, she realized she'd only seen Linda in a long evening gown and slacks. Now in a short skirt, Linda's fat ankles were visible. *An imperfection!* Alex thought with feline satisfaction.

Linda bent down and whispered something to Jon.

Alex watched Linda speak to her child, mother him. She was amazed at the ease with which Linda had slipped into her space, stolen her identity as wife and mother.

Seth stroked her back, his voice low and warm. "This'll be over soon, and Gabe thinks he has nothing to fear. Just wait. Medicare isn't something to fool with."

Suddenly, Jon burst free from Linda's grasp and ran to Alex. "Mommy!"

Before Jon reached Alex, Gabe sternly called, "Jon-a-than."

Jon froze in midstride, glancing first at Gabe and then at Alex.

Gabe instructed, "Linda, take my boys to the cafeteria and get them settled, will you?"

Linda clamped a hand on Jon's shoulder and motioned for Daniel and Eric to follow as she led them away.

Stay calm, Alex told herself as she watched Linda's possessive herding of Jon, Daniel, and Eric.

Seth glanced at his watch. "Alex, we should go to the courtroom."

"No. I've got to go to the cafeteria to talk to the boys," she said, fearing this might be the last time she'd have with them before they'd see her through Gabe's filter.

She pushed open the cafeteria door.

Eric moved away as though fearful she'd derail him from a decision he'd already made.

"Hi, Mom," Daniel said, smiling up at her from the table where he'd spread out his homework.

Clutching his bear with the missing ear and the repaired innards, Jon ran to Alex.

"Wait outside in the hall, Linda," Alex said. Trying to remain as composed as possible, she knew if she lashed out, then Gabe's allegations about her irrationality would be substantiated.

"Gabe told me to stay with them," Linda said.

"Get out." Alex put her hands on her hips and stood between Linda and her sons.

Linda took a step back, her shock evident.

Alex saw Eric's startled expression and Daniel's smile.

"Linda, my children and I would like some privacy."

"Mommy," Jon whispered.

"What, Cookie-face?" Alex asked and then glared at Linda.

"Daddy told me it's irrespecting to call her Linda, 'cause she's the mother of his house."

"What?" Alex said, wanting to scream, protest, and explain that Linda was not the mother.

Linda patted Jon's head. "Jon, sweetie, I'll be right back. Don't worry."

"Out, Linda. Now!" Alex pointed to the cafeteria exit and then motioned to the boys. "Time for a family meeting, guys, so gather around."

"But Daddy said you're not part of the family anymore," Jon said.

Daniel's chair screeched on the linoleum as he jumped up, ran to Jon, and placed a reassuring hand on his little brother's shoulder.

Alex knew Jon hadn't meant to rip her heart out. He was just parroting Gabe, but his innocent words tore at her heart.

Jon put his teddy on the table. "I don't like it here."

"I hate this!" Eric announced loudly as he approached the table.

Alex agreed. She would never have brought the boys to the courthouse, but it seemed Gabe had decided to parade them in front of her. He probably sought to unnerve her prior to her testimony, or he might have some other plan to use the boys to bolster his case. Nothing was beneath Dr. Gabriel Rose.

Jon snuggled into her as Eric and Daniel sat in nearby chairs.

Seth moved to a table on the far right of the cafeteria, giving them as much privacy as the open area would allow.

"Guys," she said, "I'm going to tell you the truth." She started with a cliché, exactly as Gabe had when he'd erased her from his life on the drive from Las Vegas.

"Mom, why don't we just wait for the judge to tell us what to do?" Eric asked.

"Boys, I want you to live with me, but—"

Jon tugged on his bear's good ear. "What if my bear's stomach opens again?"

"I'd sew it up for you," she said.

"Daddy's the only one who can fix people by sewing," Jon said and burst into tears.

Glancing across the room, Alex met Seth's warm gaze. Then she saw Daniel make a sewing motion with a pretend length of string and a needle, and her heart warmed.

Eric scowled. "Danny, what weirdo thing are you doing now?"

Alex looped her arm around Daniel. "Do you know how much I love you?"

"What's he doing?" Eric repeated.

"Daniel's letting me know that, whatever the judge decides, we're still connected."

"Not true," Eric said.

"Yes, it's true," she said. "The judge doesn't always see every-thing clearly. Sometimes he sees only what's shown to him, and he can't always see the love."

"I love you, Mommy," Jon said. "And I see good."

"I know, Cookie Face." She brushed a strand of hair out of his eyes.

"It's like this," she said. "You're up at bat, a ball is pitched, and if you let the ball go by, it can either be a strike or a ball. The umpire decides. If he calls it a strike and you're sure it was a ball, what do you do?"

"You have to listen to the ump," Eric said.

"Well, Dad and I both love you guys, and we both want you to live with us, but the judge is going to decide who'll do the best job."

Eric shook his head. "Why don't you and Dad just cut us in half and each take a part?" Then he moved close, stiffy at first. "Mom, I really hate this."

"I know." She hugged him tightly, making sure he felt her love.

"No cutting," Jon cried. "I don't want my daddy to sew me back like my bear."

Daniel leaned over and straightened his mother's collar.

Her gaze encompassing them all, she said, "I love you more than you'll ever know."

Linda burst into the cafeteria "They're ready in the courtroom. My sister's here to watch the boys." She pointed to the younger woman behind her.

Alex kissed her sons and proceeded to the courtroom.

CHAPTER 49

The First Friday Book Club women were standing outside the courtroom door.

"I can't believe you're all here," Alex said, appreciative of these four women, her community.

"That's what friends are for," Judi sang out.

Alex smiled weakly. Judi's singing was a little too upbeat, especially now. But then again, that was Judi.

"Judi might have come up with something even better than Silver Cloud," Liz said.

"Silver Cloud might still be important," Terrie said. "I had a patient—"

"Listen to what Judi has to say." Liz twirled her long strand of pearls.

Judi nodded. "Since the patient who died was covered by Medicare, the hospital is opening Gabe's locker today. Rumor also has it Gabe might have been stealing drugs, and that could've been the reason he's been acting so irrationally. They're conducting a full investigation. I told my hubby to text the minute he hears anything at the hospital."

"Let's hope your husband gets some proof before *my* husband takes my children," Alex said.

"If I get confirmation, I'll testify," Judi said.

"You're not on the witness list." Alex dismissed her offer.

"I can be added," Judi said. "With proper protocol, it's usually allowed."

Seth looked at his watch. "Time to go in."

Alex hugged her friends and followed Seth into the courtroom. She took her seat behind the responder placard, turned, and saw Linda lean over and stroke Gabe's back. He patted Linda's hand as though he were a loving man, not someone capable of hiring another man to harm the woman he'd once loved. Then he took a document from his attorney, pointed to something, and winked at Linda. She smiled and winked back.

As though spying on a forbidden scene, Alex couldn't look away. She had to watch Gabe, the man with whom she'd been one flesh, entwine himself with another. It was like the horrific sideshow at a circus where she knew she shouldn't stare but found herself staring nonetheless.

"Stay focused. I'm right here for you," Seth whispered.

Alex glanced across the table and saw Gabe's attorney's new Hermes attaché case. She stared at Mr. Leventhal's cheap, weathered briefcase. She motioned to Seth to move close and whispered, "Look at Leventhal's briefcase. There's no way he can fight Gabe's lawyer."

"It's the truth they want, not the one who has the best briefcase," Seth whispered and turned to go to the back of the courtroom.

"Right," Alex said sarcastically and looked to the right of the judge's bench where the court reporter was adjusting her steno stand. The reporter inserted a register-sized paper roll into her machine. Alex watched, her chest tightening. She knew soon all the accusations, lies, and life-altering judgments would transform themselves into black squiggly marks on white rolls of paper.

As Alex watched Gabe's attorney line up all his documents like soldiers ready for battle, she wondered if this time the judge would hear the truth or if, once more, he'd be swayed by Gabe's lies.

The judge took the bench and announced he was ready to proceed.

Gabe's attorney was called to present his opening statement:

"I'm Howard Wright, attorney for the petitioner." He explained that the evidence would show why sole legal and physical custody had to be granted to Dr. Gabriel Rose. He described Alexandra Rose as an unfit mother who burned her son and habitually failed to arrive home in time to take the children to their games.

Before Mr. Wright could continue with a litany of unsavory and inappropriate acts, Alex stood up and yelled, "I only missed one game." Then, in rapid fire, she explained how competent she was as a mother.

Immediately, the bailiff walked toward Alex, stood right next to her, and moved his right index finger from side to side.

Leventhal put his hand on Alex's wrist and waited for the judge to call him to present his opening statement. He introduced himself as Mr. Joshua Leventhal, attorney for the respondent. He explained that Alex was a responsible doctor of chiropractic whose partnership provided her the flexibility to meet all of her children's needs, including transportation. He provided a log consisting of the dates and times of games and practices to which Alex had transported the children, the parent–teacher conferences she'd attended, and the recreational activities, such as movies and park excursions, to which she'd taken the boys. Leventhal concluded his opening statement and nodded to Alex, confident he had diffused all of Gabe's accusations.

"Mr. Wright, please call your first witness," the judge instructed.

Dr. Gabriel Rose was sworn in, and, in response to Wright's questions, he drew a portrait of Alex as a danger to the children.

Then he proceeded to describe his competency. "As a cardiologist," Gabe said, "I'm able to support my boys. My soon-to-be wife has quit her job in order to provide a stable home." He glanced dismissively at Alex.

Alex's stomach churned. Gabe spoke as though the words "wife" and "work" were mutually exclusive, in contrast to words like "husband" and "provider," which were inextricably intertwined.

Leventhal stood up and looked at Gabe. "Doctor, please explain to the judge how you'll be able to care for the boys while embroiled in a Medicare investigation."

Gabe shot to his feet. "There's no—"

"I request a break to confer with my client," Gabe's attorney said.

"Granted." The judge took off his smudged glasses. "But first, I want both attorneys to approach the bench."

As the judge and the two attorneys spoke in hushed tones, Alex and Gabe glared at each other. Gabe's eyes nervously darted back and forth. She looked straight at him with unwavering clarity and saw the other side of love, the one that got twisted inside out and was ugly.

After consulting with the attorneys, the judge said, "The Medicare issue is speculative, and since it wasn't in the original proceedings, I'm not going to allow it."

"What?" Alex sat back in her chair, shocked by the judge's seemingly dismissive attitude.

Gabe smirked.

She hated that smirk. It was the same expression he'd had after he'd described her ineptitude. After criticizing her, he'd tell her he would forgive her because he was magnanimous enough to overlook her flaws. She'd thank him, grateful for whatever crumbs he'd given her. Now she knew it was control, not love, he'd offered. She would never again accept crumbs. She was worth more.

Then Gabriel's mother, the children's grandmother, was called to the stand. After being sworn in, she explained how, whenever the boys were at her house, Alex was always "extremely tardy" when she'd pick up the children.

"That's not true," Alex called out.

Again, the bailiff walked over and signaled her to calm down.

The judge cautioned, "If you do that one more time, I'm going to hold you in contempt of court."

Then, just as Gabe had threatened, Dr. Kaplan was called and sworn in. Wright asked him to explain the circumstances under which he'd last seen Alexandra. He explained she was not diligent about immediately transporting Jon to the hospital, and, in his opinion, she'd acted inappropriately. Magnifying the severity of the burn, he described Alex's blasé attitude toward Jon when he was in such horrific pain.

Upon Leventhal's interrogation, Dr. Kaplan did concur that she had tried to soothe Jon.

The witnesses for Gabe continued to give their testimonies for another hour, each witness attesting to Gabe's impeccable character and loving parenting.

Then it was Alex's attorney's turn. He called her first.

After she was sworn in, Mr. Leventhal questioned her, demonstrating her professional credentials and competent personal attributes.

When it was Mr. Wright's turn to question her, he addressed her as "Mrs. Rose."

"Dr. Rose," Alex said with quiet dignity.

"If you were to be given joint custody of your three children, Mrs. Rose, what would your financial expectations be from my client?"

"I'd expect him to share equally."

"So you're dependent upon Dr. Rose's financial help for the children?" Wright demanded.

"He is their father, and I believe he has certain responsibilities to our children," Alex said.

"Yes, Dr. Gabriel Rose is the custodial parent," Wright agreed with her.

The word "parent" used exclusively for Gabe made her gasp. Although she wanted to extricate Gabe from her life, she knew he'd been a caring father. He'd sewn up Jon's bear, cheered for the boys at their football games, and made their home secure within his embrace. Or had she just imagined they'd been secure? That was until his heart found another home.

"Mrs. Rose, as I was saying ..." Wright narrowed his gaze. "Why don't you tell us how you intend to care for the boys with your busy, um, schedule?" he said mockingly.

"I can work around my children's schedules. My partner understands my commitment to my boys and is willing to accommodate their needs." Alex wondered whether Gabe and his attorney knew about Seth's plans to move.

Wright cleared his throat as though something distasteful had lodged there.

She tensed, fearing he was about to hurl questions at her designed to reveal poor judgment, inappropriate behavior. She hoped the judge would understand how vulnerable she'd been, how Gabe had set her up, and how she'd fallen in love or lust. But she'd changed. After Luke's horrific debasement, she had faced the abyss. Now, she was more determined than ever. Now, she was a powerful woman who could protect and nurture her children.

"Why don't you tell us about your clubbing and drinking at all hours of the night?" Wright asked.

At first, when she'd seen the allegation in the petition, she'd thought it was Judi who'd informed Gabe. She'd been reluctant to confront Judi, but she'd never suspected it was Gabe who'd put Luke up to taking her out.

"Objection. Hearsay, and it was not substantiated," Leventhal said, but, of course, the judge had already heard the allegations of alcohol use and irresponsibility.

"Sustained," the judge said.

Mr. Wright nodded and asked, "What about almost missing Dr. Weisbarth's appointment for a deer-hunting trip?"

"Objection," Leventhal said. "Dr. Gabriel Rose insisted she take that appointment due to his schedule and then told her that he didn't need her to switch. It was *he* who was going on a trip."

"Sustained," the judge said.

"All that aside," Wright said, making sure it wasn't aside, "I want to discuss what you've done to control the 'behavior' that caused this custody case in the first place."

Alex froze. She would never deliberately harm her child; however, there was a fleeting second when she'd thought of her own mother and had almost believed she'd burned Jon on purpose, just like Gabe had said. Somehow, from the moment she'd become Gabriel's wife, she'd viewed the world through his prism. Often, when he wasn't by her side, she'd heard herself voice opinions that were clearly his. She'd heard herself say "Gabe thinks" instead of "I think" too many times. Once she'd become his wife, she'd watched herself disappear as easily as chalk on a blackboard. But she wasn't going to be erased from her children's lives.

"I think the Seven-Thirty report confirms joint custody is appropriate," Leventhal said.

Alex recalled when Leventhal had presented her with the Seven-Thirty report from Dr. Weisbarth, she'd been so relieved upon reading his recommendation for joint custody. Leventhal had told her Weisbarth was known for granting full custody to the mothers, but this was the best they could have hoped for, considering Gabe's probable connection with Weisbarth.

"The Seven-Thirty report was neutral, I concur, but we have a body of evidence confirming Mrs. Rose's irresponsibility," Wright said and proceeded with other questions designed to discredit her.

Alex remained strong throughout the interrogation.

Then Alex's witnesses were called. Seth and Liz both provided excellent testimony and were unintimidated by Mr. Wright's interrogation. Terri and Meredith had wanted to give their testimonies, but Alex's attorney insisted it would be more powerful to have the people who continually witnessed her interactions with the children.

Just as the judge was instructing the attorneys about presenting their closing arguments after lunch, the courtroom door opened.

Alex turned around and gasped.

Gabe put his head in his hands.

Alex wrote a note to Leventhal.

"Your Honor, we have a witness to add," Leventhal stated.

The judge nodded. "We'll break for lunch, then, as I started to explain, we'll have the attorneys each produce their closing arguments. However, I'll consider the witness and provide my opinion when we reconvene."

CHAPTER 50

Unable to eat, Alex sat in the cafeteria with Leventhal, who wolfed down a tuna sandwich. Seth and the First Friday women decided they'd rather take a walk. Alex and Leventhal discussed everything Luke had told her: the bribery, the warnings, the tape.

"We're going for broke," Leventhal said.

"Luke could be jailed." Alex shook her head.

"Alex, you've got to take care of yourself."

Reluctantly at first, then with determination, she agreed. "Who asks him the questions?"

Leventhal explained the *voir dire* procedure in which the opposing counsel could ask the witness questions designed to discredit him and show that he would not "speak the truth," which, Leventhal said, was the literal meaning of the term *voir dire*. Leventhal explained the opposing counsel would usually try to convince the judge the witness was not truthful; therefore, he shouldn't be permitted to testify.

"Does it happen?" Alex asked.

"Sometimes." Leventhal stood up. "Time to go back to the courtroom."

◆◆◆

The judge returned to the bench. "Now we have the issue of whether or not we'll hear the witness who's not on the list."

Just as Leventhal had explained, Wright asked, "Your Honor, may I take the witness on *voir dire?*"

The judge ruled Luke was to be *voir dired* by Mr. Wright.

Wright asked Luke how he knew Dr. Gabriel Rose.

Luke recounted how he'd met Gabe and how Gabe had hired him to distract Alex and then, ultimately, to get rid of her.

Wright asked Luke why he would have agreed to such a request.

"Money," Luke said and explained how he was in debt after his daughter's death. He explained how the deal was supposed to have been easy—just take Alex out a few times, get her a little drunk, and that was it. Then he explained how Gabe had escalated and, finally, insisted he do away with her. He stated that he even had it taped.

Wright asked him whether he'd obtained Dr. Gabriel Rose's permission to tape the conversation, to which Luke confessed he had not. Wright proceeded to ask him questions about his motives, his background, and the explicit nature of his relationship with Alex. At the conclusion of Wright's interrogation, Luke emerged as a dangerous hunter who had PTSD, possessed a stockpile of guns, and would do anything for money.

Then it was Leventhal's turn to question Luke. In response to his questions, Luke explained how he'd agreed to a few innocent meetings, and then Gabe and his wife had framed him. He requested permission to play the tape.

"I'll allow the witness," the judge announced.

"Here's the proof," Luke said, turning on his cell phone.

"I want you to end it now." The voice was harsh, raspy, but clearly Gabe's.

"Linda, your fucked-up plan is going to—" Gabe stood up, went to the back, and grabbed Linda's hand. He pulled her to her feet. "We're out of here."

"Gabriel Rose, stop now," the judge instructed.

Gabe sat down.

The judge explained, "The allegation of solicitation for assault will be addressed. But first I'll render my decision on the custody issue at hand."

Alex rubbed her wrist.

The judge removed his glasses. "While Alexandra might have shown some indiscretions, I ..."

Alex tensed. The judge had to understand how she had tried to travel as far away from Gabriel Rose as possible, and Luke Jackson's world had offered that distance.

"... am going to rule on the proceedings and then report to the district attorney, explaining that I have what appears to be evidence of a crime. I'm seizing Mr. Jackson's cell phone and will hold it for the district attorney's review." The judge turned to his computer and hit the keys.

"The children?" Alex wrote on the pad and pushed the pad toward Leventhal.

Leventhal wrote back, "Stay calm."

The judge ordered the attorneys to present their closing arguments. At the conclusion of the final arguments, he said, "There's no evidence that Alexandra Rose intentionally harmed her child or would do so in the future." Then he pointed to Gabe. "Dr. Gabriel Rose, I had decided not to give any weight to your alleged Medicare investigation, although, as we all know, if you were convicted, that would be a criminal charge."

Alex's heart pounded.

"However, conspiracy to commit murder has been alleged." The judge folded his arms across his chest.

Gabe put his head down.

The judge looked from Alex to Gabe. "Considering the best interests of the children, I will make an order to return the children to their mother's custody."

She turned to look at Luke. He brought his fingers to his lips, kissed them, and pointed to her. His eyes no longer had the glint of the hunter. Instead, he had the dull look of the defeated. Alex felt chilled. There was something eerily familiar about those eyes. She'd seen them many times before—on her mother whenever Alex would challenge her. Then she recalled the time the fat lady in the circus terrified her. They all had the same sad, scared eyes.

The First Friday Book Club women rushed to Alex.

"I knew you'd win," Liz said and hugged her.

Terrie kissed Alex's cheek.

"And *moi*?" Meredith said, pushing her way into the circle.

Judi joined them. "Friends are like stars. You might not always see them, but they're always there, twinkling at you."

Seth drew Alex into his arms.

Linda's sister walked into the courtroom with the boys.

"What happened?" Daniel asked.

"I'll explain everything when we get home," Alex said.

"I thought we were going home with Dad," Eric insisted.

Alex scooped Jon into her arms and placed him securely on her left hip. Daniel put his arm around her waist. She pulled Eric to her. He tensed but didn't pull away.

Seth kissed Alex's forehead.

"Boys, let's go home," Alex said.

"Will Honey be there?" Jon asked.

"Doofus." Eric shook his head. "Don't you remember she ran out in front of a car and got killed?"

Jon started to cry. "I don't want Honey to be dead."

"I'm sure Mommy'll get us a new dog," Daniel said.

"No," Jon protested. "I don't want a new dog. I need my Honey."

Alex kissed Jon's cheek. "Sometimes we lose the ones we love the most."

EPILOGUE

Six months later, as Alex was dressing for Meredith's wedding, Eric walked into her room.

"Why do I have to wear this tie?" he asked and handed it to Alex.

"I'll help," she said. And as she leaned over to tie it, her hand brushed along his freshly shaven chin, the only part of his handsome face that now sprouted stray whiskers. "You smell wonderful."

"It's the stuff you gave me for my birthday," he said.

She smiled at him. "And you insisted you'd never use it."

"I put it on me too," Jon said as he ran into the room with Lucky, the black Labrador retriever, wagging her tail and sprinting in front of him.

"You put on just a little too much cologne," she said and delighted in how cute he looked in the little tuxedo jacket and short pants, an outfit Meredith picked out and decided was absolutely divine. The burns on his legs had healed with only two barely discernable scars which showed just below his knees.

"I like the smell," he said.

"Oh, I think we have to wash some off." Alex laughed.

"But I need it on account of I'm the 'ringbear' at Merrybeth's wedding," Jon said.

"Meredith's wedding," Alex corrected and grabbed Jon to give him a kiss.

"Doofus, they're supposed to see you, not smell you." Eric patted Lucky's head and went back to his room to get his jacket.

"Mommy, are you dressed up like the most beautiful woman in the world?" Jon asked and tossed Lucky a toy.

"I'm wearing a fancy dress for Meredith's wedding, just like you guys are in your special clothes." She stroked Lucky's ears.

"No," Jon said. "I mean like the mother in the story you told me long ago."

"Which one?" She smoothed her long black dress.

"You know, the kid who thought his mother was the most beautiful woman in the world, but she was ugly. Are you trying to be like her?" Jon asked as she washed off some of the after-shave lotion.

Daniel came into the room holding Lucky's leash. "I'm taking Lucky out for a walk."

"Hurry, or we'll be late for Meredith's wedding," she said and finished applying her makeup.

As soon as Daniel returned, she helped him with his tie. Then Jon gave Lucky a treat and a good-bye hug, Eric grabbed the present for Meredith, and they all piled into the Land Cruiser. Alex buckled Jon in his car seat, and Daniel sat next to him. Eric put the gift on the floor and buckled himself in the front seat.

Just as she approached the freeway, Jon yelled, "Stop. I need to go home."

"Why?" Alex asked.

"I need to get my bear if I'm supposed to be the 'ringbear.'"

"No." Alex said. "You're the ring bearer like you practiced. "You don't need your bear."

Jon started to cry.

"We'll be late," Alex said.

"I'll run in and get it," Daniel said. "I'm sure he'll forget about it when he walks down the aisle."

"I'd never forget about my teddy." Jon crossed his hands over his chest.

"If you really need him, I'll go back," she said.

"Teddy always makes me happy."

Grateful her little boy knew exactly what it took to make him happy, she wished it could be that easy for the older boys who seemed to be struggling with life now that Gabe wasn't around. She drove back to the house.

Daniel ran in and returned with the bear, the one with the missing ear and the stomach that had been perfectly sewn up by Dr. Gabriel Rose.

Jon clutched his bear to his chest. "Bear, I love you."

"Doofus, how come you never gave him a name all this time?" Eric asked.

"Sometimes I call him Honey because I loved Honey so much," Jon said.

"That's lame." Eric turned back to the front. "I'm taking a nap."

"Football practice must have been exhausting," she said, amazed at how he'd sprouted up so quickly these past few months, shaving and voice deepening, and recently, he'd been sweeter to her than he'd ever been.

"Jon, you'll be up very late, so I'd like you to try to sleep too," Alex said.

"I'm not tired," Jon said, rubbed his teddy bear against his cheek, and was asleep within a few minutes.

"Daniel, did you put away the ribbon and wrapping paper?" she asked, glancing at him through the rearview mirror.

"Yeah, I put them in the pantry."

"Good," she said. "I was afraid Lucky would try to play with it and get tangled up in the ribbon like Honey did when she was a puppy."

"I still miss Honey," Daniel said.

"I know," she said. "Do you remember the night you guys told me you were going to live with your dad, and I told you about the string that would tie us forever?"

"I remember," he said solemnly.

Alex knew he missed not only Honey but also Gabe. She hated talking about Gabe, but she knew the boys needed their father. Since Gabe had a jail sentence pending, the boys were having difficulty coping.

"Remember I told you how the string would tie you to me forever? Well, you can use the same pretend string and tie your father to you." It was painful for her to say kind things about Gabe, but the older boys had already faced the community's gossip. They couldn't handle any more negativity.

"Love you," Daniel said and that made her heart swell.

As she pulled up to the valet at the St. Regis Hotel, she saw Meredith getting out of the limo. Beautiful, she did look like Catherine Zeta-Jones—actually, even more dramatic.

"Boys, wake up," Alex called to Eric and Jon.

"I'm ready," Jon said with a start. Then he unbuckled the straps and bounded out of his car seat.

"Jon and I have to go to take pictures," Alex said. "Will you boys be okay?"

"We'll wait in the lobby," Daniel said.

Alex and Jon went to join the wedding party.

Meredith was directing everyone. Terrie, the matron of honor, was busy trying to comply with all of Meredith's directives. Although Terrie had initially refused, Meredith had the makeup artist work on Terrie. And Terrie, usually pale and plain, looked divine.

"Our Meredith marrying. Who would have thought?" Liz chided. As always, she was stylish in her tea-length black dress with rhinestones draped down the back and her long strand of glistening pearls.

"What's that supposed to mean?" Meredith snapped.

"Calm down," Liz snapped back.

"Bride's nerves," Terrie said, a soft apology for Meredith.

Just as they were finishing up with the pictures, Judi arrived. "My mom wasn't feeling well, again," she lamented but quickly turned her attention to the bride. "Meredith, you look breathtaking."

"That was my plan." Meredith winked.

"At least you gave up on us wearing tuxedos," Alex said.

Meredith had eventually backed down and agreed that it would be fine for the First Friday Book Club women to wear dresses, as long as they were black. Providing a dramatic background for her white gown was imperative.

The procession was ready. First the justice of the peace walked down. Then Meredith's nephew walked her mother down the aisle.

The groom's parents followed.

Each one of the First Friday women walked down the aisle with a groomsman: Terrie walked with Warren's older brother, Judi was escorted by Warren's business partner, Liz walked with Warren's best friend, and Alex linked arms with Warren's younger brother. They stood, flanking the justice of the peace, two couples on each side of the altar.

Warren, the groom, approached and the wedding party and guests all turned around.

Then Alex watched as Gracie, the adorable flower girl, and Jon stood in the back, giggling together. They didn't appear to be paying attention. Alex was worried Jon wasn't going to walk down the aisle. But, just as they'd practiced, Jon walked down the aisle with the rings *and* the bear on the pillow. Gracie followed, sprinkling rose petals all over the rolled-out white satin aisle.

Then, to "Here Comes the Bride," Meredith, radiant beyond belief, walked down the aisle with her father.

As Meredith and Warren exchanged vows, she appeared to soften. She even let Warren swoop her off her feet when he kissed her.

After the ceremony, the bride and groom left the chapel, followed by the wedding party. The guests exited, row by row. While everyone mingled outside the ballroom, white-gloved waiters offered steak kebabs, stuffed mushrooms, and jumbo shrimp.

Alex watched as the ballroom doors were opened. Inside the room, the chandeliers twinkled onto the tables, each with a white linen tablecloth and a dozen red roses in a Lalique crystal vase—breathtaking.

Before taking her seat, Alex went over to check on her children, who were seated with Meredith's nephews and Gracie, Warren's niece. Jon and Gracie were still giggling, and the older boys were chatting with Meredith's nephews. Eric gave her a look, imploring her to leave. Since everything seemed fine, she proceeded to her table.

At the First Friday table, the women and their spouses were already seated. There was one chair left for Alex. The perfectly choreographed celebration began: Meredith and Warren danced their first dance, "The Wind Beneath My Wings." Then couples joined them on the dance floor.

It was at times like this when she missed Seth. She'd also missed him every day at work. He'd given her the entire practice, refused to take anything for his share, and moved to Arizona to be with his children. Although the practice had become extremely successful, she missed the camaraderie Seth had afforded her. But, she realized, friends can't always become lovers just because we wish them to be.

The band leader then called the parents of the bride and groom to the dance floor and played "Sunrise, Sunset."

Wistfully, Alex turned and looked over at the children's table. Eric got up from his chair and walked up to her. Certain he was going to insist on going home, she asked, "What's wrong?"

"May I have this dance?" he asked.

Pleasantly surprised, Alex smiled. "Of course. I'd love to dance with such a handsome gentleman."

It was something Daniel would have done, but Eric's request pleased her. It reaffirmed the sweetness each of her boys possessed. While she and Eric danced to "Sunrise, Sunset," her father's favorite song, she started to cry. Here she was dancing with her own son, a world away from her past.

"Thank you for the loveliest dance of my life," she said and kissed Eric on the cheek. Then she walked him back to his table. She checked on Daniel and Jon, both of whom appeared to be having a great time, seemingly engaged in animated conversations with the other kids.

As Alex started back to her seat, she stopped and looked at him.

He smiled at her, obviously recognizing her.

Her knees weakened. She walked toward him.

He stood up, even taller and handsomer than she remembered.

She looked into his green eyes, the color of the glass from the old Coca-Cola bottles. "What are you doing here?" she asked, surprised to see David, the gynecologist from the Flying Samaritans.

"I'm the groom's ... um ... my wife was Warren's sister." He pointed to Gracie. "My daughter's the flower girl."

"But I didn't see you at the rehearsal or when we were taking pictures," Alex said.

"I had to finish up at the hospital," he said. "Her grand-mother brought her here and helped her get dressed. It's been two years since I lost my wife, and I'm still not good at the girl stuff."

"I didn't know," she said.

"I don't talk about it," he said. "It hurts too much. I can forget at work, especially the Flying Sams, but when we're home at night, I feel so bad for Gracie."

"David, why didn't you come up to me after you saw me walk down the aisle?"

"Warren and I don't really keep in touch. When I saw you walk down the aisle with his brother, I figured you were married to him. I saw a ring on your finger, and ..."

"Oh, this," she said, wondering why she'd never taken off the ring from Luke, the one with the two hearts entwined. Maybe she wore it as a reminder of the other side of love—where dreams implode and no one is who he seems.

"Let's dance." David took her hand.

Magical—the only word to describe their dance.

After the music stopped, Alex and David stood, unable to part.

He motioned to Gracie and Jon, still engrossed in conversa-tion. "What could they possibly have to talk about?"

"Jon can carry on about anything for as long as someone will listen, and it looks like Gracie's enjoying it," she said.

"She only has me, and I guess I'm not as much fun."

As they started to walk back to their respective tables, the emcee announced it was time for the bouquet toss. Alex knew her friends would push her back to the dance floor, so she didn't even try to slip away.

Dramatic as ever, Meredith held the bouquet—feigning inability to part with it—and finally tossed it.

Alex didn't get the bouquet, but when she looked across the dance floor and saw her sons, her First Friday Book Club women, and David, she realized sometimes, when we lose the ones we love, we find ourselves.

ACKNOWLEDGMENTS

There were many talented people who helped me along the long road from gestation to publication of *Sex Happens*. I want to give a heartfelt thank you to the following: First and foremost, I want to thank Lindi Stoler, a book strategist, who helped me with many of the details and guided it down the right path. I also want to thank Sandy Ponsot and Tessa Kershnar for believing in my novel even before I did, Ryan Rivera for creating the fantastic cover, Tracey Trottenberg and Ruth Klein for convincing me that my dream was within reach, Louella Nelson and the Wednesday night writers' group for their valuable critiques, and Bethany Kelly of Publishing Partner for expertly and professionally handling the details of the publishing process. I am also grateful for the support and friendships of my eWomenNetwork and National Association of Professional Women communities. And last, but definitely not least, I want to thank my family for their love and encouragement during the entire process.

THE PEOPLE I WISH I HAD KNOWN THEN...

Ann Bennett. Brilliant brand profit builder, author, and international speaker. Creator of Renegade Branding, helping conscious entrepreneurs to liberate their rebel spirit, express their authentic voice, and build a profitable brand platform so they can be visionary leaders. Website: www.AnnBennettMarketing. com. Phone: 646-345-6671

Sandra Biskind works with business owners, leaders, and entrepreneurs to help them have an even greater impact in the world by discovering and deleting the unconscious blocks stopping them from having the prosperity, love, health, and well-being they are meant to have. Transformational life coach, speaker, international #1 best-selling author of the Codebreaker Platinum Series: *Peace: Power Up Your Life*; *Love: Ignite The Secret To Your Success;* and *Awareness: Discover How Life Really Works*. Website: www.thebiskinds.com

Chellie Campbell created the Financial Stress Reduction® Workshops and is the author of *The Wealthy Spirit* and *From Worry to Wealthy*. Email: chellie@chellie.com. Phone: 310-476-1622.

Reina Carrillo is the "Future Mayor of Inglewood in 2022." "I am about Self, Health, and Wealth." Working with World Financial Group, she helps families and individuals save and make money. Her crusade is "No Families Left Behind." Website: https://reinacarrillo.wfgopportunity. com/ Email: rcarrillo.wfg@gmail.com. Phone: 323-627-0855

Wendy Darling is a relationship and results expert, creator of the transformational change system, the Miraculous Living Method. She works with singles who want to finally attract love, couples who want to replenish their relationship, and executives and their teams (train and certify coaches/practitioners in the MLMethodology and programs). Website: www.wendydarling.com. Phone: 760-231-8234

Ruth Klein is a brand strategist and productivity guru, author of six best-selling books, and an international speaker who helps people find their voice and craft their brand message in order to become thought leaders in their industry. She's been featured in *O, The Oprah Magazine*, and is a winner of the Woman of Achievement Award—National Association of Professional Women. Website: www.RuthKlein.com. Phone: 310-741-1583

Stacey Golden-Lisnock. Unlimited legal consultation and identity theft protection is available for individuals, families, and business owners for a low monthly membership fee. Power is in knowledge and access to legal counsel, without the fear of daunting expenses. Visit the website to see the features, benefits, videos, and pricing. Website: www.staceygolden. legalshieldassociate.com. Phone: 714-642-1771

Liz Papagni. Marketing Initiative Worx (MIW) is a strategic marketing and branding firm that helps companies drive their business by taking their marketing to the next level. Website: www.marketingiw.com. Email: lpapagni@marketingiw.com. Phone: 714-595-0963

Renée Piane. International love designer and relationship re-invention expert, author of *GET Real about LOVE*. Voted Top International Love Coach, TV and radio personality, and inspirational speaker. Get back in the game of love with this powerful role model and mentor for people who are looking for love, healing a broken heart, or wanting to reignite passion in their existing relationships. Website: www.ReneePiane.com. Phone: 310-827-1100

Cappi Pidwell is Ms. Mindset. I help people reprogram their subconscious mind for fast, easy, powerful change from inside out. Address: 23276 South Pointe Dr. #112, Laguna Hills, CA 92653. Phone: 949-510-2510

Sue Podany. Berkshire Hathaway California Properties. When your life is changing and you need to move, I am here for you! Website: www. OCSue.com. Email: suepodany@bhhscal.com. Phone: 949-632-6343

Stacey Podres. Sky Diamonds Inc. Purchasing fine jewelry since 1938, including gold, diamonds, coins, sterling flatware sets, Rolex & Cartier. Email: www.SkyDiamondsInc.com. Phone: 949-230-8005

Terese A. Santos. Business, beauty, and self-care coach and speaker, and co-founder of Youlab Ageless Living. Look-Feel-Age "Younger" with Youlab's CLEAN Skin Care & Plant-based Nutrition Therapy. Website: www.liveyounger.youlabglobal.com. Email: proagelessliving@gmail.com. Phone: 949-421-8071

Tracey Trottenberg. Founder & CEO Amazing Women International Inc. Best-selling co-author of *Faces of the New Feminine Leadership*. An award-winning speaker and feminine leadership and conscious communication expert, Tracey has taught thousands of women—entrepreneurs, executives, coaches, speakers, and authors—how to dig deeper within to pull out the gold to share their story, speak from any stage, and stay feminine. Enjoy our free "Speak Your Truth" 3-part video training series: www.speakwithsoul.com/videos. Website: www.amazingwomen.org. Phone: 310-930-1296

Eric Catania-Turcio. Spiritual healer/medium, television personality. I work to make relationships better each day. Palm Springs, CA. Website: www.angelmessagesbyeric.com. Email: info@angelmessagesbyeric.com

Audra Wrightson. Award-winning interior designer, specializing in kitchens and bathrooms, and complete home remodeling. Delivering your dream home, the first time around! Owner of Audra Interiors Inc., founder of "Suite Dreams"—Interiors for Nurseries, Kids & Teen Spaces. Website: www.audrainteriors.com. Email: audra@audrainteriors.com. Phone: 714-904-7431

Tiffany Alyse Yelverton. Founder and chief sexinista of Entice Me Soirees Inc. and Sexy Survivors.org. Master of talking about sex in a way that makes even the most demure feel at ease. She and her team of sexinistas educate and entice women, men, and couples to have more fulfilling, pleasurable, and healthy sex lives, either with or without a partner. Websites: www.enticeme.com, www.facebook.com/enticemesoirees. Email: info@enticeme.com. Phone: 714-386-9684

Katherine Sai Wichmann Zacharias. Living benefits and safe money expert, Five Rings Financial. As an angel investor who loves investing in women-owned startups, I love supporting new business owners and watching them succeed! As a safe money expert and living benefits specialist, I help my tax-free retirement clients invest in accounts where they never lose money again. Websites/Twitter: www.twitter.com/TheWic, www.FiveRingsFinancial.com, www.FiveRingsEducation.com. Phone: 619-208-7717

ORGANIZATIONS I WISH I HAD KNOWN THEN:

NAPW, National Association of Professional Women, provides the opportunity to network with over 700,000 women in 200 local chapters. This vibrant networking community provides a personal forum to promote your business, product, or service, share ideas, and expand your network. NAPW local chapters also help make a difference in their communities and the world through monthly philanthropic initiatives that raise awareness of issues and causes impacting their communities and the world. Website: www.NAPW.com. Phone: 866-540-6279.

eWomenNetwork, Diana Sabatino, Managing Director of Orange County chapter. Widely recognized as the premier women's business network in North America, we have a dynamic, diversified culture that celebrates the brilliance of women entrepreneurs, business owners, and corporate professionals. There are 118 chapters in the United States and Canada. Website: www.ewomennetwork.com/chapter/OrangeCounty Email: dianasabatino@ewomennetwork.com

Made in the USA
San Bernardino, CA
20 December 2016